THE OTHER SIDE OF BROKEN

WHISPER OF THE PINES BOOK 3

SUSAN HAUGHT

FourCaratPress.com

TABLE OF CONTENTS

COPYRIGHT

THE OTHER SIDE OF BROKEN

AUTHOR'S NOTE

This book was previously published under the title
A SONG FOR LADYBUG

The cover and title have been changed—
the manuscript remains the same.

DEDICATION

To the victims
Stay strong
You're not alone
#MeToo

DISCLAIMER

*This work of fiction contains subject matter
which some readers may find disturbing.*

ONE

*T*he envelope trembled in her hands. Maybe if she didn't
open it, the darkness would stay hidden in the creases.
Maybe it wouldn't burst open and scatter bits of her sanity across the
snow. And maybe the memories wouldn't threaten to consume her.

She'd worked hard to forgive. Even harder to forget. With so much
emphasis on the present, she'd forgotten how much time had come
and gone, and life's cruel editor had spliced the past headlong into the
present. It hadn't tapped her on the shoulder. It hadn't whispered in
her ear. It hadn't knocked on the door. It had come from hell and
grabbed her by the throat.

She stuffed the unopened letter into her coat pocket.

"I thought I'd find you here." He swept a hand in the direction of
the spruce-lined hollow and eased himself to the bench beside her.
"Whisper of the Pines, this little valley, the bench, they're special to
you. It's your place."

Rachel Caldarone nodded but didn't turn. If she did, if she looked
into her grandfather's quiet eyes, the thin thread holding her together
would snap. Instead, she reached inside her coat and found Zoe's
sweet spot, massaging the hollow just below the little dog's ears. Her

gift. Her companion. One who asked for nothing but a warm lap or shoulder to snuggle into now and then.

Marshall Gowen leaned into the bench, the cold wood groaning, drowning out the pop and creak of brittle bones. "I wondered if you'd received the letter."

She turned toward him, his thoughts hidden in the lines of a weathered face. The cold had been hard on him, the ache lodged deep in unforgiving bones and once carefree smile. Five years he'd endured the frigid winters. Five years he'd grieved her husband's disappearance and apparent death alongside her. Five years he'd been there to catch her if the weight became too much to bear. Not once had he complained.

"I can't go through that again."

Her grandfather thrust his chin out, the way he always did when pondering a suitable reply, the pause as deafening as the silence between snowflakes. Not the silence that came with the peace of falling snow but that of inward thought. "You can't change the past, Rachel. But you can change the way it affects you. And others."

"What good will it do, Grandpa?" Cold air stung her lungs, her words tinged with ice. A whorl of mist floated in front of her as she exhaled, the cloud as transparent as the question and as opaque as the answer.

He draped an arm across her shoulders, gloved hands possessing the assurance and unconditional love of confidante, friend, and advisor, taking up the roles of both father and mother she'd lost so many years ago. "You're a strong woman. Stronger than you think."

Rachel dug a boot into the snow taking in the ordinary feel of the movement, the warmth inside a buffer to the cold creeping under her skin. "I'm a coward."

"You're wrong."

"Then why can't I face this?" She ground the words into a ragged question.

Grandpa rubbed his leg, stalling for time or warming his limbs she couldn't say, but the longer he paused the more constricted her throat became. "There's never been a need."

Moving her foot back and forth, she carved a compacted furrow in the ankle-deep snow. "Don't ask me to do this. Please."

"I understand your hesitation."

"I'm not hesitating. I can't do it."

"Can't? Or won't?"

"Both." She stripped the word of any charity, the period marking the end of an unwanted conversation. "I'd better get back or I'll be late for work."

She cradled Zoe and stood, but he took her elbow. "Sit."

"I need to go." He let her go, but she remained standing.

"You're the supervisor. You can be late."

"That's not setting a good example for the rest of the nursing staff."

"Molly is covering for you." He looked away and then back to her. "This is important. You must consider it carefully."

Rachel clutched her scarf, the same one she'd worn the past five winters. His scent had long since faded from the threads, but she couldn't part with the connection it offered. To Nico. To what could have been. She sank back into the bench, tightening the scarf around her.

She shoved a hand into her pocket and wadded the letter into a tight ball. "I have *considered* it," she said, drenching the word with contempt, "every day for fifteen years. I've *considered* it night after night when I wake from the nightmares and I have no one to make them go away. I've *considered* it every time I hug my daughter and wonder how the hell I can protect her from monsters like him. And every time I touch the cold granite of my dead husband's headstone I've *considered* it."

"Rachel—"

"How many times do you think that bastard considered my pleas, my fear, or what it would do to *me* while he was raping me?" The last words broke from her lips and her throat closed around them. "Oh, Grandpa." She hadn't meant to dredge up the past and drag him into it, but she had, and her heart split in two. She scooted beside him, raking him into a fierce embrace. "I didn't mean—"

"I know." He held her at arm's length, the tremors bleeding through heavily lined leather gloves. "Rachel, listen to me."

A light snow had begun to fall. He blinked, moisture gathering in thoughtful blue eyes. The ones he'd given her mother. The same ones her mother had given her. It wasn't only the moisture from the brisk morning that pooled there but empathy for what an unspeakable monster had done, his tears the confession of years of hell—years he'd shared as much or more than he'd shared her joy.

"It's not just about you this time."

The odd comment settled uneasily and she paused. "What are you talking about?"

"The letter. Did you read it?"

She shook her head.

She didn't want to read it. Didn't want to see the bastard's name. Didn't want to re-create the past, bring it back to life. If she didn't acknowledge it, she could pretend it wasn't real. Inching her hand into her pocket, she tightened her fist around the wad, forcing the reality to remain hidden.

"Given his prison record," he said, clearly choosing his words carefully, "he could be released early."

"That's not possible." She put a finger to her temple and traced the remnants of the scar, the remembrance digging beyond her flesh but the evidence nothing more than a thin silvery line. "Is it?"

The lines between his brows deepened. "He's applied for commutation of sentence, and there's another—"

"I don't understand." The implications gathered in a fog of disbelief, rooting her to the bench. "How can they shorten his sentence? According to Arizona law, he has to serve the full term."

"The how and why aren't relevant at this point. The Board of Executive Clemency has already passed it on to a Phase II hearing, and I think it would be wise to attend. He's been a model prisoner and that will serve in his favor."

"Model rapist, you mean." She clamped down hard on the urge to scream.

"I've spoken to Everett Dumas. He's the DA now, and—"

She turned abruptly.

Grandpa raised and then lowered his hands. "Please hear me out. Dumas has been through this with you. He knows this case. Knows how to prosecute a sexual offense."

Sexual offense.

The term rolled over her like a wave on the edge of breaking, primed to take her with it. "That term sounds so...weak."

Grandpa set his jaw. "Dumas is anxious to keep Chastain—"

"Don't—"

"Refusing to acknowledge his name," he said, turning away and then slowly back to her, "doesn't make him any less real, Rachel."

Anger wrapped its hardened fingers around her chest and squeezed. "Don't ever say his name. Not to me."

Grandpa rubbed a gloved hand across a neatly trimmed white beard and cleared the hesitation from his throat. "Dumas is determined he stays behind bars."

"I'd have to go back to Phoenix." Fear's groping fingers crawled up her spine and nausea rose as the words bumped off the walls of her stomach. "But if I don't..."

"There's no guarantee regardless of your testimony, but Dumas thinks the chances are better if you testify. The board needs to see your face, to hear what you've gone through because of what that bastard did and how it's affected your life." He pounded a fist on his thigh, but the illness had stolen the strength behind it.

Her head ached, each throb a reminder of the darkness that lurked in the places she'd tried to hide from her everyday world. Rachel raised the scarf to cover her nose. Where had Nico's scent gone? Had she spent so much time trying to forget the past that she couldn't remember him? The details, those small little things that crept into her thoughts at the oddest times? He'd been there to catch her when the nightmares tormented her and helped her through them one step at a time.

But Nico was gone.

The mountain had seen to that, burying him in its icy tomb. She lowered her lashes, cold lids soothing on burning eyes.

The jaws of the Rockies jutted into the sky, surrounding her in their forbidden majesty. A shiver rippled over her skin, crept its way to her heart and chilled her outside to inside as though she stood naked and vulnerable in the snow. Would this ever be over? The longing for a normal life remained distant, a dream for those whose sleep came easy.

"I'll think about it. Where's Bug?"

"I left Nicole at The Villages with Miles. I found him pacing the hall. He looked like he hadn't slept, but he said he'd walk her to day care."

"Thanks, Grandpa."

"She's taken quite a shine to him." He brushed a dusting of snow from his shoulders, the corners of his mouth curling slightly. "Seems all my girls have."

Despite the bone-aching chill, warmth crept into her cheeks. The local veterinarian had a way with animals, an inherent empathy they sensed. Including Zoe. The little therapy dog made a beeline for Miles no matter whose lap she happened to be perched on. But Bug had a reserved side with strangers—except when it came to Miles. An instant bond had formed, and she trusted Miles with them both.

"Zoe loves her vet and I know Bug's safe if Miles walked her to day care."

Zoe popped her head out of Rachel's coat.

"There's our little girl." A smile feathered the hard lines of Grandpa's brow.

Zoe wiggled free, hopped to Grandpa's lap, and gave his nose a thorough welcome. The residents loved the little therapy dog and looked forward to her 'booger kisses.' So did she. And the compulsion to curb Zoe's habit for licking noses had long passed.

Grandpa tucked Zoe into his elbow nice and snug, massaged her ears, and gave the Yorkie an exaggerated smooch on top of her head. She shivered, squirmed from his arms, and wiggled her way back inside Rachel's warm coat.

"She's quite the little dog. Your butterfly wish."

"She and Bug are everything to me."

Nico had promised her a thousand butterfly wishes, but all she'd ever wanted was one—to be normal, to live and love without fear and to have a child. He'd broken through her fear of intimacy and blessed her with a daughter, but Zoe had been the first butterfly wish Nico had given her.

Her little companion helped absorb the pain of losing Nico, a tiny heartbeat comforting her in a way no human could. The one who'd endured the lonely nights, snuggled into the hollow under her chin, kissing away tears no one else saw. Even after all these years, every now and then she'd find Zoe standing by the door, never giving up hope Nico would someday walk through it.

Grandpa splayed his fingers and massaged each one in succession. "Do you want me to stay with you awhile longer?"

"I need some time. Alone. Do you mind?"

"Zoe?" Zoe wiggled her nose into the cold air, blinking at the snowflakes landing on her eyes and swiping her tiny pink tongue at the ones on her black button nose. "Take care of my girl."

Zoe sneezed and retreated back inside Rachel's coat.

"She takes good care of me, Grandpa."

"You must read the letter, Button." Grandpa patted her thigh and pushed slowly to his feet, squinting through a grimace. He adjusted the knit beanie over his ears, a quantity of white eyebrows peeking from below the brim. "You can do this. You're not alone," he said with a deliberate pause. "But don't do it for Bug, for me, or for anyone. Do it for you."

He made his way through the accumulating snow, taking one cautious step after another, each short stride a deliberate lift and set until he was out of sight.

It was the same as it had always been, this place. Whisper of the Pines Resort with its cobbled paths and horse-drawn sleigh hadn't changed in the countless times she'd returned. It had stolen her heart the first time Nico had brought her here, and two years later she'd left it—exposed, raw, and shattered. If time could be measured with an hourglass, she could flip it over and start again. But unlike the steady stream of sand flowing from one end to the other, her thoughts were fragmented and scattered like bits of broken glass caught in the mirrors of a kaleidoscope.

"What do I do, Nico?"

The question drifted into the air and lay there, heavy and cold and unanswered. Once, he'd been her savior. He'd loosened the chains that bound her to the past and then he'd been taken from her—another notch on her heart, each one a missing piece for those she'd lost. She balled her hands into fists and pounded her thighs. "Damn you for leaving me."

The mountains were as formidable and breathtaking as they'd been then and as cruel as she had come to know. They rose around her, their secrets buried in the jagged chasm walls and frozen within its icy glaciers. Even the wind refused to speak, bough and needle still. And in the silence came the loss—not the tangible absence of flesh— but the profound loss of his presence. He'd once been there, in the sough of wind, the rustle of trees, and in the quiet of the falling snow.

Today the silence was deafening.

Snow fell in whispers, first in tiny stinging pellets and then in fat feathery flakes, the shift as uncertain as the changing seasons. Rachel lifted her face to the sky and closed her eyes. Cold, gray morning light cast images across the backs of her eyelids, the way negatives form on a filmstrip—a hiccup in time captured for eternity.

The prospect of a normal life loomed large and ragged, a mirror of the mountains that had taken her husband. The longing for what had been stolen from her lay heavy in her memory, but the sting of the wound had faded, scarred over with the passage of time. Nights had swallowed up the days, days had merged into weeks, and weeks had gathered and grown into years.

Nearly five years—if you counted backward to the day the mountain had claimed Nico. And a little more than four since a part of him had been given back to her. Nicole. Named for her father. The little girl everyone called Bug. Their daughter. Though he was gone, a part of him lived.

She wanted *before*. A do-over. But that was selfish. That wasn't fair to her grandfather. To Bug. Least of all to herself. Afraid she'd drift too far into the past, she opened her eyes.

Bug needed her to be strong. Her attorney needed her to be brave. And her grandpa had faith she'd do the right thing. Even Zoe depended on her. Hope bubbled inside her, a small thing waiting to be nurtured, a seedling striving to break through the crust.

The battle waged and she wanted—needed—to be free of the stigma, and the only way to free herself would be to move forward.

One step at a time.

The way Nico had promised.

TWO

*R*achel swiped her key card and the glass doors beyond the main entrance to The Villages at Alpine Ridge parted. Zoe whined, anxious to get to the business of doling out kisses and receiving twice her share of attention from the elderly residents. Rachel set her down, and the Yorkie took off in a blur across the lobby.

Bug was at day care and Molly could be counted on to take up the slack, but phone calls to Everett Dumas and her director, Kristina Kaufman, needed to be made and she'd spent more time at Whisper of the Pines than she had intended. Rachel glanced at her watch and automatically picked up her pace.

The train whistle blew softly, marking the eleven o'clock hour. Mentally ticking off the items on her to-do list, Rachel removed her gloves, stuffed them into the corresponding pockets, and walked across the cobblestoned lobby. Unlike the retirement community at Woodland Hills in Arizona where she'd started her nursing career, the unique atmosphere of The Villages mimicked the latest Swedish concepts with an enclosed miniature shopping area, a "street" designed with a 1950s vibe, a children's rehab center, and a day care adjacent to the medical facility and retirement community. Kristina's latest innovation for a small movie theater neared completion, and it was all centered around a lobby that could pass as a vintage railway station with one exception—the illusion was simply that—an illusion.

There wasn't anything the COO of Wentworth-Cavanaugh Properties hadn't incorporated in the state-of-the-art facility, and Kristina's nose for seeking out the best employees added to her inherent abilities in the retirement community business. She'd stolen Nico from Woodland Hills as the facility's first operations administrator. And Nico had stolen Rachel's heart and convinced her to come with him to Colorado and accept Kristina's offer to head the children's rehab center. She loved the kids—God knows she did—but her heart belonged to the elderly, and after Nico's disappearance and official declaration of his death, she could transfer into his department. The transition hadn't been easy at first. Her patients' memories of Nico overwhelmed her at times, but their stories were as much a salve for the residents as they were for her.

The train whistle blew again and "All aboard" rang through the lobby as Rachel crossed the imitation railroad tracks, checking emails and messages on her phone.

Across the lobby, Zoe leapt into Inga Heinrich's lap. Inga sat with ankles crossed on a bench clutching a pocketbook to her squat body, toes barely reaching the cobbles beneath her. Rachel slipped her iPhone into her purse and followed the little dog.

"Guten morgen, Krankenschwester Rachel," Inga said, the mild German inflection muffled in Zoe's fur. "Fräulein Zoe is such a precious love. No day is good day without welpe kisses." Inga nuzzled the little Yorkie. Zoe gifted her with a booger kiss and Inga erupted in a series of animated titters.

"Zoe loves you too, Inga."

"Danke, danke."

"What brings you out today? Is Hans under the weather?"

"Nein, Hans ist well. Ist Herr Malone, ja? He wants assistance with...*pulling the plug*." The last three words resulted in a whisper between the rows of too-big-for-her-mouth teeth.

Rachel tugged on her bottom lip. Randall Malone had come to The

Villages to recover from hip replacement surgery and had profoundly professed he was dying every time the physical therapists came near him. But according to his chart, the only thing dying was Randall's stay. The last time she'd checked on him, he'd been scheduled for release, and his son, Miles—Zoe's vet and frequent visitor to the facility—had all but physically gagged him to keep him from terrorizing the staff with his colorful remarks.

"I wait here for our little Nola. She come soon to fetch me, to see Dr. Albrecht and bring him here. For Herr Malone's...*request.*" Inga raised her chin slightly and reclined into the back of the bench. "He will consider it mercy to pull plug." She stroked Zoe between the ears with such eagerness the dog's eyes bulged with each backward movement.

The idea short-circuited around Rachel's heart. "Let's go inside, Inga, and then I can check on Mr. Malone. Hans is probably waiting for you."

Inga scooted to the edge of the bench and with a slight hop, placed her feet firmly on the ground. A white powdery fingerprint frosted her cheek, and Rachel wagged a finger at the stout woman's face.

"Oh, ist flour from my plätzchens. For Fraulein Bug. Ist Tuesday tomorrow, nein?" Inga wiped her cheek, and then promptly rubbed it down her apron. "I make ladybugs for her." Inga Heinrich's prowess in the kitchen was known community-wide and every kraut bierock, grebble, butterball, or plätzchen had left its faint reminder on the lacy cloth of the well-used apron.

"She certainly looks forward to them every week."

"Plätzchens ready...but Herr Malone..." She shook her head slowly, the tsk, tsk, tsk that accompanied the statement keeping time to the small movement.

Rachel's brows pinched together. "Inga, how long ago did you see Mr. Malone?"

Inga took Rachel's elbow and set Zoe down. She straightened the front of her frock, but paid little attention to the red indentations the sleeves had made on her overabundant upper arms.

"Why, before I come to wait for Nola, and where have you been?

Herr Malone—the young, pretty one—asks for you." She tugged at Rachel's sleeve. "You should not keep him waiting, nein?"

Rachel's mouth opened and then closed, the second half of the comment failing to register. She kicked it into second gear, Inga's tiny feet moving in double-time to keep up, and Zoe leading her charge at a set pace beside her.

The double doors into the main facility parted.

"There you are, Inga." Molly threw her hands into the air, bright auburn braid swishing back and forth to the nurse's hurried steps, and came to an abrupt halt in front of Inga and Rachel. "Hey, Rach, I'm glad you're back. Miles Malone has been looking for you and Nurse Angie is frantic because you, Inga Heinrich," she said, bright green eyes flashing below dark auburn lashes, "slipped away from the activity room right under her nose. I'm thinking an ankle monitor might be in your future." Molly took Inga's elbow.

Rachel pasted her knuckles against her mouth to keep a laugh from escaping in front of the little lady. "Angie's a new nurse, Molly. A tenderfoot. She'll get the hang of keeping tabs on the wanderers."

A wistful longing threw her off-kilter. It hadn't been that long ago she'd been a *tenderfoot*. An inexperienced nurse with big ideas that rules were meant to be ignored even if it meant losing your job. She'd nearly done just that on a number of occasions, but now she didn't have her supervisor Judith lurking around every corner trying to catch her in some wayward adventure. Rachel had a blatant disregard for the rules then, but she was the one who enforced them now.

"Earth to Rachel." Molly let out a soft whistle and waved a hand in front of Rachel's face. "Remind you of old times at Woodland Hills?"

The longing for those days weighed on her at times, but she was quick to set it aside. She had a daughter now and losing her job wasn't part of the plan to provide for her and keep her safe.

"Yeah, except there's no Judith to contend with."

"Thank God. Makes me cringe."

Rachel took Inga's other elbow. "We need to get Inga back to Hans and I need to check on Randall Malone."

Molly's expression went lax, as if someone had cut the strings holding its untroubled upward tilt. A bad feeling reared its ugly head in Rachel's stomach.

"He took a nasty turn after your last shift." Molly's green eyes glistened but not from their usual spark of playfulness, and the sprinkling of tiny ruddy freckles across her nose and cheeks seemed to fade.

Rachel counted backward. Two days. Her hand went to her pocket, the letter crinkling in her fisted hand. A lot can happen in forty-eight hours.

"He's in ICU. Miles hasn't left his side except to take Bug to day care."

Inga's jowls jostled as she volleyed between the two, keeping up with the back and forth conversation.

"Go check on him." Molly tucked Inga's hand through the crook of her elbow and patted her hand. "I'll walk Inga back."

Inga anchored her short, stout body and reclaimed her hands. "Nein."

Zoe sat at their heels and both nurses hemmed Inga between laser shots of scrutiny.

"Nein. I have no apples for my Hans' favorite strudel." Her entire face puckered, and the urgency in her tone matched the odd hand-wringing she'd suddenly taken up.

"Well, that's easily solved. C'mon," Rachel said, taking Inga's elbow once again. "I'll escort you to the Village Mercantile."

Inga gave her arm a quick squeeze. "Our son ist mürrisch. Grumpy. Not allow access."

Rachel sorted through a mental list of residents, and the Heinrichs were on the list of those approved to have access to the mini-mall. "What happened?"

Inga stood on tiptoes and scooped a hand around Rachel's ear. "They say my Hans has sticky fingers," she whispered, wiggling the fingers.

"I see."

"I keep good eye on my Hans, but nein, nein, ungrateful son say visits to store no more. And I need apples. Today."

Molly flipped her braid over her shoulder. "The new directive came through while you were gone, Rach." A serious calm swept over Molly's face, the calm she reserved to deliver a blow, and gave Rachel the *he doesn't have long* barely perceptible nod.

Inga's urgency to bake her husband an apple strudel made perfect sense. So did the significance of ending the life of someone you loved but couldn't bear to see suffer. The first she could do something about. The other was out of her hands (and heart) though it wouldn't budge from her mind.

"C'mon." Rachel urged Inga forward with a gentle nudge. "I haven't seen your new directive, you need apples, and there's only one way to get them." Adrenaline-infused blood pulsed in her temples and for an instant, she could have sworn she heard Nico's voice warning her to stay out of trouble. But it was Desi, the big old lumberjack at Woodland Hills whose words sneaked into her head.

"You should listen to your head instead of your heart, Nurse Rachel. Gonna get you in trouble one of these days."

Rachel stood in the center of the double glass doors to keep them from closing while the other two walked through.

"You break rule for Inga and my Hans?"

Rachel placed her hand gently on Inga's cheek and nodded.

Inga's shoulders slumped as if someone had released a valve and let the air out. "Inga good with secret, Krankenschwester Rachel."

In the five years she'd been with The Villages, Rachel had steered clear of the types of misadventures that had nearly cost her her job at Woodland Hills—she had Bug to think about now. But sometimes rules were nothing but an annoying inconvenience, and one small divergence to buy apples wouldn't hurt anyone.

"It's settled, then."

"Wait. I'll take her," Molly said, stepping in front of them. "You can't afford to get caught."

"And you can?"

Molly lifted her shoulders and held them there as if they'd stuck, and then let them drop with a sigh as exaggerated as the shrug. "Who's going to catch me? You?" The sharpened hue of overripe strawberries stained Molly's freckles back into noticeable existence, and they danced to the upward movement of a playful grin. "Just like old times, Rach, only this time I get to do the sleuthing."

Rachel sent the two women on their way through the east corridor with an unseen wave and glanced down the adjoining halls. No one seemed to notice anything unusual. But she had. The gesture had been a small token—nothing like the stunts she'd pulled at Woodland Hills —but the sense of fulfillment had been there even if she wasn't the one escorting Inga.

Anxiousness wormed its way into her mind, but she stuffed it into a mental trash can and buried it among the extra clutter. "C'mon, Zoe. Better put it in second gear if we want to check on Randall Malone."

Zoe whined. She swiveled her head toward the lobby but didn't move from her perch beside Rachel. Whined again.

"What's up, Zoe?"

Rachel peeked back into the lobby. "There's no one here, little girl." She stooped and picked up the dog with one hand and kissed her between the eyes. Zoe returned the token with a swift booger kiss. Rachel laughed under her breath, adjusted the therapy vest, and set her back down. "There. All set. Time to go to work?" Zoe locked eyes with Rachel and stayed in a sitting position until Rachel waved her hand and said, "Rounds, Zoe."

Zoe took off down the west corridor. Her first stop would be in the assisted living wing with Archie Comstock, who always had a dried sweet potato treat waiting. Nico had called him Rocket Man, like the song, and would whistle the tune whenever he visited. His wife called him Archie Bunker. Rachel never asked why. But besides Rachel, Zoe was the only one who didn't fall asleep when Archie spoke in his unique language of thermodynamics, aerospace propulsion, and a whole lot of math that mixed numbers and letters. Zoe loved the treats. Rachel loved the Space Shuttle romance he'd told her so many times she'd lost count. Or maybe it was because she listened. Most didn't. The language of the exclusive design team for NASA was an oblique, foreign thing her brain didn't often grasp, but she loved the story and adored Archie.

The train whistle blew, the echo passing through the center of her bones, forlorn and hollow as if she were a part of the air, adrift in the continual movement. If only she could turn the hourglass over…

"It is not a preferred measure to wish away our past, Miss Rachel, but to use it as it guides us into the future."

Rachel tensed and threw a hand to her throat. It had been years, but the palpable calm, the odd intonation and the kaleidoscope of butterflies had once been a catharsis.

She turned slowly toward the familiar voice with no expectations save the longing of the impossible.

THREE

*S*ilver-blue eyes as clear and perceptive as she remembered met hers, and a boyish grin peeked through too much white mustache. Years had come and gone since she'd last seen him, yet the suggestion of time had passed him by. How could one so old seven years ago have changed so little?

"Wilford Langhorne D'Ambrose." Disbelief formed the name in breathy syllables. "Ambrose, for all intents and purposes."

He straightened and then tilted his head forward in his customary greeting. "It is I, Miss Rachel," he said, the voice, the form, the lanky shadow as figurative as it was absolute. "At your service." As he had done in their first encounter, he straightened one leg, clamped a hand around his waist and bent into a deep, formal bow. His long black coat nearly reached the floor.

She took in the surrounding lobby. "Where? How?" Her mouth formed the words, but her mind refused to process the equation.

"I am quite gifted at appearing," he said, air quoting the last word, "when need arises."

Ambrose's timing seemed odd, an apparition of the mind showing up and disappearing at will. She clasped and unclasped her hands. "I remember your last visit like it was yesterday."

"Ah yes, Miss Rachel, as do I." He waved his cane toward the bench. "Would you take offense if we sit?"

She looked up. The clock above the ticket booth read a quarter past eleven. "I can't stay...I need to get to work." Ignoring the niggling worry, she took a seat on the bench and scooted to one side to allow him room.

He lowered his weight to the bench, a noisy exhale adding to the chorus of creaky bones.

"Ah yes, indeed. However, there is no need for worry. You shall find the nurse Molly back at her duties and you to yours as if no time has passed."

"Still speaking in riddles, I see."

"I speak only of truth."

The old man did speak of truth, but it was one that teetered on the edge of some uncanny insight that baffled her on their first visit and obviously hadn't changed.

"I'm afraid to ask why you're here. You seem to show up when things go all haywire." She had an idea why he was here, but saying it out loud would awaken the fear lying dormant in its fragile case.

He crossed aged hands over his cane and leaned into it. "I find it imperative to arrive when circumstances are not as they seem. Or shall we say, when it is determined a state of affairs becomes muddled and are in need of a gentle nudge." He paused, peering about as if prying answers from the air. "And an ambassador to do the nudging."

Rachel fidgeted with the buttons on her coat. "Terrific."

He turned a thoughtful eye to her, one that saw past the inevitable and beheld her soul. "Little escapes my realm of insight, and there is less I do not know when it comes to you."

The same shimmer of mischief she'd seen many years ago crimped the corners of his pallid blue eyes in a spirited wink, yet no sign of the additional years creased his face. Restlessness thickened the air. Rachel stood, crossed her arms, and faced him. "I really don't have time for games or riddles. I need to go."

He raised a hand. "Your need is greater than you imagine."

The insolent remark uprooted an already uneasy stomach and she shifted from one foot to the other. "What's that supposed to mean?"

Ambrose leaned back and tapped the bench with his cane. "Sit," he said, twirling his mustache between long, gnarled fingers. "I assure you I will take precious little of your time."

Rachel glanced at her watch. Tapped the face. Her mouth dropped open. She sat. The numbers read a quarter past eleven, the same as it had several minutes ago.

"Life is a vicious circle." Ambrose raised a hand and sketched a wide arc in the air. "Those things we abhor, those we find painful we push aside, disguised by what we cherish and those we love. We tuck them away, far removed from conscious thought into a place too distant to recall. Circles keep things out. And circles, Miss Rachel, keep things in."

The back of the bench gave little support to the enigmatic old man's comment.

"Consider a stone tossed into still water. The ripples created are well-defined and their effect on the water is quite evident." Rachel didn't look up. "As it is in life. Whether we fear the ripples—things that cause us pause—in our lives or love them, they are as discernable as ripples on a pond of calm water. Alas, as they continue to spread outward," he said, splaying a palm in front of him, "they dissipate and are no longer visible. But nonetheless the effects, the reminders, remain."

"This doesn't make any sense." Her arms fell limply to her knees.

"Indulge an old man if you will." Ambrose massaged his thigh, an awkward span of silence passing between them.

The state of his pain came rushing back, the recollection like a splinter festering after a season of absence. He'd never mentioned it when they'd met at Woodland Hills, but she was familiar with the aches of the elderly, and the anguish of it squeezed her heart without need of explanation.

Rachel crossed her ankles and waved Ambrose on.

"Circles, Miss Rachel. A comfort and a crutch."

"I'm a nurse, Ambrose, angles and circles aren't my strong suit."

A small noise that wasn't quite a laugh deepened the lines around his eyes. "Imaginary circles keep us safe within them by keeping our troubles from breaking through. The one chosen to break through your barrier, your circle," he said, nodding in her direction, "was a gift. One selfless enough to give his life to you so yours may be given back."

"Nico." The name formed as a murmured sigh, a remembrance that filled her with the warmth of a tended fire, and the joy of his presence evident in the light in their daughter's eyes. His memory was alive yet safe within the confines of her heart. "Nico kept me safe."

"Nico Caldarone broke through your circle. As was meant to be." His gaze was fixed at what lay beyond and yet nothing at all. "There are things of this world no one truly understands. The ripples Nico created in your life continue to expand and I am here because it is time to allow another to break through the circle."

A prickle skated up her neck. "I have no desire...I haven't considered... No. I have Bug and Grandpa and Zoe. They're all I need."

"Love is ageless, my dear Miss Rachel. When it is right, it shall withstand the boundaries of time. It is written, if you love someone you must give them wings, and if they return, they shall be yours forever."

"That's a joke." A humorless mutter marked her words. "Too many of those I loved never came back." Maybe she hadn't loved them enough. Or maybe too much?

"Circles."

"Stop talking in riddles!"

He leaned forward. "Your heart knows no boundaries, Miss Rachel. You give it selflessly to others. But it is time...you are ready to open yours to the love of another. To open your circle."

"I have Bug and Grandpa. Zoe. My patients. They're my life now. I don't need anyone."

"They are your life because you cannot confront your own."

Ignoring his response, she leapt to her feet. "I chose to be here with these people. If you recall, we met at a retirement community."

"Ah, yes, my dear Miss Rachel." He waved an index finger. "We did indeed meet seven years ago, but I knew you long before Woodland Hills. Knew of your troubles past and those you must yet encounter."

She blinked, but the ability to compose an apt reply escaped her.

"For now, you must go. Other matters await you, ones which shall test your courage to trust and believe." Ambrose leaned into his cane and pushed himself upright. He made an attempt at a bow, but Rachel reached for his hands and covered them with hers—an unspoken compromise they'd made seven years ago. "The one who holds your heart is in need of you as much as you are of him. The one who adores your daughter. The one who shall step through your circle, who will replace your nightmares with dreams once again." He held a tightly clenched fist to his heart. "You need not trouble yourself, Rachel Everly Caldarone, for if you let him go—"

"No," she said with a deliberate edge.

"He shall return. Always."

"Stop. Please."

"Trust the one who loves you, the one who sees beyond your sorrow, your anger, and your silence. Trust the one who takes these as his own and leaves happiness in its place."

His words bore a smooth inflection and the elegance and style of a foregone era, a fine wine among spoken language. This eccentric old man held the power to mesmerize her, to calm her, and yet to ignite questions for which she had no answers. So why did his words feel like sixty grit sandpaper, grinding away at cleverly disguised clues?

"What are you talking about, Ambrose? Why not just tell me outright?"

"Do not allow the past to steal your future. Stand up to it. Allow those around you to offer love and support. Now, you must go. Find the one who will break through your circle. Find the one who looks after Nicole and Zoe as he will you. With love and with honor."

"Miles?" Unexpected laughter peppered the name. "You've lost your touch, Ambrose. He's a friend. Nothing more."

"Perhaps for now. But you must first face a challenge you have chosen to ignore." He dipped his chin toward her pocket.

Her ineffable silence met a knowing tilt of the head.

"A friend is not outside the circle of those we choose to love."

Rachel shut her eyes, kneading the space between them. "Of course not, but—"

"Never underestimate love, for I have borne witness to its power. Thus it is said. Therefore, it shall be. Until we meet again, my dear, sweet Rachel."

"I can't think about this right now." She opened her eyes and spun a full circle, the questions about his existence resurfacing. She hadn't imagined him seven years ago, nor had she today. And yet, he'd vanished as if she had.

She checked her watch. Shook it. "This can't be right."

The pendulum on the antique clock above the ticket booth swung freely, the hands marking the hour at a quarter past eleven.

FOUR

*R*achel rounded the corner to the nurses' station at the same time Zoe made a beeline for Molly, but the expression on Molly's face kicked Rachel in the gut.

"Mr. Malone?"

Molly's long eyelashes fluttered as she tapped the tablet with a short, clean nail. Zoe sat patiently at her feet ogling the nurse. She handed Zoe a treat and the little dog spun in a circle, gently took the treat, and sped off down the hallway. "Miles wants to see you right away, Rach."

The bad feeling nudged her stomach again. "How's his dad?"

"Infection set in two days ago. There's been no change."

"Sepsis?"

Molly's eyes glistened, and she dipped her head and nodded, her compassion pushing aside the policy that prohibited becoming attached to the patients.

"Crap." Rachel's throat constricted, but she pushed past the dryness. "You said he's in ICU?" Molly pointed the tablet down the adjoining hallway. "Cover for me?"

"Go. I'm here 'til you get back or if you need anything."

In seconds she stood at the doorway to Randall's room. A lightweight blanket had been tucked neatly around him, the rise and fall of his chest and the monitor's steady beep the sole indications of life. Two days had made a marked difference in his appearance.

Miles was asleep in a chair next to his father, yet he wore the weight of passing hours and fear of the unknown. Randall's aged hand lay nestled in Miles' large ones—the lifeline of family tethered in the connection—and Zoe had curled herself into the narrow gap between them, a perfect niche for the six-pound Yorkie.

Rachel checked Randall's chart and then leaned against the doorframe, afraid to disturb the subtle balance of the rest and relief sleep provides. The doctor's notes indicated Randall's body and the antibiotics fought the deadly infection, morphine fought the pain, and both men fought time.

Rachel couldn't take her eyes from father and son in the midst of unspoken goodbyes—an opportunity that had never presented itself with her parents. One minute they'd been there, the next they were gone. She hadn't gone to the morgue, and Grandpa had told her closed caskets were for the best. She told herself it was for the best. As the years passed she'd convinced herself it didn't matter. But the silent tether between father and son punctuated the misconception with an uneasy pang. It mattered. Family mattered. The good, the bad, the downright ugly, and the joy and pain that went with it. Second chances were rare.

Rising voices echoed from the hallway. The commotion stirred Miles and he grimaced, gripped his neck, and sat upright, turning abruptly toward the monitor's steady beeps, and then checked the clock above the door. "Rachel."

"Molly said you were asking for me?"

Zoe set a paw on Miles' forearm. He scooped her up, pushed the chair aside, and stood. "Hey, little girl," he said and squinted a second too late. Zoe had christened him with a kiss to the nose, scrambled out of his arms, leapt from the bed, and took off out the door. The therapy dog had rounds to make. Even the ICU wasn't off her radar—when she could get away with it.

"Thanks for coming." Miles crossed the room and leaned against the wall beside her. "I need to talk to you."

Too close.

Rachel scooted to the left just out of reach, the action taken before she could think. Why? Why did it bother her? He was about to lose his father...he wasn't trying to...no, nothing more than a grieving son. "What can I do to help?"

His dark blond hair was tousled and his eyes heavy and so shadowed she couldn't see past the turmoil. She'd witnessed death. At times it wasn't easy on the dying, but it was the living whose suffering turned her heart to mush.

Miles' Adam's apple bobbed as he swallowed whatever words he tried to form, and she had the sudden urge to swaddle him like a child who'd become unstrung. And lost.

"We're friends, Miles. You've helped me through Zoe's ordeals, and I'm here for you, to help you through this with your father."

He leaned his head back and rubbed his face as if to wash away the hesitation, two days stubble an audible rasp in the quiet room. "Is he in pain?" Grief and lack of sleep mangled the words into ragged sounds.

"I don't think so. He's on a steady morphine drip."

Miles looked at his father and then back to her. "Can he comprehend?"

"There are theories." She fiddled with her stethoscope but paid no attention to the process. "But I can't say for sure."

"Does he know me?"

"Maybe."

"Can he hear me?"

"Every patient is different."

Watching his father cling to life had drained the spark from his eyes and spread its pale shadow over his face. "Does my father know I'm here?"

"I'm sorry, but I don't have an answer." She hoped the brief lift of her mouth expressed the inadequate apology. "I've seen people speak coherently moments before death and I've seen them unresponsive for days."

"Days. Jesus. I can't stomach the thought of him suffering." For the normally composed veterinarian, the shortness in his tone was rough and out of character. "I'm a vet, Rachel. When someone's pet, when there's no hope—"

"There's always hope." Invisible fingers tightened around her throat. Was it merciful? Love at its greatest capacity? Yet, to end a life was final. No comma. No question mark. No words surrounded by parentheses. The period at the end of a sentence. The mere suggestion tipped her off-kilter. "You're a doctor, Miles. A healer."

"I know. I know. But isn't there some way to alleviate…some way to know when to—"

"We're making him as comfortable as possible."

"Is it enough?"

"I know you're under tremendous stress." She gave his forearm a gentle squeeze. "It's not easy, but what you're contemplating isn't necessary at this point." She made a conscious effort to form the words. "No one knows what the next few hours may bring."

Miles slapped the wall and wheeled around. "What, a miracle?"

"I don't believe in miracles." Miracles were for the chosen few. Miracles were for the lucky lottery winner. And she'd never held a winning ticket for either. "I believe in science. In the healing power of doctors and medicine. And compassion."

"He's dying, Rachel. Slipping away right in front of my eyes." His voice was low and broken and on the verge of collapse. "I can't stand that I can't help him."

"We may be a small facility, but we have some of the best doctors caring for him."

"I'm well aware of that. I've been here often enough." The severity in his voice evened. "With Search and Rescue. Lives have been saved here. And lost…but those people weren't my father."

Search and Rescue. Nico. He'd been there. Searching for her husband.

"He's in capable hands. The best."

"Do you think he has a chance in hell of surviving this?" The creases around his eyes and across his forehead deepened. It matched the desperation in the sleep-deprived voice and took the short route straight to her heart and squeezed.

"Yes, I do." She reached for his hand and he took it with the alacrity of a drowning swimmer grasping a lifeline. "There's always hope."

He squeezed her hand, his silent plea speaking more than words. She needed him to trust her instinct. Trust her knowledge and the medical center's competency. And then he brought her into his arms, his embrace one of affirmation, of desperation, and one of mutual understanding. And something more. Her body molded to his and she gave what she could in return—a place to let go of the grief, a place to rest, and for the spark of hope to grow.

She drew back, her fingers trailing from his in a slow, deliberate movement, the immediate distance both a comfort and relief.

"You're exhausted, Miles. I'll come by after my shift and stay with your dad so you can get some rest."

Miles parked his hands on his hips and paced the length of his father's bed. "I can't leave him."

The children's day care center wasn't but a few hallways away, but he'd left his father to walk Bug there. "I'll have a rollaway brought in for you. I'll be your eyes and ears and you won't need to leave."

Miles stopped pacing, his face void of expression.

"It's one of the perks of being the nursing supervisor. I have a little pull around here."

"What about Bug?"

"Grandpa can pick her up from day care. He's big on ice cream for dinner," she said with a hint of amusement.

"Who could turn down an offer like that?" The upward turn of his mouth paled in comparison to the sudden sparkle in his eyes. "Doesn't sound so bad, actually."

"If she doesn't contract rickets and end up a bow-legged, pint-sized human." Rachel backed toward the doorway.

"Ice cream has plenty of vitamin D."

She braced herself against the doorframe and wrinkled her nose. "So says the doctor whose patients eat pellets made of green stuff."

"You make it sound like soylent green."

She opened her mouth and then closed it.

"It's from a '70s movie. With Charlton Heston?"

She stopped short of the corridor. "Oh." The explanation was as puzzling as the initial comment, but she let it slide into the corner of her mind reserved for inconsequential trivia. "Thank you for walking Bug to day care earlier."

"Didn't take long and it did me good to listen to her chatter. Took my mind off my dad for a few minutes."

Bug's chattering and non-stop questions could distract a mosquito in the process of sucking the lifeblood from a particularly juicy victim. "I'll be back after my shift."

Outside Randall's room, Rachel slumped against the wall, the hopeful words she'd spoken to Miles coiling inside her like a snake alerted to danger. Randall's vitals weren't good. His odds weren't good. She prayed she hadn't given Miles an illusion, a sense of hope where none existed.

A silent killer had invaded Randall Malone's body.

FIVE

The intensive care unit never truly sleeps, but in the small hours of early morning, the normal bustle turned down its dial in restful relief, and all was quiet.

Rachel cradled Randall's hand and brought it to her cheek. The fever had broken sometime during the night, his skin cool against hers. Even so, he had yet to stir.

"Well, Button?"

The gentle touch of the voice brought her fully awake. "Grandpa? How long have you been here? You shouldn't be in here."

"Bug woke up early and was asking for you." He removed his beanie and held it in front of him. "I brought her and Zoe a little early though neither one was fully awake. Neither were you, so I let you rest for a bit."

"I must have dozed off." She attacked her unwitting curls with a brisk finger-comb and then stretched the sleep from her stiff muscles, a groan tagging along for the ride. "God, do I need coffee."

"I'm not the Almighty and I'm skeptical of my skills in turning water into wine, but I think I can transform plain water into coffee." Normally more counselor than comedian, Grandpa's heavy Santa Claus eyebrows lifted, quite pleased with the rare display of humor.

"I'll go so you don't get into trouble for breaking the rules and allowing a non-relative in the ICU." He shot her a dubious look. "You stay here with your patient."

"He's not my patient. Just a friend."

He tipped his chin toward the rollaway. "Him too?"

She followed Grandpa's gesture to the cot.

Bug had fallen asleep curled next to Miles, dark curls askew from her braids, and her stuffed ladybug clutched to her chest in a tangle of little girl arms and fleece ladybug feet. Oblivious to the invasion of his less-than-adequate accommodations, Miles had contorted his tall, athletic body into a denim-clad pretzel to afford her room. He'd thrown one long arm over Bug, the other swiped absently at the curls tickling his chin. Zoe had sneaked in too, and had wiggled her tiny four-legged body in the small space between their shoulders.

On the days she'd been to the vet clinic or seen him in passing, she'd found him crisply dressed, a sprouting of whiskers neatly land-scaped, and longish hair swept away from his face—a reserved repre-sentation of his profession. But refusing to leave his father's bedside had further enhanced the *just crawled out of bed* thing he had going on —thick, tousled hair hanging just past his ears and tumbling over his forehead—a parallel to the wild adventurer.

Frustration, fatigue, and worry linked hands and drained from her body, and an inward smile spilled into the abandoned space. The earth ceased to spin, space and time crawling into nonexistence. Messy and rumpled with a noticeable stubble, Miles Malone was completely undone and perfectly put together huddled next to her daughter.

The sterile room dulled into a wash of blurred color, and she blinked away the watery onset, silent breaths and the invisible beating of their hearts the only sounds save the distinct rush of blood pumping in her ears.

"How is he?"

"Perfect." The answer escaped as a whispered sigh.

Grandpa twirled his beanie in a full circle and cleared his throat. "I agree, Button. But that's not exactly who I meant."

Rachel's brain processed the mindless remark, heat crawling up her cheeks. She rose quickly, chair grating across the tiles. Zoe peeked precariously at her with one eye, and Bug curled her little arm tighter around her stuffed toy, her other next to Miles, long fingers splayed across his cheek. Miles didn't move, save the lazy quirk of his mouth in the untroubled way of sleepy smiles.

She gripped the chair, her legs moments from melting into a puddle.

Passing the disquieting rumination off as fatigue, Rachel took the stethoscope from around her neck and checked Randall's vitals. The vein in his neck beat steady and strong, adding to the positive findings in the attending doctor's notes from last night's late rounds. Rachel draped the instrument back around her neck and stroked Randall's cheek. "Mr. Malone is going to be fine, Grandpa. Just fine."

"You still up for coffee?"

Rachel's eyelids fluttered, the unseen weight of fatigue pulling them down. "I could use the caffeine. I'm exhausted." She scrubbed both hands over her face. "Seems I'm speaking nonsensical gibberish this morning."

He jutted his chin and puckered his lips, the pause as pronounced as the glint in his eye. "If you say so, Button."

"Coffee, Grandpa. I need coffee."

"Coming right up." He raised a shoulder and let it drop as if he'd changed his mind to speak, turned, and left the room. Her rear was as tired as the rest of her and she paced the room, anxious for the caffeine jump-start.

On her fourth trip around the cramped space, Grandpa returned with two coffees, and she quickly flipped open the plastic spout, the aroma waking her senses. She sipped cautiously. "Oh…this is heaven."

"It's hospital coffee, Rachel."

"You don't know our director. It's the same coffee they offer at Koffee Korner in the Village Square. Everything in this community is high-end, including the freshly ground coffee beans and Charmin Ultra. Kristina Kaufman doesn't do anything halfway."

"Good to know if I'm ever quizzed on The Villages' trivia." He raised the tall paper cup. "This is for Miles when he wakes up." He set it on the tray beside him. "I have an appointment, so I need to get moving before they start without me."

"I wouldn't want you to miss breakfast with the ROMEOs." The group of Retired Old Men Eating Out met every Tuesday and though he seemed to attract attention wherever he went because of his resemblance to Santa Claus, the breakfast date gave him an excuse to socialize. Rachel took another sip of coffee, lifting her cup in silent salute. "Thanks for bringing my girls."

Grandpa's kiss landed lightly on her cheek. "Get some rest, Button."

"I will. Please be careful. The roads are slick."

Her grandfather clung to the doorway, his muscles slow to react to his mind's commands, and then he disappeared into the hallway. The marked deterioration of his coordination knotted the barbed wire around her heart and she turned away from the fading footsteps. Careful not to bump the six-inch incision along Randall's hip, she tucked the blanket under his ribs. "You can wake up any time, Mr. Malone, Miles is waiting for you."

Randall's dry, cracked lips parted. "I doubt...that."

"There you are, young man." Rachel squeezed his hand.

"I feel like a damned freight train...ran me over." He tried to swallow and grimaced. "Twice."

"I'll let your doctor know you're awake and bring you some ice chips for that dry throat."

"How about some gin to go with it?"

"Maybe tomorrow, Mr. Malone."

"Might be dead tomorrow."

"You're too damned ornery to die, Pop."

The voice, raspy and rough with sleep, startled her and she turned to see Miles lifting Bug, her sleeping daughter as limp as a rag doll against his shoulder. At four years old, she was a bit big to be packing around, but Miles handled her as if she were no heavier than a snoozing golden retriever puppy.

Miles approached the bed. "Welcome back, old man."

Randall squinted. "Hell, I can't die." Though on the edge of sleep again, his mouth twitched. "You're not ready. Neither is your sister."

Miles adjusted Bug and squeezed his father's hand. "Ready for what?"

Randall glanced from one to the other. "Kissed her yet?"

Zoe jumped onto Randall's bed in one leap and licked his nose in a sweet booger kiss, her tail in a blur of wiggles. Satisfied with her doggie ministrations, she sniffed the area around the incision, and then nudged the blankets above it.

"Must be the drugs, Dad, you're not making sense." Miles switched Bug to his other side. "And Madison's got a flight out of Switzerland late tonight."

"Call your sister...tell her...save her ticket."

Rachel swabbed Randall's nose and oxygen tube with an alcohol wipe, but Randall waved her away. "Leave me be. Isn't every day I get a nice wet kiss from a pretty girl."

"Bug and Zoe shouldn't be in here anyway."

"Hogwash. I'm paying through the nose for this little home away from home. I say who stays."

Rachel smirked. She was used to breaking rules, but Randall Malone had proven to be a comparable adversary. As if she understood who had final say in the matter, Zoe curled nose to tail into a compact ball of Yorkie fur, peeked up at Rachel, and slipped into doggie dreams with a contented sigh.

"Want to tell me what you're jabbering about, Pop?" Miles scratched Zoe's ears and then her withers under her therapy vest. A lazy roll allowed him full access to her tummy.

Miles waited for an answer, but his father had fallen back into morphine dreams, a slight quirk to his mouth.

"Rest is the best thing right now. He'll sleep for some time."

"Good." A thread of hair had fallen over his forehead, blond streaks woven between the darker ones, kissing his brow. "My cell's ready to die and it'll give me time to charge it and reach my sister. I don't think it'll hurt her feelings to cancel."

"She doesn't get along with your parents?"

"My little sister's found herself a blond Norseman. A Viking god." Miles punctuated the colorful description with a noisy smirk. "Her words, not mine. She wasn't anxious to leave him, but she was concerned about Dad. This will make her day, I'm sure."

"I didn't know you had a sister."

"Spoiled rotten. Did an internship in Sweden right after college then got a job in Switzerland. Hasn't been home much since." The evidence of his sister's absence drew his expression inward, a distance that stretched beyond physical miles. "I miss the little brat."

"Speaking of which," Rachel said, pointing to Bug, "you don't have to carry her."

"Bug and I have a mutual agreement. She asks. I agree."

"To what?"

Miles brushed a stray curl from Bug's cheek. "Anything she wants."

"Terrific. Just what a parent wants to hear."

They approached the doorway and Rachel looked back on Randall, pain and frustration lying temporarily beneath the peaceful guise of drug-induced sleep.

"I must have been asleep when Dr. Benton made his evaluation, but his fever broke during the night and his notes indicate he'll be fine, though there may be some residual effects from the sepsis."

Arm muscles tensed under Bug's weight as Miles listened intently, the strength of his compassion palpable.

"He could have a long recovery from the infection and setback from surgery, which I don't think he's going to be happy about. His doctor will fill you in with the details."

"He's not happy about much of anything unless he's in command."

"He seems to enjoy taking charge. Especially in PT."

"He's got little patience when it comes to depending on others." Miles stared at his father as though he expected him to sit up and take command of the situation.

"Rachel." Bug ground her face into Miles' shoulder, breaking the ensuing pause. "About last night…" The words fell short as if cut by a knife.

"You don't have to explain…seeing your father in that condition—"

"I...no, that's not what I meant although I couldn't have...gone through with it without..." Miles drew his brows together, the concession pinched into deep creases. "I wanted to apologize...for overstepping—"

Her knees suddenly lacked substance and began to shake. "I understand. Really."

People in emotional situations often did things uncharacteristic to their nature, but when he'd taken her in his arms an apology hadn't entered her mind. But then, he was used to showing the same outward compassion to his patients' owners. She'd been on the receiving end at his clinic and she'd be foolish to think this had been anything other than the need for human touch, a need to connect with something solid, something real in a tense situation.

"I'm a nurse, Miles. People need human contact and a little reassurance sometimes." To assure him it meant nothing more was the right thing to do. Yet, what seemed the right thing to say, didn't feel right at all. Tossing the contradictory thoughts aside, she pointed to the counter. "Grandpa brought you coffee."

"Bullshit." The cracked sound turned them both in Randall's direction.

Miles slipped in beside his father. "What, Pop?"

"Cut the crap, son, and get on with it." The blank expression Miles gave him matched his silence. "Cute kid," Randall said, his raised hand dropping like a stone.

"Dad, this is Nicole. Everyone calls her Bug."

"Yours?"

Bug squirmed on his shoulder. "You're a little high on morphine."

"I think maybe you should've...kissed her first."

Miles responded with a slow, questionable shake of the head.

"Mommy?" Bug rubbed her eyes. "Where's Ladybug?"

Rachel scanned the room in search of the stuffed toy. "Miles, have you seen Ladybug? Bug was sleeping with her and—"

Miles reached into his back pocket, produced the toy, and wiggled it in front of Bug. "This little guy?"

"No. Not a yucky guy." Bug's nose scrunched, and with the intensity reserved for most any creepy crawler with multiple legs, she inspected Ladybug carefully. "Ladybug is a girl," she said with a dramatic pout. "Like me."

Rachel buried a snort behind a fist.

"Could be a boy ladybug. Maybe?"

"How?"

Miles scraped a hand over his chin, snagged the coffee cup, and took a long drink. "I think you're right, Bug. She's pink, so I'm sure she's a girl." He swallowed the weak response with another drink.

Bug took each fleece leg in turn, a curious frown buckling her brow. "How can you tell she's not a yucky boy?"

Miles sputtered and set the cup down.

Rachel couldn't stop an unladylike snort. "Okay, mister veterinarian, you're the biology-animal-critter-geek, and I can't wait to hear your answer to this one."

He opened his mouth to speak, but Bug beat him to it. "It's okay. We forgive you." She giggled and poked the toy into Miles' face. "Kiss and make up."

Startled—and judging by the color rising from neck to ears, more than mildly embarrassed—Miles leaned forward.

Rachel held back another snort as the brawny vet hesitantly kissed the stuffed toy.

"She's as pretty as you are, so I have no doubt she's a girl." He winked and brushed her nose with his finger.

Bug held Ladybug to Rachel. "Your turn, Mommy. Kiss, kiss."

Rachel kissed the ladybug with an audible "mwah" and Bug's giggle crinkled her eyes into a firework of joy. "Now all of us." Bug welcomed them with arms opened wide. "Kiss, kiss, kiss."

Panic drained Miles' face of color, and Rachel returned an inquisitive grin. "Anything she wants. Right, Dr. Malone?"

He hesitated and then leaned in, and Rachel followed his lead and the three of them smothered the stuffed ladybug in noisy, animated kisses.

For an instant of recall, the connection was as strong as the effects of a narcotic. For an instant, they were one. For an instant, she was part of a family. Her long ago family. Her mother, father, and her. And her own stuffed puppy, as worn from love as her daughter's ladybug.

Bug shimmied restlessly and Miles set her down. Zoe jumped from Randall's bed and ran from the room, her legs a blur of motion and fur.

With an alarming squeak, Bug bolted after her.

Her daughter's name hung suspended in Rachel's throat. She couldn't call out. Not here. Not in Intensive Care. What had gotten into them? Zoe was a trained, certified therapy dog and frequently left by herself to visit the residents, but Bug was forbidden to follow.

Rachel bolted into the hallway.

"Rachel, wait!"

A fire alarm screeched. Adrenaline heated her blood. Confused visitors lurked. Nurses prepared.

Medical staff rushed by on both sides. She turned. Scanned the hallway in both directions. Her skin prickled. She spun, searching, palms crushed to her temples, and froze.

Him.

Small, cold feet skidded over her skin in a full-body shiver and the memory seized control.

She froze.

The silhouette. Long nose. Tight-combed, coiffed hair.

The air stilled. Sound ceased. Her lungs quit.

And then the smell crashed through her defenses. Distinct. Vile. She tried to swallow the sweet-hot bile searing her throat, to make it stop. To make it go away.

No-no-no-no-no.

It couldn't be. He was in prison, wasn't he?

"Given his prison record, he could be released early."

Someone jarred her elbow.

Apologized.

Swept by.

The crowd reacted swiftly, but her muscles refused the command to run.

And then the man at the end of the hallway turned his back away from the crowd. Away from her.

The earth shifted.

Zoe was missing. And so was her baby.

And the man she'd put behind bars for raping her vanished into the shadows.

SIX

"Whoa, there." Miles reached Rachel in time to keep her from collapsing. "I've got you."

"He's here."

Miles held her steady, rubbing her arms. "Who?"

"I can't lose her, too. I…"

The plea turned liquid in her blue eyes. Acute. Intense. Deep. The pain tore at him and in the quiet of his heart, he grieved with her. "They couldn't have gone far."

The flight or fight response pulsed against his skin in little shock waves. Calming a puppy, a kitten, a horse, or their owner with words and a compassionate touch was instinctive. But words seemed inadequate, and he couldn't put it into spoken thought even if he'd wanted to. He'd never experienced anything equal to this connection. Not even with…*Brenna.*

He sidelined the unexpected reminder.

"I have to find her and Zoe." Authority seasoned her words. "Now!"

"We'll find them. You have my word." He spoke calmly, but the distant drill of the alarm punctuated each word. The tightness in his gut grew. "Zoe's trained for emergencies. I'm sure she's fine and Bug is close."

"You don't understand. He'll hurt her."

"Who, Rachel?"

An intern ran past, slowed, turned. "No worries, Nurse Rachel, the fire was contained in the Village Square Movie Theater across campus next to day care."

"The children?"

"Fire's already out. More a nuisance than it was a real emergency. At least we know the alarm works." The intern's words shriveled as he wove through a small knot of nurses and orderlies.

The alarm died. The bustle subsided into the normal chaos of an emergency wing but lacked any sign a child had gone missing.

"Let me go." Rachel jerked free of his grip. "I have to find my daughter."

Miles took her elbow and led her into a small cubby. "Talk to me, Rachel. Who's here?"

She gulped for air but didn't speak.

"If we work together, we'll find them. But I need to know what's going on."

Distance crowded out the terror in her eyes as if she were wary prey on the verge of being devoured. She leaned against him limp and trembling, and he folded his arms around her. "Who, Rachel?"

"I can't...I don't want to tell you."

"I understand your concern, but something else is going on here. I want to help find them and I'll do everything in my power to keep them safe, but you have to confide in me."

"I saw..." She turned a cheek, dropped her chin to her chest, and after a moment's hesitation, she swiped a finger under her eye. "I saw...*him*. The man who...raped me." Her voice splintered. The fragments burrowed beneath his skin, shattering his insides to useless pieces.

Her background was public knowledge, but the sucker punch the admission carried nearly toppled him. The damn leeches at the local paper had run the story when her husband had gone missing. He'd been there the night the police told her Nico had disappeared on Flattop Mountain, and he'd been the one to give her the scarf he'd found near The Drift. He'd been there, searching for her husband, fearing the outcome but never giving up. And she had the same distant expression then as she did now—the silent, stormy plea that begged for someone to make it go away.

Miles fell against the wall and took her with him, smoothing her hair, comforting her now the way he'd wanted to then. The night her husband had disappeared and was presumed dead, he'd held her, loathing himself for his envy. Envy for a man who'd died tragically hours before. She'd been pregnant with Bug. Nico's baby. As the days, weeks, and months passed, the envy he'd grappled with had faded into something deeper, something he couldn't deny. But he no longer envied a man who'd been dead for five years.

Forcing himself from the dregs of the past, Miles lifted her chin. "We'll find Bug and Zoe."

"What about...*him?*" Desperation marked the question.

"I know you're scared," he said, toggling from one red, moisture-heavy eye to the other. "But Demetri Chastain—"

"Don't!" She pushed away. "Don't say his name to me. Ever."

"I'm sorry," he said, filing away the unsettling request. "I can respect that and I won't say it again." The words crept from him in a low whisper.

"I have to find Bug."

Miles withdrew his phone.

"Who are you calling?"

"The police and campus security."

"No police, no security. Please." New tears bubbled on the edge of her eyes. "He'll hurt her. To punish me."

"Detective O'Bannion is a friend. He can help." Miles took her shoulders and held her at arm's length.

"I saw him...in the hallway." She glimpsed over her shoulder as if a stalker lurked in the shadows.

"Rachel, please look at me." Miles turned her chin. She trembled, the force of it humming through his fingers.

Moisture clung to her lashes the same way she clung to her resolve, yet in the midst of the panic ebbed a glimmer of trust. A sudden desire to trace her lips with his thumb left him without words, without the will to stand. But this wasn't the time or place to act on suppressed desires.

"I promise we'll find them, but I have to ask...why do you think Bug's in danger? It happened a long time before she was born."

"He threatened to...kill me. And my family. Why would he be here if he didn't know about my baby? Don't you see? I put him in prison." A gulp of air turned into a ragged breath. "He's a...monster...he'll hurt her to get back at me."

"I won't give up until we find them, but we should alert the police."

"You're right." She shook her head, but little conviction went with it. "I'm sure she's not far. I...panicked...with the fire alarm and seeing..." She looked directly at him, not merely asking but begging for a response. "He's applied for commutation of sentence, but he's still in prison, isn't he?"

"If we call Detective O'Bannion he can check." He managed to keep the niggling concerns at bay, but the residual doubt lay rooted in his center. "It may take some time before he gets back to us with an answer."

Her eyes grew wide. "Oh, God." She dug her fingers into her upper arms and backed away. "I don't know...I don't remember what my baby was wearing."

"Her ladybug sweatshirt."

Rachel's mouth parted and she blinked.

"She wears it every Tuesday." He shrugged. "And pink stretchy pant things." He waved a hand down his legs. "And her light-up snow boots."

Without warning, Rachel turned and fled.

"Rachel!" He lunged but caught nothing but air. Her Skechers and pink flowered scrubs disappeared into the hallway in a blur. "Damn it." With the exclamation, he began to search in the opposite direction Rachel had gone.

He'd never had kids, but he understood the urgency for a mother to find her child. Instinct drove animals to protect their offspring at any cost, the distinction inscribed on their soul. Rachel, a mother before whatever else defined her, had set paralyzing fear aside to find and protect her little girl, one who loved insects, her dog, and her stuffed ladybug.

He searched hallway after hallway, but didn't have access to the places employees would and eventually found himself at the daycare center. His gaze wandered over the double doors, decorated with insects and flowers.

And then he remembered their conversation.

Ladybugs. Callerpitters (as Bug called them) that turn into butterflies. Katydids and dragonflies.

She'd been over the moon with the proposed insect displays in the new theater building, which was still under construction, and told him how Zoe chased lizards, squirrels, and beetles, and had cornered a centipede once. Two days ago, Bug had told him she'd watched Zoe chase a cat into the theater, and giggled when the cat hissed and swatted her nose.

The intern's words. The fire. And a hunch.

The sweet-hot rush of adrenaline fueled him into action.

SEVEN

*W*ith nothing except a crazy hunch, Miles slapped the wall, milled his way through the corridor, and blew through the heavy clinic doors into the cold air. In the chaos surrounding the alarm and Bug's disappearance, he'd given no regard to the weather and he'd left his jacket in his father's room. The tactical pullover and dress shirt underneath would have to do.

Miles took off at a dead run toward the theater. After he was off the covered portico, he slowed his pace to navigate the snowy landscape, and making the most of the slow trek, he pulled out his phone. Though only a sliver of charge remained, he dialed.

The other end picked up right away. "Hey, buddy, we on for Saturday on Flattop?"

"Chris, remember the Caldarone case?" Misty breaths whirled in clouds around his face.

"Sure, why?"

"Might not be exactly legal, but I need a favor. You game?"

Chris offered a noisy pause. "I'm a cop, Malone. I'll make that decision when you tell me what this is about."

"I need to know if the man charged in the sexual assault against

Rachel Caldarone..." He picked up his step across a small area of exposed earth. "...has been released from prison."

"Jesus, why do you want to know about that fucking scumbag?"

"I have my reasons. Has he been released?"

"You haven't seen last Friday's *Estes Park News*? The miserable reporter who dragged all this up when Nico went missing has an article on the front page about Demetri Chastain, aka the fucking scumbag. He's applied for commutation of sentence. Phase II hearing takes place in a couple of weeks."

"Is he free right now?"

"If the Board of Executive Clemency hasn't met, the decision couldn't have been handed down."

"Can you find out for sure?"

"Might take a few phone calls, but yeah, I can."

"Thanks, buddy." His shoulders deflated and the sick feeling in his gut morphed into an anxious knot. "I owe you."

"Enough to let me beat you down Flattop Mountain Saturday?"

"Not a chance. I have a reputation to uphold." He smiled briefly. "Thanks, Chris." There was no response, and he pulled the phone away from his ear. The screen was black. "Shit." He shoved the useless phone back into his pocket and covered the last few yards as fast as he could without falling on his ass.

Barricade tape blocked the theater's entrances. Despite the recent snow and cold temperatures, sweat prickled his forehead and he wiped a sleeve across his brow.

The *FIRE LINE—DO NOT CROSS* tape quivered in the breeze, and black soot covered the snow where it had been tromped. He inspected the ground around him. No visible sign of either Bug's or Zoe's presence could be distinguished from the construction crew's or firefighter's footprints. Only the ugly reminders of the fire remained—a sloppy mess and the smoldering stench of wet ash.

Scanning the grounds in both directions and then behind him, Miles ducked under the tape and tested the rear service door. Locked. Of course it would be—all the entrances would be locked and off limits until the fire marshal could inspect for origin and cause, building safety, and then clean up could begin. But he had to check. It made sense. He had to get inside, but to do that he'd have to think like a four-year-old kid.

Thirty-six years had passed since he'd been Bug's age, and he'd been a foolish ten-year-old kid the time he'd tried to sneak into a theater—and he didn't care to think about the consequences that particularly bright idea had cost. He was far from a kid acting on a dare. But he was driven by something quite different than watching a movie for free.

With a personal stake in its completion, he'd spoken regularly to the crew foreman and kept tabs on the theater's construction, and followed the exterior to the side facing the heavily wooded forest. At least his nefarious acts of breaking and entering would be hidden from The Village Square and main complex. Hiding them from his conscience was a different story.

The north side of the building is where he needed to be. Tracking down someone with access would take more time than he was willing to give up, and breaking a window wasn't on his list of approved alternatives. The crawl space was the only way he knew of to get inside.

"Dammit."

According to Rachel, he'd skirted the rules of Parenting 101 when it came to the little girl. And he'd ignored his own long-standing rule of remaining neutral when it came to the opposite sex since...*Brenna.* Jesus, how long had it been since he'd thought of her without jamming a ski pole into an icy snowbank? And one cold, snowy day his hard and fast rule of not mixing work with his personal life had toppled.

He'd tried to bury the feel of Rachel in his arms the night her husband had gone missing. Had tried to bury the memory. Had convinced himself his reaction had been entirely inappropriate and he'd immersed himself in his work. But the day the nurse dressed in pink work scrubs brought her Yorkie into his clinic, the steadfast rule disintegrated.

It had been the first time he'd seen her since Nico's disappearance.

The tiny therapy dog had suffered from a severe ear infection, and he'd been forced to put her under anesthesia to scrape a sample of the debris for microscopic examination and thoroughly flush and clean the ear canal. And he'd nearly had to scrape Rachel off the floor when she signed for the procedure, her heart as tender and vulnerable as Zoe's inflamed ears.

He'd written the rule in stone. But when it came to Bug and Rachel, the foundation of that particular proclamation had fast become a pile of rubble.

The crawl space access to the theater was no more than two feet by two feet. Easy for a child no heavier than a half-grown Newfoundland to crawl through, but stuffing shoulders that overcompensated for a six-foot-two frame appeared dubious at best.

He sank to his knees. Mushy, sooty snow blossomed into dark patches on his jeans. The cold spread quickly up his legs and the melting snow dribbled into his boots. Ignoring the chill erupting in gooseflesh over his body, he sat on his butt, turned his shoulders at an angle to the widest part of the space, grabbed the inside of the frame, and pulled himself through. Or at least he tried.

Midway, he stuck.

"Okay, Malone, you've been in this situation before." He squeezed the words through clenched teeth and inched backward. "You've dragged your ass through narrower ice caves and couloirs." He realigned his shoulders so the right would go slightly ahead of the left and with a move reminiscent of a man half his size, he shimmied through the opening.

The landing wasn't as easy. His ass collided with the dry dirt three feet below ground level with a thud that jarred his bones.

"Shit, that was graceful." He flipped into a crouching position. The underside of the building reeked of wet ash and smoke but was more spacious than he'd anticipated. He had to bend at the waist to keep from hitting the floor joists, but the opposite side of the crawl space grew taller with the natural downward slope of the earth. As his eyes adjusted to the darkness, they caught a sliver of light on the far side.

Cold, wet, covered in mud, and folded in half, he made his way across the open span, assessing the best way to gain access into the building. Ahead, a gaping hole opened to the upper floor. Insulation hung dripping from the floor joists, and burnt, splintered wood and pine studs lay scattered on the ground below the opening. The fire department had made jagged toothpicks out of the teak floor.

Able to stand upright, he approached the opening. He gripped the edge of the floor and braced his foot on a loose stack of boards. The lumber shifted under him. Slipped. Settled. He poked his head through the opening into the lobby, squinting at the increased light.

Listened.

Drip...drip...drip.

The floor creaked. Popped.

Drip...drip...drip.

A faint rustle. And then silence.

He turned. Didn't breathe. Didn't move. The sounds of silence grew more haunting with each second. A minute. Two. And then... there. A whimper. A small voice competing with the blood hammering in his ears. Panic and urgency collided with a second of relief and he found solid footing, tested the purchase, bent his knees, and jumped.

His upper body muscles burst into action. He hoisted himself up, his full weight slamming into the floor's jagged edge. Splintered wood pierced his gut. Pain ignited like a flame set to gasoline and his body stiffened, feet dangling helplessly below him.

"Ahhhh, shit!" Spit baptized the words. The floorboards groaned. A sweet-hot adrenaline fire pulsed through his veins as he heaved himself up, ignoring the tearing cloth and blinding pain ripping through his abdomen.

"Bug!"

Another whimper sent a shudder through his core. "It's Dr. Miles. Can you hear me? Where are you, baby?"

"In...here."

The timid voice coiled around every nerve, and he blinked slow and hard to stay focused.

Get it together, Malone. Just another rescue.

But in some quiet space, some region of his heart he rarely accessed, he knew this wasn't an ordinary rescue. "It's going to be okay, baby girl. I'm coming to get you." Holding his gut, Miles headed toward the muffled sounds.

"Zoe won't wake up." Usually riddled with giggles and non-stop chatter, her voice wavered between wet sniffles. "I tried to wake her up, but she's sleeping."

Miles turned toward the sound. "Keep talking, Bug. Are you hurt?"

"I'm cold and my teeth are talking." Her voice grew louder. Stronger. "And it smells yucky. Zoe needs a bath and Mommy will be mad because we broke the rules." A small child's hiccup fractured her words, and did the same to his heart. "We didn't mind her. We didn't mind Mommy." She sobbed, the sounds growing nearer, but did nothing to lessen the ache each word, each sob painted on his heart.

"I'll check Zoe when I get there. Are you hurt?" She didn't answer, but a faint thump made him spin to his right. "Can you make that noise again, Bug?"

Another soft knock echoed from the pile of studs...no, it came from his left, and he spun again, searching for the origin. Cardboard boxes were stacked in the corner ready for recycle, except one. One big enough to shelter a child. A few long strides and he was there, sank to his knees, and tore at the flaps.

Bug peeked at him from inside, cheeks smeared with soot and tears. "I'm scared." The small, quiet words stole his air. "Zoe won't wake up and I lost Ladybug." Her chin quivered, small and round and candid in youth, and soft, puppy eyes turned liquid, ready to spill all the scary things and deposit them with the growing ache inside his chest.

"You and Zoe are safe now." Relief eclipsed the worry but he grappled with the impulse to disregard protocol and wrap this sweet girl in his arms, or stick to the strict rules of survival training. "We'll find Ladybug and your mommy. She's looking for you too, but we have to get you out of here."

Bug reached for him, the trust in her outstretched arms dissolving his heart into a puddle until nothing stood between them but the overwhelming desire to keep her safe. To dry her tears. Lessen her fear. Her small hands disappeared in his as he helped her from the box.

His gut screamed at the exertion, but he hugged her, drawing her into what warmth he could offer. Still, she shivered against him.

"Are you hurt?"

"No." She nestled against his chest, and he held her there, protocol be damned. "Wait," she said and crawled back inside the box. Miles took the few seconds of her absence and held his gut. He drew his hand cautiously away, rubbing warm, sticky blood between his fingers, and then wiping the evidence on his shirt.

Bug backed out, Zoe limp in her arms. "Oh, God." Panic struck him as if he'd been hit with the backlash of a tree limb. "Zoe."

"Can you wake her up?" New tears streaked Bug's cheeks. "Is she going to die like our cat Alexandra?"

He'd seen that expression before. Not in Bug's soft brown eyes, but in her mother's crystal blue ones. The same urgency. The same plea. And it had been as palpable today as it had been the night of Nico's disappearance. He hadn't known the answer then, and he certainly didn't know how to tell a child he didn't know the answer now.

"Please wake her up, Dr. Miles." She looked not at him but into him, the empathy staring back shredding the framework of his soul.

A tiny pink tongue lolled from the side of her mouth, but Zoe wasn't moving.

EIGHT

$\mathcal{E}$ach flash of pink raised her hopes. Each shadow or tall, dark-haired man shivered her insides. Rachel's mental list of Bug's favorite places had been checked and rechecked. She'd scoured them all, but Bug was nowhere to be found.

Molly hadn't seen her. None of the nurses had seen her. Bug made a beeline for Inga's cookies on Tuesdays. Always. Yet Inga's sugar cookies decorated into red and pink ladybugs remained in the activity room, uneaten. And more than one of the residents had asked where Zoe was. Zoe loved the residents (especially Archie, who always gave her a treat in exchange for one of her booger kisses) and rarely missed an opportunity to make the rounds. This wasn't like her. Or Bug.

No one had seen either of her babies.

She made one last tour of the lobby—the first and last place on her list—and taking hold of the metal arm, she sank against the wooden bench.

Where could they be?

She hadn't kept them safe, and a worm of guilt agitated a stomach ready to revolt. It was her fault Bug was missing—she should've been more attentive. It was her fault Zoe had taken off—she should've stepped up her training. Her fault her parents never made it home—

she shouldn't have argued with them that night. And it had been her fault that night in the parking lot. If she'd fought harder—

And it was her fault Nico hadn't made it off the ski slopes. Her fault. Because she loved him too much. Loved them all too much. Maybe if she hadn't loved them…

~

H is instincts took over. "Let's get her vest off. She needs room so she can breathe easier."

Miles held Zoe's head and Bug unfastened the vest with the speed of a seasoned pro. He found Zoe's pulse on the inside of her thigh, the slow, steady beat and shallow rise and fall of her chest reassuring, but the tiny spot of blood from her nose concerned him more. She was alive. But he had to get her to his clinic. Quickly.

"Hold your hands out." He placed Zoe in Bug's outstretched hands, and she hugged the little dog to her chest, rocking side to side. Miles yanked the pullover over his head, wincing. The blood stain on the shirt underneath was larger than he'd expected, but he wasted no time and eased the pullover over Bug. It swallowed them both but still held the warmth from his body. "What happened, Bug?"

She handed Zoe back and poked her arms through sleeves that hung past her knees. "Zoe ran away and I wanted her to come back so we wouldn't get in trouble but I couldn't find her." She gave him a dose of bleary, red-rimmed eye blinks. "And then I came in here because…because…"

"Because Zoe came in the theater?"

"Like before." The air wobbled as she gulped in a big breath. "I wanted her to come back, so I followed her and I came in here." She pointed to the entrance doors. "And I looked and looked but I couldn't find her."

"Did you ask the construction workers?"

"No, because they were all outside and they'd tell Mommy and I just wanted my doggie back and not get in trouble, so I was really,

really quiet and pretended we were playing hide and seek. Will Mommy be mad at us?"

The question rose as a plea in her big chocolate drop eyes, and if he hadn't glanced away, he'd have been picking up the pieces of his heart from the teakwood floor.

"I think your mommy will be very happy to see both of you. Do you hurt anywhere? Do your lungs feel funny?"

She shook her head vigorously.

"Good." He mentally sorted the details for both Bug and Zoe. The more he knew the better.

"And then I smelled yucky smoke and the workers were shouting really loud." She shivered and he rubbed her arms, the friction adding a hint of warmth. "The fire alarm went off and I know what that is because Mommy made me listen one time. It's too loud." She covered her ears and squeezed her eyes shut. "I know what to do at home, but not here, and when everyone left I got really scared." Her lower lip quivered and she wiped her face with the grimy sleeve of his pullover.

"It's okay, Bug. The fire's out and you're safe now."

A little arm wrapped around him in a hug meant to circle his neck, got all tangled up in a detour, and circled his heart along with it. "Then what happened?"

"Zoe barked and so I looked for her over there." This time she pointed to the area where the firemen had broken through the floor. "There she was and I was so happy but she wouldn't come to me. I tried and tried to make her mind." Her lip quivered but it was accompanied by a serious frown. "She was being a naughty dog and I tried to pick her up and go back to Mommy's work, but she wouldn't let me and kept running over to those boards."

Random lengths of two-by-fours lay in a scattered heap like kindling tented to start a fire.

"Zoe ran under them and wouldn't come out and I scolded her and told her to 'come this minute'." The lights on Bug's boots flashed as she stomped her foot and pushed back the dark curls corkscrewed around her face, small painted fingernails black with soot.

"Finally, she came out. But then...a big piece of wood...fell down and hit her and I was so scared and I ran over to her and moved the wood and I picked her up and we hid in the box because I didn't know what to do and someone was coming back." Sooty, tear-stained cheeks puffed as Bug blew out a breath. "Zoe didn't even cry."

"She's a very brave dog."

Bug sniffed and used Miles' other sleeve to wipe her nose.

"You were very brave too, but we need to get Zoe to the clinic." Miles tried to stand, but pain checked him halfway and he sucked in a breath, but kept the urge to cry out behind gritted teeth. He hunched over. "We need to get out of here." He fought the need to call out, to blast the pain from his gut. "Through the crawl space." Blood pulsed like a flood of fiery rain to his injury, the heat and chills and razor-sharp pain pooling in beads of sweat across his brow. "And get you home to your mommy."

"I don't want to go that way because it's dark and scary. Can we go out the doors instead? The big ones? A man came in and looked all around while I was hiding. Can we go that way?"

A wave of uneasiness punctured the pain. Surely it couldn't be the man Rachel had seen, but how would he know? He'd never seen him. "What did the man look like, Bug?"

"Like a fireman."

Miles laughed, but it came out more of a groan.

Bug tugged at his sleeve. "There's blood on your shirt, Dr. Miles." She touched the stained area, the innocence of the four-year-old masked by concern. "My mommy's a nurse. She can fix you right up good as new."

Though warm liquid greeted his palm as he pressed the blood-soaked shirt to his belly, he gave her a brief smile. "It's okay, Bug. It's just a scratch. But I need your help."

"I'll help you, Dr. Miles. I know how because I'm big. I'm almost five." Bug took hold of his free arm, the slight pressure calm and composed. "Don't you worry."

A helper. A kind heart. A rule-breaker. So much like her mother. Countless stories from those whose lives she'd touched circulated through the small town, and Molly wasn't one to hold back on

Rachel's adventures (or misadventures as Molly put it) at Woodland Hills in Arizona. Rachel was known to do most anything for a patient, even if it meant breaking a few rules. Hadn't she proven it by bringing in the cot for him? And allowing Bug and Zoe to stay in his father's room?

"Can you carry Zoe for me?"

Bug took Zoe and kissed her tiny ear. "Please wake up, Zoe. Please wake up so Dr. Miles can make you all better."

"Hold her head up and try to keep her steady, okay?"

She nodded and poked Zoe's tiny pink tongue. "Why is she sticking her tongue out?"

"She can't help it. It happens sometimes when they're unconscious." The prospect of being knocked out, of being numb to the pain was a hell of an appealing concept. With one arm around Bug, Miles clamped the other to his gut to hold intact what was surely the slow unraveling of his intestines.

"Wait!" Bug gasped and handed Zoe back. "We can't leave yet." She scrambled back into the box, backed out, and then plopped on her rear. A smile as wide as the Colorado Rocky Mountains blossomed on her face.

Miles gaped at her. "Oh boy."

Bug and Zoe hadn't been hiding in the box alone.

NINE

*T*he main entrance doors opened with a whoosh and Rachel stepped outside. Nothing stirred save the occasional bird foraging for seeds in the ankle-deep snow and her rapid breaths swirling in a foggy cloud. A blast of cold air burrowed through her scrubs and long-sleeved T-shirt as she scoured the area for small foot-prints, and she rubbed her arms to calm a shiver born not solely from the cold, but the lack of any sign of her daughter.

Back inside, her Skechers gripped the tiled floor. For each stride forward her stomach plunged backward, the queasiness multiplying with a vengeance.

"Where's Zoe today?" Harriet Dilloway, who insisted on taking her half out of the middle of the hallway no matter which way Rachel moved, waved her down. Rachel slowed and reached for her arm in greeting. "No one's seen her. It's Tuesday, you know."

"I…I don't know." Her throat tightened as if the admission had grown fingers and squeezed. "I have to go, Harriet," she said, scooting by her. "I'm sorry."

"Don't be sorry, dear. I just miss that precious little dog of yours and I didn't get my puppy kisses."

The ache for both her daughter and her dog was more than Rachel could put into words. She waved at Harriet instead.

Her phone buzzed. She pulled it from her pocket and stared at it as if answering would detonate some automatic explosion.

"Molly?"

"Bug's with me in the activity room, Rach. She's fine." There was a rustle on the other end.

"Hi, Mommy!" Bug's voice drained the tension from every one of Rachel's muscles like a fully opened artery. "It's me and you know what? Dr. Miles rescued me and Zoe and said I was brave and I'm fine because the other doctor said so. And you know what? Dr. Miles will make Zoe all better. Don't worry, okay?"

Rachel forced back tears but couldn't stop the wobble in her voice or her knees and leaned into the wall. "Thank God you're okay. I'll be there soon, baby. Will you be okay with Nurse Molly for a few minutes until I get there?"

"Yes because Dr. Miles said I could have ladybug cookies, so I'm eating some right now and Nurse Molly gave me some milk to dunk them in and it turned pink. Is it okay if I have one more? Just one more I promise."

"Yes, baby. One more." At this point she didn't care if she ate the whole batch, and the proof leaked out in a nervous titter. "Can you put Molly back on the phone?"

"Bye, Mommy. I have to go now because my milk is getting warm and warm milk is yucky."

There was a momentary pause and Rachel pulled in a very long breath.

"She'll be fine 'til you get here, Rach. Angie took my rounds."

"Thanks, Molly." Rachel collected the last of her doubts and swallowed them.

"Don't thank me. It was Miles. See you when you get here."

Rachel opened her mouth to ask about Zoe, but the line had gone dead. Bug was safe, but renewed fear niggled at her.

Why did Miles need to fix her?

Rachel sped through the hallway and around the corner. Out of breath, she stood in the doorway of the activity room sputtering, and at the sight of her daughter, her knees gave way.

"Mommy!" Bug bolted into her arms.

Rachel hugged her as if letting go would pluck her from her arms forever. "My baby girl. Are you okay? Let me look at you." She held her at arm's length. "Where were you and where'd you get this pullover? It's huge."

Bug took hold of the hem and held it out. "Dr. Miles put it on me because my teeth were talking. It's warm and I like it." She hugged the extra material to her tiny body. "But look," she said, raising Miles' shirt. "My ladybug sweatshirt got really yucky."

Dark red stains covered the lower part of the pullover and Bug's sweatshirt. "Are you hurt?" Rachel turned her around, inspecting for cuts and scrapes.

Bug nudged Rachel's hands away. "No, Mommy, stop."

"Are you sure?"

"Yes. Dr. Miles said so." Bug tugged the oversized pullover back into place and put her hands on her hips. "And he said I was brave."

"I bet you were." Rachel kissed her daughter's forehead, unable to quench the feeling she couldn't get close enough or hold on tight enough and gathered the wayward locks of the hair from Bug's smudged face and curled them around her ears. "We'll find another ladybug sweatshirt."

Bug's chin quivered. "You aren't mad? Dr. Miles said you wouldn't be mad at me and Zoe." Bug patted her mother's cheek. A moment of silence crowded beside the delicate touch of her daughter's baby-soft skin and the urgent need to pick her up and lock her away. Then Bug's small palm cupped her cheek as if she were the one being consoled. "Why are you crying, Mommy?"

"Because I'm so happy you're safe and because I'm worried about Zoe." Rachel lifted Bug's braid and sniffed. "How'd you get so dirty? I smell...campfire." The dots connected, but her insides dropped. "Were you near the fire?"

Bug's head bobbed up and down in a slow, unsure fashion.

"You're not in trouble, but I need to know if you were there."

"I was really, really scared," she said, her lower lip quivering. "There were fireman and everything, and then Dr. Miles came and got me and Zoe and he said I was brave and Zoe was brave too, but she wouldn't wake up."

"It's okay, baby. I'm not upset with you or Zoe. I'm just glad you're safe." She smoothed Bug's hair and turned to Molly. "Who's on duty in ER?"

"Bug's been checked, if that's what you're thinking. Dr. Malone took her straight there. Dr. DeSpain said she's fine and to come see him if you have any questions. I told him I'd let you know but I didn't have my phone so I couldn't call you right away."

"Thanks, Molly." The weight of one issue rolled from her shoulders and crashed to the floor. "I have to check on Zoe."

"Dr. Miles took her to his hospital and he told me to stay with Nurse Molly."

Rachel clamped onto Bug's hand and stood.

"Mommy, let go." Bug wiggled her hand free.

"Molly, what did Miles say?"

"Not much, but Zoe was unconscious and Miles was bleeding."

"Dr. Miles had lots of blood on his tummy, right here." Bug patted her left side. "And I told him you could fix him right up, but he said it was only a scratch."

Molly gripped her stethoscope with both hands. "I tried to stop him so I could take a look, but he brushed me off and said Zoe couldn't wait."

Worry elbowed its way into Rachel's throat and stuck. "How bad is she?"

"Said not to worry about Zoe but my God, Rachel, Miles was bleeding badly. Seemed like more than a scratch to me."

"I need your help." Molly offered an affirmative nod before Rachel finished the sentence. "Can you stay with Nicole until Grandpa gets here?"

"No!" Bug bounced on her toes. "I want to go with you and see Zoe."

Rachel exchanged a keen look with Molly and then knelt beside

Bug. "I'll come get you as soon as I can, but right now you need to do what Dr. Miles asked and stay with Molly until Grandpa can come get you. Can you do that for me, baby? Be good for Molly and Grandpa?"

Bug slipped her hand into Molly's and huddled against her. "Okay."

"Thanks, Molly. I don't want her at the vet clinic if—"

"No worries, Rach, we'll be fine." Molly had the annoying habit of butting into a conversation, but this time chose the perfect time to interrupt before Rachel spewed the terrifying thought out aloud. "And I'll call the nurse on standby to fill in for you. Take your time, it's noon and I can have her here by one. We've got you covered."

Rachel walked backward toward the door. "I'll come get you as quick as I can, Bug."

"Give Zoe a booger kiss from me, okay, Mommy?"

"I'll give her lots of love from all of us. Behave for Grandpa."

"Do I have to take a bath?" Bug peeked out from Molly's scrubs.

"Yes." Rachel pointed a finger at her. "And don't argue with Grandpa."

"Wait, Rach. Your coat and purse. I grabbed them from your office."

"I guess I wasn't thinking."

"Understandable."

With a slow shake of the head, she took them. "Thanks."

"Go."

Her daughter was dirty but unharmed and safe and the urge to get to Zoe took over and she fled from the room, down the west entrance hallway and into the parking lot. She fumbled the key fob from her purse, dropped it, and stooped to pick it up.

"Your wee companion is quite safe, I assure you."

Rachel sprang upright. Fell against the Jeep. Dropped her key fob again. "God! Where in hell did you come from?"

TEN

"You have my complete assurance I am neither divinity, nor do I keep company with those of the underworld."

"No? Well maybe next time you happen to pop in," she said, waving her hands frantically, "you could cough or tap your cane or something before you scare the crap out of me? You're like a freakin' tornado touching down without warning."

"I do apologize. I did not mean to frighten you." Ambrose leaned over his cane in a shortened version of a formal bow. "I merely 'popped in' as you say, to assure you your wee dog is in good hands. All will be well."

"You saw Zoe?" She took his arm gently, the heavy coat not much of a buffer for his frail frame. "Molly and Bug said she was unconscious. Is she okay?"

"It is quite a story." As was Ambrose's way, he neither confirmed nor denied her question. "Your concern is understandable, but you can rest assured she is being aptly cared for."

She looked directly at him, the comfort of truth staring back at her, though one eye drifted slightly, the one she had assumed years ago saw nothing beyond darkness. "Bug is safe, but how do you know Zoe's going to be okay?"

"That is neither here nor there, Miss Rachel, only that it is so."

"I hope you're right."

"Belief and hope are gifts given freely. Belief is the key. Hope your future. You know of my ways, given up as the way of truth." The response parked itself in the momentary upward tilt of his mustache.

"I need to see Zoe for myself."

"Ah, yes, you must alleviate the fear you harbor for your companion, your wish whispered upon the wings of a Monarch butterfly—the most regal of the species—granted by the Great Spirit, and given to you through Nico."

She eyed him warily. "How'd you know about the butterfly wish? I've told no one except Grandpa." She knew his ways were unique, of something beyond ordinary explanation. She'd seen proof at Woodland Hills, and yet his elusive ways still baffled her.

"As I have stated many times, there is little I do not know about you Rachel Everly Gowen Caldarone." He reached into his coat and handed her a stuffed toy. "And I do believe this belongs to Miss Nicole, the wee one you refer to as Bug."

"Ladybug?" Stunned, Rachel reached for the stuffed toy and pressed it to her nose. Strawberry shampoo. Sugar cookies—or was it icing? And the subtle hint of baby skin, scented lightly with soap. The reminders of babyhood hidden deep within the threads.

The smile quivering the corners of her mouth vanished, and a million pieces of Rachel's heart spilled down her cheeks. "Where'd you find this?"

Ambrose waved a leather-gloved hand. "The how and why is neither here nor there." He stepped closer and wiped her cheek as gently as her grandfather would. "Your tears are proof of your love and are never wasted."

"You creep me out sometimes, Ambrose." A ragged smile joined a noisy sniffle as she traced the stuffed ladybug's glass eyes with her index finger.

"A common misconception among those I favor." Ambrose took his weight from one foot and leaned into his cane, searching the lot as if standing sentinel. "I merely nudge those along their path who are in need of a little push."

"I think I can find my own way."

"It will do no good to choose otherwise. You must find it in you to trust in someone who shall find a way to lessen the fears you keep locked away. Yes, I know of the fear which consumes you today."

Rachel clutched the stuffed toy. "You know...about that too?" Rachel nudged her foot back and forth, building little piles into the fast-melting snow. The cold, slushy mess seeped into her Skechers. "I thought I saw the man who—"

"Emotions aroused by what we perceive as impending danger or evil—"

"Evil?" She glared at him, her nerves a sudden bundle of misfired responses. "He's a monster." Rachel shrank against the car, clutching the stuffed toy. "You think I imagined seeing him, don't you?"

"No...and yes," he said with a head-tilt so slight it could easily have gone unnoticed. "When presented with that which we assume is real, it feeds our fear. It grows larger. Stronger. Manifests in ways we cannot imagine." He folded his hands across his cane. "Much the way a malformed cell multiplies into a cancerous tumor until it is recognized for what it is and is cut away."

"I know what I saw."

"Emotion which we allow to fester, whether imagined or not, is indeed quite real. It feeds the subconscious. Becomes the fuel for nightmares."

"It if wasn't him, then who did I see?"

"The man by whom your nightmares are fueled remains imprisoned."

Her thoughts boiled and bumped like thunderheads adding to a queue of questions. "So this was just some ghost I conjured from my subconscious?" She raised her hands and let them fall to her thighs with a slap, the stuffed toy dangling from her fingers, its wobbling, spindly legs drawing to a stop.

He scrutinized her, narrowed eyes twitching above puffy pillows. "Not precisely." Deep-set features and a frowsy mop of silver hair moved in a slow side-to-side swath. "You are not one prone to squandering your sensibilities on apparitions." He fell quiet, gazing from one end of the parking lot to the other.

"Then who did I see? Is someone else stalking Estes Park who happens to look like him?" Hot liquid anger flowed down her cheeks and she swiped at the uninvited intrusion.

He raised his chin, unruly eyebrows crowding together. "Demetri Chastain—"

"Don't!" The name spewed into the air hot and thick and rancid. "Don't say his name."

In a gesture meant to still her words, he perched his index finger on his lips. "You must not fear—"

"You're damn right. I don't fear him." She glared at him, resentful words hungry to be unleashed, and they reverberated inside her, reality choking the memory. "I'm terrified of him."

"Fear not the name, but the act with which it is associated."

She leaned away from the car, but her legs froze in an unsteady stance. "There's no difference." She squeezed the stuffed toy, her nails digging into the round body until it no longer resembled the cute ladybug.

"I implore you, fear not his name, for the saying of it shall set you free."

Her grip on Bug's stuffed toy tightened. Loosened. She turned abruptly. Her hands shook, but she managed the proper button to open the car door. "I have to go to Zoe."

"Never underestimate the power of love. Trust the one who loves you beyond doubt."

She tossed her purse and the stuffed toy into the Jeep, the toy tumbling between the seat and console.

"Thus it is said. Therefore, it shall be. I would venture to add, 'until we meet again', but I shall not. For love is ageless and spans all time."

She gathered her scarf, tucked it inside her coat and turned back around. Ambrose had gone, and there would be no sign of the elusive old man. Of that, she was certain.

"Doesn't surprise me, Wilford Langhorne D'Ambrose." A slow smile turned into a conscious laugh. "Not this time."

ELEVEN

he motor turned over and the Jeep's heater came to life.
The clock read noon. She'd left Molly and Bug at noon.
How was it possible no time had passed? With a steady grip on the
steering wheel, Rachel leaned forward and shut her eyes. When it
came to the enigmatic old man, nothing made sense. Or perhaps
adults weren't immune to imaginary friends.

Zoe—her butterfly wish—was her concern now. Miles had found
Bug and taken care of her, and he'd take care of Zoe. He always had.
She wanted to pray, but to whom? God? Would her concerns over a
dog be heard? He sure as hell hadn't listened any other time to prayers
for those she loved.

As she drove the back streets of Estes Park toward the vet clinic,
Miles' name scrolled through her mind—slow and sunny and safe. A
friend. A vet. And he'd help Zoe get better. It said so on his sign—Safe
Haven Pet Care ~ All Creatures Great & Small.

Since the day Nico had gone missing, Miles had always been there.
He'd scheduled visits to The Villages with the idea of a petting zoo for
the residents, unexpectedly appeared at their social gatherings, and
had taken time from his practice to educate the kids at day care about
animals. She'd lost count of the times she'd seen him engrossed in a

book, puzzle, or game with Bug during his visits, and how many exceptions had he made for Zoe after hours?

An odd sensation stilled her in the same way a sip of wine passed from fresh sampling on her tongue to a soothing, warm glow in her belly. And though it didn't take long to drive across the small town, she drove into the clinic parking lot with little knowledge of how she got there.

Except for Miles' white Chevy pickup, the lot was empty, the Closed sign hanging crookedly from the entrance door. It made sense that he'd closed the clinic to be by his father's side for a few days. Rachel parked next to the four-wheel-drive, killed the engine, and took a moment to steady her footing on the unplowed pavement. She took a careful step and froze.

The driver's side door of his truck was smeared with blood.

The sight of blood didn't normally startle her, yet she swallowed several times before she stood at the clinic entrance. Grabbing the handle, she yanked and the door swung open.

"Miles?" The name echoed through the small waiting room, accompanied by the airy twang of disinfectant. She tossed her coat and scarf across a chair and invited herself to the exam room near the rear of the building.

The room tilted, or maybe it was her. She clutched the doorframe. The tiny black and copper pup whose normal energy level was nothing less than a kangaroo on steroids, lay motionless on the steel industrial table. A large portion of her baby's chest had been shaved, and an IV catheter attached to her front leg dripped into a tiny vein.

Rachel's stomach plunged to her ankles.

Miles didn't look up. "Take a seat, Rachel." He worked diligently, deftly piecing together muscle tissue and skin.

Ignoring the request, Rachel took a step forward, afraid to look and terrified not to. "Is she…"

"She regained consciousness after we got here, but she was out long enough to take x-rays and run the tests I needed. There's no skull fracture."

The room swayed. Compressed her lungs.

"I'm treating her for a contusion, which is a—"

"I know what a contusion is." The huffy remark slid from brain to mouth before she could stop it, or at least color it with somewhat less insolence.

Miles grinned at the surly response, the mask covering most of his features crinkling with the effort. "And this wound on her side needed a few sutures."

She counted six.

The muscles in his forearms tensed and twisted, fingers strong and sure as if the connection from brain to hand were forgotten in the intuitive movements. One more loop and the last of nine nylon stitches ended in a neat black knot. Miles clipped the end and dropped the suture scissors into a metal tray.

Zoe hadn't moved. Rachel stroked her ear, the short, fine hair a touch of velvet. So small. So defenseless. So affectionate.

A butterfly wish.

"Is she...she's not going to...?" The question rolled off her tongue in fragmented pieces, afraid the asking of it would make it so.

Miles yanked off the mask and let it fall around his neck and then took her arm with the same tender compassion he'd shown her other times at Zoe's expense. "She's not going to die," he said, wiping the sweat from his brow with his free arm. "I won't let her. I'll do every-thing in my power to get her...and you...through this."

The gentle pressure of his grip seeped through her cotton sleeve, warming her, assuring her. She didn't move. Didn't breathe. Didn't speak. She looked at him then, acutely aware of the determination etched on his face, as deep as the compassion that pooled in his eyes. And in them he held the power and strength to keep her together. And the heart to heal her tiny companion.

"I've got her on a saline drip. Mannitol to help with cerebral swelling. Heart rate's steady." He glanced from IV to patient, his concern evident. "And she's breathing on her own. Bug didn't show any signs of smoke inhalation. Zoe's fine there too."

Bug.

"Bug's okay...because of you. I don't know what I would've

done…" she grabbed the edge of the table, words bunched into a dry knot, "if something had happened to her."

"She's a brave little girl. You should be proud." He massaged the little dog's ear, inside and out. "So is this little lady."

A wobbly nod was all she could muster. Losing either one crawled over her skin in an icy shiver. "Is she in pain?"

"I've given her a mild opioid for the pain and valium so she can rest, Rach."

The way he said her name soaked through her defenses. Her vision blurred, the impending emotion she'd fought to suppress rising to a crescendo. She pinched her bottom lip between her teeth and clamped down on the faulty display of control.

"She's one stubborn Yorkie. Healthy and strong." He removed the surgical gloves, tossed them to the table, and gathered her into his arms. The closeness and comfort of his body heat radiated through his scrubs and into her. "She's not giving up and neither will I."

She nodded and pulled away. His hands slipped from hers, disconnecting the comforting assurance he offered and yet giving back the distance she craved.

Miles tossed the gloves into the nearby trash and buckled over with the effort.

"Miles!" Rachel caught him around the waist.

"I'm fine. I shouldn't have turned like that."

"Bug and Molly said you were bleeding. Let me see."

Miles didn't move, but a painful grimace pinched his features. "I'm fine." If he'd meant to be reassuring, he'd failed dismally. "You just want me out of my clothes." This time the comment teased the corners of his eyes.

"Just your scrubs, Doctor." She put an end to the accusation, but the tender skin below her ears tingled as she led him to a chair. He sat without protest and she knelt beside him, motioning for him to raise his scrubs.

"I'm a doctor, Rachel," he said, holding his left side. "I've got this."

The blood on his scrubs could have come from Zoe's wound, yet somehow the refusal to let her check him did little to ease her concern. "For four-legged critters. Not humans."

"I'm fine and I'm not leaving Zoe."

"Neither am I."

"No sense both of us hanging around, so why not go home, snuggle up with Bug and get some rest?"

"If you're staying, I'm staying. It's not up for discussion."

"You're about as stubborn as that damn Yorkie."

Rachel crossed her arms, a smile escaping the prison of the last few days. "I think that's the nicest thing anyone's ever said to me, Dr. Malone."

He put his weight on the chair arm and hoisted himself up. "In that case, Nurse Caldarone," he said, mimicking the cynicism, "you should probably find a new circle of friends." In a few hesitant steps, Miles was back at the surgical table, fixed his feet, and checked Zoe's vitals. "I'll get this little girl situated in a recovery crate. She's going to be more comfortable than you or I will be."

"I seem to recall I spent last night sleeping next to a hospital bed using my arms as a pillow, and you didn't have a problem with that."

"I was asleep, sharing a rollaway with a pipsqueak, a stuffed lady-bug, and a canine. I've shared my bed with worse." Color instantly rose on his neck and skidded over his forehead.

A smile ganged up on her. "Oh?"

"I meant animals. You know. Animals are my thing."

"Care to elaborate, Dr. Malone?"

Miles produced a half-smile, salted with amusement. "I'm digging myself into a precarious hole, aren't I?"

"Pretty much. But please," she said and leaned against the wall, "I'd love to hear about this thing you have for sharing your bed with four-legged critters."

Ignoring her, Miles lifted Zoe's limp body from the stainless-steel table.

"Wait." Rachel took a step forward. "Can I?"

"By all means. I encourage the interaction even if she's still asleep. She knows you're here."

Rachel stroked the little dog's nose and Zoe opened her eyes half-way. "There's my brave little girl." A tear fell to her fur and she squinted as Rachel massaged the moisture away. Zoe's eyes rolled back and lids heavy with sleep closed over them. Miles laid her inside a special surgical crate and positioned her comfortably.

The crate was spacious and lined in clean, white fleece. It wasn't the accommodations that squeezed her heart but the way the vet's big hands smoothed the hair from Zoe's face, empathy leaking from his pores, and the soft curve of his mouth as he spoke quietly, reassuring her she'd feel better soon.

"She'll be okay."

"Thank you," she said, coaxing the words from a too-tight throat.

"For what?" He adjusted the IV drip and closed the latch. "Doing my job?"

"For saving both my girls today."

Miles gently brushed away the curls that had found their way across her cheek, and somewhere between his touch and unspoken words, she ceased to function.

"How's Bug?"

"Dirty."

"Yeah, well, so was I until I scrubbed to stitch Zoe."

She pointed to his jeans and shoes. "You're still a bit on the muddy side." A moment passed, or it could have been several. "I don't know how to thank you properly."

Impish amusement played at the corners of his mouth. "By paying your bill on time."

"I'm sure Heather will make sure your services aren't neglected. She'd have *payment is expected at the time services are rendered* stamped on her forehead if she could."

"She's wicked handy to have around to handle the business side of the practice."

"Thanks again." Reflecting back on the incidents soured a brief smile. "For saving them."

"We're not out of the woods yet." He took a step back. "It's going to be a long afternoon. Maybe through the night."

Miles slipped into the back and brought out a folding cot, pillow, and a heavy blanket. "It's the best I can do."

"I'll take first watch." She nabbed a chair next to Zoe's crate. "You've had less sleep than I have over the last couple of days."

"You're exhausted. Stress will do that, you know."

"Yes, Doctor, I do know. Besides, I couldn't sleep anyway."

"I'm not going to change your mind, am I?" Seconds drifted into a long pause. "Right, then. But don't hesitate to wake me. There's a full bath beyond the surgery suite if you need to splash your face." His phone dinged. A ragged intake of air accompanied an obvious attempt to suppress a grimace as he retrieved it from the charger. "Molly," he said, lifting the phone, "set it up so I get hourly updates on Dad. Seems he's being his ornery self."

"That's a good sign."

"I agree, except I feel for the nurses."

"The night shift will manage just fine. Connie doesn't take any crap." She took his arm as he walked past. "Please let me take a look at that wound."

"It's nothing. Just a nasty scratch. I've doused it with half a bottle of antiseptic." His voice carried the graveled hoarseness of fatigue. He stuck a hand to his side and eased himself to the cot. "It's fine."

Moments before, he'd hidden behind a surgical mask concentrating on his patient, a comforting expression she'd seen often. But the flicker of pain that deepened its intensity was no stranger either. Though he'd turned his back, the marked muscle tension, the sudden air intakes, and the pain he tried to brush off as nothing did little to ease her suspicions, or stop a shiver that started at her neck and shimmied to her toes.

"Miles, please, just a quick look."

Miles raised a hand, shutting down the inquisition.

Resigned to his stubborn insistence, she turned back to Zoe's crate, watching her tiny chest move rhythmically and the slow drip of the IV. And it wasn't long before Miles' heavy breaths of exhaustion-filled sleep filtered through the quiet. She took the lull in activity to call Molly.

Though she ached to hold her daughter, Bug would have to stay with Grandpa tonight. She sent him a text, apologizing for the short notice. The text back consisted of several smiley faces and one ice cream emoji.

The hours passed from afternoon to night in dreadful silence. She curled up with the blanket. Paced. Checked every corner of the room and the ones beyond. Marked with the distinct tinge of disinfectant and simplicity of a small-town atmosphere, the clinic was rudimentary but equipped with a complexity that would rival any big city animal hospital. Everything Miles needed medically to heal Zoe was at his disposal. Everything he possessed intellectually and an endless supply of empathy ran instinctively through his veins.

Besides Zoe, there were no other critters, nothing else to keep her from replaying the events of the day. Recalling the image of *him*. Each time she did, her insides turned upside down and she'd check it with a firm mental slap and a visit to Zoe's crate.

The chill in the room—maintained to keep bacteria from rousing their uninvited buddies to a social gathering—wasn't overly cold, yet Miles shivered. Rachel removed a stylishly beat up brown leather jacket from the coat rack for herself and draped the blanket over Miles. He flinched but didn't wake.

She checked on Zoe at regular intervals, speaking quietly when she'd lift her head and stroking her tiny companion in her favorite spot between the eyes. Once, she swore Zoe wagged her stumpy tail. In the small hours of a new day, Miles and Zoe continued to rest, the rise and fall of easy breathing a comfort to the tiny feet of dread crawling in and out of her thoughts.

She sat across from Miles in a wide chair with her knees drawn to her chest and the jacket draped over her, counting his slow breaths, each one a quiet confirmation. He'd bent his knees and crossed his arms on top of the blanket, eyes moving erratically in the way of dreams. Were his dreams filled with his mountain adventures? Other than their sheer beauty, the magnetic pull of the mountains eluded her. Miles lived it. Nico had sensed it too, and he'd died chasing their adventurous lure.

The sudden recall awakened the hair on her arms. She snugged the jacket tighter around her and buried her nose in the leather. Traces of antiseptic and Miles' musky, masculine scent lingered there, in the lines and creases of a profusion of yesterdays. Lost in his scent, the sounds of silence folded its arms around her.

She'd dozed in erratic spurts during the quiet hours of early morning, checking first one patient and then the other. But over the last hour, Miles had grown restless and she'd come fully awake.

Rachel crept to the cot and placed a hand on his neck. The hair resting on his collar was damp, the skin clammy. Heat radiated from him.

Too much heat.

He jerked awake and fell to his back clutching his gut. "Shit, that smarts." He sat up, guarding a fierce grimace.

The hoarse, pointed words sent a rash of signals to her brain. Why hadn't she insisted she examine the injury?

Miles eased the garment slowly away from his body and his hand went instinctively to the pain, crushing it against his abdomen. He flinched and then raised the bloody hand and turned it slowly in front of him, front to back, back to front as if scrutinizing a foreign object.

"Oh God, Miles, that's fresh blood." She knelt in front of him. Without permission and before he could spout another round of protests, she pushed his hands away and lifted his scrubs. The shirt underneath was caked in dried blood, fresh blood, soot, and reeked of copper and wet ashes.

And infection.

"This shirt is filthy. You should've taken it off before you put on clean scrubs. Why didn't you change?" He was a doctor, yet her question was as void of an answer as his face was of color.

"I didn't want you to get the wrong idea." He twisted away from her. "Besides—"

"Hold still."

"I was preoccupied with a patient."

"So am I. Now be still while I get this nasty shirt away from this little scratch." The last word was met with a significant amount of sarcasm and a salty glance up.

"It can wait. Heather will be here soon and I have an errand to run." He swiped at her hands but hesitated to stand. "I have to go back to the theater. It's important."

"You aren't going anywhere."

He lifted a hand in surrender, his jaw tensing rapidly. "Rip the damn thing off then, and get it over with."

"You'd enjoy that about as much as you would an enema."

He took another hard look at his gut.

She stood and pivoted on one foot. "Clean towels?"

He lifted his chin in the direction of the supply cabinet. "Left side bottom."

"Tweezers, gloves, scissors?"

What color he had left turned pasty. "Uh…Heather stores the sterilized instruments there." He pointed a bloody finger at a bank of drawers. "Gloves right side of the supply cabinet next to the instruments. She's anal about keeping things stocked."

"She knows what she's doing." Rachel snapped the gloves on, moistened a towel with hot, soapy water, and knelt beside him. "Lay down."

Miles shot her a look that went beyond the intensity of any hard-nosed tough guy, but he did as he was told and laid back.

The fabric was stuck to the scabbed areas. She made a ragged cut and rolled the loose portion farther up his chest and began to scrub. Dried blood covered a good portion of his abdomen and chest and she carefully loosened the scabbed areas, a routine she'd mastered—yet nothing about it resembled anything remotely routine. She wasn't in the retirement facility. She wasn't in a hospital or the ER. And this wasn't a stranger. A crazy course of flutters took flight in her stomach.

Her hands slowed, moving with her wandering eyes to the birthmark—a tiny coffee-colored teardrop—taking shelter in the space above his right clavicle. The slow circular motion scrubbing down a patient had never wavered. Never paused. Never questioned. The dark mat of chest hair nestled around his navel and firm pecs consumed her haste. How long had it been since she'd admired a man's bare chest without flinching? Without revulsion? Admired the unbridled lure of it? And what lay beyond? One man had stripped her of the beauty, artistry, and elegance of intimate contact. One man had given it back. Could she be the woman she once was with someone else? What once terrified her, she longed to admire. To touch...

"Rachel?"

The sound startled her and she scrubbed with earnest. "I've got to loosen the cloth—"

"I know, I know. Can you hurry it up?"

She peeled the shirt back inch by inch as she wiped the dried blood with the hot, moist towel. "Do you use Lidocaine on animals? If you have some do you want me to use it?"

"Yes. And no, I don't want any. Just get it over with."

"How about a bullet?"

"What?"

"Shirt's clear, but this next part isn't going to be pleasant." She set a clean towel next to him and took hold of the tweezers, preparing to enter the wound and remove a generous splinter—not very big, but it was definitely going to feel like she was pulling out a hunk of lumber. "You might want a bullet to bite down on, tough guy." She cleared herself of emotion and parted the muscle tissue.

"I've done this a million times—"

She dug the tweezers into the wound.

"Shit-fire and damnation!" The exclamation came out choppy and laced with spit.

"Gotcha, little fella."

"Jesus! Did you poke a hot iron in there?"

"Not in, Dr. Malone. Out." She held up the tweezers and examined the culprit, a piece of wood about half the girth and length of her pinky. "Baby splinter anxious to take root and work its way into your intestinal tract."

"You sure it wasn't the whole damn tree?"

"Just a redwood twig."

"Teak. The theater floor is made of teak." Lifting up on an elbow, he surveyed the damage.

She nudged his hand away and handed him a clean towel. "I don't care if it's made of steel, you know better than to touch an open wound without gloves."

He grumbled something incomprehensible, pressed the towel to the wound and then wiped his free hand across his scrubs, leaving a fresh, bloody smear. He sat up and swiveled his feet to the floor. "Zoe and I share an acute affinity."

"Stubbornness?"

He scowled.

She grinned.

"Seems I might need a stitch or two."

TWELVE

Suturing dogs and cats or the occasional horse or goat was a hell of a lot more acceptable than being on the receiving end. It had occurred to him to skip it altogether, but Rachel had been right; a doctor who sewed humans back together was in his best interest if he wanted to keep his entrails intact. Now that it was over, he could admit the procedure hadn't been near as traumatic (or painful) as removing the chunk of timber had been without the benefit of a local anesthetic.

"I'm sorry."

The warmth of her words drifted past his ear and he looked over his shoulder, the stitches in his abdomen unyielding, certain the doctor had sewn his head directly to the tendons. "For what?"

"For hurting you."

"Doc said you did a good job."

"I'm selfish that way."

"How's that?"

"My dog needs her vet."

"Ah. I see." He slid a hand across his face with an audible rasp. "So, had I not been Zoe's vet you would have let me die?"

"You were far from dying, Doctor. It was just a nasty scratch."

Rachel laughed, the first time he'd heard her do so since Bug had gone missing more than twenty-four hours ago. The fresh, light sound breezed over him, spreading through his body like waves of musical notes.

"How long before I can get out of here?" He rose on one elbow. "I need to check on Zoe."

"Relax." Rachel moved to his side. "I called Heather. Zoe's doing great. Besides, Doc said you need a tetanus booster, a heavy-duty dose of antibiotics, and your prescriptions for oral antibiotics and pain meds before you leave."

"If those last two are oral, the first two are—"

"Intramuscular."

"Crap."

"Don't care for injections?"

He fell back onto the pillow with a little too much emphasis, the pain shooting into tissues not blissfully numb. "Shit shit shit." Every muscle in his recently-turned-forty body screamed at him.

She fluffed his pillow. He snatched it from her and punched it with an attempt to remove the smirk.

The smirk grew wider. "Need someone to hold your hand while Doc gives you the injections?"

His imagination had taken him on more than one excursion with her hand in his, and none of them had anything to do with piercing his ass with a needle. On the other hand, in order to get to the site where this intramuscular thing was to take place on a human, she'd have to...

"Miles?"

The sound popped his thought bubble and he coughed into his fist, praying his musings didn't show in his expression. Or anywhere else for that matter. "Yeah?"

"Would you like me to hold your hand while Doc gives you your injections, or would you rather I did the honors?"

"Thanks, no." Miles responded with a throaty chuff charged with sarcasm. "I've seen you in action."

The exam curtains zipped open. The doctor on duty—who

couldn't be any older than Detective O'Bannion's high school sopho-more—sidled up to Rachel with two syringes, long, hefty needles glinting in the overhead light.

"Good morning, Dr. Malone. I apologize for not properly intro-ducing myself earlier when I was digging half the burnt theater floor from your lower torso."

The apology didn't register, but the needles in her hand did.

"Rachel was correct. This nasty little scratch, as you so described it, needed prompt attention. Another half inch and surgery would have been necessary to sew your bowel back together." She reached a hand out. "I'm Dr. Who."

Terrific. Much too young, female, *and* a direct descendent of a time-traveling alien. Despite the pearl of suspicion poking around his newly sutured gut, they shook hands.

"Shall we get this over with?" With a respectable amount of smug cynicism, Dr. Who handed the syringes to Rachel. Rachel snapped her gloves convincingly and took them, then raised them one by one, and pressed the plunger until a dribble of liquid oozed from the tip. "When was your last tetanus booster?"

"Too long ago to talk you out of jabbing me with that needle, I expect." He squirmed. "What's in that thing? It's the size of a damn cannon barrel."

"I take it you're not fond of needles?"

"Not when I'm on the receiving end, no. What's in it?"

Rachel leaned forward. "Healing."

Miles massaged his temple, but it did little to ease his concern for the immediate future. "Uh...no offense, ladies," he said, peering out the tiny gap in the curtains, "but isn't there a, you know—"

"I'm the sole doctor on duty, Doctor." The glint in Dr. Who's gray eyes was so subtle, he nearly missed the slight upturn of her mouth. "Trust me, you've got nothing I haven't seen before."

He toggled from one to the other, deciding which one he'd prefer puncture his backside. The answer was clear, but he chased that particular scene out of his mind before it became audible. Or visible. He gave a reluctant nod to the teenage doctor.

"Sorry, Rachel. If you'll excuse us, my patient needs his injections."

Rachel backed through the curtains, whipped them shut, and then poked her head back in, the curtains drawn into a tight circle around her face. A scene from *The Shining* came briefly to his mind. "Bend over and crack a smile for the doctor, Doctor." A Cheshire grin blossomed on her face and she closed the curtains with a whip-snap and a noise he swore was a highly ramped-up snicker.

He eased himself off the exam table and braced for impact.

"It's actually quite common, Dr. Malone." She lifted the gown, swabbed the area, and sank the beast of a needle into his left butt-check.

Air came sudden and fierce between his teeth. "What is?" He shook his hand to restore the blood flow to his knuckles and braced for the next round.

"The fear of needles." The second pinprick was taking forever. Or maybe it was over? "It's more common than you'd think. You can stand up straight now. Tetanus goes in your shoulder."

"Terrific."

She pinched his shoulder and he pinched his eyes. "There. All done." Dr. Who patted his shoulder with the hangdog expression reserved for a terrified child. "Would you care for a sucker for being so brave?"

That statement had Rachel written all over it. "Sure. If it's laced with whiskey."

"No alcohol, Doctor." She handed him the prescriptions and a formulated smile. "Follow up with me in a week and we'll remove the stitches. Number's on the scrip." She turned to leave. "Oh, and muscle tissue may become sore from the injections, so having them massaged might be a good idea." The cynicism returned. "And by the way, my name's not actually Who."

He smirked. "That's reassuring."

"This whole thing," she said, waving the needles as if brandishing a pair of swords and then tossing them into the sharps container which in his opinion, was where they belonged, "was Rachel's idea."

Miles parked the confession to hash over later, read the prescription label, jerked his head up, and grabbed his newly bandaged gut. "Are you serious? Lecter?"

Dr. Who-slash-Lecter raised both palms and let them fall, an attempted smile mutating into a sinister stitch-ripping grin.

"Please don't tell me you have a fondness for fava beans."

"There's no such thing as a good fava bean." The sinister grin migrated to her eyes. "Not even paired with a nice chianti."

"Thanks, Doc." Miles hid a glimmer of mirth behind the raised prescription. "For not being a serial killer or an alien."

"You're quite welcome." Her grin faded into seriousness. "You're a doctor, so I don't need to remind you to take all your medication even if you feel better. Follow the instructions and you'll be fine. You can get dressed."

"How long before I can travel?"

"Give it a few days. That was one nasty scratch. It needs time to heal internally."

"Ski? I'm SAR—search and rescue."

She shot him a serious look infused with a generous amount of caution. "No. And no. Not until after your follow-up. We'll discuss it then." The curtain closed and she left him to dress.

Saturday's race down Flattop with Chris would have to wait. Miles grimaced inwardly at his muddy jeans, ruined shirt and stained scrubs, but slipped back into them anyway. A fresh change of clothes had been the least of his worries, but he could have brought a clean set of scrubs.

Rachel popped through the opening. "No sucker?"

"She didn't have one made of whiskey and don't you believe in knocking?"

"There's no door and this is my turf. Besides, I enjoy surprises. You know, throwing open the curtain to find the Great and Powerful Oz."

A lewd thought came to mind, but he decided against giving it a voice. "Classic movie."

"I'll make you some whiskey suckers next time you watch it."

"Only if you and Bug watch with me."

"I don't think she'd watch it if Santa Claus held her in his lap. The flying monkeys scare her."

"Can't say I blame her."

Rachel passed him his discharge papers. "Sign these and you're free to go."

He took his time guiding each button through its matching hole and followed along as she watched each twist and turn, thankful he hadn't tossed the ruined shirt after all. "*Charlotte's Web.*"

"What? Oh. Her favorite movie." Several curls had come loose from her ponytail, and she made a futile attempt at restraining them. "How'd you know?"

Miles tucked what remained of his ripped shirt into the waistband of his jeans, wincing as he reached to the back. Rachel shooed his hands away and finished the job. "I take animals to the day care center and let the kids play. Bug's always the first one to..." he squinted, deciding which verb from a growing mental list best described the little girl's actions, "...instruct the other kids the proper way to handle them."

"Sounds like her bossy little self."

Miles chuckled. "She asks me to stay and watch *Charlotte's Web* with her. Or *A Bug's Life.*"

Rachel tilted her head, the bottom corner of her lip pinched between her teeth. "You're good with her. With kids. Do you have children?"

The question balled up in his throat and then fell to his stomach as if someone had dropped a rock in it. "I've never...no. No kids. My wife..." He slipped into his jacket and slid the papers from the table. "Correction, my almost-wife decided she didn't want to have a baby."

"I'm sorry. I didn't mean to pry."

"It's been a long time. Thirteen years." *Lucky thirteen* he thought with a silent scoff. He motioned for her to go ahead of him, spread the curtain, and followed. "Brenna was a smart, ambitious woman." Miles handed the signed papers to the nurse at reception and shoved the rest into his back pocket—the automatic motion proving to be a ruthless bitch. He placed his hand on the small of Rachel's back and led her out of the ER and into the hallway.

"Brenna and I..." he paused to slow the pace but more to align the story in a *Reader's Digest* condensed version, "we didn't want kids right away. She'd been out of college for a year and I was set to graduate, when her fledgling PR business took off. She was adamant about waiting and I agreed. We weren't married yet and I didn't have a job in my field."

A wiggle of a line formed between Rachel's brows and she clasped her hands. "I assumed all vets had their own practices, or belonged to a group similar to medical doctors."

"My degree at the time was in wildlife management which meant I'd have to relocate. Brenna didn't appreciate the idea of leaving Denver, and I didn't blame her. I thought we loved each other enough to work it out. But..." The weighty pause grew heavy with the recollection. "I don't think she wanted kids. At least not with me."

"She'd have changed her mind, wouldn't she? After her business got off the ground?"

Though he had a suspicion it would be easy talking with Rachel, he hadn't planned to dive into his past. He supposed it was her compassion for her patients. He supposed, in a roundabout way, he was her patient and it was her obligation to listen. Besides, he couldn't go anywhere without her; she was his ride out of here.

"Brenna gave up on us a week before our wedding."

"Oh." Rachel turned abruptly. "I'm sorry."

He slowed and leaned a shoulder against the wall, looked away briefly, and then down at his feet.

A small knot of nurses and orderlies buzzing with the latest gossip weaved around them.

"You don't have to talk about it, but I consider you my friend and I'm here if you want to." She touched his upper arm briefly. "Any time. If you want."

"Brenna kept the ring." He kicked one sole of his Sorels with the other, a smattering of dried mud tumbling to the tiled floor. "I got drunk on a plane bound for the Florida Keys, and a few weeks later I enlisted in the Marines. My all-expenses-paid two-year honeymoon. No exchanges. No refunds."

"Afghanistan?" The uneasiness in her tone was as marked as a sniper's bullet.

"Iraq." Her lips parted, but he eased the uncertainty with a smile laced with assurance. "In a way, it was the best thing that ever happened to me, Rachel. I trained alongside a Navy medical corpsman and learned everything I could but found treating the few injured animals we came across interested me more." She rewarded the comment with a curious vacancy. "I'll tell you about it someday." He pushed away from the wall and led her the few steps to another room.

"Might be an intriguing story coming from a man who chose desert camo and combat boots over counting elk and deer."

He laughed, the deep sound foreign. He'd lost track of the last time he'd done so without any artificial wheedling. And he took an extra moment to absorb hers, an open, flawless reflection of the woman without reservation.

"Molly assured me Dad's out of the woods, but do you mind if I check in on him?"

"Of course not. I checked his chart while your nasty scratch was being stitched and I assumed that's where we were headed. He's out of ICU and according to the nurses, he's favoring his ornery side." A sheepish grin deflated the seriousness. "I'm fairly certain he's on the mend."

The description fostered a mild chuckle, and he used the subtle break to rest his hand on her back again, enjoying the feel of a perfect fit. "Doesn't surprise me. He's always been cantankerous and outspoken." He leaned in close to her ear, the scent of her hair and skin stirring him to linger there a second longer. "Dad might be old, but he had quite a crush on my fiancée. I think he was more torn up over my split with Brenna than he was over my enlistment."

"That's not true...is it?"

"You don't know my father."

They shared an uncomplicated moment and walked through the

doorway together, but he dropped his hand from Rachel's back as if his brain had disconnected the signals.

"Hello, darling." The flourish in her words hadn't changed. Her compulsion to visit had. Miles stepped into her outstretched arms and into the signature cloud of Gucci's Guilty perfume. "Hey, Mom."

Rachel gaped from one to the other.

"Rachel, this is my mother, Glenda. Mom, Rachel Caldarone."

Rachel reached out a hand. "Very nice to meet you, Mrs. Malone."

"Ha!" Randall bellowed so loudly a passing orderly poked his head in the doorway. Rachel quickly waved him on his way.

Glenda glared at Randall, scrutinizing the immobile man. Then, taking Rachel's hand in both of hers, she patted it gently, and with the keen interest of a bird of prey, scanned Rachel from the top of her misbehaving curls loosed from the pony tail, to the soles of her Skechers. "I guess Miles hasn't confided in you, my dear."

Randall Malone considered the three of them with intense curiosity. "She's not a Malone, Nurse Rachel. At least not for long if I have anything to say about it. She's Glinda," he said, overemphasizing the 'i' in the pronunciation. "The Wicked Witch of the West."

"That's Glenda—with an 'e' you half-witted enginerd. And," she said, raising her chin, "Glinda happens to be the good witch."

"Not in my fairy tale." Randall shoved his glasses upward, the frames sliding easily through a thick head of silver hair. "No difference if you ask me."

"Who asked you?"

"Nobody with any sense would marry the old bag."

Glenda shot him a cursory look. "You did!"

"Because I was too damn young, horny, and blind as a bat."

"Okay, okay. That's enough." Miles inched his mother away from an imminent public meltdown. They'd always bickered and fumed, and as perfectly contentious as *Goodbye Girl*'s Elliot and Paula, and threatened divorce every other week. And he was stuck in the middle acting as referee in a fiery game with no hard and fast rules. "Mom, what are you doing here?"

"I was told my soon-to-be-ex was about to kick the bucket and I wanted a front row seat."

"Front row at the reading of the will, you mean."

Glenda raised her chin and took a forward step, but Miles held her back. "We're not divorced yet, you...you..."

Listening from the confines of his bed, Randall crossed his arms, a gracious smirk appearing at Glenda's obvious inability to appropriate a suitable insult.

Rachel took a cautious step and slipped between them. "Glenda, I'm a nurse and I need for you to speak in a more soothing tone."

"Soothing?"

"Please. For the patient's sake."

Glenda gave her the once-over again, steeled features giving way to a thickening smile. "So, my son has a new love interest?"

Rachel swiveled faster than a spinning top and confronted Miles, eyes accusingly wide.

"I've heard enough." A chunk of gauze and a good length of surgical tape would have been put to good use had he had access. "Rachel's a nurse. She and I..." Miles toggled between the two of them. "I needed a few stitches and Rachel offered to drive me to the clinic, and now with the pain meds in me—"

"What?" Glenda spun him around. "I assumed your scrubs were bloody from surgery. On a Clydesdale." She snagged the hem of his shirt and moved it aside, eyes screaming louder than the gasp she'd contained with her hand. "What did this woman do to you?"

He winced, promptly removing his mother's hand from his shirt. "I injured myself while searching for her daughter."

"Daughter?" The question bore the weight of a sizzling insinuation he didn't care to hear. And then she leaned in close to Rachel's ear. "Miles has been hurt. And deeply."

"Mom! Jesus!" His stomach did an involuntary flip, his mother's brilliance in art history and charitable endeavors outdone by her mordant affinity for inappropriate remarks.

Ignoring the outburst, Glenda took a stray blonde curl, stretched it, and let it go. Startled at the gesture, Rachel turned a cheek. "I don't take kindly to women who have a penchant for dragging my son through hell."

Rachel stepped back, depositing the curl behind an ear. "I'm sorry...your assumption... Miles and I aren't—"

"Are you ready to go home, son?" Glenda took hold of his arm, but he set his feet firmly in place.

He glanced at Rachel, but she'd turned away. Damn, why did his parents find it necessary to be so antagonistic in public? It was part of some annoying repertoire they had for garnering attention, and this was no way to introduce his parents to Rachel.

Rachel took Randall's hand to take his pulse. She wasn't his attending nurse, but his father beamed like a teenager holding hands with the prettiest girl in school.

"Thanks, Mom, but no. It's taken care of."

"Your sister decided not to come. Do you know anything about that?" The accusation came bundled in a piercing glare.

"Switzerland is halfway around the world." Miles mentally ducked to avoid the silent recrimination. "Madison's busy and Dad's going to be fine. She'll be home soon."

"After she dumps Lancelot."

"Lars. His name is Lars."

Glenda shrugged and approached Miles, poised to finger-comb his hair the way she'd done when he was a kid, but he stepped aside. At least she hadn't licked her fingers. "We could stop at my salon and have Sonya trim this mop on the way home."

Two small steps and he was far enough away to avoid any further intrusions. "Maybe next time, Mom."

A commotion at the door diverted his attention, and they all turned in unison. A wispy old man shuffled through the door and greeted each in succession with a jerky nod.

"Is he dead?"

THIRTEEN

"*W*ell? Is he dead?" Halton Grimm—resident wannabe bookie and apt storyteller—turned first to Rachel and then to Miles and Randall, setting his wattles jiggling with each nod. "I've got one hefty wager on the outcome." When he set his gaze on Glenda, he smiled and his eyes coupled into mere slits. He laced his hands together and cracked his knuckles in a practiced movement.

Halton Grimm was used to winning. His stories were legendary and Rachel had been privy to them more than once. He'd spent his life cashing in on bets too mundane for Las Vegas bookies and too lackluster for the local mob. And when he wasn't cashing in—one winning ticket at a time—he slogged through boredom by breaking into homes, breaking into safes, and breaking hearts.

But he took no pleasure in stealing. Not really. The challenge and the title, he'd said, were his motivation. Not the mess that went along with it. Prison, for one. The only thing Halton said he'd ever stolen was another notch on his belt of conquests. And with his advanced age, he wasn't opposed to telling the world of his talents, increasingly masterful as the years passed. Though most of his captive audience assumed he was nothing but a braggart, when Halton made the rounds through The Villages at Alpine Ridge, everyone kept a tight rein on their belongings.

Rachel approached Halton and took him by the arm, the mysterious obsession with placing bets on whether someone lived or died crawling around in her stomach like a restless heap of wiggling worms.

"What brings you out today, Halton?"

"A beautiful woman, it seems." Halton slipped free, slicked back a thin crop of white hair, and with a slight shift in attitude, added to his height by at least an inch topping out under Rachel's nose. He'd risen in stature and took aim on his newest enterprise—Glenda Malone. "Looks like I got here just in time to steal her heart."

"Halton, this is Glenda and Randall Malone, and their son, Miles."

"I know the doc. Shows up a lot around here."

With an obvious disinterest in anyone other than Glenda, Halton moved closer to her, and Miles ushered Rachel into the hallway sporting a mischievous grin.

"Remember the errand I mentioned? I need to go back to the theater building. Soon." The grin wavered and he looked dubiously at his bandaged abdomen. "Do you think your keycard will work? To let me in?"

"What's so important you have to go back?"

A half-nervous smile turned the corners of his mouth, and the warmth of it slid up her neck and embraced her scalp. "It's time sensitive. Trust me on this?"

She opened her mouth to speak, but he severed the words before they'd formed.

"I don't want to cause you any trouble, but I have to get in that building." Whatever else he'd openly displayed morphed into instant distress. "I've tried the fire department and there's some sort of training exercise going on and they can't respond except for an emergency."

"I'm sorry," she said, frowning, "but the building is under construction and the technology for our security system hasn't been installed.

My keycard won't work. The fire department probably has their own locks in place anyway."

"Getting inside isn't an option. I can manage the crawl space again if I have to." The words were barely audible but ripe with uneasiness.

"No way you're going back in there," she said, eyeing his bandages. "With or without my keycard."

Ignoring the remark, he paced the hallway and then turned and repeated the action. "Maybe with Halton's visit—"

"You're not listening."

"Maybe I'll have time to sneak over there and if Mom refuses to leave at least she'll be civil with a stranger in the room."

"Unfortunately, nothing is safe around Halton Grimm, not even your parents' civility. He'd probably steal that and their sanity if he thought there was a possible reward involved."

"Hmm. Do you think he'd take a horse, two goats, and three chickens in exchange?"

"That's not terribly nice, Miles."

"Neither is my mother."

"She's not always like that, is she?"

"No, she's not. She's got a big heart actually. It's only when she's got a stick up her ass and Dad has a keen way of obliging just by opening his mouth."

"Miles!"

"Sorry. Mom's just Mom and Dad eggs it on. They're quite fond of each other when they aren't in the same room together. If that makes sense." A shred of amusement seeped through the exhaustion and stress of an invalid father and embarrassing mother. "So...this Halton Grimm—as in the fairy tales Grimm?"

"Spelled the same, but I can't vouch for his heritage. Halton is a thief by trade." An idea began to percolate, but processing a full-fledged plot needed a bit more thought. As the nursing supervisor with a daughter to think of, she wasn't an employee with no obligations or responsibilities now, and breaking the rules would take some consideration. "He has a big mouth and finds humor in bragging about his so-called conquests."

"That's not exactly something—"

"He's also a professional locksmith-slash-burglar."

"There's such a thing?"

"Halton's got more fairy tales than Jacob and Wilhelm. You wouldn't believe the interesting clique of people we have living here. They've lived storied lives and love to talk. And I adore listening to them. I'm a sucker for history, and what better place than a retirement community?" Afraid she'd lose the budding formation of a plot, she waved a hand to dismiss the comment.

Inga's entrance into The Village Square had been Molly's caper, but she'd been made an accomplice by ignoring it, and a delicious worm of adventure caught her unaware, one she hadn't experienced in a long time. Not since her last transgression to deliver a forbidden letter for a self-proclaimed mobster. Not since leaving Woodland Hills had she broken the rules. Not since she'd made the promise to Nico and her boss to keep her nose clean and not cross the lines. Not since Bug's birth.

Rachel laid a hand on Miles' chest. "I have an idea." For an instant, the connection she'd once had with Nico surfaced, and the times they'd shared a daring escapade came rumbling back. The adrenaline rush. The plot. Nico's protective nature, his tenacity and willingness to go along with her outrageous schemes. And there was the tremendous feeling of completion, the tenderness the residents had shown her each time she'd assisted with a simple request. A wish they'd never realized without her.

Longing for those times nudged her squarely in the heart. "Are you up for a little breaking and entering?"

"Breaking the law isn't something I do on a regular basis. At least not since I was ten."

"I prefer to call it breaking bad."

"As in drug deals?" He lowered his voice to an incredulous croak. "Chemical recipes for crack?"

"I think it's meth." The visitors passing by waved and nodded at the candid exchange and Rachel's boisterous laugh. *Breaking Bad* isn't solely the name of a TV show. It means to 'defy authority' and I had quite the reputation at Woodland Hills—before I came here."

Miles leaned against the wall, the air whooshing from his lungs. "For a minute there I thought you were going Hollywood on me."

"Not quite, but it does sorta involve breaking the rules. I could get in trouble, but trust me I won't. I'm good at stealth."

"Your so-called proficiencies become more interesting by the day."

Raised voices and laughter drifted from Randall's room, and an enticing aroma of something buttery wafted from the hallway along with the clatter of noon meal trays.

"I'd better make sure my parents haven't killed each other and see my mother gets out of here before Dad's lunch ends up in his lap and your friend kidnaps her—which actually," he said, scraping a hand over his chin, "might not be such a bad deal."

"You take care of your mother, and I'll see if Halton is up for the mission." She shot Miles a look meant to be fearless, hoping the tinge of apprehension hadn't collapsed it entirely. "He's our only way into the theater."

"You sure about this?"

"Do you want in that building?"

"Yes, but not at your expense."

"This is mild compared to what I'm used to. Game, or not?"

Miles didn't respond right away, but desperation peeked through an uncertain nod. "What are we waiting for?"

When the sense of impending adventure turned into liquid adrenaline, it didn't take Rachel long to formulate a plan to sneak Halton out of the building. It was easier than it had been at Woodland Hills simply because she didn't have her supervisor, Judith, to contend with. She was the supervisor and she was certain she could get them out and back before anyone noticed a missing resident. And with Molly as backup (she'd opted in without hesitation) this tiny infraction would be a piece of cake, a mere blip in a retirement community bustling with busybodies.

Miles had successfully extricated his mother from the room after promising to meet her for dinner, and Halton had been giddy at the chance to show Rachel his lock-picking "equipment," prove his bragging rights, and his enthusiasm for leaving the premises (the part about lack of permission an added bonus) to pick a lock added to his stature by at least another inch. She'd never seen his spine so straight or his smile so wide.

Their plan set in motion, Miles and Rachel made their way across the grounds through what was left of yesterday's snow, each with an arm looped with Halton's. The locksmith's steps were guarded and slow, but a few paces from the door he stopped, threw his shoulders back, and took a deep breath worthy of a twenty-year-old athlete.

"Nothing beats the fragrance of a Vegas heist. I know we aren't in Sin City kids, but goddamn this is as exciting as the lights on Freemont Street." Halton slithered from their grasp, rooted around inside his gray wool overcoat, and plucked a long, exceedingly fat cigar from an inside pocket. Swept it under his nose. "What happens in Vegas stays in Vegas and by God nothing compares to a good Black Dragon to ensure a successful outcome."

"We don't have much time, Halton, can we keep moving?" Afraid the frail man would fall, Rachel took hold of him again. If anything went wrong...

"How much time we got, sweetheart?" The last word came out distinctly animated and more like *schweethawt*—a clichéd throwback from a B mobster movie.

They'd squandered several minutes with the slow stroll across the grounds. "Not long," she said, glancing at her watch. "Another twenty minutes."

Halton reached into another pocket, removed a custom matchbox, retrieved a small instrument and deftly snipped the end of the cigar. Tapping it lightly, he then chose a matchstick from the box and lit it. A tall yellow flame hissed and then burned quietly as he turned the end of the cigar in the flame. He chucked it between his teeth and began puffing steadily until the end glowed bright orange.

Rachel coughed and waved a hand through the hazy cloud. "Must you?"

"I cannot properly perform my duties, my dear, without the accompaniment of a soothing smoke." He turned in her direction and blew a perfect line of smoke rings into the air, proceeded to the theater entrance, and with Miles' help, knelt down in front of the double doors. A goliath lock secured a heavy chain looped through the handles.

Miles scanned the area as if casing the perimeter for unwanted guests. "This is taking forever."

"A little nervous are we, Doc?" Rings of gray smoke circled the words. Halton removed his gloves and then placed them neatly on the ground next to him, the smelly stogie stuck between his teeth. Reaching inside his coat again, he dug a small worn black case from yet another coat pocket. "No worries, young man. Nurse Rachel's got your back."

Rachel swallowed a response.

Halton opened the case with a nimble yet careful movement, chose two small tools, and inspected the locks. "They've secured the self-locking doors with a Master lock—high end, extra security, extra pins —your tax dollars at work here, folks."

"Mr. Grimm," Miles said, turning his back to the doors, "how much longer?"

Halton glanced warily at Miles, one eye closed to the swirling cigar smoke. "Patience, son." With his ear parked near the lock, he inserted first one instrument and then another. "Most household locks are easily manipulated."

Rachel's limbs went limp and she leaned against the building to steady herself. "My home isn't safe?"

Yellowed teeth bit into the meat of the tobacco. "Depends on your security system."

"I don't have one, but I always lock the doors and windows."

"Locks merely give the illusion of safety."

Her imagination painted a vivid picture, and a cold shiver infected her like a rampant virus. "Bug."

Miles approached her and took her hands, his offer of assurance reflecting in his eyes, his voice low. "She's safe, Rachel. She's with your grandfather. He'd call if—"

"But what if he's out there?" The image she'd seen in the hallway grew stronger, her words weaker.

An unspoken missive passed between them. "As soon as we're done here, we'll go pick her up. Sound okay?"

The rigid posture her fear held in place relaxed. "Thank you, Miles."

"Besides...Halton might be blowing smoke. This lock business sounds like fairy tales—"

The lock sprung free. "Bingo!" Halton raised his hands in triumph, his inflated stories taking on a new dimension of authenticity.

"So much for fairy tales." Miles stretched out a hand to help him up and Halton took it. "Are all locks this easy to crack? If you're not a pro?"

"If you've got two hands and pick set, anyone can pick a lock, my friend." He shuffled closer to the double doors. "Alarms and sophisticated security systems take a bit of practice." Holding onto the door handle, Halton manipulated his tools once, made an adjustment, and yanked again. The heavy bar lock clanked, and he pushed one side open. He bowed deeply. "After you."

"Rachel, you and Mr. Grimm can wait here. This won't take long." He took a step and turned around, walking backward. "Though maybe longer than the sixty seconds it took to break in."

Rachel stuck a short two-by-four between the doors to keep them from closing. Halton puffed away on his cigar, smoke drifting in lazy circles in the still air. She hated to admit it, but Halton's Black Dragon outranked the stench of wet ash by at least a millimeter.

Miles returned shortly, cradling an arm across his partially zipped jacket, his expression and body assembled in cheerful celebration. He motioned to them, and when they peeked inside his jacket, three small, furry heads turned toward the sound, their eyes closed and ears pinned to their heads.

"So that's what all the fuss was about." Rachel stroked the velvety fur between their unopened eyes. "They're precious. So tiny."

The delight on Miles' face painted the composite of the man within, the kittens' soft fur an intimation of the slow, sure melting of her heart.

"Well done, Doc." Halton winked and took two small steps back to allow Rachel access to the kittens.

There were three, two white as a ghost with ears and noses that looked as though they'd been dipped in milk chocolate, and the runt a soft, dusty gray with markings the color of the underbelly of storm cloud. Three small fluffy powder puffs.

"Are they Siamese?"

"Himalayan, but I think they're of mixed breed. Their mother had the markings but not the long coat."

Rachel couldn't face him. "Where's their mother?"

"Without examining her, I'd guess she succumbed to smoke inhalation, but I don't know for sure. Feral cats are tough and she'd have moved her kittens to safety before the smoke got to them if she was able. Whatever it was, she lived long enough to keep her kittens alive." He stroked each one in turn, taking a little more time with the runt. A chorus of high-pitched mews came from inside the coat of the man with a soft heart ready to protect the motherless kittens, nurture them, and love them without preamble. "They wouldn't have made it much longer."

"What will you do with the mother?"

"If you'll take the kittens, I'll go get her and we can take her to the clinic."

"What are you going to carry her in exactly?"

Miles retrieved something from his back pocket. "I grabbed an animal body bag before we left the clinic. There's a small plot for unclaimed pets. I'll bury her there."

If she took a step, her legs would surely give way—not from the cold or fear of discovery, but the pure compassion of someone who'd risk anything to save a life. And he'd saved these three babies today. Just as he had saved two of hers.

"My job here is complete." Halton rocked back on his heels. "No locksmith on earth needs to unlock your heart, Doc. There's room in there for a convoy of Mack trucks." Sporting a yellow-toothed grin, he leaned into Rachel's ear. "From the looks of it there's room for you too, my dear." With a waggle of old man eyebrows, he winked at Miles. "A blind person could see that."

Rachel opened her coat and Miles transferred the kittens. They nestled inside, snuggling into each other. Miles returned with the mother hugged securely between arm and waist.

The locksmith-slash-burglar shuffled to the door and pushed it open. "Shall we?" he asked through a tunnel of smoke rings. "Maybe I can catch the dribbles of what's left of lunch. It's Wednesday. Cook's got a knack for meatloaf."

"Let's get these little guys to the clinic. I've got a lactating mother in the barn I hope will adopt them," Miles said, his tone climbing in obvious enthusiasm. "Maybe we should get them settled and then get Bug. Is that okay with you?"

Not looking from the kittens, Rachel nodded.

Halton cleared his throat. "Might need this."

"What the—? Where'd you get that?"

Halton punctuated a shrewd smirk with a wink—not his usual wink, but one of considerable mystery.

"Aside from your various other talents," Miles said, reclaiming his wallet, "you're a pickpocket too?"

"Institute of higher learning. Post-graduate work."

"I'm a big proponent of higher education," Miles said, the statement seasoned with a rich chuckle.

"You catch on quick, Doc."

"You've raised breaking and entering and picking pockets to a fine art." Rachel polished the statement with a note of amusement.

"You're never too old to learn a new trick, Nurse Rachel." Halton snuffed the cigar on the concrete and tucked the half-smoked stogie back into his pocket with an affectionate pat.

"Now you can add kitten rescuer to your résumé under unusual skills." She secured the kittens and Halton raised his elbow. Rachel took one, Miles his other.

Near the entrance to the retirement community, Halton wiggled free and launched into a gear three times faster and waited at the door tapping a foot. Rachel swiped her key card and he burst through the door with a brief backward wave.

The door closed and Miles took her arm and they headed to the parking lot.

"This was an awesome thing you did, Miles. Rescuing them."

"I couldn't have done it without Bug and Zoe."

Any sort of reply shriveled and died before Rachel could voice it.

"Zoe found them and Bug protected them."

"So that's why Zoe ran away? She must have smelled the smoke and her instincts kicked in even before the alarm went off." She exchanged a look of wistful understanding with Miles. "Zoe knew the kittens were there."

"Yorkies are natural hunters and a particularly smart breed. Yeah, her instincts were spot on."

"And Bug followed Zoe. To bring her back. To keep her safe." Profound love bubbled inside her, but a dagger of fear popped the fragile shell. "How can I keep her safe, Miles?" She looked to him for assurance, to ease the noose around her heart. "The locks...oh God... if he's out there—"

"Do you trust me?"

Rachel's knees threatened to desert her, and she tightened her coat around the kittens. "Of course I do."

"Good," he said, picking up the pace. "I have an idea."

FOURTEEN

"Mommy! Mommy!" Bug leapt into Rachel's outstretched arms, curls bouncing across her back and shoulders. "Mommy, Dr. Miles has kitties." She pushed away and grabbed Rachel's hand with both of hers, tugging her toward the crate. "And Zoe is going to be okay because Dr. Miles fixed her all up with stitches and medicine and I gave her a big booger kiss like she gives me."

Rachel took her daughter by the shoulders and smoothed her hair. "We have to talk quietly, baby, can you do that for Dr. Miles and for the kittens and Zoe?"

Bug nodded vigorously. "Did I wake Zoe or the mama cat up? I didn't mean to."

"The mother cat's name is Prim. It's short for Primrose. Zoe's still sleepy from the medicine, but we don't want to frighten her, Prim, or the kittens," Miles said, reaching for a chair.

Rachel beat him to it, tossed him a *you're determined to rip those stitches* look and set the chair next to the crate. He'd wanted to bury the mama cat, but Rachel had insisted he hire someone. Since a repeat visit to Dr. Who-slash-Lecter wasn't high on his list of do-overs, he'd asked Heather to take care of it—one of the few times the stubborn vet listened to her.

"One, two, three babies." Bug slid into the chair, crossed her arms, and rested her chin there, peering into the crate. "Their eyes aren't open yet and Dr. Miles said they're very young and their mommy isn't around and they have to have milk from Prim. She likes it because she's purring. That means Prim's happy, right, Dr. Miles?" Bug's attention never wavered from the crate, her question lost in a tangle of feline fur, purring, and tiny, kneading paws.

"That's right." Miles took hold of the table and squatted, Bug's petite shoulders disappearing as he draped an arm over them. "It takes a special mama cat to be willing to adopt another mother's babies. And that makes me happy."

A mother's instinct is as inherent in animals as it is in humans. Miles had settled Prim who'd bristled at first when confronted with the orphaned kittens, and then curled into a corner and allowed the kittens to root around until they each found a nipple to suckle.

"She loves them, right, Dr. Miles?"

Miles turned his head toward her, a lazy smile growing wide. "Yes, she does." He stood slowly, grimacing at the strain, and retrieved Zoe —still not quite her lively self—and handed her to Rachel. Tears stung Rachel's eyes, and she and Bug lathered her with kisses and cuddles and were in turn rewarded with a string of booger kisses. Bug giggled and Rachel put a finger to her lips.

Miles reached inside Prim's crate and lifted one tiny head.

"What are you doing, Dr. Miles?"

"Checking to make sure the kittens are getting enough to eat." Milk dripped from the kitten's mouth and Prim hissed in an obvious attempt to protect her newly adopted family.

"She doesn't like you touching her babies. I think you better stop that."

"I think you're right, and I think all my patients have had enough stimulation for one day, Bug. We should probably let them rest."

"They need to sleep like Mommy says I do so I can grow up big.

The kitties need to get big so they can play and get into trouble. Mommy says kitties get into lots of trouble. Is that bad, Dr. Miles?"

"I think it's part of their nature." A low chuckle tagged along with the answer. "They get a little rambunctious sometimes. And they're babies, so they're curious." Miles turned to Rachel and winked, a slow thing meant to tease. "Oh, I almost forgot. Look who I found, Bug." Miles pulled the stuffed ladybug from his back pocket. "Found her hiding in your mom's Jeep."

"Ladybug!" Bug hugged the toy to her cheek, her ears disappearing in an exaggerated shrug. A smile leapt across her face, wide and joyful, her father's smile, the marked signature of her inheritance. Yet, the one that graced Miles' face was just as wide. Just as joyful.

Rachel's insides turned watery. So did her eyes. She looked away and blinked several times. Zoe was safe here at the clinic. Bug was safe with her and had been reunited with her favorite stuffed toy. Under Heather's and Miles' care, Zoe would grow stronger every day, but so did the knot in her stomach. How could she let her guard down when that man could be out there? She couldn't have imagined it. It had been too real. She was losing ground with the mental quarrel.

"C'mon, baby. It's time to go."

"Wait, I have to say goodbye to Zoe and the kitties and Prim." Bug's lower lip trembled, but she brushed her hair off her forehead and gave Prim and each kitten an easy pat, and Zoe a kiss on the nose. "Prim didn't hiss at me, Dr. Miles."

"I think she's quite fond of you."

Bug beamed and Rachel coaxed her away from the kittens, out of the clinic, and into the back seat of the Jeep. She buckled her in and opened the front passenger side door for Miles.

"Time to take you home, Doctor. We can drop Bug off at Grandpa's on the way."

"Why not bring her?"

Rachel shifted her weight. "You sure?"

"I'd like nothing better."

Bug held Ladybug snugly between her chin and shoulder, the small arm wrapped around the toy rising and falling with each carefree breath. Long, dark eyelashes floated just above the contour of round cheeks whose innocence would someday give way to high cheekbones and olive skin of a stunning young woman. The sudden longing to touch her daughter's face, to stop time and watch her sleep paralyzed her.

"My God, she's something." Miles turned away and cleared his throat.

Rachel gently closed the car door. "She's exhausted and I think she'd be better off at Grandpa's. I won't be long at your place, so I think we should drop her off first."

"Whatever's best for Bug has my vote."

Yesterday's snow littered the shaded areas of the forest, and the usual frozen drifts had dwindled to nothing more than pockets of mush along Fall River Road. Winter always held the reins in her tight grip as the coldest months waned in the Rocky Mountains, but this year she'd loosened her foothold early and March had wound down and turned into April with only the slightest gasp. On the cusp of bursting forth, spring merely held its breath.

Rachel kept an eye on Miles, who'd done more than his share of squirming. "I didn't realize you lived this far out of town."

Miles seized the seat belt and loosened it from the bandaged area on his abdomen. "The way my gut is protesting this seat belt, I'd give my right..." he rubbed a knuckle under his nose, "my right arm to blink and be there. Not exactly thrilled at the prospect of turning off the asphalt." With due caution, he leaned forward. "It's the next left."

She clamped her hands on the steering wheel. "Why are we turning here?"

"Because it's where I live."

She turned off the asphalt onto a dirt road. "This is the road to Whisper of the Pines Resort. Do you live there?"

"No. Yes. Sorta." Miles adjusted his position. "Shit! That was a mistake." He let out a breath he'd been nursing. "When I bought the practice in Estes Park I found myself up to my eyeballs in debt and used the clinic as both animal hospital and residence."

"That's the reason for the cot and full bath?"

He nodded. "The owner of the resort, Logan Cavanaugh, is a friend of mine. He'd recently purchased the property but didn't want to mess with the two outbuildings and offered me a smokin' deal. Told me if I wanted one of them, it was mine and I could stay there as long as I needed. They weren't much more than log cabins used for storage and shelter for an entire colony of mice and one cheeky raccoon family. But after two years of living at the clinic, it was a slice of heaven."

"Somehow that doesn't surprise me about Logan."

"You know him?"

She hit the first pothole with a jolt and she clutched the steering wheel with renewed vigor, and left Miles holding his gut and glaring at her.

"Sorry."

"It's okay. This time. Hit another pothole and I may have to put your life on the line and drive under the influence."

"Fat chance."

"At least I know where the potholes are."

Not keen on the alternative, she wiggled her bottom and leaned forward for a clearer view of the road. "We'll see about that."

"First, slow down and then tell me how you know Logan."

She eased off the gas and averted another pothole. "He's the CEO of Wentworth-Cavanaugh Properties and his cousin, Kristina Kaufman, is the COO and director of their conglomerate of retirement communities. And my boss."

"I've had the pleasure of meeting her."

The confession held a cat-like wariness that spoke of something beyond generalized meaning. "You know Kristina, too?"

"You could say that."

What lay behind the ambiguous answer was none of her business, yet her curiosity wasn't playing fairly. "I met her and Logan at Woodland Hills, where I began my nursing career. Kristina's the reason Nico and I came to The Villages."

Miles turned his attention to the window, the movement discernible through her side vision. Had she said something wrong? He knew Nico. Knew their story. The disengagement pooled in a heavy cloud of silence.

The muddy, rutted road was anything but civil toward a score of stitches whose temporary numbness had most likely worn off some time ago. Unfamiliar with the dirt road, she hit yet another pothole, and muddy water splashed in an arc around the Jeep. Miles grabbed the center console and the dash simultaneously and left a few choice words echoing in the cab of the Cherokee.

"Logan's usually not this lacking in the road maintenance department. I have a suspicion you two are co-conspirators in my demise."

"I'm so sorry. I'm not used to dirt roads and I assumed the Cherokee would be more comfortable than your beast of a truck."

Miles relaxed into the seat, gesturing up and down. "You'll get us there. Eventually. If the jarring doesn't pop the stitches and spill my guts all over your leather seats."

She took more pressure off the gas, wishing she could poke a button and hover over the bumps. This was taking forever. They'd filled his scrips after dropping off Bug, but Miles hadn't eaten anything and Rachel had warned him about the possible repercussions of taking pain meds on an empty stomach or his guts may not be the only thing he spilled. A round of dry heaves would add another nasty layer of discomfort to the six internal stitches needed to tie the muscle tissue together, and a dozen surface stitches to brag about on the outside.

"Tell me more about your place." The distraction might take his mind off how sore he was, but the heat of his gaze proved her ulterior motives hadn't gone unheeded.

"Sure, but first you need to take the fork up ahead or you'll end up at the resort."

She slowed and eased into the turn with more expertise than the last one, driving off the road to avoid a puddle that spanned the width of the road. Miles let go of the breath he'd held from beginning to end of the sizable pothole.

"Hey, I'm a fast learner."

"I'll make an off-road girl out of you yet."

She slowed to a stop and engaged the four-wheel drive. All four tires grabbed as she maneuvered the Cherokee along the road that had taken on a keen resemblance to Swiss cheese. "Please continue your story."

Miles visibly relaxed. So did she. "For the first few years I sank every spare dime into the clinic. I had no extra cash to work on the cabin, so I refurbished what was there. As my practice picked up, I added on and started sprucing up the second cabin."

"Sounds like a lot of work."

"I was young and it suits me. It's secluded yet close enough to town if there's an emergency at the clinic. So..." He tensed as they neared another pothole. "I met with Logan a few years ago to rehash the terms of our agreement. I wanted the full five acres and both cabins, but only if he allowed me to buy it from him. He agreed, had the property surveyed, and I took out a mortgage."

"Wait...both cabins?"

"I rent the other to Shephard Dawson, Logan's handyman slash horse whisperer." He bit down on an abrupt chuckle and held his side. "He's a park ranger and teaches me which hiking trails to take, which ski runs are the best, and how to keep the bears away. In exchange, I teach him how to care for the resort horses and wounded animals he comes across while he's playing park ranger."

"Bears?"

"Bear, elk, deer. Raccoons. The occasional bighorn sheep. My only neighbors besides Shep."

Forest shadows filled her peripheral vision, every movement the alarming image of lurking bears.

"Don't worry. Bears rarely visit unannounced."

"What...do they wear bells to announce their arrival?"

Miles grabbed the dash and then relaxed when she expertly maneuvered around the pothole.

"Chicken."

"Not a fan of potholes. The numbness wore off a while ago and sonofabitch if it doesn't hurt. Fortunately, we're almost there. And no, the animals don't wear bells, but Strider lets me know if there's something or someone in the vicinity. He's not the least bit chicken."

"Who's Strider?"

"You'll meet him soon I expect."

"Looking forward to it." She said it confidently but wasn't sure if she meant it. "And to meeting Shep."

"Shep's the most experienced volunteer on our SAR team. A man of many talents. Writes music, plays a mean guitar, and sings at the resort on weekends. Guy's got mad skills. Handsome too."

"Sounds intriguing."

"You should come sometime. To hear him and his band play."

"I'd like that." The last swooping bend seemed to take forever and no time at all. She'd welcomed the distraction for his sake, but had been mesmerized at the account and speculated why a man of his capacity for compassion, his community standing, and how one as handsome as the tall, sandy-haired veterinarian remained single.

"Is Shep single?"

Miles jerked his head in her direction. "Why? Do you want me to ask him out for you?"

"No!" Heat prickled her neck and she pierced him with a look meant to avenge the uninvited embarrassment. "No, I'm not...I was curious...if he shared his house with anyone I knew."

"He's divorced. No one special in his life right now, but he'd be a great catch." Something lurked in the statement...a hint of something she couldn't pinpoint. "For someone who has a thing for handsome, guitar-playing, outdoorsy, write-me-a-song type of guy who happens to be loaded."

"He's rich?"

"Got your attention now?"

"No." The curt answer came wrapped in a curt smile. "I wondered if he'd written any songs I'm familiar with."

"He's not broken any billboard charts with his music. Maybe a few hearts. Made his fortune on Wall Street."

"Interesting combination." She paused, trying to place how he'd come from the hustle of Wall Street to the middle of nowhere in a mountain cabin at the base of the Rockies. "If he's got the money, why does he rent?"

"He's too busy playing mountain man. Wants nothing to do with the responsibility of his own place. Works out for both of us."

"I see."

"I'll introduce you sometime." He finished the comment with a mumbled, "or not" he didn't think she heard.

"Sounds like a plan." Rachel pulled up to the cabin and slipped the Cherokee into Park. She killed the engine and took hold of the steering wheel with both hands at high noon. The tic, tic, tic of the cooling engine kept time with her fingers tapping the steering wheel.

"You're not moving. Is there something wrong?"

She took a second—or six—to respond. "I thought you said this was a storage cabin."

"Used to be." He laughed and grabbed his side. "Are you going to come in or leave me in the wilderness without a ride?"

She closed her misbehaving mouth. "I can't wait to see the inside of your little storage shed."

Miles reached for his door.

"Wait." Regaining her focus, she popped the seat belt and slipped quickly from the Jeep around to the passenger side and opened his door.

"I believe a gentleman should open the door for a woman, not the other way around."

"Zip it. I thought I made it clear when you wanted to dig a grave for the mother cat that you shouldn't be exerting pressure on those stitches."

Miles slid gingerly from the seat, pea-sized gravel crunching under his feet. Rachel closed the door behind them and then with exaggerated animation, swiveled her head in all directions.

"Looking for something?"

"A gentleman."

He mumbled something under his breath that sounded suspiciously like *"very funny."* She offered him a cockeyed glance as assurance she had heard.

Winter hadn't completely given in to spring. Its willful breeze bit cheek and nose and whipped her hair, whispering secrets through boughs of spruce and fir and the skeletal white branches of quaking aspen. But an underlying sound not quite audible, not quite silent trickled through the silence.

"Do I hear water?"

"Fall River's a few yards from the back of the house and running big this year with the early spring thaw."

"Some back yard." She stepped next to him, taking in the surrounding woods.

"The neighboring elk feast on the apples in late summer, but they're quiet. Unless they're in the rut." He took her hand. "But that's not until fall."

She glanced up, unsure whether to pull away or allow his fingers to twine with hers.

"There's still some slush on the ground." The answer came as a tender squeeze, the heat warm through leather gloves. "I might fall." Though the intention was meant to keep him upright, an impish smile —a glimpse of the boy he must have been—quirked one side of his mouth. Playful yet with a sincerity that wove the fibers of the adventurous man. He looped her arm through his elbow and gave it a pat. "There. Safe in your care. Now I pray you're a better guide than you are a driver."

"I take good care of my patients."

"I'm not your patient."

"You are now."

Something huge and black broke her peripheral vision and she turned abruptly. She froze, an animal loping toward them at a fast, lunging gate. "I certainly hope that's your dog?" The end of the sentence took on the same upward pitch as her eyebrows.

Miles whistled. A series of rich, deep barks accompanied the lengthening strides. The closer the animal got, the larger it loomed, a big pink tongue bobbing below a nose that held an acute resemblance to a bear.

"Miles?" The tension in her voice tightened along with her two-handed grip.

"Rachel, you're about to meet Strider."

"That's Strider?"

"Named for Aragorn in *Lord of the Rings*."

"I was thinking more along the line of wee Hobbits." She pressed two fingers together. "Not Treebeard."

"Strider's an oaf. Might knock you out with his tail, but he wouldn't hurt a fly."

The huge dog brushed by her to get to Miles, knocking her off balance. "I'm pretty sure Zoe would make a nice appetizer. What is he, besides huge?"

"A Newfoundland."

The gigantic dog nuzzled his way under her arm and she had no choice but to let loose of Miles to scratch the dog's big wet head. It was an easy feat as the dog (aka small horse) stood level with her waist, and big brown eyes like pools of melted chocolate drooped contentedly. A gentle soul inside a burly exterior, a mirror to the one who fed him.

"Rescued as a pup."

"I can't imagine this monster as a puppy."

"Bigger than Zoe is now."

"I think the egg he was conceived from was bigger than Zoe." Strider stuck his nose in the air and howled. "I think he's happy you're home."

"He's just hungry. Thinks he's starving when he's not sleeping. C'mon, you big moose." Miles left a wet handprint on his jeans. "You can stay on the deck, but you're not coming in until you dry off."

"Aren't vets predisposed to being nice to their animals?"

"I am nice. I also happen to be smarter than my dog."

Rachel pinched her mouth to contain a smile on the verge of erupting into an undignified snort.

"I made the mistake of letting him come inside wet once and when he shook, well, let's just say lesson learned."

"Right." The single syllable stretched into three long beats.

Strider's tail swished in a fierce back and forth movement that would produce a nice breeze if their breaths weren't freezing into white clouds.

With her arm tucked securely into his elbow, Miles wrapped his free hand around his middle and led her inside, blocking Strider's way. The dog's tail lost its vigor and drooped, and he plopped to the deck with a pitiful groan.

Rachel let go of Miles, backpedaled and stooped to pet the dog, his fur thick and soft and exceedingly wet. He whined, a mournful sound that looped around her heart. "If he doesn't let you in soon, I will. I promise."

Rachel shut both doors and caught up to Miles.

"Make yourself at home," he said, tossing both jackets across the back of a chair. "There's pods underneath the Keurig, or wine if you're so inclined. Beer in the fridge. I'll shower and change—"

"Oh, no you won't!"

He turned, staring blankly at her.

"Didn't you read your discharge instructions?" He shook his head. "You're a vet, you should know your stitches shouldn't get wet for twenty-four hours. You can remove the bandage tomorrow and then you can shower."

"Spit baths aren't exactly my thing."

"Tough."

"Nothing gets by you, does it?" He raised his hands in surrender, slapped them mechanically to his sides, and headed toward the bedroom. He took two short steps and then turned back around and pointed a finger, his gaping mouth primed to spill forth an objection.

"No shower," she said with a playful grin. "I'm not going to be happy if I have to replace the bandage because you can't follow simple instructions. Unless, of course, you'd like another visit to Dr. Lecter?"

He left the room mumbling to himself.

"I'll stand guard if I have to."

He turned around and pinned her with a dogged flash of blue. "That can be arranged."

She severed eye contact and peered around the expansive living room. "Men," she muttered, eyeing the huge exposed beams that held the ceiling in place, chinked log walls and an impressive stone fireplace in the center of one wall. The room was massive and rugged and...*warm*. The ambiance of a cozy home and the man who called it his.

A bank of windows spanned the entire wall opposite the fireplace. She slipped out of her coat, approached them, and looked beyond the house and river, beyond the endless sky and jagged ridges of the Rockies and into the frayed edges of memory.

A chill penetrated the cozy warmth. Her hand went instinctively to her neck where a gold band once hung from a chain—the mate to the one her husband had worn—ghosts of what had been etched in the small nicks and scratches, the unwritten melody of their short life together. Her half of a pair. In spite of the mountains, in spite of the memories held within their crags and icy caverns, her heart smiled.

You took my husband from me but you can never take my memories.

Her memories took her back, but she no longer mourned Nico's passing, the ache of a deep wound eased by the passage of time—the scar still palpable but no longer painful. His presence had given her the freedom to dream, their daughter the reminder that he'd never be more than an arm's length away. And finally, she'd taken the chain from around her neck and put it away.

Miles slipped in beside her. "You okay?"

"Yes." She looked up and into the concern buried behind soulful eyes, his hair damp and disheveled and falling in thick threads over his forehead. "Just thinking."

"They're good listeners. The mountains. I give my troubles, my concerns to them." A contemplative pause squeezed between them. "I gave Nico his first ski lessons. Some people are born for the slopes and he was one of those people. He was a good skier, Rachel. I didn't know him well, but Chris speaks highly of him." He turned her to face him. "I'm sorry things turned out the way they did."

The concern had vanished and in its place was something she'd not seen before. Was it sadness? Or perhaps suppressed uneasiness?

"I'm fine. Really. The mountain took him, Miles, but the hurt, the pain..." The burden of memory touched his features and she had to look away, back to the mountains where the pain of Nico's absence had begun, acute and bitter and cold, now nothing but a distant memory frozen in time. Over the months and years the pain had faded, each season of deep snow burying it deeper within the blanket of acceptance.

"The pain isn't there anymore. It's like a little fire that burns inside me now, but there's no anger, no denial, no bargaining with God." The saying of it—the saying aloud of the words stung with the admission yet carried the solace of acceptance. "The what ifs have been put to rest. Nico's fire is like a slow-burning candle flame—a reminder that there's warmth in his memory, but no longer the awful pain of loss." She paused, hands resting calmly in front of her. And then she turned them over and then back, as if the answers to unasked questions lay hidden in the movement. "And I expect his spirit will reside inside me for as long as I draw breath."

"As it should be." His jaw tightened as if struggling to voice his concerns. "I've never given up the search for him, Rachel." The lines between Miles' eyes grew together, his voice deep and choked. "I couldn't. Not after the way you looked right through me that night, through O'Bannion, and waited for him to walk through the door. You never let hope die. How could I?"

"He's been gone for five years." Even after all this time, she still found it hard to say. *Dead.* The word had a finality to it that she'd not completely grasped.

"The mountain doesn't fight fair. It can be cruel and unforgiving. God knows I've pulled more than my share of casualties from its bowels, but I couldn't...I can't give up. Maybe...I don't know...if I give up searching for him, I'm giving up and the mountain wins." The tenacity with which he spoke matched the steel-blue of his eyes. He skimmed her arms, the slow motion of his hands one of affirmation and of assurance, and then they fell to his sides as he turned again toward the mountains. "I'll never give up searching."

The intimation washed over her like the flow of molasses on a cold day, the flavor sweet yet tinged with the essence of truth. Rachel took his hand then and brought it to her cheek, the cool skin a balm to the fever of feelings clashing inside her. And then she took his other and faced him.

His eyes deepened from steel-blue to the darkest gray, drawing her to a place longing for touch. A place to seek refuge. A place sheltered from the shadows. He brought their clasped hands to his chest and held them there, both anchor—the way in, the safe harbor and security to stay—and lifeline, the way out, with enough rope to let her go.

The eyes don't lie.

A symphony of rapid heartbeats pulsed against her hands, the fragrance of soap and wilderness and the promise of tomorrow rousing her senses. Rachel rose to her toes, every muscle, tissue, and cell holding her together dissolving to mush as his strength invited her in. She held his gaze and touched her lips to his in a tentative kiss she hadn't meant to give. And when she drew away from what wasn't hers to take, he took it back, soft enough to allow her hesitation, but power enough to gain her trust.

A smile ripened against her mouth, the shadow of a thickening beard delicately rough and vividly alive against her skin, awakening sensations buried under the visage of time.

Miles rested his forehead against hers. "I've spent many sleepless nights dreaming of how sweet this would be, Rachel Caldarone." He whispered the words, his breath minty and warm and seasoned with the same palpable shivers of hesitation. "And I've only one thing to say."

She looked up, waiting for a reply that stretched for miles, though no distance separated them.

"Hello." And he leaned in and took her mouth, this time with no hesitation, his tongue meeting hers in a soft joust that soared past greeting and into invitation—one she took willingly and gave back in a breathless exchange.

"If our first kiss was hello, what was that one for?"

"Healing."

With her head nestled firmly in his palms and thumb grazing her cheek, he kissed her again.

FIFTEEN

*R*achel stepped away, the separation as cold as the glacier walls he'd scaled, yet his lips and tongue still simmered with the taste of her. But he knew enough to hold back the longing to give more, to allow her space and pray she'd respond to what was real and not the ghost of the man who'd been dead for nearly five long years.

Sometimes this relationship thing was tricky, an equation as complex as a chemical formula. One small misstep and it blew up in your face. He'd learned his lesson the first time with Brenna and he didn't particularly care to repeat it. And though he held a bachelor's degree in two majors and the certificate hanging in the clinic proved he'd earned the DVM behind his name, the ability to think rationally in that moment left his head empty.

She increased the distance between them, stopping at the shelves flanking both sides of the fireplace and then turned briefly. "You said earlier you had an idea? About what?"

One foot in front of the other, Malone, it isn't rocket science.

"I'm worried about you and Bug."

"Did you talk to Chris? He's free, isn't he?" Her eyes darted beyond him, the panic well-rooted. "I need to go. I have to make sure Bug's safe."

He moved closer and waited for her to acknowledge the closeness before he took her hand. "I spoke to Chris but he hasn't called me back. But that's not what I meant. You need to see for yourself Chast —" She yanked her hand free, but he slowly took it back, stroking her knuckles. "I think if you see for yourself he's behind bars, you'll be reassured he can't harm you. Or Bug."

She speared him with a direct scowl, the contempt pouring from her rigid features gouging a fresh wound, ripping another hole in him that couldn't be stitched.

Her fingers slipped from his. She turned her back and paced the shelves lined with DVDs. She removed one and put it back. Took another. Flipped it over, absently scanning the fine print, tapped it against her palm, and then returned it to its space.

"Are these all Oscar winners?"

"Most. Some are just favorites. Ones I find worthy of owning."

"Hobby?"

"Yes. I have quite a collection…some quite rare." He rubbed a finger over an eyebrow and then dropped his hand to his side. "I'd be happy to discuss my movie obsession with you another time."

She turned around, lips pursed into a thin, white line, a dam ready to give way. "You want me to go to the prison? To *face* him?"

He twined a hand around Rachel's waist. "You wouldn't have to face him or speak to him." Confronting the monster who had violated her had his guts twisting, but it could never compare to the panic leaking from her, trembling against his hand. He'd been the complacent champion with Brenna and he wouldn't make that mistake again. He would protect Rachel, her heart, her life, and her daughter, whatever the cost to himself. "Correct me if I'm wrong, but I think in this case seeing is believing."

She squirmed free, and with her hands curled tightly over the edge of a shelf, she settled her weight between them. "You can't travel yet."

"Doc said a few days. I'll reopen the clinic tomorrow, but it'll take a week or so to catch up on routine exams and surgeries and do some rescheduling of patients, and see if Dr. Pennington is willing to swap on-call emergencies. And I want to make certain Zoe is ready to go home." He leaned against the back of the sofa. "Which reminds me, fire department discovered the source of the fire."

"So fast?"

"Bucket of rags used for staining the banisters spontaneously combusted. One of the construction workers fessed up to the foreman, foreman to the fire department. Open and shut case."

"I'm sorry about the mother cat, but I'm glad no one else was injured." Rachel looked up briefly, picked up a DVD, and tapped it against her palm, but her attention was focused somewhere beyond him, beyond the room. And then she found purchase in the present and stared at the floor. "I can't do this, Miles."

Words can be easily misconstrued and he prayed she was talking about the prison visit and not what they'd shared moments ago. He chose the one he could live with best.

"It's just a suggestion, and you won't have to go alone. I'll be there with you." He sought some sort of acknowledgement, but she gave him nothing in return. He stepped away from the sofa, interrupting the clumsy hesitation with a quiet sigh. "Think about it, and whatever you decide is okay with me. For now, make yourself comfortable. I've got phone calls to make and then we can talk."

Rachel didn't look up, her reply caught somewhere between a nod and a shake.

Stepping beside her, Miles slid his arm over her shoulder, a small recoil evident under his touch. He disguised the movement with a gentle squeeze. "I'll be in my study if you'd care to join me?"

She leaned into him, the movement a minute thing that rolled through him as expansive as the mountains surrounding them, but it was enough for now. The need to soothe her, to break through the barrier standing between them tightened his chest. If she'd let him. If she could look at him without seeing the past and the ghosts that haunted her. He lifted her chin and wiped the warm moisture from her cheeks, his thumb kissing away the remnants of her thoughts.

"I won't be long."

Rachel responded with a brief smile that left him with a mixture of
want and need to take away the sadness and replace it with a smile
that wouldn't fade. One as bright as the Colorado summer sun. One
that crinkled her eyes. A smile nothing—or no one—could wipe away.

"Will you be okay by yourself for a few minutes?"

She raised the DVD. "I'll pop this in while I wait."

"Care to watch it in the home theater?"

"Where?"

"It's the movie obsession thing." He accented the candid statement
with a small chuckle. "It's the reason I built a special room for view-
ing, and why I knew so quickly about the cause of the fire at The
Villages."

"I don't see the connection."

"Kristina Kaufman came to me with the idea for the theater at The
Villages, so I spoke with Logan about it." An odd laugh accompanied
his answer. "He had to cover the phone to recover from a fit of
laughter and said if I was wise, I'd put my money in something with a
much better return on investment, but didn't think I could put it
anywhere that would give me more satisfaction."

"I think highly of them both and respect their opinion."

"I'm a sucker for anything movie related, so it didn't take much
coaxing for me to decide to invest with Wentworth-Cavanaugh. So,"
he said with a short intake of air, "now that you know my weakness
and reason for a home theater, would you like me to set you up with
your movie?"

"Maybe later?" She motioned for him to go on about his business.
"I'll be fine right here."

Heather had dropped the phone when Miles had spoken to her
about his impending absence. She'd recovered quickly,
jumping at the chance to run things while he was gone, and assured
him she'd take care of everything during his five or six day absence. A
one-woman office manager and vet tech, Heather was a crackerjack in

every form of the word and would carry out his instructions to a tee and most likely invent a few of her own.

Heather suggested Bug come help feed the kittens if her mother agreed, and Grandpa Gowen was able to drive her over. Since the kittens were strays and Bug had officially rescued them, they belonged to her.

He'd agreed and made a mental note to give the woman a raise.

Heather's idea gave him an excuse to postpone placing the last phone call on his list to Detective O'Bannion and run the idea by Rachel. But barging in on her thoughts wasn't high on his agenda. Memories and ghosts were hard bastards to compete against.

Halfway out the study door, he stopped. Rachel wasn't in sight. He checked the kitchen. Then a big black head popped up, groaned, and sank back into the sofa. He made his way across the room, but when he opened his mouth to shoo the dog off the furniture, his breaths came to a full stop. A mass of blonde curls was splayed over the pillows and he stared at the landscape before him, as flawless as a hand-painted canvas.

His houseguest had fallen asleep with Strider in full stretch beside her.

The video had been muted, the familiar wiggling pink pig and literate spider in full animated character. It was plain to see the movie had been a way to link herself to her daughter. She missed her. So did he. The planned and unplanned trips to day care educating little ones about animals and how to handle them had become a way of life. And an innocuous way to see a special little Ladybug.

Rachel lay partially hidden under the black hairy dog and a mountain of pillows confiscated from around the room, and a fleece throw covered her from the waist down. With a pillow tucked under an arm and another snuggled under her chin, she'd curled herself around Strider. The big oaf had perched his huge head on Rachel's thigh and she'd fallen asleep with her hand in the thick fur behind Strider's ear.

Miles knelt beside her, a stealth movement meant to go unnoticed. Two nights of uncomfortable, interrupted sleep had caught up to her and he had no intention of disturbing the angel sent to awaken what had been long dead inside him. An angel sent to guide his way back to the living.

Blonde curls lay limp against her cheek and the need to touch her overshadowed the desire to leave her undisturbed. He brushed the curls aside and then pulled the throw over her shoulder, the shallow rise and fall of her breathing giving way to the flutter of sleepy eyes.

"Sweet dreams, my love. My ray of sunshine." He'd spoken aloud, the words barely a whisper but abundant in truth, and a mere suggestion of things he longed to say but didn't dare.

Would she have him? Could she leave a man she loved, step over a new threshold and let him in? He was ready. Ready for it all—every good thing was his to cherish, every doubt his to turn to belief, every fear his to calm, and every moment his to make new memories. Perhaps his patience had finally paid off.

Her eyes fluttered, closed again, and then opened halfway. She stretched an arm over her head. "Hey." A sleepy smile turned the corners of her mouth and it took all the restraint he could muster to keep from kissing each corner, plant another in the center and allow them to simmer.

"I didn't mean to wake you."

"Bug's not the only one who's a little tired."

"No reason for you to stay awake, Sunshine." He hadn't meant for the nickname to slip, but she made no effort to correct him.

"You'll go with me?" A sense of trepidation crept into the words, forming a crease between her eyes once solemn and peaceful in sleep. "To Arizona? To the prison?"

"Of course I will." He took her hand and held it against his chest, wincing at the unplanned movement.

"I can't do this alone."

"I'll be there every step of the way."

"But I don't know about the hearing." She frowned and dug at her lip.

"We'll take it one step at a time, Rachel. Together. Whatever you can handle. I'll be there for you. And for Bug." The tension eased from her features, growing slack as exhaustion tipped her over the edge of sleep. Her chest rose and fell with the slow motion of easy rest, drifting into dreams. His dreams to grant. Big ones and little ones and all of them between. "I'll always be right here," he said and gently stroked her cheek with the back of his hand. "I'll be the one you can count on." *For the rest of my life.* "For now, sleep well, Sunshine."

Unwilling to let the moment go, he stayed, caressing her with his eyes, tracing the fine lines around her eyes and nose and mouth—lines he longed to deepen with her smile and the passage of time.

He rose, walked to the long bank of windows, and stood gazing into the mountains, waiting for them to give voice to inward thought. "Let's do this, Nico. Let's do this for her." He spoke not to himself but to the ghost that guarded her future and plagued the past.

On his way back to the study, his stomach growled, protesting its neglect. He stopped in the kitchen and opened the fridge. Deciding on deli turkey, provolone cheese, crisp lettuce, and sliced dill pickles slathered in a generous amount of sriracha mayo, he assembled two sandwiches. One, he wrapped in cellophane for when she woke, and one for himself now. If he didn't get some pain meds in him soon, he'd never catch up to the growing ball of fire igniting the fuse to his kidneys and lower back. He grabbed a beer from the fridge, twisted the top, and flung the cap in the trash. With two swallows, he downed the pills without regard to the warning to avoid alcohol while taking pain meds.

The missed call reminder on his iPhone buzzed. He took a bite of sandwich and glanced back at Rachel and Strider curled into the sofa. The sight of her swept peacefully into sleep reached up and seized his heart, sure his brain had misfired instructions to beat. Willing himself to move, he reached the door to the study and shut it to within an inch of closing so the phone calls wouldn't disturb her. He rescheduled the dinner date with his mother first and then hit the redial button and took another pull on his beer.

Chris picked up on the first ring. "Hey, buddy, glad you called back. I've got some news."

"Chastain?"

"Yeah. Scumbag's sittin' pretty inside the Arizona State Prison in Florence, southeast of Phoenix."

"Good. Fucking pervert deserves to be on death row. A slow, painful death by exposure to radiation would be too good for him. Nor would I be opposed to feeding his nut sack to the wolves. Still attached."

"You're making me a little nervous, Doc. Our new puppy will be in need of neutering in a few months." There was a silent pause on the other end. "Why the sudden interest in this guy?"

"It's Rachel." Miles made his way around the desk and sank into the oversized leather chair. It gave way with a mild squeak. "She's afraid Chastain's out of prison and will come after her and her daughter."

"That's impossible."

"Try convincing her of that. She's terrified enough to imagine seeing him around every corner."

"Wow. That's heavy stuff, buddy. You know, though..." Chris ended a moment's pause with a small cough. "Our families were close, and after Nico's death she kept to herself and then when the story came out in the *Estes Park News,* she severed the ties completely. It was a difficult time. But I still don't get your connection..." His voice trailed off as if someone had stolen the end of his thought. "Wait a sec. Are you finally—"

"I'm helping her out."

"Now I get the picture."

Miles inspected the ceiling. A small chink between the logs would need repairing. "Do you? I don't even know if I get it." He got up and paced the room in a carousel of circles, the steady squeak of his Sorels conducting a minor ovation across the wood floor.

"It's none of my business, but I've known for a long time you've had a thing for her."

"Look, Chris..." He started to explain but yielded to the fact he'd never been good at hiding anything from the detective whose DNA consisted of part bloodhound. "Shit. That obvious?"

"Let me put it this way." Chris' hesitation reeked of casual appreciation. "Women practically throw themselves at you, and you've never given anyone, including Brenna—"

"Leave Brenna out of this." The name ground between his teeth.

"I'm just saying you've never looked at a woman the way you look at Rachel. Not as long as I've known you. What took you so long?"

"You know her history."

"Suppose you're right. The assault and then losing Nico couldn't have been easy to get over."

"I don't know that she is."

"It's been what, fourteen years since the assault and almost five years since Nico's death?"

"Fifteen. Took a year to prosecute the sonofabitch but the amount of time isn't the issue."

"Then what's this about?"

"I want to convince her to take a road trip to Arizona to prove Chastain's still in prison and isn't a threat to her or her daughter. Didn't help that damn thief told her the locks on her house aren't safe. Nothing like proving a point."

"Thief? What kind of company have you been keeping?"

"He's one of Rachel's patients who helped us break into the theater—"

"That, my friend, I did not hear."

"If I have to, I'll hire security and keep her here, at my place, so I know she and Bug and her grandfather are safe." Miles ceased pacing and threw a hand on his hip. "I want to kill the sonofabitch who did this to her."

"Me too, buddy. Me too."

The common bond they shared calmed his troubled nerves into something more conducive to conversation. "I've got some other calls to make. Logan Cavanaugh's got connections in Arizona and I need to ask him if he can pull a few strings."

"The Cavanaughs have connections all over the world. Whatever you need, Logan can probably provide it. Something to do with the hearing?"

"Hearings are usually conducted via videoconferencing. Maybe he knows someone close to the Board of Executive Clemency who could suggest a change of policy." He wavered on the end of a mental shrug, unsure whether to continue. "An in-person hearing."

"Are you fucking kidding me?"

"Trust me, Chris. It's not what I want to see happen, but I think it might be necessary."

"For Christ's sake I hope you know what you're doing."

"I don't. Just a gut feeling." The apparent apprehension in Chris' pause matched his, a tight coiling in his gut. "If you hear anything else give me a call."

"There is one more thing. This isn't public knowledge so forget where it came from." Chris' vigilant detective's tone seeped into his voice. "Another victim has come forward with an allegation of rape. A kid. Or at least he was when the fucking pervert *allegedly* raped him. He's in his thirties now, but in Arizona there's no statute of limitations on sexual assault against a child."

A fog of disbelief spoiled the air. "A child?" The words formed as a whispered cry, a child's innocence stolen in a blink of an eye. *Bug.* The little girl with the wild curly hair. The little girl who had attached herself to his heart and pulled the strings so tight he'd never recover. The idea of someone touching her, or any child in that way rose as thick sludge in the back of his throat but did little to incinerate the vile thought.

"How could anyone...?" The question died as quickly as it had been given voice, and Miles took pause to acclimate to an unspeakable deed.

"I've worked these cases. The damage...it's worse than you can imagine. It's bad enough when an adult is involved. Death is too good for these sick bastards, and all too often they go free or the incidents are never reported." The disdain was audible in Chris' tone and heavy breaths. "Chastain's hearing is coming up, and let's pray the victim doesn't retract his statement."

"And if he's convicted of a second offense?"

"He could spend the rest of his life in prison with no possibility of pardon or commutation of sentence."

"Not long enough in my book. Spending eternity in hell would be a more fitting ending."

"If he's guilty of statutory rape of a minor, he'll probably die in prison if the inmates don't get to him first. Rapists are prison lowlifes, even among inmates. I hate to say this, Miles, but Rachel should testify whether by video or in person. To give them a taste of the hell he's made of her life. And to support the other victim."

"Shit." Miles tapped a fist against his chin several times. "I was hoping you'd say it would be a waste of time and talk me out of it."

"Sorry, buddy, it won't be a waste of time."

Semper fi.

Improvise. Adapt. Overcome.

He'd first given those words life lying in a makeshift bunker in the moonlit Iraqi desert. He, the first lieutenant, had improvised. The unit had adapted. But as dawn broke and shed light on the mission, he'd had to overcome more than he'd bargained for. And he had to do the same for Rachel. To be her strength.

Miles braced a leg across the desk and then withdrew it, holding his breath until his gut quit cursing the movement. He leaned against the desk instead. "I'll speak to her, and no matter what happens, I'll see her through this new development."

"Good luck, buddy."

Miles disconnected the call, Chris' words echoing in his mind.

The door to the study opened.

"What new development?"

SIXTEEN

*E*ven the tan from winter skiing couldn't hide his pasty color. "Miles, when was the last time you took your pain medication?"

He dismissed the question with a wave. "A few minutes ago. I'm fine." He stood, grabbed his gut with one hand, the desk with the other. The first few days of an abdominal puncture weren't pleasant, but the pain etched on his face wasn't of the physical variety. She recognized both.

"You don't look fine." She approached him and lifted his shirt. "And if you've taken your pain meds, you shouldn't be drinking. Didn't you read the warning labels?"

He pushed her hand away, but she didn't move. "You're persistent, I'll give you that."

"I'm used to resistance. Men think they're invincible."

"I thought maybe you wanted me out of my shirt again."

She glowered at him and continued her inspection. "Bandage looks good and you're not bleeding." She lowered his shirttail, burying a trite comeback beneath it. "Now that we've established you're not in need of another trip to Dr. Who—"

"Lecter." His features corkscrewed and he put his weight against the desk. "As in *Silence of the Lambs.*"

"Whatever. You'll be in la-la land when the meds kick in so tell me about this new development."

If his color blanched any further, he'd be as white as fresh snow. He turned first one Sorel and then the next, his attention focused on the splatters of mud and dried blood stuck to the boots. He looked up and cleared his throat. "I made you a turkey sandwich and there's beer in the fridge."

"I'm not hungry and you're changing the subject."

He stood, downed the last swallow of his beer, and locked an arm around her waist. "I'll tell you, but first you're going to eat something. I'm just a vet. You said yourself I'm qualified to mend critters, not people and I don't intend to peel you off the floor when you faint from lack of nourishment."

The words pouring into her ear had nothing to do with the issue at hand, but she played along. "I'm not going to faint."

"Swoon then?"

"No." She invited him into the half-answer with an animated half-grin. "Well, once…"

"I knew it." With his hand pressed to the small of her back, he guided her toward the kitchen.

"I do not swoon!" She slid onto a barstool.

Miles tossed his empty bottle into the recycle bin, peered into the fridge and came back with the sandwich and opened a fresh beer, fizz escaping in a misty whorl. The bottle cap clattered on the countertop and then he crumpled the cellophane, the tight ball unfurling as if touched by magic. "You admitted to swooning."

"Technically speaking."

He arranged her lunch on a plate in front of her, handed her the beer, and added a bowl of strawberries and a paper napkin. "Now I'm curious."

The anxiety had eased to the somber, rugged complacency he wore when relaxed, a balanced mixture of concern and waggish playfulness.

His features carried a certain intensity, the solid line of his jaw equal to the benevolence in his sobering blue eyes.

She lifted the bottle and took a drink, resisting the urge to scrunch her nose. "My dad and I were waiting for Grandpa at Sky Harbor airport and a guy with a guitar strung across his back nearly ran me over." She took another swallow, this time the unpleasant fizz subsided into a warm ember in her belly. "My purse went flying, his papers scattered, and he caught me in time to keep me from splattering myself all over Southwest Airlines' gate three. A very embarrassed Jon Bon Jovi heartily apologized several times while we gathered everything." She tilted her head. "The papers had scribbles of music and what I assumed were lyrics."

He propped his elbows on the bar. "A new song?"

"Maybe. Anyway, he apologized again, winked, and was off. I spent my ten seconds of fame in the arms of Jon Bon Jovi and all his glorious hair."

"Did he say anything else?"

"I was thirteen and too busy *swooning* to recall." She leaned back and parked the back of her hand against her forehead in a perfect rendition of an eighteenth-century swoon.

When Miles laughed, it wasn't loud but deeply intense. It monopolized his entire face and lingered long after the sound had left the room. But this time the effervescence fizzled as quickly as it had appeared.

Rachel took another drink, squinting.

"I take it you don't care for beer?"

She picked absently at the label, torn bits forming a neat little pile. "Reminds me of rotten corn cobs." She took a bite of the sandwich and stopped chewing. A plucked pickle belly-flopped on the plate.

"Or pickles?"

"Just dill. But I don't think my alcoholic or pickle preference is what's on your mind."

Miles came around the bar and took the barstool across from her, one boot on her footrest. He leaned forward and took her chin in one hand, the napkin with the other. "You've got mayo," he said, dabbing her mouth, "right here."

"You're stalling." She snatched the napkin from him. "What's going on?"

Miles leaned into the barstool's low back. "I spoke with Detective O'Bannion. There's been a change in Chast—" Rachel clenched her teeth. "Something's happened that could affect the hearing."

"I receive word if anything..." Tension knotted her muscles. Her throat tightened around a rising wad of panic and the room heaved sideways. "He's not...he's not in Colorado, is he?".

Miles took her hand and skimmed a thumb over her knuckles, the back and forth motion soothing the seesaw pitch. "He's still behind bars."

"But I saw him. I know it was him." The mind is a powerful organ, capable of incredible feats. She'd seen it time after time with the elderly. Had it been her imagination? Had she imagined him taunting her among the crowd?

"I believe you think you saw him, Rachel, but you have to trust the authorities." His Adam's apple bobbed as if he were trying to swallow something horrid and couldn't get it down. "But there's been a development you need to know about."

She hesitated, digesting the meaning of carefully placed words. "Just tell me."

"Someone else has come forward."

Miles spoke gently, evenly, but the words fell in an awkward, garbled heap. She batted at them, swatting the mental word pictures away. Like the hands of a clock, she wanted to force them back around. Rewind. A do-over. Isn't that what kids asked for? A second chance because somehow the rules had been skewed and the end result wasn't fair?

"That can't be. He's been in prison for the last fourteen years."

"Happened before he was convicted. The victim," he said, distress breaking the barrier of his normally calm voice, "is a grown man now."

A putrid sludge filled the space between the words and crawled into her gut.

"He was a kid when the alleged sexual assault took place."

"It's rape, Miles." The word seethed through her teeth. "Why does everyone want to take the brutality from it? To turn it into something that sounds so apathetic?"

"I didn't mean to come across that way."

"Then don't make it sound less than what it is." She slid from the stool, the legs grating across the hardwood floor. She punched her hands in her jeans pockets and peered out the bank of windows. She could hide there, in the mountain, disappear among the snowy crags and crevices. Nico had. Why couldn't she? "A *child?*"

"The bastard's not particular about age. Or gender."

"A boy." Unable to process the concept, she mouthed the words, helpless to bring them to full form, and yet they were too loud to disappear.

"I don't know exactly how the legal system works, but it seems to me the more evidence against his release, the better."

If this was exposed, would more victims come forward? Would there be another trial? Would he prey on new victims if he was released?

"Chris believes your presence at the hearing is crucial." Miles joined her at the window and draped an arm around her. "It would be advantageous to testify in person, to show the board the impact he's had on your life. And it would add a level of reassurance to the victim coming forward. If he's found guilty of a second offense, there's a good chance he'd spend the rest of his life in prison with no chance of release. Ever."

Would this ever be over? Would she ever be rid of him? A cruel shiver rippled over her skin.

"You won't be alone." Miles brought her to him, her back tight against his chest. "I'll be there with you."

No, she wouldn't be alone. Not in the physical sense. Miles would stand beside her, but he'd never be a part of the private, polluted club to which she'd been unwillingly initiated. But there was someone who shared membership. Shared the flashbacks. Shared in the devastation of a dream. Maybe together…

The memories would never die. Not completely. But if she chose to testify at the hearing and Dumas made good on the new charges, she could put to rest a portion of her twisted past. To put an end to the physical threat. She wanted to do the right thing. Be strong. Brave.

But she was none of those things.

"You can do this, Rach. I'll be right beside you. One step at a time."

The voice belonged to Miles, but his words had once belonged to Nico. And Nico had set a part of her free—the part to be the woman she was despite the brutality she'd endured. She turned in his arms and looked up at him and he held her, the connection running not around them, but through skin and muscle and bone, knitting body and soul together.

"Whatever you need, it's yours. All you have to do is ask."

The strength she needed came with his words and with the way he looked not at her but into her and seized her burdens for himself. "You." She laced her arms around his waist and held on as if she'd taken hold of a log adrift in an open sea. "I need you."

"I'm here."

"I don't know if I have the courage to do this." The longing to shove it all aside and go home and hold onto her daughter outweighed her crumbling courage.

"I'll be your courage. Your strength. I'll be whatever you need me to be. One thing for certain, you won't be alone because I swear I won't let you out of my sight."

She leaned into his shoulder, the steady beat of his heart a lullaby, his presence the strength she could depend on. The pleasure of his arms around her a cocoon, the safe haven he offered openly and without hesitation.

The urge to run, to hide from the ugly truth spread like the resurgence of an angry fever. She put her palms to his chest and Miles covered her hands with his, uncertainty melting beneath his touch.

Yes, her tiny family needed her to be strong. Her eyes misted, but she blinked back the burn and found his, ones whose power penetrated her with the fortitude of a battleship and the empathy of the healer within.

"It's about as appealing as drinking antifreeze, but I think you're right. I have to see for myself he's in prison." Despite the dryness in her throat, she seized the next words before they could shrivel and disappear.

"When do we leave?"

SEVENTEEN

*R*ain in Arizona is a rare treat, the way the last swirl of caramel at the bottom of the ice cream bowl is always the sweetest. A rainy day late in April usually means the pungent odor of sagebrush drifting in the breeze, air heavy with moisture, and the weight of the storm settling the dust.

But this wasn't a usual rainy day.

The steady swish-thump-swish-thump of the Chevy four-by-four's wipers lulled the drone of the tires on the empty stretch of asphalt. They were close. Close enough to smell it. Rachel had never seen a maximum-security prison. Never been inside one. But the stench hit her—an instant of recall—caustic cologne, sweaty hands, rain-drenched asphalt.

The fence grew taller, thicker, heavier. Concertina wire corkscrewed atop the heavy-duty chain link, and the storm's weight descended around her, seeping into the cracks of unsound armor. The lunch they'd stopped for in Show Low—an Italian antipasto she'd shared with Miles—sank like a boulder in a deep pond, dragging her stomach with it.

Miles slowed and pulled to the shoulder, gravel grating beneath the tires. Rachel shrank into the center console as far from the ghastly fence as she could. He shoved the gearshift into Park, leaned across the console, and took her arm, his touch warm and firm on unsteady nerves. Still, she shivered.

"We don't have to do this. There's plenty of room to turn around."

The overwhelming urge to act on his suggestion hummed in her thighs. Twitched in her foot. Blood hammered double time in the places it shouldn't be heard or felt. Ears. Stomach. Head.

The memory screamed to be set free.

"Rachel?"

The muffled sound of her name punched through the grayness. Slowly, she turned toward it, inching further into the console. Away from the razor wire. Away from the memory. Away from the perimeter of the past.

"Please talk to me." He took her chin then and guided her face toward him, the movement shaky and stiff. "I can't help unless you talk to me. Let me in."

Lines of fatigue stretched across his face, but the expression was dipped in determination, the sort of thing he might have worn on the battlefields of Iraq. But this was her war, and the battle raging inside her bloomed full force with no defense save a feeble armor of fabricated courage.

"What the hell was I thinking? I should never have brought you here." Miles dropped the truck into Drive, waited for a silver SUV to pass, and then swung the steering wheel in the opposite direction.

Rain pattered against the windshield. The wipers swished back and forth in a cadence mocking the tic-tic-tic of the turn signal.

"No." The command faltered, but it was enough for Miles to hit the brakes. "You were right. *Are* right. I have to do this."

"There's no harm in changing your mind. We can be back in Show Low in a couple of hours. Or return by way of Hidden Falls. I'll leave it up to you."

Thoughts of Hidden Falls and Woodland Hills cut through the despair in a moment of reprieve. Dottie. Ruthie. The Colonel. "I want to turn around so badly I can barely breathe." Her chin quivered and she strained the words through a barrier thick with doubt.

"But I can't keep running from this, from him, for the rest of my life."

"If you're sure." Miles fell back against the seat, drumming his index finger on the steering wheel. "But if you want to turn around... now would be a good time. Once we get inside," he said, taking her hand firmly, "it's not going to be easy. Probably a lot worse."

She swallowed a sob. "That's what I'm afraid of."

He leaned over and took her mouth, kissing her gently but deeply, the power of it hidden in the unspoken authority. "I won't leave your side, but you say the word and we're out of there. Deal?"

She nodded, the confirmation a crude mix of torture and resignation.

The few minutes it took to drive the remaining distance passed in fractured seconds, and before she could utter a change of mind, they were parked in the rain-soaked lot of the Arizona State Prison.

Surrounded.

She shivered. Metal chain-link fencing and concertina wire surrounded them, and the all-knowing, all-seeing eye of the watch-tower peered through the windshield. The rain had cooled the temperatures to the seventies, but hell freezing over couldn't feel any colder.

Miles slid from the truck, met her on the passenger side, and opened her door. "Here," he said, handing her his sweatshirt. "The hood will keep you dry."

She poked her arms through the openings and cinched it around her, the outside world stealing the warmth it offered. Encased in his scent, she traced the clinic's logo and for an instant she was back in Estes Park with her daughter, Grandpa, and in increasing measures, Miles. She slid from the seat but her knees collapsed.

Miles crushed her against him, his strength bleeding into her as if they shared a direct connection. "You've got this and I've got you." He raised the hood and tucked it around her chin.

Raindrops gathered on his lashes like tiny drops of dew and his hair had fallen over his forehead, the accumulating drizzle slipping from the strands. Drip...drip...drip. The movement, small and inconsequential, settled on her heart. Wads of his shirt balled in her fists and she reached for, and took his mouth, fast and hard and hungry. Nothing mattered—not rain or wet or chill—but the feel of him, the palpable surety of his presence and the power in the simple connection. And he gave back what she had taken.

He tipped his forehead to hers. "Ready?"

"I am now."

"I won't leave your side, Rachel. That's a promise. And I don't make promises I don't intend to keep." He tilted her chin toward the sky. "Look there, do you see it?"

She shaded her eyes, squinting as she scanned the sky. Gray clouds bumped and rolled and then split open to a crystal blue sky and the perfect arch of twin rainbows.

"Rainbows are a symbol of a bridge to a brighter place." He punctuated the remark with a lopsided smile, an offer of momentary reprieve.

Rachel tilted her head toward the guard tower. "I'd rather step over it in search of that elusive pot of gold."

"I promise I'll be beside you through whatever storms come our way, and together we'll find that pot of gold." He finger-combed his rain-soaked hair, draped an arm around her shoulders and urged her forward.

The closer they got to the entrance, the bigger her anxiety grew, but Miles didn't waver. Didn't hesitate. Confidence and resolve amplified each step. Wrapped in the strength of his invisible cocoon, she followed, escorted by the low hum of the electrified fence vibrating in tune to her nerves.

Once inside, the minutes passed in a blur, a disjointed confusion of apathy and perception, a match of wits pushing and pulling her along on some automated system of forward motion. Had they checked in? Signed her name? She recalled removing her shoes. Retying the loops. Had Miles done the same? She couldn't put the recollections in order, but surely they'd passed all the security requirements. She had no intention of bringing the bastard cookies or a pack of gum, let alone smuggle contraband.

Heavy feet moved in automatic motion, her movements synced by the subtle twists and turns of Miles' hand as if he were the lead in some absurd dance with no music, no rhyme, no reason. Someone had joined them, his voice a muffled drone. Metal and noise and disinfectant stung her senses and she stopped abruptly, turning in the direction they had come.

"You okay?" Miles' voice filtered through the confusion.

"I don't..." She spun a vicious circle. "Where'd we come in? Where's the exit? I need to find the way out of here." Her vision blurred.

"The exit is behind us, and the guard knows where all of them are." Miles buried her head in his chest. "It's okay."

The guard came up beside her decked in full uniform. His nametag read S. DeLuca, but his expression said empathy and subtle inquest.

"I sympathize with your reluctance to go forward, Mrs. Caldarone." The guard placed his hand loosely on his gun belt. "The warden made sure all the bases were covered for this visit, and I'll be with you and Mr. Malone the entire time. You're safe."

"Where's your gun?" The words tumbled from her mouth and her eyes flicked from the guard's gun belt to his face.

"The tower gunmen who overlook the grounds are armed. We carry stun guns and pepper spray. Radios."

Rachel leaned into Miles' side and he tightened his grip.

"The prisoners won't be able to see you, Mrs. Caldarone. They won't know you're there. I hope that helps alleviate some of the apprehension you're feeling."

She huddled closer to Miles, hesitation fracturing the assurance in her nod.

"The warden made special provisions for this visit, Rachel, but we're only allowed a few minutes." Miles spoke softly and then nodded in the guard's direction. "We need to keep going."

They followed close behind the guard, but she was closer to Miles, the friction as denim brushed denim a rough yet soothing comfort.

They were soon inside a long hallway. Too narrow. Too many doors. Too much sweat and pine disinfectant. The walls pitched.

Ceiling shifted. She clenched Miles' hand, fingers tingling. He responded with a quick squeeze back but didn't speak. He didn't question. And he didn't let go.

Officer DeLuca opened a heavy metal door. "Right through here," he said, motioning them ahead.

The door sealed behind them. The heavy thud compressed her lungs, the air stale and too heavy to breathe. DeLuca checked security, and she wrestled the impulse to shove the men aside and burst into the open hallway.

The walls of the small room turned sideways, closing in around a conference-type table, several cushioned folding chairs, and a long, narrow window. "The window is actually a one-way mirror. You can see them, but they can't see you."

"They?" she asked, biting back the urge to scream.

"There's a classroom on the other side of the glass. The prisoners learn skills to help them adjust to the outside upon their release."

Rachel's legs let go. Miles eased her into a chair. She couldn't bring herself to look, the resistance holding her back as ruthless as if the Jaws of Life held her in place.

"I can't, Miles." Sweat moistened her skin, but her mouth went dry. "I can't do this."

"I'd be happy to step outside." DeLuca's tone was decisive yet soft.

"No!" Rachel scooted to the edge of her seat. "No, please stay...I feel safer with you here. Please."

The guard gave Miles a long look and took a step back, clearing her line of sight.

Miles reached for her hand and brought her to a standing position, his body a shield between her and the glass. "I'm going to step aside—"

"Don't leave me!"

"I won't leave you, but I'm going to step aside so you can see for yourself Demetri Chastain—"

A gasp died between parted lips.

"As long as he's in custody he can't harm you, Bug, or your family."

Tears blurred her vision, and she squeezed her eyes shut.

Miles stepped to her side but held her close, his strong arms a lifeline attached at her waist. "Open your eyes, Rachel."

She stiffened, her body in stark appeal to the request. Willing herself to respond, she gulped air and slowly opened her eyes.

Color and form blended, a wash of images with no shape, no definition, no intelligible form. She blinked once and then again. Orange jumpsuits, shaved heads and dreadlocks, powerful arms and thin necks riddled with tattoos stabilized, grew steadier, and then came into full focus. The shape of their heads. Skin color. Hair and hands distinct. The movement of fingers, eyes, mouths, each one a pockmark, each one a toxic mark of hell. So diverse. So alike.

Faces of poisoned souls.

She scanned the room. Steadied on one. Fixed on the target, her mental crosshairs drew him in, magnifying him until his face, his body, his presence, his nearness drained her of feeling. Blood surged fiery-hot and thick. Body and mind contracted, stiffened. Her body disconnected from her brain, ceased to function.

Him.

The weight of the memory crushed her. Adrenaline shot through her veins in hot spasms. Putrid, noxious breath curdled her stomach. Cold, greedy hands groped her and she flung her arms, squirming against the vile grip. Arms bound her. Silence devoured her screams. She lashed out. Limbs flailed and her head thrashed in vain effort.

No-no-no-no-no!

"Let me go!" Inflamed words burned her throat and she spit them out like acid rain. "Get off me!"

"It's me, Rachel. You're safe. I won't let go. I'll never let go."

A scream tangled and died before it could break free. The guard lunged forward but then backed off.

Why didn't he help her?

Strong arms gripped her, a vise around her chest. Still, she struggled.

"Let me go!"

"You're okay. It's me. You're safe."

Words died on her lips. Pinpricks of light danced behind her eyes, a meteor shower of panic. Silent screams shattered her. Left her exposed. Warned her.

Don't struggle. He'll kill you. Let him. Let him take you.

She gave in and let him drag her into the dregs of hell.

"I'm right here." The tone and effort of the voice grew softer and his grip around her eased. "You're okay, Rachel. I won't let anyone hurt you." The voice—deep and subdued and resolute—penetrated the memory like an ice pick splintering solid ice. "Come back to me, Sunshine." A cracked sob floundered and he held her—not as a prisoner. Not as prey.

Not the memory.

She clutched her arms to her chest as he turned her slowly around.

Safety.

Limp arms fell to her sides. She dissolved, torment spilling in silent, wet circles and soaked his shirt. "I'm...sorry." Barely a whisper, the words faltered.

"No need of apology, Rach."

The endearment another man had given her wrapped around her heart and squeezed, yanking her from the past into the present. Her mind and body unwound. Stilled.

Miles smoothed her hair, threading the loose curls between his fingers. "Guard," he said, "we're done here."

Officer DeLuca poised to open the door.

"Wait." Rachel kept hold of Miles but pulled away, the muscles in his forearms trembling under her palm. "Not yet."

A frown crippled his forehead, a thin sheen of moisture glistening in the creases.

She swallowed and then swallowed again to flush the decision and the misgiving that went with it. "I have to...look at him."

"I can't put you through that again."

"It's my decision." A sudden punch hit her in the gut, but she punched back. "I need to confront him or I'll never be able to testify at the hearing."

"Rachel, please. This is tearing you up!" Battle-gray eyes turned his pain liquid, and the urge to look away, to distance herself from it pierced her heart. "Jesus, Rachel, it's tearing *me* up to see you like this!"

"I need to do this."

Miles tossed his head back and stared at the ceiling as if the answer lay hidden in the lines and seams. "I love you, and seeing you in pain is tearing me apart." The words trembled, fractured by the obvious torment, the truth scribbled in an unwritten language.

It hit her full force. Those words. When had this happened? This can't happen. She can't let it. Yet it filled her with a wave of recognition, of need, and a courage she didn't think would ever surface again.

"I need to face him. Without falling apart."

He took a deep, sobering breath and tipped his head once.

So did she.

"Promise you won't let go?"

"You have my word." He took her hands in his and pressed them to his heart, stroking each of her knuckles in turn. "I'm right here. Always."

Miles let one hand drop, the other he held with a firm grasp. Rachel swallowed the last of her reservations, and turning slowly around, focused on the bastard who had taken her against her will, violated and broken her, and left her body, mind, and soul shattered on the rain-soaked asphalt.

She pinned him with her eyes the same way he'd pinned her that night, fury and volition trembling through her flesh. Miles tightened his grip and left no distance between them.

Every muscle in her body rebelled. Commanded her to flee. The urge to turn away tugged at her, to vomit the vile image and spew it to the ground like the overpowering side of a tug of war. But need grew and ripened. The need to face him. The need to conquer. To overcome.

Seconds passed and bled into minutes.

And then he looked up, into the mirror. And straight into her.

His toxic stare tore into her, the compulsion to jerk away a powerful pull. The stench of rain on asphalt, sweat, and spent lust. His mouth formed words she couldn't hear, yet the years flew backward…

"Hello, Angel." Hot, putrid breath primed in whisky burned my ear. "You shouldn't make your needs known to the public. Someone might take you up on them."

The memory rewound as vivid as the sweaty palm choking her air and rancid breath on her neck. The curtain fell, playing out that night in grand detail, sight-sound-smell flooding her in a puddle of instant recall. She wanted to break through the glass, to hurt him, to find revenge. And she wanted to turn and run, hard and fast and far.

Always a step behind.

Thick, hot bile climbed her throat. Her lungs collapsed, a giant fist squeezing until no air remained. The room pitched, tilted sideways, and took her stomach with it. Her knees gave. Miles gripped her firmly, the constant amid a world teetering out of control. "I think I'm going to be sick."

DeLuca grabbed the trash can and she hugged it without mercy. Miles held her hair back as the waves hit one after another and she purged the memory, releasing it in putrid heaves until nothing remained but a sick stench. The stench of memory. The stench of *him*. She clutched the metal can, searching the sickness for strength.

Miles set the trash can aside, took a handkerchief from his pocket, and wiped the sweat from her forehead, dabbed her eyes and then her mouth. The tenderness of his touch spoke of the inherent compassion to see past the symptoms, find the injury, and heal the pain. "Better?"

Nodding, she reached for his hand. He took it and squeezed, and with renewed conviction, she turned back to the window.

Protocol separated them. Her on one side, him the other. Opposite sides of something few understood, sharing a bond no one would ever completely sever—a sick, noxious thing that had brought them together, but an unbreakable bond nonetheless. He may be the one sitting behind bars, but it could never compare to the prison he'd locked her in.

She took a hesitant step forward, dragging Miles with her. Raised a hand to the window. Her warm palm left a ghostly imprint on the cold barrier, the invisible connection they shared barred by a sheet of glass.

Had he been this thin back then? She recalled the strength. Forced power. Leaning back in his front row seat, he turned away, breaking the connection. His hand went in the air, the model rapist turned model student's left hand waved as effortless as a kite in the wind. A gold band glinted in the fluorescent light. Married? He'd confessed to a bitter divorce that night and wore no ring. Had he lied? Or had he lured another woman with his charm and good looks? Whoever she was, she wasn't the first, but Rachel could make damn sure she'd be the last.

"I swear you'll never hurt anyone else." Ragged from the burn of bile and choked with years of suppressed anger and pain, the words fell lucid into the world she'd kept hidden in a locked mental box. She lifted her hand from the glass. The heat of her fury had formed a foggy silhouette, a testament of her promise. "So help me God."

A sea of emotions collided. Rachel swiped her cheeks and turned from the nightmare. Miles held her, the power of his presence leaping into bones carved hollow by the fingers of rage. With the simplicity of his touch, and each slow, steady heartbeat against her cheek, the pain eased. And Miles was here with her, and she could disappear into him and everything would be okay.

Yes, her family needed her. And so did the other victim, the man whose childhood, whose innocence and trust had been stripped from him as a young boy and whose nightmares had followed him into manhood.

"I'm ready to go, Officer DeLuca." Taking a step back, she straightened. "I've got a hearing to prepare for."

EIGHTEEN

$\mathcal{T}$he timing couldn't have worked out better.

From the time it took to contact the prison for a visit he'd requested pursuant to Arizona law under the "extraordinary circumstances" clause, Miles had managed to work around his patients and schedule Rachel's visit within days of the impending hearing.

She'd crumbled at first sight of the bastard. And then with nothing short of sheer tenacity, she'd fought to confront her demon and take the damn thing by the horns and send it back to hell. If Rachel had refused to attend the hearing after seeing Chastain in prison, nothing would have been lost—she could send her testimony in absentia by mail. But she'd fought the devil himself and won. And damn if he wasn't proud of her.

He believed he knew her. Had been there the day Nico had gone missing and had witnessed how stalwart she could be in the face of unmitigated circumstances. Had watched her for years at The Villages, her job bringing both laughter and heartache, yet she remained the epitome of strength and compassion for her patients, holding out hope when there was none. He believed he knew her and definitely loved the woman who walked into his heart five years ago.

But in a small, stuffy prison room with a one-way mirror into hell, he'd fallen deeply and irreparably in love.

Miles lifted his fork and paused. Rachel was idly nudging the chopped pieces of arugula and red romaine in a splash of red wine vinaigrette. Kalamata olives remained untouched. A vague distance paled her cheeks, though a while ago they bore the telltale mark of the desert sun.

The waiter returned with the bottle of Arizona chardonnay he'd kindly recommended and refilled Rachel's glass. Miles placed his hand atop the neck of his beer and asked the waiter to leave the bottle of wine at their table.

He set his fork down, pushed his empty salad plate away, and crossed his arms on the table. "Not hungry?"

The beginning of a smile went as limp as the salad greens. "I guess not. Not really." Candlelight wavered in quiet blue eyes and he'd give his life to take away the apprehension and dread lurking beneath the façade she had openly displayed over the last two days. Fun in the sun, they'd said. And it had been—with the exception of a somber visit to her parents' graves.

They'd spent the days traipsing from adobe-sided shops filled with southwestern fare, to the sanctity of Butterfly Wonderland, where she'd taken a million pictures on her phone to send to Grandpa to show Bug, and spent an unusual amount of time pondering the Native American butterfly legend. And then it was off to Chase Field and a Diamondbacks vs. Rockies baseball game, where she'd swiped all the mac and cheese from both halves of the Mega Dog hotdog. And she'd deliberately ignored his protests and shoved his mouth full of cotton candy, but he'd reciprocated by topping off the shared sweetness with a kiss that lingered through the seventh inning stretch and ended for all to see on the jumbotron. The Rockies lost. But he considered it nothing short of a shutout.

The pale blue dress she'd chosen matched her eyes, and they'd laughed about it earlier, her wearing a dress as foreign to her as he was in a dress jacket. The evening concluded at a quaint western-style bar with a live local band and he'd made an attempt at the two-step but his feet (and hers too, it seemed) had refused to obey the simple instructions.

The last two days had been uninhibited and a hell of a lot of fun. Miles drained the remainder of his beer, scooted his chair back and dragged it next to hers.

With an elbow sneaking its way onto the table, Rachel leaned into her palm. "What in the world are you doing, Dr. Malone?"

He adjusted the gray jacket he wore and scooted as close as he could until their legs touched. She shied away, but he put a hand on her knee and held it there with a little pressure, the simple gesture one of several he'd discovered did more to ease her than words. "I know you're scared, Rach."

She gulped the wine, crumpled her napkin, and tossed it next to her unfinished salad. "I don't care to discuss it."

"Please hear me out." When she didn't respond, Miles continued. "What you're doing is beyond commendable, and it's going to take a shitload of courage." A curl had come loose from her messy bun and he touched it briefly, but left it to frame her chin. "But after tomorrow, you'll never have to think about it again."

"You can't know that for sure." Uncertainty scribbled a frown between her brows. "What if the decision goes in his favor?"

"It won't."

She stared into her lap, turning her hands over and then over again. Small studded diamonds circled her watchband, sparkling in the subdued light. "I hope you're right." Not a trace of confidence adorned the statement.

Miles stilled her hands, raised them to his mouth, and kissed her fingers in sequence. "Trust me."

The lines sprinkled around her eyes eased. "I do, but—"

"Good. Now," he said, scooting his chair back, "let's get out of here."

"What about dinner?"

"I have something else in mind."

She paled and turned away, the remark he'd meant as a means to quantify an abrupt departure hanging heavily between them.

"What about the wine?" She stared at the bottle with as much reverence as a lover's departing kiss. "We can't leave it here half-empty."

"Can't drive with an open bottle, but there's nothing stopping us from walking with one." Miles stood and mentally calculated the waiter's time, a decent bottle of chardonnay, a beer, and two unfinished dinners. He tossed a hundred-dollar bill and a twenty on the table and reached for her hand, squeezing a risky grin into the deal. "I think ice cream is next on our menu."

A sedate smile blossomed and she took his hand and stood, adjusting the clutch over her shoulder. He made no effort to leave and took her face in his hands, the lines and curves of lips and mouth soft beneath his thumb.

Her eyes closed. "Miles..." A sigh swallowed his name.

A shock of sooty lashes caressed her cheek, restless eyes hidden behind lids softened with a sable glow. God how he missed them in that instant, her eyes, the bluest ones that sparkled when she smiled, the deep azure ones that forewarned of displeasure, and the baby blue ones she saved for her daughter—for Bug—for the sanctity of love.

"Sometimes words aren't enough, Sunshine." He kissed her, hesitantly at first, and then he pressed for more, parting her mouth with his tongue. And she let him in, the wine's sweet smoky flavor mixed with her unique taste erupting in a shower of sensations.

Forks stilled. A scattered round of applause rose above the murmurs and they broke apart, onlookers sharing a mixture of satisfaction and longing. If only they could experience what standing in his shoes was like—but then again, he had no intention of sharing.

Pink blotches dotted Rachel's cheeks. "We're causing a scene."

"Good. Gives them something to shoot for."

"Miles!"

"C'mon, let's get out of here."

He caught sight of an elderly woman with her chin in her palm staring at them. He dipped his head at her, took Rachel's hand and kissed it sweetly, and then winked, dressing it with his best flirtatious smile. The woman turned to her husband, busy mashing butter and sour cream into his baked potato. The blissful expression disintegrated and she smacked his arm, bits of potato leaping from the old man's fork.

Not eager to see the end of the foray, Miles took Rachel's waist, gesturing toward the exit.

"Wait." She snatched the partially consumed bottle of wine and tucked it under her arm.

Miles reacted with a quiet chuckle and led her out of the restaurant.

Crickets guided their steps as they strolled along a winding path, and something floral lingered in the cool evening air.

"This place is lovely," she said, looping a hand through his elbow. He held it close to his side, the connection one he would never tire of —to keep her near, to protect her always. And in all ways.

Sunset painted the sky in orange and pink, silhouetting the palm trees against the push of twilight. The pathways came alive with the soft glow of evening lights, and children laughing in the distance complemented the chatter of birds.

He slowed to a stop near a stone bench. "You miss Bug." He'd said it for her, but the notion echoed his own inclination.

"Very much."

"Why not give her a call?"

"I spoke to her before dinner."

"It's almost her bedtime. Little girls need to be tucked in, even if they're eight hundred miles away."

With little prodding, Rachel sat with the phone to her ear, legs crossed and Bug on the line. Her foot danced to and fro as she spoke candidly, the back of the simple white pumps slipping off her heel.

Miles took a few steps away to give her some privacy, but it wasn't long and she waved him over, patting the seat beside her.

"And guess what we're having for dinner?" Rachel wrinkled her nose and spoke in a hushed, conspiratorial whisper. "Ice cream."

Bug squealed.

Rachel squinted, yanked the phone away from her ear, and laughed aloud. The echo of happiness from the two girls sparked every nerve in his body, and he wished there was some way he could bottle the sound.

"She wants to say goodnight to *her* Dr. Miles," Rachel said, handing him the phone.

He pressed it to his ear. "Hey, how's our little Ladybug tonight?"

"You know what, Dr. Miles? Grandpa took me to your hospital after day school and I gave the ponies and goats some hay and emptied their water cuz it was yucky. Miss Heather let me help and Grandpa said it was okay." She paused long enough to suck in a lungful of air.

He'd seen her perfect round face explode with excitement on numerous occasions, and a knowing smile grew alongside the lively image.

"And she let me have ice cream with lots and lots of sprinkles. But don't tell Mommy." She'd lowered her voice and he envisioned her little hands with painted pink nails cupped tightly around the phone in the way of secrets. "Cuz Miss Heather said it was a secret and then guess what? I got to feed the babies, Dr. Miles, because Prim is running low on milk from her tummy. She's not their real mama. She's a...a..."

"Surrogate."

"That's cuz the babies are 'dopted and I got to feed them all by myself with a special bottle like a real baby and hold them like a real baby. But they're not real babies, they're baby kitties, but I could give a real baby sister a bottle, right, Dr. Miles?"

"Sure." He choked a little on that one, reluctant to go anywhere near the birds and the bees thing again. "I bet you were a big help to Heather today."

"I am cuz I'm big now. I'm almost five." An animated breath puffed through the phone line and he imagined her holding up five long, dimpled fingers. "And guess what, Dr. Miles? You won't ever guess what the babies can do."

"What can they do, Bug?" Amusement crept into his words.

"They can purr! I heard them and so did Miss Heather."

"They're growing up fast."

"And then Miss Heather said I could name them. Can I, Dr. Miles?"

"I think that's a perfect idea."

"Grandpa, Grandpa!" Miles put some distance between the phone and his ear to soften the wild enthusiasm. "Dr. Miles said I could name the kitties anything I want."

A muffled voice filtered in from the background and Miles was sure Marshall had agreed. How could he not? "Do you have names picked out?"

He imagined her flawless little girl face scrunched into her thoughtful, inquisitive expression, the one he'd seen at day care when he'd brought pets for the kids to play with or played games with her.

"No," she said, stretching the word into several syllables, "because my grandpa says I have to get to know them but I already do and I'm going to name them when Mommy comes home." Bug paused, a rare occurrence for the chatterbox with no apparent Off switch. "Are you taking care of my mommy, Dr. Miles? Grandpa said you would and I'm taking good care of the kitties and Zoe, but Zoe can't go back to mommy's work until Mommy comes home. I think Archie and Molly and Inga miss her. 'Specially Archie. I really, really think Archie does cuz he doesn't feel so good, but Nurse Molly said he's a fighter. Do you think they miss her?"

"I'm sure they do. Zoe's special to them."

"When are you coming home? I miss my mommy and I miss you too." Her voice wobbled and she sniffled, sound and voice winding together in a tether and pulling—a keen, conscious tug—from somewhere deep inside him, somewhere he hadn't known existed, and pieces of his heart spilled to the ground in a muddled heap.

"I'm taking good care of your mommy. I promise. And we'll be home in a couple of days, okay?"

She didn't respond, but he sensed acknowledgement in the little girl's silence. She sniffed again and said, "Do they have callerpitters at the butterfly place? They turn into butterflies, you know. Grandpa told me 'Zona has scorpions and he showed me a picture. Did you see one?" If he could see her, she surely would have scrunched her nose and buried it in her hand in sheer excitement. "Do they have sparkle bugs there? I want to see a sparkle bug, Dr. Miles. Really, really bad."

If he had his way, there was one insect he'd squash until its guts lay spread on the asphalt to fry in the Arizona sun, but the Chastains of the world weren't the kind Bug meant.

"Someday I'll show you sparkle bugs. They're fireflies. Some people call them lightning bugs. They don't have them here, but I'll bring you a preserved scorpion for now. How does that sound?"

Rachel shot him a look of wide-eyed outrage and adamantly shook her head.

"Deal," Bug said, satisfaction percolating in the compromise.

"I have to give the phone back to your mommy now."

"Okay."

"Good night, Ladybug. Sweet dreams."

"Good night, Dr. Miles, I love you."

His heart stuttered. A lump the size of the Rocky Mountains lodged in his throat, but somehow he managed to form words. "I love you too, Ladybug." Caught off-guard, his response had bloomed effortlessly from his heart, formed words, and spoken without reservation. He handed the phone to Rachel, got to his feet, and stepped away, a stomach of fluttering wings along for the ride.

After what must have been a fair amount of protesting from the other end of the line, Rachel said good night for the fourth time, ended the call, and dropped the phone into her purse.

He collected his thoughts into something remotely composed (for the most part) before she joined him.

She touched his back and he turned. "You two had a lot to discuss."

He cleared the hoarseness strangling the ability to speak. "She's something."

The lines punctuating her smile deepened. "Her heart is hard-wired to her mouth without a shutoff valve. Says what she feels." She adjusted her purse strap. "She truly does love you, you know."

"The feeling is mutual." Miles took her hand. "Doesn't take her long to wrap herself around your little finger." *Or heart.*

"Which reminds me." Rachel wrinkled her nose. "A scorpion?"

"We have an agreement."

"Yeah, some agreement. She asks. You say yes."

Unwilling to deny it, he offered his best artful grin and hand-in-hand they walked around the last bend in the path.

"This way." He skirted around an expansive group of shrubs with palm-sized red flowers, giant potted plants, and leaves as large as elephant ears. "I think you're going to enjoy this."

NINETEEN

The shrubbery opened to a swimming pool secluded amid a forest of tropical foliage and palm trees. Sand covered the man-made beach and bottom of the pool, enhancing the ambiance of gaslight torches, twittering birds, and sultry air. Not quite the briny scent of the ocean, but an enchanting beach experience in the middle of the desert city.

Miles sank the wine bottle into the lagoon's wet sand with a few twists. Standing at an angle, it resembled a bottle washed ashore after a journey at sea.

"How'd you find this place?"

Amusement lifted his shoulder and then dropped out of sight. "There's a map in the room."

"No, silly," she said with a playful jab. "This resort?"

A warm breeze teased the torch flames, the flickering light reflecting in her eyes. A moment of peace penetrated the apprehension and he took pause, pinning to memory the untroubled expression.

Simple. Natural. Genuine.

The depth of damage that bastard had caused was beyond what

he'd ever imagined, and witnessing firsthand the hell she'd suppressed for years had shredded his insides. But staring at her now with the serenity of simple pleasures fresh on her face, he vowed to bring back her smile. The one that sought nothing but the simplicity of life's wonders. The one that had soothed him when he woke in a cold sweat, reliving the nightmares of battle. The smile that completely undid him the first time she'd looked his way.

"Well?" A smirk accompanied her unabashed appraisal.

"It's a deep subject."

She parked a remark in a saucy grin. Slipping out of her shoes, she laid her purse on a beach chair, and looped her arm through his.

"I stumbled across the site on the internet while making the arrangements for this trip, and I know you have a thing for the Mediterranean."

"How'd you know about that?"

"You mentioned it once," he said, the memory sloshing uncomfortably in his stomach. "You told me about an island in the Mediterranean off the coast of Italy."

The torchlight burnished her hair with sparks of copper and gold, and the breeze took the wisps that had come free and brushed them across her face. She pushed them away. "Sardinia."

"It must be important to you." Sardinia had been foreign to him, but when she'd mentioned it, he'd been a quick study. Though he preferred snow, mountain streams and rapids, evergreens and big game wildlife, the tropical feel of the Mediterranean beaches held a certain appeal. "Bug would love the pink sandy beaches and the red-eyed damselflies."

"Yes, she would." Sadness shimmered in her eyes that bore a heaviness he couldn't explain. "Nico has family in Sardinia."

The hitch in his chest startled him, but he kept it from his voice. "Which means you and Bug have family there. Family is important. You should visit someday."

She paused, staring at him. The sadness had dimmed and an easy countenance softened her features. "You're an amazing man, Miles

Malone. That's a lovely idea. Maybe someday we will." She breathed in, the slow inhale and exhale a soothing movement on his arm. "The ornamental orange trees are in bloom. I've always loved the scent." She dug her toes in the sand. "I miss that about Phoenix."

"I can see the attraction. The weather. No snow to shovel." He rested his chin on her head, the scent of her hair reminiscent of summer rain. "Would you ever consider moving back?" Air drained from his lungs and he waited for her answer.

"I never wanted to see this place again." She loosened her grip and slowly stepped away. "Would you want to live somewhere where there was nothing left but memories you can barely face but have to live with?"

"I'm sorry, that didn't come out right." He reached for her hands to fix what he'd screwed up before she could pull any farther away. "I wanted to know...I guess I was afraid." Words abandoned the unfin-ished thoughts and fizzled out.

"Afraid of what, Miles?" She yanked free, the fragile bubble he'd formed to shelter her shattered as if popped with a pin. "I don't see you visiting your parents or a spouse in a graveyard, facing a hearing tomorrow, or sitting across the room from a man who cut your soul to pieces and left it to die with his spent seed dribbling down your leg." Her chest heaved. "Or trying to reclaim your life, waking every day hoping this day will be better than the day before or wishing you had an hourglass you could flip and start over. Or terrified every time a man looks at you or every single moment you can't protect your daughter from the monsters under the bed." She flung herself on the nearest beach chair and covered her face with her hands. "Or from the monsters..." Her voice stumbled. "...those you meet every day... monsters disguised as normal people."

His insides broke apart as the years of fury, unbridled fear, and endless doubt spilled down her cheeks, and he didn't know which way his guts would end up, which way to put right what he couldn't take back.

"I'm sorry, Rach." The hurt reflected on her face, her eyes, and dammit to hell he wanted to take it back. But he couldn't and he said the only thing he could, the truth hidden in his thoughts. "I'm afraid of losing you."

Stunned into silence, she looked up.

Miles knelt beside her and cupped her tear-stained face in both hands. She tried to pull away, but he held her, the aggregate of her pain leaking in a quiet stream.

"I can't begin to know what you've been through and I never meant to stir up the past tonight. Jesus, not tonight." He gathered mismatched thoughts and ground them between his teeth. His jaw ached. What he wanted to do was clamp his hands around Chastain's neck and strangle the life from the bastard's lungs. "I…I couldn't stand the idea of you moving back here after this is over. I'm sorry, it was selfish and thoughtless." He fell back on his butt. "I couldn't stand to lose you, Rachel." The words he wanted to say wouldn't form. The ones that did were too few and too vague and too simple to convey the unraveling of his heart.

Rachel swiveled around, tucked her dress, and kneeled into the sand between his legs. "I shouldn't have said those things…I don't know why I…" She pleated the fabric of her dress between her fingers. "I used my own anxiety…about tomorrow…I'm sorry. I shouldn't have."

"Rachel." He raised her chin, but her eyes didn't follow. "Please look at me."

She looked up slowly, reluctance and remorse battling for domination.

"There's no need to be sorry. Not with me." He traced the sleek line of chin and jaw with his thumb, the skin moist with the unrest overflowing from her heart. "I'm the one who should be apologizing. None of this has been easy and tomorrow won't be any easier. Harder, most likely." She lowered her lashes and he rested his hands on her shoulders. "I get it. But I need you to believe me when I tell you I'd never leave you to face this alone." He brushed away a strand of hair that had fallen to a moist cheek. "I love you—"

"No." She shook her head with renewed firmness. "Don't say that."

"I will say it. And I'll say it over and over until you believe it. I love you and I'll be there for you tomorrow, the day after, and the day after that. If you want me to be."

She looked away.

"Do you?"

The silence that ensued held an uncertainty, piercing him with a blow that sucked the air from his lungs.

"I can't...I—"

He placed a finger to her lips, drifting into the void he'd vowed never to enter again. "It's okay." Words he'd heard before. Words that had severed the life from him. "I guess I assumed something that wasn't there, that we were headed in the same direction."

A gentle hand touched his cheek. A healer's hand. One designed to ease the pain—to heal the hurt—and it trembled against his skin. As her silence grew, the ache grew with it.

And then she pressed her lips hard to his and he absorbed the salty, wet truth. It was the sweetest thing he'd ever tasted and the most bitter.

Goodbye kisses usually were.

She neatened her skirt and got to her feet. "I can't love you, Miles," she said, the unspoken apology polluting the air. Polluting his mind. Polluting his dreams.

The desire to reach for her, to make sense from chaos trembled from every part of him.

She brushed the sand from her bottom and walked to the edge of the water, the thin fabric of her dress swaying in the breeze.

Miles rose and stepped beside her. He had no words, no coherent thought to attach them to. The pool quivered, the stillness broken. Reflections rippled and bent, each crest dipped in sunset gold.

"Don't you see?"

"No. I don't." Torn flesh and infected wounds he could handle, he could fix, but not her words, the harshness of them tearing the fabric of his soul. "I thought...I guess I didn't think."

Curls loosed from their tethers trailed along her neck and shoulders, her silhouette golden in the torchlight—too distant to touch, too close to let go. Unstable moments passed quietly between them and his heart collapsed.

"Everyone I've ever loved has been taken from me," she said, the words a whisper on the wind. "My parents. Too many patients to count. Nico." The breeze took his name and swallowed it, and she lowered her lashes and wrung her hands in a slow, repeated pattern. "Bug and my grandfather are all I have left."

The insinuation left its cold handprint on his soul. "I'm not going anywhere."

She shook her head slowly, her shoulders assuming the job of absorbing renewed tears. "I can't take that chance."

"Rachel, please listen to me." He couldn't articulate the plea into a proper semblance of words. Didn't want to. Didn't want to hear her response, words that would unravel the threads, the ones she'd given him to mend a soul that had once been ripped apart. "I'll be there for you and for Bug. Always."

"How can you say that?" The pitch in her voice matched a pinched brow. "You're an audacious skier. You kayak swollen rivers and climb mountains and repel into ice caves and one day that damn mountain will bury you and you won't come back."

The words hit him full force, his shoulders sagging under the weight.

She turned abruptly toward him. "You'll leave too, like Nico and everyone else I've ever loved, and I can't go through that again. I can't." Sobs ignited her words and she pounded her fists to his chest. "I won't, damn you."

Hard deliberate blows lashed out as she let go, transferring the bottled anger, pain, and loss to him. And he absorbed it. The pain of loss. The emptiness. The lonely days and forever nights. And he cried with her, the past colliding head-on with the present.

She gave way and he held her, quieting the sobs as she trembled in his arms.

"I can't say what our future holds. No one can." He lifted her chin.

"But I'll tell you one thing I know for certain, Rachel Caldarone. The day I fell in love with you I fell off a bottomless cliff, and the only thing that hurt me then and every day since has been the ache in my heart every time I looked at you and couldn't have you."

"Stop—"

"There's nothing in this world that can stop me from loving you, coming home to you, and keeping you and Bug safe."

Disbelief hovered in the absence of her words. "I can't do this again...I can't love you." She shut her eyes, new tears bleeding through lashes pointed at the sand. She didn't move, seemed scarcely to breathe. Torchlight danced and swerved, casting her features in opaque shadow. And when she opened her eyes again, the shadows gave way and an extraordinary change came over her. "But I do."

The storm in her subsided and his world came together and righted itself. "Don't be afraid, Rach. Don't be afraid to love again. My heart is yours. And I'll protect yours and Bug's with all I have to give. I see the way you care for her, the way you love her, and I feel her joy and yours. And I'll do everything in my power to keep both of you safe from the hurtful things in life."

"I'm scared."

"I promise you have nothing to fear."

"You can't make that promise. My track record speaks for itself."

"If we don't take a chance, take that first step, we'll never know."

She laid her cheek on his chest and looped her arms around him. "Hold me."

He wrapped his promise securely around her in a firm embrace. "I don't make promises I don't intend to keep. But if you'll have me, I swear to God I'll be there for you. Always."

They stayed that way, entwined in the present and each other until full night folded its arms around them.

Miles turned his gaze to the stars and his heart to her. "I love you, Rachel Caldarone." He lifted her chin and met her tears with a slow, deep kiss, one meant to seal the promises of tomorrow and take the pain from the past. And she kissed him back, one he took without reservation, to take into the future one step, one touch, one kiss at a time.

They broke apart, breathless. "I will love you always. Will you allow me to attend your needs, care for you, and realize your dreams? Be there for you? For your daughter?"

Moisture fractured the light in her eyes. "Yes," she said, her moist, salty lips pressing against his.

The last few moments gathered in a fog, flickers of hope growing from the roots of doubt. "I can't promise there won't be pain, but I promise to share the good times and see you through the bad."

"The first time you kissed me—"

"It was my promise then, my promise now."

"You've made a lot of them. Promises, I mean."

"None I don't intend to keep." Her smile grew against his mouth. "Do you find this amusing?"

She lowered her lashes, heavy with the remnants of his words. "I've committed myself for all of ten seconds and you've already broken a promise."

"I couldn't have—"

"You promised me ice cream." Moisture accented a playful grin.

Miles removed his jacket and tossed it across the beach chair. "Not just yet." Hopping from one foot to the other, he flipped off his shoes, and then took her hand and dragged her toward the water.

"No-o-o-o, you don't." She tried to pull free, bare feet digging into the sand. "That promise said nothing about getting wet!"

"And I made no promise not to."

"You said ice cream, Miles Malone—" She squeaked and dug her heels farther into the sand.

He outweighed her, towered over her, and was used to hoisting dead weight straight up a glacier wall. Coaxing a petite female a few feet into the water whether protesting or not, would be a piece of cake.

He didn't have to.

Her skirt hit the water and she lunged, tipping him backward, and sending them both under water. They came up sputtering. Soaked, he picked her up and carried her from the water with his mouth glued to hers.

The cool April evening raised ripples of gooseflesh on her bare arms. He set her down and draped his jacket over her shoulders.

"I didn't know you were a lifeguard."

"I'm not. But I will guard you with my life. You're not my first rescue, nor will you be the last, but you're the only one that matters."

TWENTY

*W*hether the dress came through the unexpected dip in a chlorine pool seemed of little consequence. The gauzy chiffon had clung to her, the temperature of certain body parts quite obvious. But the chill had nothing to do with wet clothing and everything to do with Miles.

Three words.

Keeping herself in check had lapsed when Miles breached the subject. How thoughtless she'd been—taking it out on him when he'd taken charge, made all the arrangements, and had guided her through this horrible ordeal from the beginning. The pain and loss had come rushing back, yet somehow, she'd regained enough courage to face the truth of those three words.

"You're a strong woman. Stronger than you think."

"Never underestimate love, for I have borne witness to its power."

Grandpa's words. Truths Ambrose spoke of. Miles' patience and understanding. Despite the dryer's warm air, the fine hairs on her arms rose in pleasant waves.

Dressed now in fashionably worn jeans and a white blousy long-sleeved top, Rachel sat on the hotel vanity seat blow-drying her hair, straightening the curls as best she could. The hot shower had flushed away the chill, but it had been Miles who had warmed her on the inside.

Setting the dryer aside, she propped an elbow on the granite vanity, taking a curl between her fingers and stretching it to full length. It bounced back and for an instant, she envied the weeks she'd been halfway free of them while pregnant with Bug. The jacked-up hormones had not only made her sick, but taken most of the curl from her hair. The hiatus, however, had been short-lived.

The dress hung in the shower, the slow drip, drip, drip a reminder of how she'd ended up under water with a guy she had known for years, but never truly knew. She'd never truly *looked* at him. In all honesty, never paid *attention*. Had she?

The answer was as clear as the water in the lagoon, a tangle of emotions skidding into dangerous territory.

How long had she known? How long had she tried to hide from the truth? From him?

If she dared search backward, she'd known for longer than she cared to admit—the stolen glances; the tickle in her belly when he spoke in that deep, even voice; the way his demeanor changed when Bug walked in the room, his entire body embracing a full-on smile. And the way her knees dissolved to mush when those steel-blue eyes looked not at her, but into her as if he held the power to reach in and cradle her heart.

Time after time she'd refused to see beyond the surface, casting it off as that of friends. Time after time she'd refused to see how much he cared for her daughter, telling herself he was compassionate about *"all creatures great and small"* assuming the idea behind his clinic's blurb included small humans. Time after time she'd let the past interrupt the future, allowing the barriers she'd built around herself to ward off the ghosts and bury any idea of pursuing a relationship—too afraid to let go of the past and terrified to embrace the future.

Could she do this again? With someone else?

She tucked her jeans inside ankle boots and stood, making a careful inspection turning one way and then the other. She sprayed a cloud of perfume into the air and walked through it.

A soft knock startled her, and she knocked the blow dryer off the vanity, lunged to catch it but tripped on the cord, caught the vanity with her shin, and the vanity seat, dryer, and her hand hit the wall in a trio of clunky thumps.

"Rachel?" The heavy hotel door muffled Miles' anxious voice. "What's going on in there? You all right?"

"Fine," she said, hobbling to the door. The locks clicked and she stepped gingerly back to allow him in. "Just a bit clumsy."

"No broken bones?" Miles leaned in and kissed her cheek, a faint hint of leather from his jacket and his signature wilderness cologne mingling with the fresh scent of soap. It clung to him in a masculine cloud, brisk and wild and musky, and she wanted to stay there, breathing in the powerful spice.

"All parts accounted for," she said, adding a dose of humor to disguise her clumsiness, "but my hair dryer and the wall may not have fared as well."

"You sure?" She nodded, and Miles folded his arms snugly around her middle. "God, you smell good. Like a bouquet of untamed wild-flowers."

"Beats smelling like bubble gum. Or Hello Kitty. Zoe tries to lick one and sneezes at the other."

He lifted the hair from her neck, his lips grazing the sensitive skin with a low murmur that startled the butterflies in her stomach to full flight. "I haven't a clue what a Hello Kitty smells like, although I know how Prim smells when she's been wallowing in the horse manure. It's neither wildflowers nor bubble gum."

"Nice." Rachel wrinkled her nose. "Bug's favorite thing is spraying me or Zoe with one or the other. It's a little girl thing."

"Hello Kitty. Bubble gum." He pointed to his temple. "Mental note taken."

He sculpted himself around her, his mere presence enclosing her in security. If only she could stay wrapped up in him and forget about what lay ahead.

"You sure you're okay?"

April nights in the desert can be cool, and she stepped back, scanning the caramel brown leather jacket he wore over a long-sleeved black shirt and flawless fit of stylishly worn jeans. His fingertips held onto hers. "Just enjoying the view."

"Agreed. However," he said, guiding her in a slow twirl under his arm, "the hotel failed to warn me how incredibly stunning the view could be."

"I had to change." Heat bloomed under her skin and she rubbed her neck to chase the sudden prickles. "My dress is dripping wet." She gestured toward the bathroom.

"When the sun rises or sets, it's breathtaking whether dressed in clouds or clear skies. What's in front of me is stunning without a doubt," he said a little breathy as he took her other hand, "but it's not what the package is wrapped in but the gift inside."

She dipped her head briefly to hide a quiet smile. "Good, because I prefer jeans, scrubs, or jammies. Clothing that includes legs."

"Jammies?" Confusion reduced his laugh to a rumble, and a lock of hair tumbled over his forehead. Even when damp and combed back it had that rumpled, messy thing going on. She reached up and tucked the strays back into place, a chill shimmying along her arm.

"You've got a lot to learn if you're going to hang with a four-year-old."

"Jammies." He repeated the word with a slight smirk. "Item two noted."

She grabbed her clutch and threw a sweater over an arm. "Ice cream may not be a suitable substitute for dinner, but my stomach says otherwise."

Miles shut the door behind them and escorted her through the hotel corridor. "I'll remind you of that the next time Bug wishes to replace her dinner." Sarcasm spewed from the comment.

"Stuck my foot in that one, didn't I?"

"Yes."

"And you're not going to forget it, are you?"

"Item three noted." The Down button on the elevator lit up. "I have a better than average memory. Although, if you ask Bug she'll tell you I stink at Animal Memory."

"I take it she always wins?"

"She lets me win now and again. I have a hard time finding both flamingos." He let out a sort of grunt, a sound seasoned with mirth and voiced in recollection. "And the turtles. Especially the turtles."

"What, no bugs?"

"I have yet to chalk up a victory at Insect & Bug Memory." He leaned into her ear. "She's got it mastered."

"Commendable, Dr. Malone." Rachel's insides fluttered. He said he'd never had children, yet his instincts were—on occasion—as sharp as any seasoned parent.

"Do I hear a brownie point somewhere in there?"

"Perhaps. Except for the crazy agreement you have with my daughter to give her anything her heart desires."

The elevator dinged and the doors parted in a quiet rumble. With a hand positioned on the small of her back, Miles ushered her inside. "Seems to me this agreement has spread from daughter to mother."

"Excuse me?"

"I'd do anything for you." Dark blue eyes softened to dove gray. "All you have to do is ask."

"Then you can order my ice cream in vanilla."

"Hmm. Not incredibly adventurous."

"You're the one who thrives on adventure. I'll stick to boring."

"You're anything but boring." The elevator bumped into its descent. Miles leaned against the handhold and gathered her next to him. "Ever been kissed in an elevator, Sunshine?"

The suggestion stirred the tiny hairs of cheek and neck, a ricochet of tiny sparks traveling over torso and limb. Slowly, she shook her head.

"Neither have I." He slid his hand in her hair, fingers curling around the nape of her neck. He drew her in with a gentle yet firm tug, the creak and subtle hint of leather the only obstacle between them.

She leaned into him, the full measure of his scent filling the small spaces of sense and time. Her mouth parted, accepting the invitation, and he bathed her lips with warm, delicate caresses and then swept his tongue inside, seeking the connection to its mate.

A conspicuous flush warmed her skin as if they'd done something illicit. "Guess we can check that off our bucket list."

"One down." The words crossed her cheek as a minty whisper. "So many more to go."

The elevator dinged. He kissed her forehead and led her into the hotel lobby.

Women ogled. Men dropped an approving glance. And why wouldn't they? The man next to her was drop-dead gorgeous—rumpled, unshaven, completely undone, and entirely put together—the adventurer tamed in the midst of the city.

R achel had opted for two scoops of vanilla ice cream with a hefty dose of caramel drizzled over the top. Miles had insisted she taste both of his unique combinations and although they were enjoyable, going off the grid wasn't. Adventure made her skittish. Even when it came to veering into unknown ice cream flavors, boring suited her just fine.

The leisurely stroll amid Old Town Scottsdale, interrupted briefly to fulfill his promise of dessert, and the simplicity of Miles' presence were the distractions she needed, crowding in beside the anxiety. But as Miles swiped her hotel keycard through the lock and the little green light flashed, the weight of it came thundering back with the attitude of a raucous thunderstorm.

Miles stuck his foot in the door and handed her back her keycard. "After you, Sunshine."

"We could go for coffee before we call it a night."

"You've got an early wake-up call tomorrow." The hesitation was momentary but unmistakable. "You need a good night's sleep."

If it came at all, sleep would be tricky and nowhere near good. Doubt stretched its long fingers, but in a gesture meant to appease him, she nodded.

Rachel set the keycard and her clutch on the dresser, tossed her sweater across the bed, and kicked off her boots. Miles draped his jacket over a chair. She unlocked the French patio doors and opened them fully.

The air lay cool and heavy with moisture from the lagoon directly below, and the sweet scent of orange blossoms drifted in with the breeze. She leaned into the railing, inhaling the tranquility of the night, the anxiety of tomorrow stuck somewhere in the exhale.

Miles slipped in beside her, laced an arm around her waist, and pulled her into his side. Despite knowing he was there, his touch roused a flurry of reflexes, but she quickly relaxed.

"Will you be okay by yourself tonight?" An air of concern surrounded the question but held no suggestion other than the gentleman he'd proven himself to be.

She faced him then, challenge parked in the quirk of her mouth. "And what would you do if I said no?"

Normally rooted in frank decision, his eyes flickered with a moment of uncertainty, but his answer would be bound in obligation —it was the kind of man he was.

"I'll be fine, Miles. I've spent the greater part of five years by myself. Another night alone in a hotel won't kill me."

A flash of something—something almost helpless and deeply uncertain—skittered across his face. Twelve hours and she'd be within feet of *him*—the demon she'd shared a life with. At times it lay dormant, a slumbering memory no more than a mental shadow. Other times it forged through every barrier she erected, a raging dragon she had yet to slay.

The gravity of it settled inside her, stealing away the tranquil hours and days she'd spent walking hand in hand with Miles, discovering mac and cheese did belong on a hot dog, baseball wasn't boring if it involved a moist kiss that spanned the seventh inning stretch, that there were flavors of ice cream more adventurous than vanilla, and butterflies came in every color of the rainbow.

Miles tucked her beneath his chin and the peace of merely being so close secured her in a comfort she'd forgotten existed. "This isn't an ordinary night, Rachel."

"Please don't remind me."

"If you need me to, I'll stay so you can rest." The words fell warm and reassuring against her scalp, the offer striking back in equal measures of need and want laced with an acute sense of uneasiness.

"I'll be fine."

"Then it's time I say goodnight."

She closed her eyes, heaved the past into the memory box, and locked it tight. She longed for him to shelter her from the day looming mere hours away, even if for nothing more than a few moments of relief lost in his kiss, lost in his body. Lost in him.

"Please look at me, Rachel."

Steel-blue eyes had gone as dark as cabochon sapphires and deeper than a starless sky, his gaze warm and soothing as if he'd caressed her skin. And then his hands threaded her hair and he took her mouth, hungry and eager and laced with a passion that matched the marked urgency growing heavy in her breasts. He parted her legs with his knee, the answer to unasked questions pressing firm and wanting against her.

"I don't want to leave. But I have to or I won't be able to."

"Then please stay."

Dusky lashes covered his eyes, but when he looked at her again, the intensity softened to a quiet tenderness. "No. Not this way." The concession came as a whisper as he stroked her cheek with the back of his hand and smiled, a sweet, lost turn of his mouth that spoke of endless things without saying a word. "When the time is right. Then I'll stay."

Rachel reached around his neck and placed a lingering kiss on his cheek, the stubble coarse and soft and all at once substantial, a translation of the man within. A shiver of longing clashed with an equal sense of relief.

"But...I want..." She couldn't form words with any logical precision and they slipped out in a jumbled mess. "I don't know..."

"I love you and there's nothing I want more than to prove how much." Miles rubbed his thumb lightly under her eye, his voice deep and honeyed. "But I won't compromise what we have. Not for a night that will end in regret."

"I would never—"

"It's the night before the hearing." He brought her hand to his mouth, the light kiss sealing his convictions and protecting her own. "You're ramped up in some strong emotions. Ones you can't see but I feel. Your body trembles with it and I won't take advantage of that or of you. I won't let this happen. Not tonight."

Miles led her from the balcony, picked up his jacket, and paused at the door. "Lock the door when I leave and make sure you close and lock the patio doors. If you need anything, call." He leaned in and kissed her lightly and then again. "My phone will be next to me and I'm only a few doors down."

"I'll be fine." His fingers caressed hers in a momentary goodnight dance, a kiss of flesh, and then he slipped out the door.

She locked the door and then shut and locked the patio doors, and threw herself on the bed. But his absence tightened the knot around her middle.

The scent of wilderness and musk rose quietly pungent from her skin and she lay curled in a ball tracing the remnants of his kiss with her finger. Minutes blurred into hours. At some point she'd dressed for bed and turned out all but one light, yet each time she closed her eyes the clap of the judge's gavel and booming voice exploded inside her head.

Commutation of sentence granted" echoed through her, hollow bone to hollow bone. The room grew heavy and hot. Sweat chilled her skin. She kicked away the suffocating sheet and a minute later yanked the comforting weight tight under her chin. The battle waged. She dozed. Woke. Dozed again. Finally, exhaustion pulled her toward sleep.

Thump!

The patio doors rattled. The curtains swayed. Settled. With a pillow clutched tight against her chest, she lay motionless in the dark, the air too heavy to breathe.

She dared not make a sound.

Blood-noise pulsed fast and loud in her head, a thunderstorm gone vicious.

Dared not move.

Neurons crashed head-on, an aftershock of tremors vibrating her body.

Dared not blink.

Eyes unwavering, unblinking, unfocused.

Dared not breathe.

Dared hell to open its doors.

TWENTY-ONE

*Y*ears as a vet and search and rescue volunteer prepared him for late night call outs, but nothing had roused him faster than the pounding on his hotel room door.

In a matter of seconds, he'd tossed the sheet and duvet to the floor, smashed his shin on the bedframe, and grabbed his sweats, hopping into them one leg at a time as he crossed the room. He flipped a switch, the sconces over the bed throwing out a muted spray of light. Without checking the peephole, he yanked open the door and braced his hip against it.

Huddled in a white hotel bathrobe, Rachel shifted from one bare foot to the other and then dove inside.

Miles sidestepped into her path and bundled her into his embrace to keep them from tumbling into the hallway in a tangle of bathrobe and sweats. "Nightmares?"

With both hands clenched under her chin and worrying her lower lip, she tossed her head side to side as if searching the hall. "I...must have dozed off and there was a noise."

Miles took a quick look in both directions down the deserted hallway, led her inside, and closed the door behind them. "Why didn't you call? I would have come to you."

"The noise...I couldn't...I panicked." Her throat moved up and down, each word a ragged hitch. "All I could think about was *him*."

The implication of how deeply the wounds had scarred her burrowed under his skin. "It's okay to be afraid. But it wasn't him. He's in prison."

Rachel backed away.

He took her hands, cold fists a shiver on his heart. "I won't let anyone or anything harm you." On any given day, she gave herself to her patients, going beyond the boundaries of normal care. She'd been there for him not so long ago, and yet he hadn't been there for her tonight and the truth of it bound his words.

Slowly, her skin warmed under his touch and he loosened her fingers one at a time. White knuckles regained their color and the tension eased from the rigid fists. Miles placed them at her side. "You're safe now."

"I'm sorry, Miles, I freaked," she said, tying and untying the belt. "I couldn't sleep after that."

The confession tore at him, the decision to leave her alone grating on spent nerves. Of course she would've said she'd be fine, but he'd seen her reaction at the prison and again at the pool, and yet he'd ignored his own reservations and left her to endure the night alone— and more vulnerable than he'd imagined.

"I have nightlights everywhere at home. A leftover habit I guess." She cinched the robe tighter and sat on the bed, distance flavoring a reminiscent smile. "When I was pregnant with Bug, I was up and down a lot during the night. But hotels don't have nightlights, so I left a light on." Shoulders draped in thick cotton terry met her ears and fell. "It was silly."

"Not at all."

"It is...when you're supposed to be a grown woman."

The woman who'd unleashed her tenacity at the prison had hidden herself in the shadows of the past.

"We do what we need to survive. It's not silly if it helps."

"I sound neurotic."

"You sound like a survivor." His tone held an unequivocal parity to the one he reserved for those he'd found buried in an avalanche, rescued from an ice cave hundreds of feet below the surface, or recovered from a river's icy rapids. Those who lived to tell their story.

"With a suitcase stuffed with mental debris."

"We all have baggage, Rach." She raised her eyebrows in neutral reply. "That aside, I'm sure there's a simple explanation for the noise." Rachel didn't reply and he used the cue to continue. "This place is crawling with young adults. Beer bottle maybe? A shoe? Could have been anything. Some species of birds are attracted to light."

Questions staggered over her face as if in a drunken queue. "A bird?"

"It's a possibility. Be happy to check for you."

"No!" She stood, twisted the ends of the terry belt around her wrist and paced the room. "I can't go back there, even if it was just a bird."

"It's settled, then." On her third trip around the room, Miles caught her sleeve, pulled her close, and stroked her back and hair, visibly settling her with the repeated motion. "You'll stay here with me. I'll be your eyes and ears so you can rest." To have her here, knowing she was safe sent pleasure seeping into the words his body couldn't speak.

"Thank you."

Her sigh touched his bare skin, warm wisps drifting over him in small ripples. And her fingers lay lithe and tentatively splayed on his chest, giving breath to nights he'd lain awake aching to put to flesh what his heart yearned for and his mind imagined. Had she called, he might have been prepared for the restless stirrings loose-fitting sweats wouldn't hide. But she hadn't, and his body responded to her touch, to the closeness with only the bathrobe hanging slack between them.

So close, yet more distant than the stars.

He drew the bathrobe together, took her forearms, and backed a half step away. He tied the belt firmly around her before things got out of hand and he wasn't able to stop his imagination from becoming reality.

"You need sleep, and you'll be safe here." Miles parked a hand in his hair while he processed the disheveled room and then sprang into action straightening the bed covers. "I know a little about calming a nervous critter. It's all about touch and tone of voice." The remark had come out nothing like he'd intended, but he ignored the embarrassment crawling up his neck and set about to tidy the bed. He fluffed the pillows, giving them an extra punch.

One of Rachel's eyebrows quirked up.

"Not that I meant you're a critter."

The other eyebrow mimicked the first, and she folded her arms in front of her.

"Or...what I meant was...I'm a vet and I sorta have this thing for calming an animal..."

"Yeah, someone once told me you had a thing for animals in your bed."

"Damn. I did say that, didn't I?" He tossed his hands up. "I give up." He reached across the dresser and raised the partially consumed bottle of wine. "Truce?"

"The wine. I forgot."

"You were too busy trying to drown me."

"I might do worse for a good bottle of wine."

"Security guard was a little pissed I'd brought a glass inside the pool gate." He turned away to hide a quirk of the mouth before a full-fledged smile broke free. "I told him it wasn't the glass I was concerned about."

"That was special. Thanks."

"My pleasure." He could only hope the dose of humor had erased the mess he'd made trying to explain his calming technique. "I thought the wine might help you sleep."

"Can't hurt. Thanks for going after it."

He took two plastic glasses from the nightstand, ripped off the protective covering, and poured them both a glass. He wrinkled his nose. "Not a beer or a shot of whiskey, but it'll do." He tossed it back in two big gulps.

Rachel raised her glass in a mock salute, swished the liquid, swallowed, and took another small sip. Rose-pink circles bloomed on her cheeks. "I want to hear more about this special veterinary super power of yours. Something about calming critters?"

"I've already stuck my foot in my mouth once tonight."

"Twice."

"I vote we change the subject." Miles set the empty cup down. "Come here, Sunshine."

Rachel set her cup next to his. He pulled her in close and she splayed her fingers in the mat of chest hair. "In all fairness, I've seen the way you treat your patients. Heard the way you talk to them. If there's any truth to the rumors—"

"Who says they're rumors?"

"Rumors are set straight by proof."

"That can be arranged."

She traced the raised red scar on his abdomen. He flinched, the two-week-old wound still tender beneath her touch. "It's healing nicely."

"Someone threatened me if I didn't follow instructions." He nudged her away from the sensitive area. He had no desire to embarrass himself—again—and picked her up in one swoop and deposited her on the bed. "You might want to cover up. The air conditioning is set on low."

Rachel took his hand before he could slip away. "Please, sit with me?"

He hesitated, grappling for any excuse to shove the sensible part of his brain out the door and not just sit with her, but make love to her. God knows he wanted to. Had since the day he'd met her and every day since. But he couldn't claim her as his own. He may have chipped his way into her heart on one level, but she belonged to someone else, someone she needed to exorcise before he could lay claim to what he wanted for himself—all of her, inside and out, not simply the shell she was willing to let him see. He may be reckless and carefree with his life, but this would be a miserable excuse for a moment of self-gratification.

And excuses were for cowards.

The mattress gave as he sat next to her and braced his elbows on his thighs. He kneaded his palms, heat building with the back and forth friction.

Rachel placed a hand over the restless movement. "I couldn't have done this without you." Her hand trembled, but her voice remained calm.

"You're a courageous woman." He raised her hand and kissed the back. "You'd have done the right thing with or without me."

She turned toward him and leaned her forehead against his shoulder. "I need you."

Jesus, he needed her too, his body in perfect tune to her every move. But he wouldn't allow her emotional state to clutter the rational part of his brain, and he lifted her chin. "I have a pretty good idea what you're thinking...what you think you need and right now it's not me. Not like this."

"You don't know what I need!" She scooted away, tightening the robe around her. "Unless you have some psychology degree you haven't told me about? Or another super-power that allows you to read minds?"

"No, of course not."

"Then don't tell me what I need." The air left her lungs as she fell back against the bed.

The urgency to protect her overpowered the salacious thoughts worming through every part of his body. Miles threw a leg over her thighs, straddling her. "Then tell me what you want me to do."

He didn't move. Neither did she.

She closed her eyes. "I...I thought."

"Tell me you want me to take you without regard to your feelings, your past, to what's going on inside your head. Tell me you want me before you're ready. Tell me!"

"No!" Her eyes flew open, fear and panic mixed with recognition. Not the recall of the memory he'd seen unfold at the prison, nor of his aggression he was certain, but the sheer power of the suggestion that she'd forfeit herself to the very thing she feared. Afraid to face the truth—and terrified not to. Willing to sacrifice herself to prove something she didn't need to prove. Not to anyone, and especially not to him.

He lifted his weight and lay down beside her, rising on one elbow. Blonde curls splayed over the duvet and mingled with her tears in a golden shimmer, yet she clutched her arms to her chest. With his thumb, he gently wiped the moisture from her cheeks, gathering the broken pieces of an intricate mosaic. One he wanted to know step by step. Piece by piece. Inch by inch.

But only when it was right.

Miles reached out his hand, reaching for her, reaching for forgiveness, and reaching beyond the here and now.

Without hesitation, she took it and he gathered her against him. Warm, wet tears fell to his chest.

"Dammit to hell, Rachel Caldarone, I love you more than you could ever know, but I'll be damned if I'll ruin what we have. What we can share when it's right." Every muscle in his body shook, the need, the worry, the frustration building and forcing itself out through his pores. "Do you think I can't feel it when you shrink from my touch?"

"I don't—"

"You do and it kills me knowing you've been hurt in this way. You say you want me with your words, but your body speaks a different language and I won't give in to greed just to have you. I'm not a kid. I'm past the age of lust, of satisfying a need with a romp between the sheets. I don't want that and I don't think you do either."

He crushed her to his chest, the need to bury her fear and distrust tensing the muscles that held her close. "I need you and *Jesus* how I want you, but I want to heal your fears, not add to them. Be your shelter and your home. Keep you safe and be everything you want and need. I don't want just the pieces you're willing to share, but those you aren't. When it's right, you'll know. We'll know."

They stayed that way, his body wrapped around her as if to shield her from the torment, from the memories, and from him. And she molded to him, sharing the same air, one heartbeat from sharing each other.

"I'm sorry," she whispered, the words both promise and supplication, and an extraordinary expression of relief drained the color from her face. "I thought if we..."

The apology she offered he took with his mouth pressed fervently against hers, the sweet ruffle of wine mingling with the underlying tang of repressed fear.

"Forgive me?" His words disappeared against her warm lips, but the forgiveness she offered he seized and seized again, their tongues dancing to the suggestion of what lay ahead in the heady aroma of the future. "You're safe, Sunshine." He pushed the curls from her temple with his index finger and then traced the faint scar hiding in the wisps of hair, a fevered mark penetrating skin and muscle and piercing his heart. "I will never hurt you or abandon your feelings to satisfy my own. All I ask for right now is your trust."

"I do trust you. That's why—"

"Shhh." He captured her words with a finger pressed to her lips. "One day it will happen. But not tonight. What you need now is sleep." He held her, want and need giving way to something nameless, something expanding inside him too big to contain and he let it go, sighing heavily into her hair. "Jesus, how could I love you any more than I do right now?"

She sucked in a sob, and he kissed her eyes in reply.

"Is there anything you need from your room?" Miles swiveled his legs over the edge of the bed. "Something besides the robe, maybe?"

She scooted to the headboard and crushed a pillow under her chin. "I could use my toothbrush and phone," she said and reached into her pocket and then handed him her keycard. "In case Grandpa calls."

"Anything else?"

She tightened the bathrobe and shook her head.

He stood. "You okay?"

"I'm in good hands now."

The mere suggestion forced him to suppress the eagerness to prove it. *Someday.* "Critters think so."

A tiny spark had returned to her eyes. "Please hurry."

Miles stooped and kissed the top of her head, tipped both keycards in the air, and walked backward toward the door. She punched the pillows, crawled under the covers, and bundled the bedclothes under her chin. It took only moments for her eyes to soften, droop, and then close. With sleep calling her to the edge of dreams, he slipped out.

The security mechanism locked into place and he leaned against the door. He'd done the right thing by refusing to give in to his selfish whims. The decision rested easy on his heart, but his body had heartily disagreed. But as long as she was safe and unharmed, he could live with the battle and accept the mental bargain. She came first—would always come first.

Once inside her room, he checked the patio. A small gray feather stuck to the glass of the French doors fluttered in the breeze. The pursuit of a small wink of light on a dark night had been the house sparrow's demise. Tiny footprints of remorse skittered through him as he dialed the front desk to have it removed and the glass cleaned.

It had taken fewer than five minutes and Miles returned with her toothbrush and her phone tucked inside a pale pink case. The locking mechanism beeped amid the laughter from a group of college-aged kids having far too much fun for a weeknight. Recalling his own adventures at that age skiing the slopes of the Rocky Mountains, kayaking the rapids of Colorado's swollen rivers, and ending the days with a few too many beers, he slipped back into his room.

Transfixed at the woman in his bed, he propped himself against the dresser. The threshold of dreams had erased the exhaustion, and the slow rise and fall of her breathing drained the heavy pressure from his chest.

One day she would be in his bed for other reasons. She may harbor ghosts (don't we all?) and he'd do everything in his power to snuff them and take her memories and the pain that went with them. His to vanquish. And only then would he love her with everything he had to give, the way a man should love a woman.

Miles approached her, set her phone and toothbrush down, and stooped to brush away a curl that had drifted across her cheek, her sleepy smile not carrying the strength to open her eyes.

"I didn't mean to wake you."

"You forgot something."

"Your phone and toothbrush are on the nightstand." He eased himself down, barely moving the mattress. "Have I forgotten something else?"

"Your super powers."

He picked up her bathrobe lying across the foot of the bed and placed it closer to her.

"No worries, Mr. Respectable veterinarian." She yawned. "I'm wearing jammies."

"You could have told me sooner." Hesitating, he lay down beside her propped on one elbow and scooped her into a spooned embrace, cocooning her backside next to him. Despite the sheet and duvet between them, she fit easily into the contours of his body as absolute as if they'd been carved from the same mold.

"I thought you knew, with your super powers and all."

A chuckle vibrated between them. "X-ray vision isn't one of them."

"That's comforting," she said, a yawn stretching the comment.

Jesus, how he wanted to kiss her as sleep folded her in its embrace and she drifted into dreams. He smoothed her hair instead, calmly stroking her as he would a trembling puppy. And then his hands played over her body, and he began to speak softly of the wonders of his world. The wilderness that lay beyond the mountains, streams brimming with fish and cattails and roaring waterfalls, wildflowers blanketing the mountainsides in spring. The images came to him and he spoke effortlessly, a continuous monotone of the abandoned cabins, beaver dens, and herds of elk and bighorn sheep he often came upon while searching for lost souls, how the wind took his dreams as he challenged a ski slope, the way the elements carved intricate designs in an ice cave hundreds of feet down, and the hearts and souls of his four-legged patients, each one he knew by name.

And he threaded her hair between his fingers and massaged her scalp and neck, her body relaxing, giving in to sleep.

Her breaths lengthened and grew shallow against his chest, his knees fitted in the backs of hers. And he reached around her waist and tightened his grip, wincing when her body stiffened at his touch and then relaxed in the bosom of sleep—he the protector, she the life force he needed against him today, tomorrow, and each day beyond.

"May this be the last night of troubled dreams, Sunshine. Your dreams are mine to fulfill now. And I swear I'll make sure every one of them comes true." The same soothing tone marked the promise of his words.

Certain she was asleep, he left the bed with as little movement as possible, the empty wine bottle proof one of them would sleep soundly.

He splashed his face with cold water, the desire to touch her without the barrier of his convictions receding much too slowly—and far too quickly.

Sleeping next to her would be the easiest thing he'd ever done, the wait ultimately the hardest. One day he would. One day he would lay with her, their bodies as one, and he'd hold her as she drifted into the shadows of sleep and he'd follow her into dreams holding her next to him.

Pulling a chair next to the bed, he sat. Sometimes the easy thing to do was also the hardest—to allow her the space she needed to want him as much as he wanted her. Without boundaries. Without regret. Without hesitation.

Without the barrier of the past.

He wouldn't challenge his convictions or his promises.

No, it wouldn't be easy, the wait.

But something worth waiting for never came easy.

TWENTY-TWO

*T*hey say the coldest part of the day occurs at dawn, moments before the sun's rays pierce the horizon. But dawn had come and gone and left its achy, cold warning embedded in her bones.

She reached out, searching for Miles' warmth. But she was alone and rolled over to find him propped in a chair next to the bed, awake. Keeping watch. Keeping her safe from the monsters under the bed.

"Hey," she said, clearing the sleep from her throat. She leaned against the headboard and crumpled a pillow in her lap.

Sometime during the night or early morning hours Miles had showered, dressed, and had hot coffee waiting. "Good morning, Sunshine." He kissed her forehead and handed her a steaming cup. "With a splash of cream."

"Perfect." Drugged with sleep, the word rolled over her tongue and she took a sip of coffee to steady it. The warmth ignited a tiny fire in her belly as she contemplated the small movements of the man who had proven to be the pillar of her strength and the source of her weakness. Whether rumpled, unshaven, and wildly adventurous, or as he stood before her now refined, dignified, and gently tamed, he was utterly charming and ferociously protective. Her fortress. Her soft landing. Her safe haven.

Perfect.

"I checked the patio and the noise you heard was a kamikaze bird. I had maintenance remove it."

She blew on the hot liquid and circled the rim with her index finger. "I'm glad I didn't have to see it." Relief drained from her shoulders but did nothing to ease the queasiness, and she slapped a hand across her belly.

"It's early, but when you're ready to dress, I'll walk you to your room."

W hen she'd paced her room for the hundredth time, Miles suggested they spend the last few minutes at the lagoon before the hour-long trip into downtown Phoenix. Water lapping at the sandy beach would be soothing, he'd said. The sun sparkling on the rippling water would be serene, he'd said. The cool morning air would be refreshing, he'd said. Yet as they stood with their hands locked together staring out over the water, all she could think of was how to tell him she'd changed her mind.

"It's about time to go." The surety he so easily displayed fixed his jaw, the neatly trimmed stubble shadowed in the filtered light. But a small crease set his brow despite the tranquility of early morning. "You ready?"

Though the air was cool, sweat trickled under her arm. She clamped down on her lip, the pain a momentary distraction. "I don't think so."

He slid his fingers under her chin and raised it with the gentleness of a healer's hands—hands that caressed a puppy as a father would his child, hands that cleansed an animal's wound with the compassion of a mother, hands that held her with what she needed and the promise of more, hands that with a single touch steadied her rapidly failing courage. "Please look at me."

In an effort to keep doubt from bursting from a carefully composed façade, she blinked. "I don't think I can go through with it."

"You're a survivor. You've more strength, more courage inside you than you know. You can do this."

"Not without you," she said with more plea than she'd intended.

"You won't have to. I'll be right beside you, but it's your courage that will get you through this. It's in here." He placed his hand near her heart and took her mouth in a sweet, light kiss and sealed it with one on the corners and a lingering one to her forehead.

The advancing sunrise had painted the sky in hues of orange, pink, and red behind a thin layer of clouds that would soon give way to vivid blue in the way of desert mornings.

"Red sky at morning, sailors take warning."

Miles drew a finger along the line of her chin and then touched her nose. "Then I promise you red skies at night."

It wasn't simply the way he looked at her or the way he knew exactly what to say, but the way he stood with such assurance, transferring all he had to give back to her. He stood beside her now, black jeans and jacket, and crisp white shirt in staunch harmony with the steadfast man. And with their hands linked, the authority and courage he lived by shifted to her.

"Guess we'd better go." She squeezed the words through a cloak of hesitation. "Rush hour traffic can be a bitch."

⌇

The commute made a liar of her, and they made the last turn off Jefferson and into the downtown parking area twenty minutes early. Plenty of time to back out.

Miles opened her door, but her legs were too heavy to move. He took her hand, reaffirming the link to the energy and strength she needed to go forward. Her feet landed securely on the ground and they skirted the parking lot to the front of the Board of Executive Clemency building.

Miles paused at the entrance. "You've got this and I've got you.

We're in this together." A solid kiss lingered on her temple, but the expansive building's gray shadowed windows stripped the warmth from his touch.

He took her hand, each step up the concrete stairs feather light and indistinct, as if her legs had come unattached.

The doors parted. Cool air lifted the hair on her arms. Her throbbing head pulsed in time to her footsteps. Without Miles to ask questions and lead the way, the urge to turn and flee would have overtaken her. But he walked confidently beside her, holding tight to her hand to keep her courage from leaking out. He wouldn't let go. But she couldn't guarantee she wouldn't.

Stale air filled her lungs, the memory growing larger and stronger, bullying its way through crumbling courage. Though she couldn't recall how or when, they'd acquired an escort. The woman pointed politely and then left them facing a door.

"Miles." The name formed as a choked, ragged syllable. "Get me out of here."

"Take a breath, Rach. You've got this." He trailed his thumb along her trembling jaw, his gaze steady and sure, everything she failed to possess residing there. "When it's over, you'll never have to go through this again. You have my word."

"I'm scared." The words trembled from her lips.

"It's okay to be afraid. You wouldn't be human if you weren't. Jesus, I'd give anything to take all of this and live it for you." His words took physical form, the burden falling at his feet. "But I know you can do this...for yourself and for every man, woman, and child who shares your fear."

Miles traced a lone tear with his thumb. The tired lines had given way, and he wore a marked determination, the same conviction he wore when he'd stitched Zoe's wound after the accident. The same expression of unshakeable decisiveness he'd had at the prison. And it was evident now, not through his words but his presence, her anchor in a roiling sea.

He swallowed, a lengthy pause going with it. "But I won't lie to you. It's not going to be easy."

"Red skies at night?"

"Always." His kiss landed as a whisper between her brows. "Take a deep breath."

She did.

Reclaiming the determination she'd let slip away, she latched onto his forearms, afraid of speaking, afraid the words would dissolve into nothing but air. She nodded instead.

"Here we go." He took her waist and together they walked through the double doors and into the waiting lion's den.

Three separate rows of desks formed a square U separating them by mutual association from a long expanse of desk that sat a few inches above the floor to their left—The Board of Executive Clemency. Two males flanking one female exchanged notes and comments. Judge and jury. She didn't know their names. She didn't know if she could recite her own. Her body grew light as if filled with air, a loose bundle of muscles and nerves moving in slow motion without form, without substance, but somehow she followed Miles to a table directly opposite the board and took a seat without falling limply into the chair.

Rachel swiveled, scanning the room. A red exit sign glared above the door.

Miles scooted as close as he could and took her hand under the table. "I'm right here, and I won't let go."

The fabric of his words covered her chilled skin in a brief moment of reprieve. A second later (or was it several?) a briefcase thumped on the table.

The portly man whose closing arguments had cinched a unanimous decision fourteen years ago placed a bottle of water in front of each of them and took the seat next to her. He landed with an exhale, setting the chair in an accommodating bounce, took Rachel's hand, and kissed the back. "It's good to see you, my dear."

The distinguished face had become more rounded over the years, the cases he'd prosecuted etched deep within the lines. But the accumulation of years and the burden of exposing the truth couldn't extinguish the empathy in clear, brown eyes.

Her heart lightened. "Hello, Mr. Dumas."

"Everett, please, Rachel. We've spent far too much time together to revert to formalities, don't you think?"

She nodded, the reply both answer to the question and challenge of uncertainty that lay ahead.

Dumas patted her hand and leaned forward. "And you must be Miles Malone?"

Miles stood, the chair scooting behind him. The sudden loss of his touch left her chilled and she rubbed her arms to ease the sudden shiver.

"Everett Dumas, District Attorney." Dumas extended his hand and Miles took it in a brief, solid handshake. "Rachel's grandfather mentioned you'd be attending today. Please give Marshall my regards, won't you?"

"We will."

"Please sit, Miles." Dumas flicked his hand. "Formalities are wildly overrated, reserved for formal occasions. This is going to be a cake-walk. If I know the board, which I do, this hearing will be open and shut." He lifted a shoulder so slightly it seemed as though he'd given in to a muscle tic. "Thirty minutes max and that sonofabitch will be taking a free ride back to Florence."

Thirty minutes of hell. Staying ahead of the seconds was exhausting, and minutes seemed to stretch for days, but each passing second would bring her closer to getting away from here, away from Arizona, and away from the memories.

Away from him.

"How can you be so sure?"

Dumas recoiled as if she'd poked him with the pointed hook of the question mark and jutted a double chin. "Trust me, Rachel."

Trust.

A word she'd lost the flavor for, but both men sitting next to her had offered theirs without question. Dose by dose, they had given and she had taken, needing no more proof than that of their actions.

"It's highly unusual for the prisoner to attend. Hearings are handled via videoconference, so someone with considerable influence must have pulled a few strings. I certainly don't have that kind of leverage." Dumas threw a staunch glance at Miles and Miles acknowledged it with a nod.

Dumas draped a stout arm over Rachel's shoulder and gave it an affectionate pat. "Give your testimony as we discussed." He drew his arm back and crossed both over a paunch that had grown considerably over the years. "I've got a few tricks up my sleeve that no one—myself included—saw coming." Leaning back in his chair, he buttoned his suit coat and clasped his hands over his belly. "I guarantee this pervert will never step foot outside the confines of concertina wire."

"We hope you're right." Miles gave Rachel's shoulder a gentle squeeze.

"I am." A single leather clasp on Dumas' briefcase snapped open and he retrieved a pile of papers from inside and raised them in sanguine display. "This one's open and shut."

The air of confidence in his words was exceeded only by that of his stature, the one that came alive in the courtroom, the one he'd laid at her feet and asked nothing in return save truth. And it was the same fortitude that had shattered, sharing her tears in the telling of it. The understanding and empathy for his clients lay hidden under the staunch persona of a driven attorney.

Dumas tidied the papers and set them directly in front of him. He punctuated a pause with a long release of air, straightened, took Rachel's forearm in a firm grip, and nodded toward a door on the opposite side of the room.

"The dog and pony show has arrived." He drummed his fingers in an unsettling chant on the hardwood table. "The circus is about to begin."

Heavy doors parted.

An unseen clock ticked. Chatter died. The *click-click-click* of a pen tapped. Her heart thumped against her ribs. The air thickened. Seconds paused. Stretched.

Tense. Vigilant. Still.

Heavy.

The doors opened—wide, toothy jaws spewing the vomit they couldn't hold back.

Flanked by two guards, the prisoner—the man who had violated her—entered the room.

TWENTY-THREE

The past collided with the present and the room dissolved in a gray soup. Shapes blurred. Light and dark images popped on and off inside her head, an automated tilt-a-whirl sideshow. She fought to slow the nauseous spin, to lighten the shadows.

To keep them from becoming *solid*.

The guards escorted the prisoner to the table to the right. He pushed back the handcuffs and locked hands with a man suited much like Dumas—navy suit and striped tie—but unlike her attorney whose days since the bar exam were too numerous to count, this one owned the next cover of *GQ*. Greeting completed, the two men sat.

"James Northwright." Dumas tagged the name with a small grunt. "Rookie pisshead thinks he can outperform a veteran quarterback," he said with an air of smugness. "I assumed the wealthy pervert sitting next to him would have taken notes at the trial. Northwright may be a partner in one of the most prestigious law firms in Phoenix, but he'll never sink his size eleven Ferragamos into the underworld of sex crimes. His ego's too big." He shook his head, a second chin wobbling with the effort. "And his balls are too small."

The humor aimed at Northwright's effectiveness skimmed by her, indifferent in their quest.

The prisoner scanned the room. Fastened on her. Wary. Perceptive. A predator stalking its prey. Fear dug its tentacles into her spine.
Inched upward. Spread. Revulsion rippled her skin, tiny hairs alive in
vain defense.

Fifteen years. Fifteen years since she'd been a slab of meat between
him and solid metal. Fifteen years of hell. But this was a new hell.
Bright as dawn. Exposed. Raw.

He smiled at the guards.

Smiled at his attorney.

Smiled at her.

She didn't.

Her defenses crumbled and her mind flooded with the shattered
pieces of her past.

Then he broke the connection and looked away.

Focus.

What had Dumas told her?

"If you find yourself overwhelmed, concentrate on your daughter."

Bug.

Miles placed a hand on her arm as if she'd spoken Bug's name out
loud. Maybe she had. He blinked, slow and mindful, a reminder of his
presence and the buffer to a malignant past. Her safe haven. Hero to
her little girl.

A little girl who bore Nico's olive skin and dark hair, her own
unruly curls, and who spoke with the same fervent sparkle in the dark
eyes her father had given her. A little girl who loved bugs more than
ice cream and Zoe more than either. Whose great-grandpa would
buckle her safely into her booster seat so she could visit the residents
in the activity room today because Inga baked butterfly-shaped
cookies on Thursdays. Today was Thursday, wasn't it? And little girls
and boys should be kept safe, to indulge in cookies and laughter and
each other without fear. Rachel blinked, the harsh overhead lights
stripping the moment.

Voices rose and fell, but one spoke above the din.

Dumas.

What had he said? A muffled *tap-tap-tap* echoed in her brain. Dumas turned the mic toward her and dipped his head once.

The chaos running loose in her head seized her voice. Someone squeezed her hand. Gave her forearm a pat. A shared connection of courage and love spilled into her from both sides and the memory exploded from the depths of hell and unshackled her voice. Her lips began to move.

"My boyfriend, Jason, and I had a disagreement that night, and a customer offered—"

"Mrs. Caldarone," the female board member said and repositioned the mic, "can you please indicate to the board who you're referring to when you speak of 'a customer'?"

One sentence spoken. One sentence questioned. How many more to go? She pushed it aside, but the answer pushed back, crushing her into the seat. Had she shaken her head? She hadn't spoken, had she? The name—the name they wanted her to speak—shattered in her mind like broken glass.

"Fear not the name...for the saying of it shall set you free."

The female board member clasped her hands, the movement small and inconsequential, but reverent eyes spoke directly to her. And then Miles wrapped both hands around her one.

"I'm right here. And always will be."

She glanced to the right. Secured in handcuffs and shackles, the prisoner steepled his hands and studied the steel bracelets, yet he remained motionless as if someone had pressed the pause button on some phantom remote control.

Then he looked up.

Even from across the room his eyes were vivid, an aggregate of amber, gold, and bronze amid solid features. The face of a chameleon—as handsome as it was feral. As charming and deceiving as it had been that night.

The customer waved his empty glass. He wasn't a regular. I'd have recognized him, and Carl's ability to associate names and faces was uncanny, but the bartender hadn't called him by name.

The man swiveled toward me. "I'd be happy to fill in for what's-his-

name." He glanced in Carl's direction. "You're in need of a scapegoat to escape whatever you're running from."

As tall and generously muscled through the shoulders and torso as Carl, the stranger blocked my view of the bartender completely, severing eye contact with my friend and co-conspirator. I had to admit if I couldn't continue to whittle Carl down until he gave in to my dubious scheme, the current view and his divine cologne made the wait somewhat easier. Though his tie had come askew, the suit shouted designer and the intensity in his gaze spoke ambitious young businessman who didn't often take no for an answer. Success at the price of tenacity. The aggregate size of him and his attached ego fit into a neat bundle of dress for success.

I offered a polite smile, though I couldn't help thinking he'd deliberately eavesdropped on my conversation. And why did everyone think I needed to escape? I just wanted Jason to get it through his head I needed to move on— that I didn't feel the same way he did. I couldn't. Couldn't fall for anyone. Not Jason. Not anyone. It was too hard. Too painful. It was easier to step away before things got seriously...messy.

"Thanks, but I just need Carl to pretend we're a thing." I pointed between myself and the churlish bartender, whose obnoxious habit of playing concerned father sometimes really ticked me off.

"Not today, Princess," Carl said and handed the stranger another double shot of Crown, shot me a look that could have seared the hairs off my arms, and wandered to the far end of the bar.

"No problem, Angel." The stranger's sultry eyes darkened. "I won't be far if you have a change of heart."

The confident businessman turned confident inmate leaned back and placed his hands nonchalantly in his lap. His lips thinned, whitened, and then curled. Bile rose from her churning gut and crawled up the back of her throat.

She'd smiled at him that night. Had thought him handsome. Had considered him merely a guy who'd had too much to drink and had offered to help her alleviate a 'situation.'

The prisoner lifted his chin and looked directly at her.

"Hello, Angel."

He mouthed the words, but they were as clear as if he'd spoken aloud. Spoken an inch from her ear. Spoken without sound. Yet the shiver of their echo ascended from the shadows of yesterday. The shadows of hell.

Miles' grip tightened and he leaned into her. "You can do this." The reality of his words enclosed her in an instant shield. "Let me be your strength, whatever you need me to be. I'm right here," he said, clearly suppressing the rage behind a quiet outward appearance. But his faith in her bled through, connecting her to the present.

Then she turned to Dumas, who gave her a modest nod steeped in encouragement.

Rachel climbed inside herself, latching onto the murmur of blood through vessel and in and out whoosh of air through lungs determined in their purpose. Back straight, she faced the board. Both men sat stalwart, washed of any sign of emotion, yet each in turn offered her a subtle nod. The woman did the same.

Rachel swallowed a sob before it could fester and leak out all blubbery and choked and...*weak*. He had reduced her to something less than human once, but never again.

Drenched in the aftertaste of vile recollection, Rachel turned and spoke directly to the prisoner. "His name is Chastain. Demetri Chastain."

TWENTY-FOUR

"You may continue, Mrs. Caldarone."

Rachel's mind doubled backward into the gray soup of total recall. "After my shift, I left the restaurant where I was employed as a waitress." She looked down briefly, knuckles void of color. "Carl, the bartender, offered to walk me to my car in case Jason followed me, but I told him I'd be fine. I got to my car and reached for the door." The images came into focus but her voice unsettled. "Someone grabbed me from behind and clamped a hand over my mouth. I assumed it was Jason."

The saying of it festered and grew until she couldn't hold it back. "Jason wouldn't hurt me." She examined the mic, the small blackness leading her down, down, down, somewhere far away yet as tangible as the thick spit inside her mouth.

One more step inside the memory and she'd be in that parking lot, smashed against wet asphalt. Hard metal. One more step and she wouldn't be able to stop it.

She tugged at the memory of Jason, the lanky art student who smelled of Sennelier oils and turpentine and wore more paint on his clothes and hair than he mixed on the palette. The one who'd wanted more than she could give. She dug deep and pulled Jason forward, a temporary shield to suppress the urge to curl into a ball and disappear.

One step at a time.

"I couldn't breathe. I couldn't tear the hand away. Jason wouldn't do this. Jason's hands were kind and soft and smelled of...of oil paints and charcoal and turpentine. But these hurt and reeked of sweat and whiskey and cologne." She fought against the renegade words and pasted a hand to her mouth. Let it drop.

"It was dark. It doesn't rain much in Arizona, but it did that night." A small hiccup doused the recollection and slid down her cheek, the trail as cold as the drops of rain. "It was so cold." Her lids refused to close, to blink away the images. "He was hurting me and I couldn't get away."

She paused and looked down, the grain of the wood swirling along the path of the memory, and she followed the lines groping her way back to the present and keeping the past from strangling her. She sniffed and found the mic, a spot of stability amid the madness.

"I fought. Kicked. Tried to break free. I tried to scream..." A noisy breath devoured the imaginary scream. "But I couldn't remember how." The words, too heavy to come out right, rose to an ugly pitch. "It didn't matter because he shoved a handkerchief in my mouth and tied it. It was too tight and it smelled like...*him*." The words came small and strangled, the recollection large and vivid on their tail. Repulsion clogged her throat. "He dragged me to his truck. It was dark. There was no moon and the security light was out. Carl sent in a request to fix it, but I guess they didn't get to it."

Rachel looked directly at the female board member. "Did he know that? About the light and parked deliberately in the darkest part I mean? I don't remember...from the trial."

The woman's expression thawed behind the stolid features, and she leaned forward, grasping an instant of solitude maybe, an instant to regain the indifference that had fled from her face. Rachel hadn't considered if this would be difficult for them. It had been. Before. During the trial. One juror studied her feet, or maybe it had been the floor. Rachel couldn't be sure. Only that the juror rarely regarded anything beyond her invisible body bubble.

"Mrs. Caldarone, we've read the trial transcripts. This is merely a hearing to decide whether Mr. Chastain is to be granted commutation for the remainder of his sentence. Do you understand?"

Rachel regarded the question, digested it, and then tossed it aside. It wasn't possible for anyone to understand unless they'd joined the exclusive club whose initiation sprang from the bowels of hell. "*You are the ones who need to understand,*" she said, the words salted with prejudice.

Someone touched her chin and she recoiled. Raised her hands. Miles caught them and brought them to his chest. Voices murmured. He shook his head at Dumas and Dumas covered the mic with his hand.

"You don't have to continue, but whatever you decide we're here for you." He considered her with an air of concern so profound he saw beyond the surface to the inner parts of her no one else had reached. Places another had approached but never entered, and he gave it again and again, the proof balanced on the edge of his eyes. "We're with you. Supporting you. Bug. Grandpa. Dumas. And me. Lean on me, Rach. I'll be your strength. Let me be whatever you need me to be."

The power of his words expanded inside her, giving back and filling the drained reservoirs. She turned back to the mic and Dumas removed his hand.

"Whenever you're ready, Mrs. Caldarone."

James Northwright bolted upright. "This isn't a trial," he said, slamming his hand on the table. "I respectfully request we forego this blatant attempt to sidestep the issue, which is to consider commutation of sentence for a man who—"

"Sit down, Mr. Northwright." The closest board member clicked a pen several times and then pinned it to the table. "We're fully aware of what's to be considered. The proceedings in this particular case are highly irregular to begin with and I suggest you refrain from escalating this into something other than exactly what it is. You and your client will have ample opportunity to present your recommendations to the board."

Was this a good sign? Why would anyone want to listen to the sick details of something so ugly she'd tried for years to block out? To stop the pity? The stares? To step away from the guilt? Stop the self-doubt and nightmares that therapy couldn't? She'd found her own way once, through another who'd delivered hope. And she turned to Miles, and he to her, the connection new, but more alive than she could remember.

Her tongue swept over rough lips, and then she focused on the mic, the black object a small tunnel of isolation. Of secrecy.

"He threw me to the asphalt. The fall bloodied my hands and knees and my hand bent sideways." Rachel grabbed her wrist, phantom pain searing past flesh straight into bone. "He dragged me up by the arms and pushed my face against the truck. I tasted blood and something crunched. Like gravel when you step on it, you know? Blood ran down my face and neck and down my throat." A wan smile formed. "It tastes like wet pennies. Blood, I mean. Did you know that?" The smile died. "Then the pain came like someone had jabbed a screwdriver into my brain. And the lights...pink and white flashes behind my eyes. I thought I was going to pass out. I wish...I wish I would have." She tried to swallow, to flush the vivid recall of blood and rising nausea. "He said not to move, that he was the scapegoat I had asked for."

Her mouth had gone paper dry and she took a sip of water, the liquid sliding down her throat, soothing it, but did nothing to cool the repulsion or steady her trembling nerves.

"He pinned my face against the truck. Grabbed my ponytail. Yanked my head back and said if I made a sound I'd never speak again nor would my family." She wrung her hands, the air rancid and heavy, pressing against her chest. "I told myself to fight, that death was better than giving up. But I couldn't. I couldn't make my legs or arms move. It was as if I was...detached somehow...from my body..." Question and answer formed into a slight tilt of the head. "...watching from somewhere else."

Tattered images formed slowly and then all at once. "He shoved my skirt over my waist. Tore my under clothing. Something metal hit the asphalt." She lowered her lashes, grasping a brief moment of reprieve and then brought them back. "He called me his angel." The word played across her mind, revulsion tied to the name a monster had given her.

A muffled groan came from beside her, and she turned slowly toward it. The muscles in Miles' jaw tensed, poised to strike at something unseen yet as visible as the rage he guarded. He buried his head in his hands.

Dumas spoke to the board. "A minute. Please." He switched off the mic and leaned in front of Rachel. "You all right, Mr. Malone?"

"No, dammit, I'm not all right. I can't stomach what that bastard did." His thigh took the blows of a ruthless fist, and deep crevices had formed across skin flushed to an angry red. "Fucking psychopath."

"You don't have to stay." The moment she said it her courage collapsed, flowing out of her like water through a cracked pipe. She wanted to take it back, to tell him she couldn't do this without him. But how could she? This was her hell, and she had no right to ask him to sink further into the nightmare.

The fury that had turned his eyes to molten steel softened. "I will not leave you."

"I understand if you need to get out of here." She'd meant them, but the words came out flat and insubstantial. "It's okay."

Miles wiped a thumb across her moist cheek. "What I need is to beat the shit out of the perverted psychopath. Slowly. And by God I'd savor every minute he suffered." Fierce admission tensed his jaw. "But it would never be enough and I'd be the one sitting in his seat, so we'll do this your way, Dumas. I hate it, but you're the expert."

Rachel looked down at her hands parked neatly in her lap and picked at a rough cuticle. "It wasn't Everett." Miles peered from one to the other, his expression fragmented with skepticism. "It was my idea to tell it like this."

Miles dropped his elbows to the table, first two fingers kneading his temples.

"I didn't want to do this. Relive it. But if they let him out..." The thought, vicious and clumsy, trembled on her lip.

"They won't." Miles looked directly at Dumas with cold, blinding voracity. "Take care of the sonofabitch. For good."

"This wasn't easy for Rachel the first time around, and maybe worse today. As long as I've been putting these perverts behind bars, it never gets any easier. Not for the victims. Not for anyone," Dumas said with a frosty bite and an uncompromising squint. "The board will vote against commutation. You have my word."

"I don't give a shit about how this affects me or you or anyone except Rachel..." He dug a hand into his hair, pushing it from his forehead. "She's my only concern." Miles sustained the DA's gaze long enough for the statement to be cemented into Dumas' brain and then turned to Rachel and gave her hand a reassuring squeeze. "I'm not leaving you. Or this room."

She nodded, groping deep inside for the strength to bring the last fragment of ugly truth to the surface to be offered up as penance for those who shared membership in her private club. Those who've fought to cope with the past. Those who struggled now to stand up to an abhorrent monster. And those of the future—the ones whose fate will throw them along this sick path. A shared horror few knew. And fewer understood.

There would be future victims. Ones who would come forward. Ones who wouldn't. Ones who added to the statistics. Ones who didn't. But this offender, this despicable monster would never again be the demon in someone's past, the cause of another stolen life.

Rachel took a sip of water, the liquid as tremulous inside their plastic prison as her nerves were inside her. She switched on the mic, and Miles took her hand, the connection coming together twice as strong, twice as secure. Twice as safe.

Past. Present. Future.

With a long glance at the stalwart man beside her, she cleared her throat. "I'm ready."

TWENTY-FIVE

*G*rateful for the short reprieve, Rachel turned her focus back to the mic. The black hole took her back, the images spewing forth once again. Shielded by the distance it afforded, an opaque, pendulous bubble enclosed her, suspending her above the scene as it played out in vivid detail, the memory unleashed for one final act.

He yanked my skirt up. Ripped my underwear. Grabbed my breasts to free them. Fully exposed, I shivered. So alone. So cold.

"Relax, Angel, and enjoy the ride."

Over and over he took me hard, penetrating, groping, pinching my nipples. He groaned. Trembled. Relaxed. Warm liquid dribbled between my legs.

"I'm sorry, Angel. But you asked for this. A silent auction to the highest bidder. A win is a win."

I collapsed and the world went black.

"He shoved me further into the nightmare with each thrust, each bruise a notch...a...a conquest in some sick game." She bit her lip. Hard. Pain took physical form and left its bloody mark. "When he... finished...he pushed me down and left me there. By his truck. Drove away as if he'd done nothing more than stop for a drink. But he took what wasn't his to take. And with each piece he took, part of me died."

A concentrated frown tightened her face. "I don't remember how I got there, but at the hospital…" The images hung suspended in her mind's eye, blocking the words. The mirror. The grotesque assortment of bruises, cuts, and broken bones she'd touched as if it were some bizarre Halloween makeup. White, sterile lights—spotlights exposing the shame the doctors and nurses tried to hide under layers of bandages and soothing talk. "They said my cheekbone was shattered, my nose and wrist broken, and I'd need metal plates in my face." Rachel traced a line from temple to ear and under her eye as if reliving the path of the surgeon's knife, the damage secured beneath the nearly invisible silvery lines. But the steel reminders refused to relinquish the physical pain. She grimaced, and then she raised her eyes to the board. "They warned me not to look. But I couldn't help it. I wanted to see what I'd *'asked'* for."

A shudder soiled her skin and she dug her nails into her arms, a feeble attempt to rid herself of the rancid memory. "When they finally allowed me to shower, the water wasn't hot enough and they didn't give me enough soap." She dissected the words between clenched teeth. Pried them apart. "I scrubbed until my skin was raw…but I couldn't get him off me."

Rachel paused, the past liquefying until the present came fully to the forefront. Then she set her jaw and raised her chin. "I may have been his angel that night. But he was my demon." The outlines of the board blurred, but she acknowledged each one in turn. "And this was hell."

The board members talked among themselves and Dumas took the opportunity to switch off the mic. He draped an arm around Rachel and pulled her briefly into his shoulder. "I know this was difficult, but you were fantastic."

"Is it over?" The question rolled off her tongue and landed somewhere in the middle of the table.

"It's over," Dumas said, the sentence deflating as if the air had been let out. "The board may have a question or two but for you my dear, it's over."

Miles embraced her, the shelter of his body accepting the shattered pieces of her past. He took them from her and gave himself back, two halves of a shared whole. He released her and she looked down at her hands, calm now, and her heart was slowly making its way back to normal—if such a thing existed.

She looked up at Dumas then, the weight of the inevitable tensing his jaw. "But it's not for you. Is it?"

"It's never over for me, Rachel. Not as long as perverts like Chastain draw breath."

"Mrs. Caldarone, we have one final question if you'll indulge the board?"

She looked first to Miles and then to Dumas, questions simmering between them. He nodded once and switched on the mic.

Miles took her hand firmly, her anchor in a sea of divergent emotion.

Dumas acknowledged the board.

It was one of the men who spoke. "At any time did Mr. Chastain threaten you with a weapon?"

Everett Dumas grasped Rachel's forearm, shook his head once, and lifted his chin to the opposing table. "Northwright is going to make an ass of himself. Right. About. Now."

Northwright slapped the table. "The answer is explained thoroughly and without question in the transcripts." The wily attorney's words remained calm, but his eyes and scarlet skin said otherwise. "At no time did my client produce or use a weapon."

The answer bore no falsehood, but the lies hidden inside the insinuation spilled into the hearing room despite Northwright's objections.

"Mr. Northwright, please try to restrain yourself."

Rachel leaned forward, her back straight. "No."

"You don't need to answer." Dumas firmed his grip.

She pulled free. "No. He did not threaten me with a weapon." Her voice steadied. "His weapon was his lack of morality. His depravity. His sick sense of entitlement."

"Mrs. Caldarone—"

"He did not threaten me with a weapon but the night he raped me..." she looked directly at the prisoner, "...Demetri Chastain took my life as certainly as if he'd slit my throat."

TWENTY-SIX

*A*ccording to the clock outside the hearing room, thirty-five minutes had passed since the first word had been spoken. Thirty-five minutes seemed like thirty-five years, and walking from the hearing room into the hallway passed in a blur.

"Excuse me, Mrs. Caldarone?"

Rachel jumped and Miles tightened his hand on her waist. She turned and looked into rounded shoulders and then the face of someone she'd never seen, yet he hid the distant disquiet behind a mask she knew well. This man had become an artist—the same mastery she'd acquired over the years—skillfully hiding behind the parody of acceptance.

"And you are?"

"Daniel Stratton." He lowered his gaze and his shoulders followed as if seeking the solace of the unpeopled floor. "I'm, I mean I was… Everett Dumas said you were…"

She took hold of his arm, acutely aware of the small flinch. She smiled and secured the link, taking the attention away from him and back to her. The humiliation of coming forward. The embarrassment of admittance. The questioning glances and pity from those who didn't share the exclusivity of their private club. "I know who you are."

He opened his mouth to speak, but nothing followed. What spurt of courage he'd mustered had vanished.

"It's an honor to meet you, Daniel." She offered her hand and Daniel took it briefly, a reflex of obligation and courtesy, but the urge to run skittered across his face. She turned to Miles and looped her arm through his elbow. "This is Miles Malone. My rock. My anchor and best friend."

The two men shook hands. Rachel shuffled her feet, Daniel's outward hesitance a mirror of her own. "I'm no expert on this...thing we share," she said, sweeping a hand between them, "but one thing I know for certain is you need someone. Someone close. Someone to lean on."

"My wife...couldn't come today." He furrowed his brow, interrupting an intelligent but cautious expression. "She..."

"Give her time." Rachel didn't know this woman, but it was obvious Daniel wasn't sure of the outcome. The same thing she'd felt with Nico. If this woman loved him enough to marry him, Rachel stood behind the belief that if given the chance she'd process the information into some sort of understanding and eventually acceptance. "One day she'll look beyond the victim and see the man. Trust in your love." She glanced at Miles, the affirmation of a shared insight clearly written in the space between them.

Daniel stuffed his hands in his pockets. "I have a son. He turned two in February. He's the reason I've come forward." Soft eyes hardened into bright green marbles. "I can't imagine someone doing to him—"

Rachel took his arm gently, allowing time enough for the apprehension to leach. "I have a daughter, Nicole. We call her Bug." The yearning she'd lived with when she thought she'd never have a child came rushing back. "I believed I'd never have a child, Daniel."

Daniel focused on his feet, not looking up at the mention of his name.

"I was too afraid to get close to anyone. I couldn't..." The memory shot through her—a heat-seeking bullet set on destruction and she clamped Miles' arm. "I couldn't be intimate with anyone, but the people who loved me helped me through it. Your wife will help you too."

Miles tightened his grip, the gesture one of acknowledgement and acceptance.

"What if she doesn't...what if she can't?" Daniel looked up then, pleading for the answer she'd once sought herself.

"What's your son's name?"

"Jason."

"For now, focus on Jason." It was the second time today she'd resurrected the name. This time it came and went and left no residue. "It's a good name. A strong name. Do this for him. For the children who may never get the chance to be a child. For those who've had their innocence stolen. But mostly do it for yourself."

"I didn't want to come here today, but I think..." He steadied himself. "I think it was okay. You've given me courage."

"I can't tell you it will be easy." She traced the nearly imperceptible cracks in the tile with her toe. "I'm so sorry, but it won't be. It will be a kind of hell you've never known."

"Worse than...?"

She mentally weighed the question, but hell's scales were tipped beyond any sort of judicial balance. "Perhaps a...different kind of hell."

"It took guts to do what you did in that hearing room. And at the trial. God," Daniel said, and the encouragement he'd managed to display dissolved. "I don't know if I can...do this."

"It's the most difficult thing you'll ever do. But you can do this."

Miles cleared his throat. "If anyone can put that sonofabitch away for good, it's Dumas. If that gives you any kind of encouragement."

"It does. Thanks." Daniel offered a brief smile, one pitched in automatic reflex that quickly went out of focus. He turned back to Rachel. "Everett said you'd help." He swallowed the words, his Adam's apple keeping time with the movement. "For support, I mean. Answer questions."

The healer in her stepped forward, overtaking the impulse to run. "Of course I'll be here for you." She held her hand out, wiggling her fingers. "Unlock your phone."

Daniel hesitated and then dug in his pocket, unlocked the iPhone, and handed it to her.

"There," she said handing it back. An instant of regret clogged her brain. Could she do this? Put herself out there? Be there for someone else though she could barely stand her own memories? She'd tried therapy and the group thing and shuddered at the recollection. "I've programmed my number in your contacts. Any time you need to talk, call."

Daniel studied the phone for a long while, tapped the screen, and then slipped it back into his pocket. "I haven't met the others. Dumas says there's more than the two of us."

Rachel's heart slammed against her chest.

"I thought I heard my name." Dumas slid in between them. "I see you two have met?"

"What the hell, Everett? More than me and Daniel?"

The District Attorney rubbed his temple in a manner meant to stall. "The board will find seventeen letters testifying to the fact that your life has been adversely affected and continues to be affected by that bastard."

"That's not what I asked."

"I have in my briefcase copies of police reports from two more alleged victims besides Daniel." He grasped Daniel's shoulder briefly. "They're willing to come forward and bring further charges against Chastain. The board will have the reports by the end of the day."

"Dear God." Rachel buried her face, Miles' firm hold steadying a rapidly disintegrating stamina.

Dumas rocked up on his toes, the extra height adding to his confidence. "In the state of Arizona, there's no statute of limitations when the alleged victim is a minor child. Two of the three who've come forward," he said, exhaling as if to rid his lungs of some slimy sludge, "were under the age of fifteen at the time of the alleged incidents and fall under the adopted statute's timeline. There's another, an adult at the time. Unfortunately, the time limitation has passed for her to press charges, but her testimony will be crucial."

Fresh bile soured her stomach. How many had he violated who had remained silent? Her nails dug crescents into her arms.

Venom pulsed through her veins, Miles' strength shielding her from the poisoned words. The din of voices, clatter of footsteps, questions, answers, and confusion were lost in his marked presence.

Dumas didn't wait for a response and switched gears. "Rachel, there's someone who's been biding his time to speak to you. He's an admirer of your strong will and submitted a letter of support as did a few others. Some may surprise you." Dumas turned and waved a tall, burly man toward them.

Rachel's surprise evaporated into a wide grin.

Time had been good to him, salting the edges of a full head of hair, muscular broad shoulders and strong, bold features as wary and kind as they'd been when he'd tended bar.

"Rachel." Carl lifted her up and spun her around as easily as any man half his age. The display of lines framing his eyes had deepened, accentuating the thoughtful man within. "How are you, Princess?"

"Carl," she said, smacking his shoulder to set her down. "My God it's good to see you."

"You BITCH!"

Five heads spun in unison toward the outburst.

A tall, slender woman wearing as much Botox as she did designer clothes set her eyes on Rachel, destined for a head-on collision.

Miles took a step ahead of Rachel, and Dumas and Carl flanked her sides, the three men a living fortress and no match for one woman, even one who was obviously ticked.

"The current Mrs. Chastain." Dumas clicked his tongue. "And I don't believe she's happy."

The click of high heels grew louder, her pissed form taller, and pinched, squinty face tauter. If not in an agitated state, the blonde, handsome woman would have made quite a different impression.

"You!" The reprimand flew between evenly spaced teeth. "You could have helped him come home." Her nostrils flared, dangly diamond earrings whipping back and forth with the force of the words.

Help him? The disgusting idea rotted and died a quick death. Rachel raised her chin but otherwise didn't move.

James Northwright took Mrs. Chastain's arm from behind. "Claudia, please, we need to leave." He ransacked his perfectly groomed coif into a disheveled mess with one hand, urging her backward with the other.

"That's the first credible thing you've said all day, Counselor." Dumas took a step forward.

Claudia Chastain wrenched free of Northwright's grip. "You haven't seen the end of this."

"And she, the second." Dumas tilted his head slyly in Claudia Chastain's direction. "We'll see you back in court, Counselor. I trust you've seen the police reports?"

Northwright shot Dumas a knowing glare—one steeped in a collective mix of discernment and caution—and escorted Demetri Chastain's wife down the hallway and out of sight.

"He's seen them. I made sure of it." The tension in his round face turned jovial. "God almighty I'd have given anything to see that cosmopolitan mug of his go all doltish." He rocked back on his heels. "I'm going to nail Chastain, and the population inside doesn't take kindly to child molesters." He ended the statement with a grunt. "Not kindly at all."

The small knot of people who'd congregated to witness the showdown slowly diminished.

Carl enclosed Rachel in a full body hug, rocking her from side to side, and then held her to arm's length. "So, Princess, have you finally settled down?" He winked, the implication coming at her not as an accusation, but from the playful, fatherly side of the bartender.

"As settled as the San Andreas Fault."

"That's the girl I remember. I've met my share of neurotic women, but you've always been my favorite." Carl kissed her forehead.

She couldn't argue the designation. "You?"

"I bought the restaurant and changed the location."

"That's fantastic. Makes me happy to know you've realized your dream."

"And I'm a grandfather. Twice." The muscular chest puffed, cheeks threatening to split in two.

"I bet Marlee's a wonderful grandma."

"Nothing compares to grandkids." He went away for a moment, a moment of recall perhaps, written in the lines and creases of a content face. "How about you, Princess? Married? Kids?"

Rachel took Miles' hand. "I have a four-year-old daughter, Nicole." Carl glanced at Miles and then back to her. "Her father passed away before she was born. This is Miles Malone—"

"A friend." Miles extended his hand. "It's a pleasure to meet you, Carl."

"Friend, eh?" Carl's smile lines sprouted into full definition. "I've tended bar most of my life, kids. You can't fool this old pro."

Rachel squeezed Miles' hand. "You were always beyond perceptive."

Carl shot Miles a hardened look. "Take care of her, son."

"That's the plan, the reason I'm here."

Carl wished them well with a parting hug, and headed to the exit, turning once with his signature two-fingered salute. Nostalgia bubbled over her in warm retrospect, acutely aware she'd never see the familiar gesture, or Carl, again.

And then he turned the corner and the past opened its arms and swallowed him.

She offered Daniel the same parting hug, which he took with both greed and an underlying hesitation. She emptied her heart on the man's shoulder as both link to their private club and the courage to face the future.

Everett Dumas gave her a carefully executed hug—one of guarded enthusiasm, one he'd mastered dealing with the varied responses of the victims—and she hugged him back without regard. He shook hands with Miles. "Take care of her, Malone. She's something special, this one."

"I couldn't agree more. It's an honor to be by her side."

"I'll call as soon as I hear anything." He puckered his mouth. "They didn't give an immediate response, so it could take a couple of weeks. In the meantime, give my regards to your grandfather and that beautiful little girl of yours."

"I will." Rachel offered him a goodbye wave.

Attorney and client headed toward the exit, heads locked in deep conversation, the attorney's hands working feverishly in keen demonstration.

"Rachel Everly Gowen Caldarone." Miles placed both hands on her hips, beaming. "You were fantastic in there today." He brought her in close. "And with Daniel."

"I don't really know how I did it." A moment of hesitation softened the comment. "But I felt an odd sort of connection with Daniel."

"You'd be good with other victims. Counseling."

The idea lodged in the pit of her stomach. "I can't think beyond today and what Dumas told us." Her piece of the universe, her private club, had been but a grain of sand, a tiny granule obscured by miles of beach. But today the private club she'd been president of and sole member had gained a few unwilling initiates. A single grain of sand had suddenly become a sandbox.

"What you did today took courage. And guts."

"It was horrible." She leaned her forehead against his chest and then looked up. "And liberating, in a sick sort of way." She fiddled with a shirt button, sending it in and out through the buttonhole. "But today wasn't about me."

Miles took her hands, calming the idle movement. "If not you, who?"

"Him. Chastain." She frowned, the saying of the name a rancid reminder. "Northwright will say he's changed. Been reformed. Who's to know for sure? And what about all the people who've been changed because of him? They'll never live the life they were meant to."

The realization mushroomed and then settled amid the rubble. She would never be the same no matter how she lived her life. No matter how fiercely she guarded herself, the memory, and those she loved. No matter who she shared her life with, she'd been irreparably changed. The scars crazed her in the same way fine china wears its tiny cracks—the outward evidence insignificant, but when examined closely, the damage ran deep and reticent like the inner churnings of a sleeping volcano.

"That bastard doesn't deserve to live and he damn sure doesn't deserve freedom. Dumas will see to that."

"He may never be free, but neither will his victims."

She'd been an adult. Had known what was happening. What had gone through the minds of those children? Whether they understood or not, they'd been scarred. Her scars ran deep—the revulsion to being touched, to intimacy—the demon she'd never truly exorcised. What had he done to them? To their fragile minds and innocent bodies? How did they process it? Could they? Did they hide from the memories as she did?

She swallowed the ugly speculations. "I came today for two reasons. For the victim—victims and to forgive myself. And him."

Miles lifted her chin, brushing her cheek with his thumb. "Forgive him?"

"I tried." Angry heat bubbled in her cheeks. "And maybe in some crazy way I did forgive him. For what he did to me. Looking back on all those years of therapy I think I finally understand why it didn't help, why it never made a difference." The knots loosened and shifted, guilt slowly disconnecting its hold. "I needed to forgive myself. And I couldn't."

"It wasn't your fault."

"I thought it was."

"No, Rachel." He slid his fingers behind her ear, his thumb lightly stroking her cheek. Confusion mingled with something deeper, something rooted in sincerity that turned quiet in his eyes. "It was never your fault."

"I can live with the pain he's caused me. I think I've forgiven him for that." Had she truly seen beyond the ugliness? Beyond judgment to the flesh of the man, the human, bypassed the need to avenge the wrong? Perhaps at this moment, the answer was yes.

"You've got a forgiving, compassionate heart, Rachel Caldarone."

"I don't know, Miles." She shook her head. "I don't know if I'll ever forgive him for what he's done to those kids."

"For that, he doesn't deserve forgiveness."

"Maybe it's not for him, but for me. For peace of mind."

Miles embraced her, his courage bleeding into her with a renewed sense of strength to embark on a new beginning. The slow, methodical massage on arms, shoulders, and back a steady source of power she could take into the next phase, not free of the memory, but free from the grip of fear.

"There's something I need to tell you."

"You can tell me anything."

"Forgiveness is one thing, but I can't forget. I'll live with the memory the rest of my life, and I don't know if I can…I thought last night…with you…I thought if I made the first move…"

"There's no need to explain. I get it."

"No, you don't." She twisted free and stared at the floor. "There were times when…with Nico, that were…ugly."

"I never thought it would be easy. I don't expect it to be."

"I won't blame you if…after today—"

"There's nothing I've heard or will hear, nothing you can tell me that could persuade me to leave you, Rachel. Nothing. We'll deal with it. Together. We've a lifetime to figure it out."

"Miles—"

Strong hands curved around her face. "Nothing." He kissed her thoroughly, one meant to set the foundation of future requests. "You're safe. You have me now. You're mine to love and protect, heart and soul and body. I won't take anything you don't want to give, and I'll honor what you do."

She smiled against his mouth to seal his words, nail the lid on the past, and take his promises of tomorrow as her own.

"It's over, Rach. Let's go home."

"I'm so tired and I could use some solitude." She tucked herself into the crook of his shoulder. "Do you think we could stay? One more night?"

The answer rumbled in her ear, the sound deep and graveled, one of testament and affirmation. And it seeped through her skin, trickled past the tiny cracks, and settled into all the abandoned spaces.

TWENTY-SEVEN

*I*t was the same hotel. Same folding luggage rack that held her suitcase. Same jewel-toned carpet and nondescript art. Same drapes, with their small cleft in the center that let the afternoon sun creep in, casting a gold band across the bedspread. Yet the similarities ended there—the balcony rising several stories higher and the breeze whipping around her as children splashed and giggled in the lagoon directly below.

The lock clicked. The bottle of Late Harvest chardonnay Miles had ordered as an after-dinner treat thumped on the dresser, and his clothes rustled with each footstep as he crossed the room to the balcony. His arms came around her and though she knew he was near, she tensed. The inherent response wouldn't be an easy one to break.

It had been a long, difficult few days and she leaned against him, the tension of the last week flowing out of her.

"You okay with this?" A delicate kiss caressed her temple, the touch as soothing as the little fire the wine she'd had at dinner had fueled. The satisfaction of Miles holding her and the first meal she'd truly enjoyed since they'd arrived added to the pleasurable fullness.

"I was curious why we took the elevator to the top floor." Rachel turned and faced him. "Why'd you change our rooms?"

"Between snowbirds and Diamondbacks' and Rockies' fans, the area during spring training and the beginning of baseball season is swamped. It wasn't an easy task booking the rooms we had, and when you mentioned you wanted to stay an extra night, I had to do some sophisticated negotiating. The only room left was this suite."

"Right." She attached a wry smile to the matter-of-fact tone.

"No need to be concerned, Sunshine," he said with a throaty chuckle. "I booked a room for myself down the street." He took her hand before she could quantify the situation with a protest. "Come. I want to show you something."

He led her through the main space to the opposite side and opened the drapes to a long bank of windows and another balcony. "I don't know the name of the mountain, but the concierge assured me we wouldn't be disappointed with the view."

The afternoon sun spilled over him, streaking his dark blond hair with gold sparks. His eyes had assumed the brightness of a summer sky, and the lines and creases marking forty years had lost their intensity and were steeped with content. Even the landscaped stubble conveyed softness, and she ached to touch it, to touch him as if for the first time.

Rachel stopped breathing. Stopped thinking. Stopped seeing— except for the man beside her. The man who had reached beyond her heart and touched her soul. The man who had given her the courage to dig deep within herself and was there to catch her when she fell. The man who had weathered the battles alongside her.

Was this the man who lived to race down snow-clad slopes? Who became one with the mountains and earth and was the extension of the animals he loved? She saw the truth of it written there, in the lines and creases that spoke of joyful purpose. The man complete.

Miles caressed her cheek, the sensation familiar but intimately new. "You okay, Rach? Is this not to your liking?"

The moment had vanished. She mourned its passing and selfishly wanted it back. She slid an arm under his shirt and around his waist, reaching for something tangible to reconnect the loss.

"It's perfect, Miles." In her heart it was he who was perfect, not the place, not the time, but the *who*. Nothing else mattered as long as he remained by her side and had strength enough for them both and strength enough to understand.

Rachel pointed through the window to the two humped peaks in the distance. "That's Camelback Mountain. You can't tell from this angle but its outline resembles a camel lying down."

"Appropriate for the desert."

"I know you're fond of the Rocky Mountains and months of snow, which lends to the idea of killing yourself by sliding down them on skinny sticks, but you've never truly seen a sunset until you've seen the sun sink over Arizona."

"They've been great so far."

"They've been typical, but there's a mare's tail in the sky tonight. Sunset promises to be stunning." A wistful sigh punctuated the observation.

"My kind of clouds." A one-syllable laugh jostled the reply. "I believe you when you said you never wanted to come back here, but I hear a hint of longing in your words."

"I'll return from time to time. To visit Mom and Dad." She strengthened her hold, his skin warm under her palm. "Otherwise, I have no desire to return." Lean, hard muscle tensed under her touch, his body toned from years of skiing the mountains, climbing glaciers, and traversing rivers. "My home is in Estes Park. What I haven't had enough of is you. And I want to be with you."

His expression matured into the one she loved, one she never wanted to see burdened again because of her. This was the man she desperately needed—the man who had both strength and courage and loved her enough to set her free—if she didn't lose him in the struggle.

Piece by piece he'd shaved the armor from her defenses. The ties that bound her to the past loosened, and the demon inside her took control, her body no longer hers.

Her mouth parted. He answered the invitation with a hunger he fought to rein in, to take his time and make love to her mouth, her eyes, and her body, to strip her of her inhibitions until she belonged to only him. And she responded without question, first with her tongue and small whimpers of unvoiced hunger, and then the desires of her body in words too loud to ignore.

She melted against him. "I think you'd better cancel that room." She reached up to stroke his cheek.

"Are you sure this is what you want?"

"Positive."

"I thought you needed solitude. After the hearing and all."

"Yes. Away from people. Not you."

"Last night—"

"Was a lifetime ago."

He gently grasped her shoulders and leaned far enough away to see her face, to read what she'd written there. "If you're sure—"

"Don't you want this?"

"Jesus, Rachel. Do you need to ask?"

She lowered her hand to his butt and squeezed, but he took it back and held it firmly against his chest.

"You're a hard man to get into bed, you know that?"

The pleasure of her comment ached in his loins, but to make this leap he'd need to take small steps. The wanting of her pressed against the constricting denim, aching to be free, the salacious compulsion to take her now colliding with the desire to nurture her wounded soul, to hold her securely and let her set the pace, let her take control. He had all the time in the world and none at all.

"I need for you to want this as much, or more than I do." He trailed his thumb along her temple, her cheek, and came to rest below her ear, the rapid beat of her heart under his thumb a parallel to his. He held her there, her breaths warm, shallow gasps against his skin.

"I want this more than you know." Her eyes drifted over him, the blue ones that sparkled like sunlight on water yet touched with the depth of hunger and steeped in need. "I need you. Not in a day. Not in a week. I don't know how to explain it, but it has to be now."

The late sun beat through the window glass bathing her skin, her scent rising in the warmth of the light.

"Jesus, Rachel, I've wanted you from the first time we met on that snowy night." He brushed her lips with his, her breath stirring his sensitive skin. "And I swear I fell in love with you right then and there and every minute I'm with you I only fall deeper." He found the tender place below her ear and kissed her there, her skin hot and cool and clammy. "But I couldn't take what wasn't mine. Not then, not now. I'll never hurt you, Sunshine, and I'll never take what you're not willing to give. What isn't mine to take."

"This isn't going to be easy, but I trust you. I trust in your strength. But you must trust me too," she said, a little hoarse and a little shy, but spiked with surety.

"Whatever you need or want, it's yours. All you have to do is ask."

"This has to be my way. This time." A hint of something hidden, something on the verge of letting loose burdened her words.

"Your needs are my needs." He took her in his arms, gently at first and then pressed her body more firmly into his. She surrendered, melting against him the same way bits of warm wax mold together into a single form. The slight build of her was that of an evening dove come to rest, and he must take care not to rush her, to take his time to mend the shattered pieces of her past. She'd been broken apart and put together piece by piece, and damn himself to hell if he should destroy what kept her whole.

"I'm here for you," he whispered and skimmed his hands along her arms, the tiny hairs coming to attention under his touch. "Your way."

"Please try to understand." She closed her eyes tight. "I've wasted so many years pretending. Pretending it didn't matter. I know what I have to do, what you have to do." The breath she drew came in hitching crests and in great relief as it left. "I can't pretend any longer. Not with you."

"I want you to be free to love, to find comfort in being together, and I want to satisfy your every need, whatever they may be."

She tucked her lip between her teeth and nodded.

Miles located his wallet and fumbled inside for the stash of condoms.

She raised an eyebrow and let it drop in what could have been approval, highlighted with a shred of relief.

"I'm a doctor. And a man." He set the line of foil packets on the nightstand. "I'm prepared."

"That veterinary super power thing?"

He raised one corner of his mouth and lifted her into his arms. "Something like that."

Rachel clasped her hands tight around his neck. Slowly making his way across the room, he bowed his head and kissed her tenderly as if a fragile piece of fine china lay in his grasp. Upon setting her to her feet next to the bed, he took her bottom and positioned her snugly against him, his erection throbbing, desperate with the need to ready her. But he must go slowly, every step taken with gentle caution.

She took his mouth hard and wanting and with a passion both fierce in its need and direct in its taking. And he let her in, to take what she needed, to pin the moment with the vehemence of the past.

He'd mentally planned this night. Planned to be gentle. Planned to offer the tenderness she needed to deliver her from the past and find the way to their future. One unobscured by anything but the freedom to be with him, open and honest and barred from unspoken inhibitions. No barriers of the past.

But when he took her arms from around his neck, she pushed his hands away. Grappled with the shirt buttons. Exposed his chest. He wrapped her in his arms to calm the sudden frenzy, her body trembling on the outside with the battle raging inside. He struggled to calm her, to calm them both as she writhed in his arms, but he couldn't stop the past from bullying its way between them.

"I love you, Rachel." Her hands balled into fists and she stiffened, limbs taut, her skin stretched tight from forehead to chin. "I love you I love you I love you. It's me. Just me. Please stay with me."

Tears fell wet and hot on his bare chest, the sting of a thousand bees searing his flesh. "It's okay, Rach. I've got you. There's no hurry. We can wait."

"No." She stared at him with an unsteady union of urgency and fury and an unbridled hunger seated deeply in eyes gone as dark as the pending night. "Now."

What he understood, or assumed he understood, rushed out of him, his conclusions tossed into a mental shredder. He understood nothing of her need. "I don't want to hurt you...I thought—"

"You don't get it!"

She pounded his chest and the pain of it echoed inside him. "No, I don't. Tell me. Tell me what you want. What you need." He wiped the tears from her cheek. "I'll do whatever you ask of me."

"You have to understand. This has to be this way." She stood on her toes and took his mouth as savagely as she had done a few moments ago. "I need...I need you to take me back to that night, to purge his presence, to rid me of the demon forever." The kind, soft-spoken woman vanished, the broken one in her place. Tears spilled, soft blonde hair a buffer to the fury seeking substance. "This is what I need."

"You can't ask me to do this. I can't hurt you, to have you like this. In this way." The pain behind the words left his mouth undisguised.

Determination burned in her eyes. "You said you'd do whatever I need."

"I'd do anything for you. You know that."

"Then do this for me," she said, more challenge than statement. "You think it's wrong. Maybe it is. But I have to go back to that night. I have to know."

"You're asking too much."

"Too much?" She blinked the flimsy question aside. "Dammit, Miles. I've lived through a decade of trying to destroy myself. Been beaten beyond recognition and raped." As the word left her mouth her skin paled, gone white as paper and as rigid as the bones beneath it. "I've lost my parents, a husband, and so many patients I've lost count. And I survived," she said, the words cursed with venom. "And dammit to hell I'll survive this! I have to stop pretending and put an end to it. To come full circle."

"You're asking me to do something I can't."

"It's the only way I know how to get past it." The urgency in her plea gathered, swelled, and leaked from her eyes. "I've lost everyone I've ever loved and I can't bear to lose you. Not over this."

"How could you think I'd leave you because of this?"

"I told you sometimes it got ugly. There were times with...Nico." She looked down through lowered lashes, but he lifted her chin gently, taking back the hesitation at the saying of his name. "I needed something more. Something he couldn't give."

"There's room for private things between us, things that belong to no one but ourselves. It's okay to have those kind of secrets. And this may be one of them. One I don't need to know."

She slapped her palms to her temples. "Yes, you do!"

He didn't want to go there. Didn't want to know. But he forced the prejudices aside and accepted it. For her. "I can't say I don't envy Nico for the time he had with you, but I won't take it from you either. He was—is—part of your past. And he's a part of our future, just as anyone is who's a significant part of our lives."

"Nico..." Her throat moved up and then down, and he watched her take in his words and bleed them out. "...was a good man."

"I don't deny that." A dart of jealousy struck his heart, more painful for its raw, unexpected appearance. No. He wasn't jealous of a dead man. His jealousy stemmed from what he couldn't give her—an untarnished past. The ability to live beyond the damage.

"And he eased the panic from being with him. With a man. Intimately. But he couldn't free me from that night." The sob came as a hiccup, and she took a step away. "He didn't understand. Didn't have what it takes to go through with it."

This wasn't what he'd imagined her to say, the confession a vice-grip squeezing his heart. "And you think I do?"

"I believe in our love, the strength of your love for me. The power to take me through this. One final battle. For us."

He closed the distance, unwilling to let her go. Unwilling to let her step away from whatever it was he could give. He'd said he'd do anything, and he'd meant it. But that didn't mean it wouldn't tear him apart, rip to shreds everything he believed and tear his guts out by honoring her wishes.

"My way. To heal."

With their eyes locked, she tore at his shirt buttons. Freed the garment. Tossed it aside. The pink cotton tee flew over her head and it joined the growing pile of discarded items strewn across the floor. Her bra followed. Disheveled curls spilled over the soft mounds of her breasts, nipples dark and erect. Gooseflesh pebbled her skin. Without looking away, she unfastened his jeans and stripped the rest of their clothing until nothing remained between them but naked air. Naked skin. Naked memories.

Jesus, she was breathtaking, a goddess before him, a woman formed of a life lived, graced with the blessings of motherhood and a beauty that comes only with the passing seasons. He took her in his arms, savoring the feel of her body against his bareness; sensations and emotions long buried surging to life. "You're everything I've dreamed of," he said, tracing the line of cheekbone with his thumb, "but this is tearing me up."

"I need this."

"I don't want to do this. Not like this."

"You must." She forced the plea through a strangled gasp.

"This isn't how I imagined our first time."

"It has to be this way."

"I can't do this to you!" He grabbed his head with both hands and squeezed, as if he could evict the disgusting suggestion. "You're asking me to do something I can't...Jesus, Rachel. You're asking me to fuck you." The words curdled in the air and curdled his gut. "I'm not a fucking animal."

"He is." The remnants of truth trickled down her cheek.

"I'm not him! I'm not that kind of man and I have no desire to fuck you." The words seethed between his teeth, but with the next breath he gentled his voice. "I want to make love to you, Rachel."

She reached for the packet, tore it open and rolled the condom over his length. With each touch, he chastised himself for his body's traitorous response.

"This isn't about love. Not this time. It's truth stripped raw and I have to go there. To know." She kissed him harder than she'd done before, the fire in it hot and angry. "I'm begging you to take me back to that night. Take the stain he's left inside me and flush it away."

The implication of what she wanted wrestled against everything he believed. She should be honored. Protected. Loved. Not taken in heated lust. And it tore at him, his heart, body, and mind fighting a battle he didn't know how to win. Maybe it was a battle that couldn't be won. Maybe he shouldn't fight it.

Maybe in order to put her back together, he must first tear her apart.

In a moment of sublime truth, the tendrils of her soul pierced his heart, laying him open, her desire a raging need pouring out of her and into him. He wasn't afraid to die for her—he'd die a million painful deaths to see her through this—but to live without her wasn't an option. He didn't own that kind of courage. But this...

She lay down, dragging him with her and he lay beside her, the urge to stop this, to stop himself a raging mental war. Torn between heaven and hell, he took her into his fierce embrace and fought to restrain her, to restrain himself.

"Take me back." The words fell heavy and rank, drenched in a power forged from fear.

Lost in her need for escape, he rolled to straddle her and anchored her within his arms. She squirmed. Fought for domination. She cursed an unseen assailant, unleashing the fury. Agony thrummed from her to him. He held tight, pinning her with his weight. Her nails dug into his back, the pain sharp and brutal, a testament to her past and confirmation of her need. She cried out, cursed him as he entered her, fought, kicked, writhed beneath him, a trapped animal clawing its way free.

She bucked beneath him, matched him thrust for thrust, tear for angry tear. Her thighs clenched around him, seizing what he hadn't wanted to give. Her teeth sank into his shoulder and his flesh gave way and in that moment, he took her rage. It drowned him and fueled him, and an inscrutable darkness seized him, a cloud between him and an assailant who'd taken what wasn't his. Reckless lust tightened his balls and filled him with blind need to rid her body. Rid her womb. Rid her of an invisible presence. Rid her of the demon that kept her from him.

Drenched in sweat, they rode the wave of his spasms as he spilled himself, her teeth buried in his shoulder. The pain seared past his flesh, to muscle and bone, its scars branded on his heart.

Still joined, she dissolved beneath him in a puddle of trembling limbs, sobs, and spent tears.

"I'm sorry, so sorry." The words mixed with his tears and shattered, but he couldn't stop the torment, couldn't stop the pain. Acute and raw, it collapsed his muscles and clogged his mind. It leaked from his pores and dripped from his eyes, spilling from him in heavy, useless splinters.

How had he allowed this to happen? Why hadn't he been more a man and found another way? But he hadn't been strong enough, hadn't had courage or strength enough for both. Guilt shattered what remained of his integrity, spent like the seed he'd buried inside her.

He wiped her face, clearing away the torment of battle debris and soaked hair and then leaned his forehead against hers. "Can you ever forgive me?"

"There's nothing to forgive." She kissed the corners of his mouth, her tears sweet and salty on his lips. "And I'm not sorry."

Afraid he'd crush her, he rolled to his side, but Rachel reached for him until they lay facing one another, skin to skin. He couldn't look at her. Couldn't allow her his weakness. Couldn't face the shame.

"Did I hurt you?" Bathed in doubt, the question emerged as a hoarse whisper.

"No," she said as tender kisses graced his cheeks and swabbed the remnants of his tears. "This hurt you. Not me. And I'm sorry for that. But sometimes going beyond the physical to the pain inside is what's necessary." She reached around him, the warmth of her body caressing him lessened the anguish knotted in his limbs.

His body grew taut, trembled, and eased as she nourished him with the touch of her hands, embracing forgiveness she hadn't asked for and seeking answers to questions she hadn't formed. She nestled against him, her body the cooling balm to the heat of torment, an instant in its making and a lifetime in its freeing. His heartbeat settled. He did not. With nothing more he could do, he let go the guilt.

She parted his hair, fingers slow and generous, gratitude and forgiveness infused in her healing touch. To throw oneself into the fires of hell, trusting another had been a leap of faith. Faith in him. Faith he'd be there to catch her.

In a solemn moment reserved for secrets, for things unsaid and known only by two, knowing lips touched his, and she gave back what he alone had been able to give. She'd taken what she needed—to relive that night and be free of it, and he'd given in to her against his will. But not against hers.

Understanding hit him full force.

A man, a monster, void of all things human had broken her. Taken what wasn't his and walked away without thought, without remorse. Walked away with her life. And she'd turned to him—to Miles—as the one to give it back.

One bond severed, another sealed.

Lost in a fog of a torment he'd never known, he took her mouth and kissed her the way a man should kiss a woman—with the promises of tomorrow his pledge; yesterday's shadows consumed, his gift.

The armor she'd worn hadn't merely chipped or been grazed with chinks, but cracked wide open, the weight of it lost to battle. In the layer beneath, the fragile shell he'd longed to peel away had crumbled, the proof of it resting in eyes she refused to take from his. Eyes reserved for tenderness left in the wake of a death so profound the speaking of it would surely break him apart. Eyes he'd seen when she spoke of her daughter, the baby blue ones reserved for the sanctity of love.

She had turned to him in need, not the fear of it but the wisdom of knowing he could provide what she needed. He hadn't given willingly.

Nor had he been certain of the outcome. But he'd seen past his own convictions and understood had he turned her away, she'd always be searching for something, some other way to escape the demon that had taken possession of her body.

The armor hadn't protected her. It had merely kept the woman and her secret locked inside.

They lay facing one another, naked and exposed and completely undone, the distance between them a whisper, her scent heavy on the air. Silence stretched and yawned, time enough to fill a heartbeat, a breath, a touch. Time enough to span a lifetime.

He took her face, her skin as unblemished as polished pearls on his palms. She held him with her eyes, reaching beyond the physical, beyond body and expectation. And in them he saw what he needed— the whole of her, the woman complete, one who'd been waiting beneath the surface.

The woman he hadn't had the pleasure to meet.

"Hello, Sunshine." He took her mouth again, this time with enough reserve to allow her space to take it back, to sever the bond before he took her to the place where they would no longer be alone, but of one body, one mind, one soul. "It's nice to meet you."

She didn't use the moment to back away but relaxed her mouth against his. "If the first kiss was 'hello,' what was this one for?"

The question lay quietly between them, the remembrance of the first time he'd tasted the pleasure of her kiss nurturing a shared smile.

"Healing."

The memory reflected in her eyes the same way it had on his lips and she skimmed her fingers over his shoulder and along the contours of side and hip and thigh. The intimacy shivered his nerves, stroking him in places she hadn't touched.

"Make love to me, Miles."

TWENTY-EIGHT

*T*he man beside her lay open to her, not the quality of being unclothed but of full exposure, of having given more of himself than he had to give simply for the sake of another. Not to imprison her in the tomb of her past as she'd asked, but a refuge from where she'd drawn strength. To offer a safe haven to let go. To heal the wounds of a shattered soul. To offer life that comes of death.

She couldn't have stopped him. Couldn't have stopped Chastain that night any more than she could've stopped Miles. She'd been selfish in the taking of it, of even asking, but it had to be this way. It wasn't the rough nature she'd needed from Miles, but the strength in the asking and of the giving. She had to know there was nothing she could have done. Had to know it wasn't her fault. And then, she could forgive herself.

Yet guilt trickled from the corner of her eyes.

She wept.

Not for herself, but for the man who'd given what no one else could. Whose salt-soaked tears fell, dissolving the defenses she'd framed from guilt.

She wept.

Not for his grief or hers, but for the passing of a woman claimed by the overpowering strength of a demon whose venom tasted of anger, despair, and shame.

She wept.

Not for what she'd asked him to do, but for the death of something that should have died years ago. A death she'd resurrected, claimed, and sent back to hell.

She wept.

Not for a battle won, but the end of a war.

"Make love to me, Miles. Your way." The whispered prayer took shape with a delicate brush of her fingertips across his lips.

Moist, tender lips kissed her eyes, erasing the reminders of her greed. "It will be my pleasure. Give me a minute to clean up?"

She nodded, but the lifting of his weight took root, the loss immediate and intense.

Miles walked around the bed, each step unguarded from her gaze. Each step a landscape of bone and muscle and flesh. She reached for him and he sat beside her, gathering the sheet around her. Then he laced his fingers with hers. "You okay?"

"I'm scared. A little."

"You took what had to be given. To purge him. To take back control."

"It's not that. I'm scared to let go. Of this moment. Of you." She curled into his back, his presence solid and sure. "Even for a second."

"It's over." He scooted halfway around. "And I'm here."

Rachel closed her eyes. "I don't know if...if it was enough."

Miles skimmed his thumb over their clasped hands. "If it takes the rest of my life, I'll make sure it is."

How could he be sure? How could she know if it had been enough? She'd learned to dissociate—before—to step away from the reality of intimacy long enough to pretend. To profess enjoyment. But this had been different. Miles had allowed her to take command and she'd forged headfirst into the wreckage, setting right what she couldn't that night or any since. And she'd fought her way through it and survived, as if she'd been the victor in some sadistic contest. If she hadn't completely unnerved him, if he stayed, maybe...maybe it would be enough.

The prospect matured in a shuddering loss for words.

"I'll be right here. Always." He pressed their joined hands to her heart, the pleasure of his promise confessed in the intimate closeness. "Even if you choose to let me go, I won't be far." He lifted a wisp of hair from her face, the touch a feather on her skin. "You can't get rid of me that easily."

Exhaustion knows no timetable and she must have closed her eyes for a minute, for when she opened them his blue ones held hers, the peaceful nature like the gentle swell of waves on a quiet Mediterranean sea. The clean scent of soap, spicy cologne, and the heightened musk of readied male shivered her skin as if he'd touched her, tiny hairs on her body rising to meet the suggestive ministrations.

"Welcome back, Sunshine."

She rolled to her side, bringing the sheet with her. "How long have you been staring?"

"Too long and not nearly long enough."

"I'm sorry I dozed off."

"I can't think of anything I'd rather feast my eyes on. The blue of a bright summer sky." He kissed her eyes, first one and then the other, his touch a whisper on her skin. "The succulent valleys." Warm, soft lips met the hollow of her neck, the tip of his tongue teasing and leaving sudden shudders in its wake. "Golden strands of silk lifting in the breeze." He swept the hair from her face, the faint brush of his fingers a caress on her cheek. "A priceless landscape I'll never tire of."

And then he tilted her chin and his mouth was on hers, tender and giving and gentle and with a careless regard for time, his tongue the seducer, hers the enticer. He took what she offered, the kiss meant to bond, to seal the unbreakable, and of becoming one.

"Rolling hills and pearled slopes." With the grace of a confident lover, he eased the sheet away from her, and she fought the tension in the wake of exposure. He paused, nurturing her hesitation, allowing her time to accept his offer. She leaned into him, her tongue sweeping the slope of his lower lip her answer.

He lowered the sheet fully, his hands slow in the asking, gentle in the seeking and a tender closed-mouth brush of his lips turned deeply intimate, the gentle pressure of his tongue parting her lips and tentative hands caressing the slope of neck, shoulders, and breasts, exploring in the dim light. Her breaths grew shallow, her breasts heavy, nipples tingling under his seasoned touch. Gentle, knowing fingers skimmed her belly, curved around her waist and cupped her bottom, and the whimper that escaped was as unexplained as the wake of shivers his fingers roused.

With his hand light yet firm against her thigh, he paused. "May I continue to touch you?"

Afraid to breathe, afraid she'd break the spell, she nodded once and closed her eyes, keen to the seductive boldness of his arousal and the heightened state of her own.

"Tell me...if you aren't comfortable...or if I go too fast."

"It's...I'm okay." She reached to draw him down to her. "I want you inside me."

"Slow and easy," he said, his words a warm whisper on her ear. "I want to take my time, to show you how much I love you, how much this means to me." A subtly placed kiss behind her ear shivered along her neck, down one side and ended at her toes. "My body is yours, as yours is mine. It's a gift. One I'll not take for granted. And if I have you now, the way it should be between a man and woman, it will be for always. A lifetime."

"You have my heart and soul. What's mine is yours."

"Then it will be an honor to love you. To take your body, and you of mine. But for now, you're mine to pleasure. Mine to love the way a man should love a woman."

"Please...show me."

"To make love to you is to pleasure you. Think of nothing but my touch, each one an intimate embrace, a kiss from my soul to yours. Relax, Sunshine, and let go."

The things he offered no one had ever given her. Courage and strength enough to face the past. Patience enough to face the present. And hope enough to face the future, to carve a life built on the cornerstone of trust. And trust him she did, with heart, mind, and soul. And for the first time without thought—she trusted a man completely with her body, hesitations of intimacy, of her nakedness safely tucked beneath the warmth of his touch.

Restless and wanting, she slid her hands through his rumpled, messy hair. The bedhead suited him. Suited her. And left her completely undone. She scooted nearer, the shadow of his beard rasping against her cheek, yet the tenderness in his touch an intimation of what lay beneath the rugged, adventurous exterior. She breathed in his scent, bold and strong, the essence of pure male sex appeal. It surrounded her in a cloud, the reciprocation of passion nudging her in the thigh.

The pleasure of knowing her effect on him grew anxious and she took him with her hand, stroking and guiding his sheathed length as she arched her back to offer the gift of invitation.

To her surprise, he pulled away.

"Mine to pleasure. Without regard to time." He cupped her between the thighs, his touch tender and possessive, both balm and ember to a rising heat. He squeezed her there, matching her subtle moves. The artistry of his skillful hands teased and stroked her from the sensitive, swollen places the pressure of his fingers aroused, to the core of her being. The rich flavor of it purled inside her, pulsed in her blood and in places crying out for more—places foreign, untouched by passion, unfed by desire. Unfamiliar, yet fully awakened.

He stilled himself and stilled her with an intimate smile. "I can take it from here," he said, words and movement seasoned with the murmurs of a language spoken without words.

~

E asing his body next to her, he stroked her back, shoulders, and thighs, savoring her nakedness. To touch the slope of graceful bone and supple skin sent a deluge of sensations thrumming through his skin into his blood and straight south, rousing him to desperation. And he couldn't contain the groan, the slow rumble primed in need, of wanting to awaken her fully and to fill her, to complete the bond between them.

The scent of her was enough to breach the boundaries, to lose all sense of time and place and take her with abandonment. Instead, he eased her shoulders to the bed, spread her thighs with his knee, and kissed her above the smudge of blonde curls.

She sucked a breath between her teeth, stroking his offer to continue.

"I'll never stop wanting to taste you here." He skimmed his hands over the swell of hip and grazed the valley of open waist, and then he dipped his tongue into the waiting folds and sucked gently, the sweet saltiness heady with her musk.

"Oh, God, Miles." Her words shriveled into whimpers as she wound fistfuls of sheet in her hands.

Gently cradling her hips, he kissed the insides of her thighs, lingering there long and slow, taking his time to give each their proper attention. "I'll never stop wanting to pleasure you here." His beard rasped against the tender skin and a quiver shivered her thigh, the sensation blending with a subtle moan that found him trembling with need.

He paused a moment to settle himself and then moved upward to her navel. "And touch you here." His tongue circled the tiny indentation. A ripple of gooseflesh pebbled her skin, and he tamed it with moist kisses.

"Miles…" She said his name but it lacked substance, spoken with neither demand nor surrender, but touched him with its rawness.

He continued upward, the swell of her breasts kissing his chest, the mating of their nipples awakening nerves beneath his flesh. He threaded his fingers in her hair and kissed her, the remnants of wine mixed with the taste of her essence sweet on his tongue, and the joy of it vibrated muscle and bone, every nerve at full peak. "Jesus, Rachel, I want to take your tongue and never give it back. To taste you here and everywhere, always."

She drew him firmly against her, her warm, bare flesh joining his in complete surrender. "Then, please, kiss me again."

With a hunger roused from a part of him buried deep within, he took her mouth. The dance of lips and tongue radiated through his body, taking up arms against the restraint he'd carefully guarded. The need to take her pulsed against her belly and she answered, arching against him.

"Don't stop." A whisper against his mouth.

"You're enjoying this, then?"

"God…the way you kiss…it's as if your mouth is connected to the rest of your body."

A small vibration tickled her lips. "Last time I checked, it was."

"You know what I mean."

"Tell me."

"Damn you…"

"Tell me, Sunshine."

"When you kiss me…your entire body…every inch of you responds."

"Practice makes perfect," he said, teasing her mouth, "so would you care to practice a bit more?"

"Damn you, Miles Malone. Do I have to spell it out?"

Again he took her mouth, his tongue selfishly seeking its mate. He took everything she offered, intimate responses nourishing his body with each touch of her fingers and hands and skin.

They broke apart, their breaths heavy and wanting, and he moved downward, away from her intoxicating kiss and the urgency to satisfy the overpowering hunger his body demanded. He could have stayed there, nursing her mouth until he emptied himself but this wasn't about him. This was about her. Only her.

He took her breasts, the mounds of flesh firm and full in his palms, nipples deeply flushed as if dipped in a full-bodied wine. He claimed one with his mouth, swirling his tongue around and over the round nub, exploring the pebbled, sensitive flesh. He suckled there, tugging gently, each account slow and deliberate yet touched with greed. It wasn't enough. He couldn't hold her close enough or love her intensely enough to satisfy the ache, the overwhelming need to seal the distance between them, to heal what was his to heal.

She arched her back and met his weight. His answer teased her, and he indulged her with a single, gentle stroke over the light crop of curls. She pressed for more and he smiled, her nipple coming loose with a small pop. Then he took the other, giving full attention in equal measure.

"Stop...*please*." The word came as a plea and he paused, not knowing whether to stop or go on. And then her arms closed over his neck with increasing force and in answer, he drew himself fully over her.

"Not yet." A low moan, almost a growl met the demand, and he tightened his arms around her, bracing himself so he wouldn't crush her with his weight. "I'll never stop wanting to hold you as I am now, knowing you want me as much as I want you, to feel you and taste you, eager and ready."

He rocked gently above her, a knowing sigh joining his movements. "And I'll never tire of the sounds you make as your need grows."

"I don't...make sounds."

"Oh, but you do, and it's driving me crazy."

"Miles...please."

"And when you open your heart and soul and grant me your body, I want to give you what you need, to pleasure you until you cry out from the wanting and dissolve with me in release."

Their tongues met, the prelude to the unhurried dance he'd choreographed without intrusion, without interruption, without the barriers of the past. One that left her putty in his hands.

"Damn you." The whimper rolled over his ear as both plea and command, and hoarse with the effort.

The wanting, the longing to be one with her went far beyond the flesh as if his heart were being squeezed. "And when we're apart, I swear I'll ache until I see you again, touch you with my eyes until I can touch you with my heart and soul and body."

And then he entered her, sliding into her ready warmth, and she opened herself, entrusting him with her care. Joined as one, she gasped, but he stayed pressed to her, not moving, filling her wholly and fully, unwilling to continue, for God help him he wouldn't be able to take it slow.

He paused for air. He'd been oxygen-deprived on mountains not fit for humans and beneath the rapids of a raging river. But this was something more—more than thin air or drowning under water—he'd filled himself wholly with her and left no room for anything less.

"You're my one love. My life. And I'm yours, one flesh, neither of us alone." He took up the rhythm then, moving inside her, holding back but giving up all within him, and each time he filled her, he became one with her, not as he had with the blindness of greed to breach the past, but with all his heart, his mind, and the fabric of his soul. "I'll never stop wanting you. Needing you. And I swear I'll never stop loving you, beyond what words could ever say. Beyond life itself."

He couldn't draw her close enough, hold her tight enough, or find words enough. And the room around him grew dim, and he lost connection with everything but her, their bodies one, not knowing where one ended and the other began. One body, one flesh. And he loved her with his touch and the murmured notes of a language spoken without words.

Her heart beat soundly against his chest. Her hips rose to meet his and she pulled him down, her grip tight around his neck, her body tense and unmoving. Sensing her response, he stilled himself and she let go and took him with her, stroking him from within. His release began with hers, deep inside her, each shockwave an echo of his love spreading from his epicenter into her, their cries not of sadness or pain, but of completion.

Two halves of a whole.

Complete.

He stayed joined with her for a time, barely able to hold himself above her. His limbs trembled, heart threatening to climb from his chest and burst into pieces. And then he lowered himself to her side, resting his forehead to hers. "God help me, Rachel, I do love you so."

They lay comfortably tangled together, her body as much his as his was hers. She curled her foot around his leg, her toes a warm tickle on ankle and calf. Gooseflesh rose, tingling where her fingers drifted over his flesh.

The waning afternoon light spilled into the room bathing her in a warm glow. Did she feel its warmth as much as he did merely in her presence? As much as he already missed being inside her? She had no idea of her power over him. No idea what she did to him, how she could possess him, weaken him with a kiss. A glance. A touch. No idea she reduced him to a quivering mess.

But she'd trusted him to be her strength. And he secured thought to motion and pulled her into his chest. In no hurry to let her go, he rested his cheek against her hair, the simple clean fragrance and the passion of their lovemaking ripe with their mingled essence. Calming perfume and enticing potion. He'd never have enough of it. Of her.

"Can I ask what you're thinking?"

"I'm not." She sighed, a lazy, blissful whisper of air. "I just want to stay right here, with you holding me like this."

"We have all night. Every night, if it's your wish, for the rest of our lives."

"I think I might just die this way." She tilted her chin and met his eyes. "But I need to tell you something. About this. About what happened."

The sudden change of tone left a cold tingle in its wake. "You can tell me anything, Sunshine."

"Promise you won't laugh?"

The question came as both relief and intrigue. "Is it funny?"

"I don't think so."

"Then I won't laugh."

She turned on her belly, idly twirling the mat of chest hair around his nipple. If she didn't stop doing that...

"No one has ever...I've never...experienced that before." She lifted a shoulder in a shy shrug.

The meaning escaped him. After all, she'd been married, yet he sensed her hesitance and didn't want to make her any more uncomfortable by asking. "You can tell me."

"I don't exactly know how."

He kissed the top of her head. "There's no one else here. No one will hear but me."

She rolled onto her back and stared at the ceiling, her cheeks tickling his side as her mouth turned up. "This was...being with you I mean, like this, in this way was...different."

He weighed the comment, but came to no obvious conclusion. He had to know what she meant. Had to know if he'd done something wrong and how to fix it. If it could be fixed. "Care to explain 'different'?"

"More like...beautiful."

"I'm not good with words, but there are several things that come to mind when I hear the word 'beautiful'." He lifted her chin. "You. The mountains. The Arizona sky. Your body is beautiful. Can you be a little more specific?"

"It's embarrassing." A nervous giggle punctuated the trite remark and she raised the sheet over her breasts, securing it under her arms.

"I'm listening."

"I thought I was going to combust. Or, implode maybe?"

"Ah." An unexpected laugh rumbled in his chest. "Good to know."

"You said you wouldn't laugh."

"It's just that, yeah, I suppose you could describe it that way."

"This was different than any time before. With anyone."

Her words had a definite way of stroking his ego, but judging by the tone there was more to it. "Sounds good so far."

She nudged his scar and he flinched.

"When you hold me, or kiss me, it's as if there's this connection between us, one I can't explain. And when you held me that way and came inside me, my entire body filled with a warm, bright light that exploded and shattered into a million pieces and rippled through the empty spaces and filled them up."

"I see." He scooped her into his side.

"I felt complete. Or whole...for the first time. I've never experienced that."

"I think I get it, but why don't you humor me?"

"For a doctor, you're not getting this."

"I'm a tactile, visual learner."

"Damn you." A deafening pause consumed a moment of hesitation. "I've never let anyone...get close enough to...and then after Chastain...I couldn't. Even throughout my marriage, no one's ever..." She clamped a hand over her eyes. "I've never reached a climax with anyone during sex before." The confession rolled from her in a single collapse of air.

He'd expected something, perhaps some profound prophetic observation worthy of contemplation, something he could learn from to please her. But the implication needed no explanation, and he chose to keep it light.

"I'm flattered."

"I knew you'd laugh."

"I'm not laughing, but I do have something to say about it."

She teased his nipple, took his mouth hard, and then softened the touch, torturing him with a delicate brush of her lips. "And I have a feeling you're going to tell me."

Miles rolled her on top of him, the mere suggestion of another round with this amazing, complicated creature stirring him to full arousal. He wasn't merely making love to her, he was building a future, tying up the loose ends of their tattered lives. And in it he'd found what he'd been searching for, and she'd lost what she needed to lose.

"It may be the first time, Sunshine, but it damn sure won't be the last."

TWENTY-NINE

*M*iles stirred first, scooped her into his embrace, and kissed her lightly on the neck. "I'm starving." He flipped his legs over the side of the bed and stood. "I'll give room service a call. Any requests?"

The place where he'd lain next to her and loved her—*loved her completely and unrestrained*—was warm, but the loss of connection, the emptiness, roused a chill.

He came around to her side of the bed and sat, raising her into a sitting position. He took her in his arms, sheet and all, but made quick remedy of the barrier and slipped the covering from her shoulders, the sheet pooling in her lap. Her breasts free, she nudged him to turn away and nestled into his back.

"That's nice." The gravel in his voice rumbled against her breasts and she leaned in close, his body warm and solid. "Your body is meant to be touched, to be worshipped, mine to honor in doing so. I'll never tire of honoring you. Of loving you."

"Miles," she said, briefly closing her eyes, and then traced the raised welts and vicious teeth marks she'd left buried in his flesh. The violent, red autographs on his shoulder and back turned her stomach. "I'm so sorry."

He glanced over his shoulder, an artful half-smile mere inches away. "Battle wounds." He hadn't flinched, allowing her full access to what she'd let loose, and offered full acceptance in return. It wasn't the first time she'd left her mark on the flesh of someone she loved but prayed it would be the last.

"Does it hurt?"

"Not much. Jezebel's bite is worse."

"That's comforting." The comment swirled uneasily and then settled. "Wait...who's Jezebel?"

"Sweet, sweet Jezebel." A dramatic sigh softened the sharp edges of the name. "She's got one hell of a pair of soft brown eyes."

Rachel poked a raised welt and then poised to offer another.

"Ow! Okay, Sunshine." This time he shied away. "I can take a hint when someone's jealous."

"I'm not jealous." She punctuated the remark with another poke.

"Shit-fire, woman." He laughed, the deep, easy sound massaging her sensitive nipples. "Okay, okay. Jezebel is Mr. Marley's cranky old mule."

"You should've said so in the first place."

"She's somewhat gnarly if she doesn't get her treat. Like someone else I know." He shifted to face her, his easy smile reflecting the tenderness of the healer, but it slid from his face. "Battle wounds leave scars. They're proof we've fought and won." He caressed her cheek, his thumb tracing the line of jaw and neck with slow, tender movements. "Proof we survived."

She slid her fingers lower, tracing the lines of a tattoo on his left shoulder. A dog's silhouette was set in the background of an eagle in flight perched over a globe. "What does 'semper fidelis' mean?"

"It's the Marine Corps motto." The muscle beneath the tattoo tensed. "Means 'always faithful'."

She reached out to touch it, to put to flesh a part of him locked behind the black and red ink.

"And is 'improvise, adapt, overcome' a part of the motto?"

"Unofficially." He lowered her hand from his shoulder. "Rachel—"

"Is this one of those secrets you don't wish to share?"

"It's no secret. I just don't talk about it."

She disentangled the sheet, and scooted around to face him. "You don't have to tell me, but you mentioned you'd been in Iraq and that it had been a good decision to enlist."

"It was the reason I became a vet." The lines between his brows deepened, eyes set on their clasped hands. He stroked her knuckles, each action an appraisal, a contemplation that roused a distant, inward look. "That part was true."

With one hand on his bare thigh, she traced the tattoo with the other. "Tell me?"

"It's not a pretty story."

"And mine is?"

"Point taken." He stood, retrieved two hotel robes, and handed one to her.

"Why do I need this?"

"Because at forty years of age I'm no spring chicken, and if you keep touching me the way you are, I'll have to surrender to you again and I think it just might do me in."

She hid her lips between her teeth to avoid the growing amusement. "What happened to those veterinary super powers?"

He draped the robe over her. "Even Superman needs to charge his batteries now and then."

She secured the robe and shimmied up against the headboard. "How long does recharging take?"

Amusement displayed itself in a spray of laugh lines.

"Just curious." Her shoulders rose and fell in a lazy shrug. "I've crossed another item off my bucket list, but I've got a hell of a lot of lost time to make up for."

He unleashed a deep rumbling chuckle. "We've all the time in the world." He wrapped himself in the identical robe and scooted in next to her. "And I plan to make every moment count." Then he looked at her and kissed her, but neither word nor lips touched her skin. "Later."

The tingle started at her toes and spread in a warm wave, ending with a delightful shiver. The sound of his voice, the way he looked at her, and his slightest touch had conceived sensations that completely unhinged her. And if loose hinges were a sign of insanity, she had gone far beyond the need for therapy. She was addicted. And the drug Miles administered came without an anecdote.

"Your turn to share. Tell me why you traded counting elk and deer for desert camo."

He leaned back, his head hitting the padded leather headboard with a faint thump. "Because of Brenna."

"Your almost-wife who left you at the altar?"

He stared at the ceiling. "She left me a week before the wedding, but I wasn't completely forthcoming about why."

One thigh peeked from the robe and she touched him there, giving him a reassuring squeeze. With a grievous glance, he tucked her wandering hand under his arm.

"Brenna was three months pregnant."

She swiveled around, gooseflesh peppering her skin. "Oh, God, Miles—"

He raised a hand in both offer and refusal. "The pregnancy wasn't planned," he said, the words a shadowed whisper. "I don't know how it happened—well, yeah, I know how it happened, but I don't know why." He coughed into his fist. Color started at his neck and spread, and he swiped it as if he could will it away. "We were young. And broke. But we could've managed."

A flood of emotions stilled her. She pushed them away, suffocating them before they had a chance to feed, the need to hear his story overpowering the desire to allow them to breed.

"Had she told me she was pregnant, I would've tried to convince her not to do what she did, but I didn't know and I wasn't a part of the…decision." He averted his eyes. "Brenna aborted our baby, murdered our child six weeks before we were to be married."

Rachel swallowed a gasp. The admission pulsed dark and cold through her veins, the echo of his remorse seeping into the space between them.

"Our baby was mine too." The hoarseness in his voice emanated with precise accuracy, the disgust and sadness bleeding through the tough mask. "Do you know how well-formed a twelve-week fetus is?"

She did know—but couldn't voice the remembrance. Bug's ultrasound photos were in her baby book, the CDs stored safely away. The tiny body perfect. Arms. Legs. Nose. Heart beating like hummingbird wings. *Alive and safe inside her body.*

Her hand went to her belly.

A pointed silence spread, his eyes glassy and dark as if the distant memory was close enough to touch. "God knows I tried to make it work. But it wasn't the same. After. I couldn't look at her without... thinking. Imagining. I couldn't look her in her eyes and not see our son or daughter, and I know she sensed it."

He secured her into his side as if she was his tether to a life preserver. "She showed no remorse. Only relief. And it was then I had my doubts that she ever wanted kids. At least not with me." His voice was steady but steeped in fatigue, the kind earned from years of unrequited loss.

A sudden longing crept up on her, the longing to see her daughter's smile, the inquisitive eyes and unruly curls, feel her little arms around her neck, good morning kisses and the way she clung to *her* Dr. Miles. She inched toward him, curling her body to fit him, to take the suffering, to allow him to assuage an unthinkable nightmare.

"Enlisting seemed a pretty damn good idea after that." A massive sigh escorted the sobering fact. "I needed a distraction. Time to bury the son or daughter I'd never have the privilege to meet."

Could you ever truly lose a child, even to death? The miracle of creation, the blood and flesh and bone a shared bond that can never be undone. To lose a child was one thing, but to never know them another—the color of their eyes, the downy softness of baby hair, tiny fingers wrapped around yours, the quiet murmurs and gurgles, or the sweet scent of baby skin. There were no memories for him to reclaim. No dreams to recall. And he had no gravesite to visit save the one he apotheosized in his mind. He'd been made childless not by choice, but by a thoughtless, selfish act.

She traced the outline of the birthmark with her finger. A

teardrop. A tattoo on the outside for the scar on the inside—for the child he'd never know. "You must have loved Brenna very much."

"Thought I did." The deep noise he made was one she could diagnose as neither admission nor denial. "I was young." Miles tucked her head under his chin. "Didn't know what it truly meant to love someone the way I loved the thought of a child."

The instinct to take his burden wound her insides into a knot. "You've never thought about having a baby with someone else?"

"No. God no. There's not been anyone...and besides..." He bathed a pause in a long exhale and tightened his arm around her. "I can sympathize with you, Rach, the losses you've endured. And maybe I'm being inconsiderate and selfish, but I couldn't bear the thought of that kind of loss again."

The loss he spoke of had ripped her apart more than once, but once for anyone was one time too many. A tear parked itself on her nose. She wiped it away.

"Once overseas I didn't have time to think between skirmishes, and after my tour was up, vet school and then my practice occupied my time." A sluggish shrug lifted one shoulder and his face squinted briefly with it. "But a confrontation with the enemy took another life I cared about."

The rest of the story teetered precariously on the edge of speech. The conflict he bore rested in the facial lines and uneven words, his need to be free of the burden as fierce as hers had been.

Rachel sat upright. "You were my strength, Miles. Let me be yours." She tucked her chin to her chest and stroked his arm through a long pause.

"My squad depended on me but I couldn't stop the bullets." He shut his eyes briefly. "Scott and Shep were marksmen and took out the sniper, but Scott saw something I didn't and lunged at me, pushed me into the ground. Jag leapt on top of us." Miles looked up with an intensity void of outward emotion, but the sheet twisted in his fist. "Jag fell. I grabbed Scott's hand. The war sounds were unending, but somehow distant. Muffled. We stayed that way for what seemed forever, locked in this odd bubble of silence." His brow creased deeply and then softened as if the memory had seized the pain. "His hand went limp and I squeezed harder, but he didn't squeeze back. He took one more breath..."

Miles swallowed, the motion pronounced in the up and down movement of his throat. "I was the commissioned officer. A first lieutenant should be the protector, not the other way around...I knew what to do, but I couldn't fix it."

Rachel took his hand and held tight, to bring him back, to save him from that night and the pain of letting go.

"Scott had a wife and son. Wasn't a year old." He looked up then, his expression distant, lost in the rubble of the past. "I should've been the one to die that day. Not Scott. Not Jag."

She'd been there, wondered why she'd been the one left unscathed when those around her had been taken. The concept weighed on her heart but she sat resolute, to take his sorrow and bridge past to present as he had done for her.

"You were meant to live, Miles. For your family and to be the healer you are. To be here for me. For Bug." A cold silence filled the lack of his response, and she groped for words to fill it. "Is that where you met Shep?"

He dipped his chin in a single nod. "Not a good idea to strike up a friendship, get close to anyone during a war." He clamped a thumb and forefinger to the bridge of his nose. "The ghosts and nightmares follow you home."

"But Shep made it back okay."

"Crazy bastard's too ornery to die." He smiled with a sort of quiet amusement, but it seemed completely disconnected from his eyes, and her stomach shifted uneasily. "But Jag didn't. Damn mutt didn't know there was a war going on."

"Jag's a dog?"

"Mascot of sorts. Scruffy damn thing. Showed up one day during mess and never left. Lived on handouts mostly. A desert rat or bird here and there." Rachel wrinkled her nose. "Had a penchant for sniffing crotches."

"Shep or the dog?" She was far from successful in curbing a smirk, and he answered with a throaty grunt.

"I wanted to name him Klinger, after the character in *M.A.S.H.* And because if one of us moved, he was right there alongside, as if attached with an invisible leash."

She'd seen reruns of the show and recalled Klinger's theatrical efforts to be discharged from the U.S. Army field hospital during the Korean War. "If the shoe fits." This time the smirk wiggled free, spilled into her fingers and they wandered to where the dog enjoyed depositing his nose.

"If you wish to hear the rest of the story…" He took her hand from his crotch and gave it back in an animated gesture.

Reluctantly, she folded her hands in her own lap. "Please."

"I outranked Shep, but he called the honors and named him Jag. Judge Advocate General. Said he'd court-martial the four-legged bastard if he sniffed his crotch." He lifted a shoulder. "The name stuck."

Perhaps the whispers of memory filled the momentary lapse, and he surveyed the ceiling as if the story were written across the expanse of white. "I kept him alive for a time, but we had to get out of there before the enemy took our entire squad. I had to stop…I had to let him go. I couldn't save the old bastard, Rach. And I couldn't save Scott."

The aggregate movements of Adam's apple and muscle reflex left a cautionary note on her skin. "Knowing when to let go is one of the toughest things in the medical profession."

"We lost three good men that night." The distance clouding his features was one of remembrance, of regret, and of sorrow. "I couldn't save any of them any more than I could have saved my child." He made a small noise, of acceptance perhaps or the need to disconnect the past with something physical. Miles smoothed her hair, the reflection of time and of recall playing out in the slow movements.

"As soon as Shep and I were stateside, we decided on the tattoo."

"He has the same one?"

An insignificant nod seemed as distant as the look in his eyes, and he offered a smile, but it held no more strength than the imposter it was. "It was Shep's idea to add the dog. I think he did it more for me than himself." The air around them sizzled in recognition of the losses between them. "I've always had a thing for animals, but I guess I found my calling that night. Med school crossed my mind, but I figured maybe if I had the tools and the proper training, I could save someone else's buddy, someone else's Jag."

"I'm glad you chose veterinary medicine. Zoe needs her doctor."

He dipped his head and kissed the top of hers. "I think of them often. They come to me in nightmares. And Jag. Crazy mutt didn't know how to lay still without wagging his tail or sporting a smile in the way of dogs."

"Zoe's a pro when she's begging for attention or a treat."

He leaned closer and whispered in her ear. "She must've learned it from you."

"I don't beg." She opened her eyes wide to quiet the response poised to spew from him. "But speaking of treats—"

Miles laughed, the sound as reassuring as the glint that had returned to his eyes. "Haven't we indulged in treats? Twice, if I recall."

"Are your batteries charged yet?"

"We'll discuss the options after I shower." The look he gave her was steeped in caution topped with a delicious dose of challenge.

Showering with him carried its own delightful intrigue, but stepping out of the comfort of the robe and downy bed seemed exhausting. Besides, it was hovering on evening. "Actually, I meant the wine. A cheese tray from room service would complement it nicely."

He got up and let his robe fall in a heap, the taut muscles of his backside tensing as he walked away, solid and dimpled and honed from shoulder to hip in the way of a beautifully made man seasoned with maturity. "I'll take care of it. You rest."

"By the way, where did Jezebel bite you?"

He turned and walked backward. "I thought we were talking food?"

The full-frontal view offered plenty of food for thought. "Inquiring minds want to know."

Amusement grew into a smart-ass grin. "In the ass."

"So that's why you have a matched set of butt dimples?"

He spread his arms and turned the corner into the bathroom. "Compliments of Jezebel."

Rachel raised the sheet over her nose to smother the audible amusement. Water splashed the shower tiles. She sighed, fluffed the pillows, and rolled onto her back, counting the ceiling tiles and contented beats of her heart until he returned.

A plate of seasonal fruit and a meat and cheese platter sat on the balcony table between two patio chairs, and the half-empty bottle of chardonnay stood alongside an ice bucket swaddling a couple of beers. The morning had left her exhausted; the afternoon limp and thoroughly giddy in its afterglow, and the two glasses of wine she'd consumed while Miles showered had enhanced her relaxed state.

A tailored assortment of sounds came from inside the room. Miles' muffled voice and activities added complement to the rustle of trees lifting their leaves in the breeze. Birds settled into their evening songs, rising above the chatter of children in the midst of pool play.

Ice rattled against the metal bucket and she turned to see Miles twisting a beer top and the quiet hiss that followed. His hair lay in wet tendrils, muscles of shoulder and back rippling with the small movements. Loose gray sweats hung low on his hips and past the tops of his bare feet.

The bottle cap clattered to the table. He took a long pull on the beer and set the bottle down. Though she'd turned back to face the mountains, she knew he'd come up behind her. Still, she tensed when he touched her shoulder, a selfless gesture he offered to make his presence known. And then he reached around and took her in his arms. Her body gave, and she leaned against his bare chest, languishing in the scents of shampoo and soap and the bold male undertones he couldn't conceal if he tried.

Early evening spread through the sky in a variety of red, gold, and orange, and a skiff of clouds lay in streaks across the horizon, their edges painted in the rich purple of a Four Peaks amethyst. The sunset magnified the mountain silhouette, and the man holding her magnified his presence a little more every day. The sunset filled her with its warm beauty, and Rachel pinned the moment to memory.

"I think we're set for the night." Miles found his way to the slope of belly beneath her robe, his touch soothing in its explorations. "Hotel's cancelled, we've got food and drink, and an amazing sunset."

"It's gorgeous, isn't it?"

"Red sky at night."

She turned to face him, allowing the robe to open fully.

"I'm a Marine, not a sailor, but Jesus, Rachel, your touch, your skin, you next to me is pure delight."

"I could stay right here until my last sunset on earth. I never want to let go of you. Of this."

He urged her closer until they were skin to skin. "You'll have to be the one to let go, because I plan to keep you right here." He took both her hands then and placed them over his heart. "Until my lungs no longer breathe and my heart beats no more."

A kiss, moist and soft and steeped in forever touched her lips. "Hello, Miles Malone. It's nice to meet you."

"Hello, Sunshine."

He deepened the kiss, his tongue seeking, finding, coaxing, and the whole of his body joined in the quest.

"That was for healing. One step, one touch, one kiss at a time."

He tasted of beer and promises and forever, and she longed to sample what he'd yet to offer. "That last part sounds nice. Your kiss tastes of beer and so much more."

"Thought you didn't care for the taste of beer?"

"It's different on you."

The flavor of the implication curled one side of his mouth. "I'm not sure I want to shower in it. Even for you."

"Not all over, silly. Here." She distinguished the observation with a brush of her lips to his. "And...there are a variety of things I have yet to taste on you. And touch." She splayed her fingers through the coarse twists of hair covering his pecs and then traced the line from navel to groin, his skin rippling beneath her fingertips. "You're a nice shade of not really dark…but not quite blond down here. I hadn't noticed."

"So are you…down there. And I have noticed."

"You don't mind?"

"What? The natural state of a woman's body?"

"Some men prefer—"

"You're perfect, Sunshine. As for the body part in question…fluffy, trimmed, or bare, it's just right." The sound he made, an unmistakable suggestion dressed in a hint of a chuckle, shivered on her skin. "Mine to enjoy, to pleasure…in whatever state."

Though the breeze held the warmth of coming summer, goose-flesh tingled her skin, and she tucked an embarrassed smile against his flesh. Miles closed the robe around her and she turned toward the sunset, content in the safe haven of his embrace.

The light had changed so slowly she'd barely noticed, the colors as fragile as stained glass. The first evening stars had popped out between a skiff of clouds, tiny pinpricks in a velvet sky.

The need for solitude would remain; those times sneaking up without warning. But the definition had changed. Miles had fused himself to her heart and he would be her anchor when being alone wasn't enough. And when he looked at her, he saw past the rape, past the victim and saw the woman whole.

Maybe she could too.

As the sun dipped behind the Arizona mountains, she said goodbye to the day, goodbye to a malignant piece of her past, and hello to a man who nourished her with the touch of his hands and with every beat of his heart, the promise of forever sealed in his kiss.

THIRTY

The snow came without warning. Not a freak storm, but one that changed the shape of impending spring. For several years, fierce snowstorms had drenched the mountains with unprecedented amounts of snowfall and temperatures far below normal, and winter often held a firm grip well into May and June. The frigid winters hadn't been easy on Grandpa, but the skiers loved it. Including Miles.

April snows weren't unusual in Estes Park, but spring had come early this year. Miles had promised a bounty of baby wildlife and hillsides of wildflowers around Emerald Lake, and her first hike in the mountains held her in the clutches of intrigue. But the late snow dampened that idea, and with Miles away on a rescue incident, Rachel's sense of dread deepened.

Outside the windows of The Villages' activity room, the remnants of winter covered the earth and the promise of spring in a fresh blanket of white. Reading a steamy historical romance wrapped up in a blanket by the fire in Miles' cabin seemed far more attractive than the stirring of restless thoughts the late spring storm stirred. At least he'd be off the mountain and safe at home.

The earth held its breath and so did she.

Despite the long-sleeved T-shirt under her scrubs, uneasiness shivered along her nerves. Unable to shake the silent alarm puncturing the peaceful fall of snow, she rubbed her arms and backed away from the wall of windows.

"He's been down this road before."

It hadn't been on good terms, but she'd heard the voice before. The woman's husband had been on the edge of death, the stress enough to set anyone's raunchiest attitude loose. Rachel swiveled around, the same steel-blue eyes Glenda had bequeathed her son staring back at her.

"I don't intend to stand by and watch my son go through that kind of heartache again, Mrs. Caldarone."

If coming across as cordial had been her intent, she'd missed the mark completely. But if her intention bordered on callous—Glenda had dosed her with a full syringe.

Glenda pursed her lips as if holding back the contents of a burgeoning dam. One finger at a time, she removed her leather gloves and then placed one on top of the other—palms facing—in a practiced ritual paced to extend the unsettling pause.

"Please call me Rachel, and I'm sorry, Glenda, but I'm afraid I'm not following what you mean."

Glenda gripped the gloves in one hand and placed her other on Rachel's forearm. Her face shone with the elegance of manufactured youth, but her hands wore the signature of age. "May I have a minute of your time?"

"Of course." Rachel glanced first at the clock above the double doors and then outside. Twilight hung in balance, escorting the last of daylight, and the snow had matured from tiny pellets smaller than grains of rice to thick, downy feathers. Apprehension nipped at her, chills chasing up her spine one vertebra at a time. "I have about ten minutes before rounds."

"I consider it safe to say I know my son better than he knows himself." She clasped her hands, the culmination of stature and determination reflected in the concise bundle. "I don't claim to know what's going on between you two, but he's got the same look about him as he had with his fiancée." She peered down a dainty, straight nose. "You do know about Brenna?"

The name quivered inside her. Pangs of jealousy? Or was it the way she'd said her name? There were no secrets between her and Miles, but Brenna's wasn't a story she cared to revisit. The question served more as the opening to a safety deposit box she had no business peeking into.

"Yes, Miles told me about her."

"Then I don't need to remind you how badly that woman hurt him."

Rachel adjusted her feet and fiddled with the stethoscope around her neck. "Mrs.—"

Glenda raised a hand. "So, am I to assume he's confided everything?"

"There are things we haven't discussed." Rachel took Glenda by the arm and turned her toward the exit.

"And I understand there are some *things* in your past," Glenda said, imposing an articulate emphasis on 'things', "that one might say could interfere with a relationship?"

The light dinner she'd consumed began to play a wicked game of cat and mouse in her stomach, but Rachel ignored it and planted her feet in the center of the doorway.

"If you're referring to the fact I was raped, then yes, Miles knows. He knows every sordid detail and he's been nothing but understanding and supportive." The urge to lash out, to temper this woman's preconceived notions tipped on the verge of spilling over. But the desire to remain resolute, for Miles if not for herself, overpowered the impulse to set this woman straight. "You've raised a remarkable man."

Glenda had averted her eyes and then brought them back around. "I happen to think so, too. I also know he's vulnerable."

Rachel crossed her arms and stuffed a response she'd regret behind a slight frown. She had considered everything Miles was, but vulnerable wasn't one of them.

"That woman chewed him up and spit him out." Glenda's pale blue eyes turned stringent. "And I will not stand by and let another woman do that to him again."

The dagger-edged comment landed in the center of her heart, but she recognized the provenance: She was his mother. He, her offspring. A bond incapable of rupture.

"He's a good man. My son needs someone who can give him what he wants. What he needs. He's got enough baggage and doesn't need the burden of anyone else's."

The words chased her and grabbed hold, a noose around her neck. She had to get back to work, away from the strangling words. Rachel seized the last bit of resolve spinning in a kaleidoscope of contradiction and pushed a smile through the rubble.

"I understand, Glenda. Perfectly." Rachel checked the time again.

"Something wrong?"

The longer Miles remained on the slopes, the heavier the knot in her stomach, already the consistency of dried cement. But she didn't want to admit it. That her dread stemmed from a skiing accident. That the longer Miles was gone, the deeper the fear he wouldn't come back.

"There's a skier missing on Flattop, and Miles left early this morning."

"Ah. I see. Search and rescue incident." Glenda's breathy complaint did little to soften the antipathy she'd embedded in the conversation. "Yes, Mrs. Caldarone, he's risking his life for someone silly enough to ski during a spring storm. People don't think, do they? It's the warmest spring we've had in five years and the combination of thaw, freeze, and new snow is an accident or God forbid, an avalanche waiting to happen. It's circumstances similar to this…"

Glenda's words dropped to the floor and skittered along the tiles unheard.

Five years

Five years since Nico had gone missing. It had been snowing that day too. A day like this one. Did these incidents always last this long? Why hadn't Miles called? The strain of his absence grew stronger, the weight too heavy to ignore.

The drone of Glenda's admonition of careless skiers collided with the past and staked its claim. Suspended in the fog of memory, she drifted into the resurrection of the past...

Officer Chris O'Bannion twirled his beanie in a nervous circle. "He was last seen on Flattop Mountain, Rachel." He cleared his throat and glanced at his partner as if seeking permission to continue. "Near The Drift."

"What do you mean last seen?"

Chris' leather police jacket groaned as he touched my arm, but I jerked away and picked up Zoe instead. She loved company, but tonight she was antsy, wiggling in my arms. I suspected she wanted them out of here as much as I did. What else would make Zoe fidget this way?

"The skiers ahead of him waited—it's an unspoken courtesy to make sure someone knows when you leave, where you're headed." Chris brushed melted snow from his collar. "They waited, Rachel...long past a reasonable amount of time for Nico to make it down, but he never showed up."

Our baby stirred, a flutter of life against my growing belly. "He must have taken a different way and it's taking him longer with the new snow, that's all." I cradled our baby, bumping and pressing from inside me, and peered over Chris' shoulder and out the window, sure the Jeep's headlights would veer into the drive any minute. Lights flickered and I willed the vehicle to turn in...but it continued up the road, dragging my heart with it.

"Mrs. Caldarone?"

I looked back. Zoe's vet. What was he doing here? He too removed his beanie. His hair fell over his forehead, melted snow a slow drip...drip...drip from his forehead to the floor.

"I'm with Larimer County Search and Rescue. We've had a crew of men and women searching for your husband for hours. We won't give up our efforts, but the storm's covered his tracks. Conditions deteriorated quickly on Flattop with the heavy snow and wind. I'm so sorry...but there's no sign of him." He removed a scarf from inside his jacket and handed it to me. "Except for this."

Miles. Zoe's vet's name is Miles. Why was he glaring at me as if I'd lost Zoe? She was in my arms. Safe. I wasn't one of his grieving pet owners. Damn him. Damn them all. He'll look the fool when Nico comes home. All of them will.

I raised the scarf to my face. A spec of debris scraped my cheek, and I closed my eyes. Still warm from Miles' body, the scarf erupted with Nico's scent, faint traces of him woven among the threads. I pressed the scarf to my face to keep his image alive—to keep him alive. Close. To keep him from leaving me. From leaving our baby.

The room shifted, or maybe it was our baby reaching for her daddy. Maybe I was the one reaching. Reaching for what wasn't there. I breathed in Nico's scent and exhaled what strength remained in my knees, and Zoe's vet was there, catching me before I hit the ground.

Missing.

Nico was missing.

THIRTY-ONE

*D*etective Chris O'Bannion squinted, glancing from Miles and then to Shep. "Care to let me in on what you're thinking?"

Miles stabbed both ski poles into the snow. "Could be hypothermia." Suspicion hung from the statement, leaving little doubt he didn't believe it. He'd worked rescues alongside Shep long enough to know the veteran wasn't buying it either.

"She sounded hysterical, not delirious." Chris brushed the accumulating snow from his shoulders.

Miles gripped his poles. "That's what's bugging me."

A quiet man by nature, Shephard Dawson lifted a pole and prodded the snow several times, an exercise fueled by impatience—one Miles had seen numerous times when the situation didn't sit right with the seasoned rescuer. Shep was as anxious as he was to act on the woman's accusations, the only way either of them could put the niggling hunch to rest.

"So…if she's not completely bonkers from advanced hypothermia, what the hell was she babbling about?" Chris toggled from one to the other.

Chris hadn't been long on the volunteer SAR squad, but having been raised at the base of the Rockies, his knowledge of the slopes was a valuable resource to the team. But he hadn't embraced the intimacy of the mountain and lacked the intuition of an experienced rescuer.

"It's more a hunch." Miles handed Shep a subtle nod, confirming the answer years of working together asked without uttering a single word.

"You think she actually saw another victim out there?"

Shep pulled the goggles from atop his head and wiped them with a gloved hand. "Won't know unless we check it out."

"Their group's been accounted for." Chris twisted a pole, widening the hole he'd punched in the frozen snow. "Incident commander said there've been no reports of missing skiers."

Miles lifted his goggles and set them on top of his helmet. "We're going back to the avalanche site to be sure." Ice and snow pelted his exposed skin, each one a punctuation, each one a stinging reminder of the volatility of a spring storm and unstable mountain. But the hunch was strong, and if someone was out there...he had to know for sure.

Shep stooped to check his bindings. "It won't take long, buddy."

"Go back to the team, Chris, and wait for us there."

"You guys are out of your fucking minds! Flattop isn't stable. The whole side of the mountain came down and they've closed the slope. And correct me if I'm wrong, but that means to all skiers. Not just the smart ones."

"Shep and I can handle this."

"Fine. Put your lives on the line again." Chris shoved his hands through the ski pole's wrist straps. "I'm going with you."

"This isn't up for debate."

"Tough shit, asshole. Last time I checked I was an adult capable of making my own decisions."

"Has nothing to do with adulthood." Miles replaced his goggles. "We need somebody to stay behind to check in with the team. To let them know where we've gone."

"I know these slopes better than either of you."

"Dammit, Chris! You have a family. If something happens—"

"Fine. Go. Get the fuck off my mountain." Heavy breaths misted into clouds. Chris sidestepped his skis, stopped suddenly and turned back. "Hey, asshole." He looked directly at Miles, opened his mouth, and then closed it as if he wasn't sure if he should speak. "I won't be the one to tell Rachel this time if this mountain swallows your sorry ass."

Miles saluted, an artificial gesture meant to assuage his friend's apprehension, but a quiet shiver went with it. So many years had come and gone without a second thought for his welfare. In the deserts of Iraq bullets whizzed by so close he swore he felt the draft and smelled the gunpowder, and yet he'd put himself between the enemy and his troops. He'd spent days and nights drowning in the bottom of a bottle after Brenna's *decision*. And the rescue incidents he'd volunteered for defied the laws of survival. He'd never had a reason to care, to set his selfish ways aside. But the idea of leaving Rachel and Bug alone seized him in a way he never expected.

"Have a cold one waiting for us." Shep grinned, a mischievous thing that took up the space his helmet and goggles didn't hide.

Chris tucked both ski poles into his side. "I'm not your fucking barmaid," he said and used both middle fingers to escort his buddies into the shitstorm.

"We love you too, Detective." Miles laughed, and Shep sent the perturbed detective a noisy kiss with both gloved hands.

They dug their poles into the snow.

"You assholes got your radios and beacons on?"

Miles and Shep each raised a pole in answer and walked their skis to the edge of the slope.

"Then why the hell do you need me to tell the team? They know damn well where you are."

Shep and Miles exchanged a knowing glance.

"Semper fi."

Miles tossed him a two-fingered salute. "Semper fi."

Shep leaned into the slope. Miles followed a few seconds behind and as he gathered speed, his skis grabbed, edges slicing through the powder and into the icy layers beneath. They made their way down the piste in a crisscross pattern, snow spraying in wide arcs from their skis.

The downhill rush expanded his lungs with frigid air, and wet snow mixed with fresh powder stung the exposed skin in the places the goggles, beanie, and helmet didn't cover. Miles moved without effort or thought, his body synced with the mountain, mind in tune with the man ahead of him. The wind rushed past, the exhilarated voice of nerve and muscle crying out for more.

Time passed in a blur of trees and the rhythm of the skier in front of him. Nearing the halfway point to their destination, Shep veered off the manicured slope, weaving in and out of trees close enough to lash at his jacket. Snow fell in clumps in front and behind his teammate. Miles plowed through them, knees bending and twisting.

"You crazy bastard." Miles half mumbled, half laughed and followed his buddy into the wilderness backcountry and through narrow limestone couloirs. The snow deepened, drifts concealed among the keen shadows of rock and evergreen.

The downward descent steepened. His pulse picked up speed.

Shep knew the shortcuts, along with the dangers in the best of conditions. So did he. With the daily thaw and refreezing at night and layers of heavy, wet snow and powder on top, the snowpack wasn't stable. It lay like the bank of a raging river, ready to slough, ready to give way and churn its way to the bottom in an unforgiving and deadly ride.

Shep whipped a tight right. His skis bit into the virgin snow, his form lost in the snowy camber of a swooping rooster tail.

"Sonofabitch. You're headed for Devil's Horn." The shortcut would take several minutes off their descent—minutes that could be the difference between life and death for a buried skier. But it didn't come by its name by being a prudent route.

The backcountry plummeted downward. Their speed increased. Adrenaline spiked his blood, the drug-like rush fueling the automatic movement of muscle and joint.

Down...down...down.

Shep leaned into his skis and shot off the cliff, nothing but airspace between body and mountain…and was gone.

Five seconds.

Six. Eight. Ten.

And then he, too, exploded off Devil's Horn. He hung suspended, weightless, an eagle drifting above a world that ceased to exist. Miles spread his legs. The rush let loose in a long bellow that fell flat in the snow-laden sky, but the reverberations hurtled through his body until gravity hurled him into the downward plunge.

The bottom milliseconds away, he bent his knees, skis busting through the thin layer of powder and into the hardpack beneath. Shock waves rippled through muscle and bone as his body absorbed the impact. Lungs burning and every nerve on fire, Miles whipped in beside Shep. Breathing hard, he glanced back at the cliff and then to his buddy.

"You're one crazy sonofabitch, you know that?"

"Takes one to know one." Shep took off, weaving in and out of trees and through chutes.

The avalanche had occurred not far from where they were, but the woman they'd rescued had seen the skier farther east. Closer to The Drift. It made sense. The Drift wasn't for the average skier, but without knowing the area, skiers often took a wrong turn and ended up in terrain they couldn't handle. He'd recovered plenty of unsuspecting skiers from mishaps, and packed his share of bodies with bloody gashes, head injuries, or bones that had splintered as easily as toothpicks from a too close encounter with a tree or a hidden drop-off like Devil's Horn.

Most wore the battle scars to tell the tale another day. Some weren't as lucky.

Shep slowed to a stop and let Miles catch up. "Got anything on your beacon?"

"Nothing."

"Might not have been wearing one." Shep lifted his goggles and scanned the area. "The Rockies are magnificent until one of these babies comes roaring down the mountain and leaves a trail of debris and shit. Looks like somebody pulled the ring on a grenade on a fucking battlefield."

"The force behind it takes anything in its path. Lives included."

"Something I'll never get used to."

Shep didn't have to spell it out. The images it conjured had nothing to do with the mountains and everything to do with an Iraqi desert—thousands of miles away in time and distance yet close enough to touch.

"Let's hope that woman was bat-shit crazy." Shep pointed to his left, breaths swirling in misty clouds. "Avalanche followed the canyon," he said and replaced his goggles.

"Said she spotted the skier east of here."

"What the hell was she doing skiing the glacier? It's spring thaw. Not the most brilliant decision."

Miles leaned on his pole. "Neither is skiing off Devil's Horn during avalanche season."

"That's different. We know the area."

"Doesn't make it any less reckless."

"Funny," Shep said, taking up his poles, "somebody who thinks they're smarter than I am followed this stupid bastard off that sixty-foot cliff."

Miles' grin offered no argument. "I'll take this end. You take the other side closer to where we found the woman."

"The avalanche could have carried her away from the sighting."

"This one will take a little ingenuity. It's a goddam maze of booby traps."

"Spring thaw's been a bitch. Not enough winter snow and it got too warm too fast." Shep pulled off a glove with his teeth, stuffed it into his armpit and checked his watch. "Doesn't leave us much time," he said, blowing on his fingers and then replacing the glove, "if this weather doesn't clear."

"Few hours tops." Miles offered his fist. Shep responded with a hearty fist-bump. "Godspeed, buddy."

"Be safe, my friend."

"Now you're concerned for my welfare after you lured me off Devil's Horn?"

"Fucking awesome, wasn't it?"

A burst of exhilaration pumped through Miles' veins. "Yeah, since we made it without causing another avie or ramming a tree up our ass."

Shep grabbed Miles' shoulder and gave it a good shake. "You've got a chance at a family now too. Don't blow it by dying out here."

"I don't plan on it."

"Good." A curious concoction of relief and droll humor marked Shep's grin. "Carrying your carcass out of here isn't high on my to-do list."

Miles laughed and took off across the scabrous terrain, dodging protruding spruce limbs, splintered trees, and debris mixed with hard, lumpy snow and icy patches. Skiers call it crud. He called it shit.

Miles surveyed the area with a soldier's keen eye, as if scanning a war zone for survivors, and then skirted the area closest to the tree line. If a skier had gone down, this was the most likely place. Dammit —where was the beacon signal? Every skier should wear one, but some people think they're invincible. Hadn't he and Shep proved that? The free-fall off Devil's Horn had pushed his adrenaline beyond the point of exhilaration—albeit not out of the realm of foolish. But damn...the rush!

The early spring thaw had slowed with the coming of the storm, but the evidence of the rapid fluctuation in temperature took with it the accumulation of years of ice and snow. Craggy rock formations jutted from places unexposed for years. Above the muffled silence of falling snow and swoosh of skis through the icy terrain, Miles listened, instincts on high alert. He moved cautiously across the wasteland, combing the area for signs of life.

Dark shapes wove silently through the trees. *Elk.* They trotted in single file away from the search area. Caution spiked his blood. Did their intuition sense something? Or were they merely escaping from unwanted intruders? Migrating to the first fresh sprigs of grasses and wildflowers in the lower meadows seemed the logical choice, and he resumed the search.

The hard snowpack beneath him creaked and groaned, bursting to life after years of unusual snowfall. Water trickled somewhere nearby, the first of dozens of waterfalls that would spring from outcrops of cliffs and overflow the creeks and rivers. Fall River would run big this year. Rachel loved the sound—water running briskly over river rocks and tumbling into the pool below his house. And with her by his side—

Miles pulled up. Set his poles. Cocked his head. Listened. Waited. The earth paused. Held its breath. So did he. An eerie quiet silenced the woods, his heartbeat the only sound breaking the stillness.

And then he heard it.

A slow rumble built to a crescendo. He cleared his goggles. A white cloud billowed across the canyon as a wall of snow and ice roared down the side of the mountain.

Fuck. Shep.

"MALONE!"

His name echoed between his ribs. The earth came alive under him. He stabbed the snow with his ski poles, but the flow took hold. Miles braced for impact. It hit him full-force, upended him, and crushed him into a rock crevice. His ribs gave. Lungs collapsed.

The roar died and his world went black.

THIRTY-TWO

*G*lenda snapped her fingers, the sound as sharp as a dry twig splitting in two. "Still with me, dear?"

The sound jolted Rachel from the voice of remembrance. "Guess my mind was elsewhere. Miles is on a mission, but he's an expert skier and the SAR team is with him."

"Mmm." The one-syllable reply was short but teeming with conjecture. "True. But when the mountain decides to turn itself inside out, even the best skiers can't outrun it. Avalanches are wicked creatures."

Rachel stubbed the callous comment into the tiles with toe of her shoe. "Has Miles contacted you by chance?"

"Good heavens, no. He knows I worry and is considerate enough not to tell me he's taken a rescue call."

The subtle insinuation wheedled its way under her skin, and she scraped her toe across the tiles squishing the remark as she would an unsavory insect. "I'm sure he'll be back soon."

"They'll search all night if they don't find the missing skier." Glenda's stark statement added another notch to Rachel's heightened state of concern.

She had to get out of here, away from this woman, the insinuations and the memories, away from the weight of mounting dread. "Is there something I can do for you, Glenda?"

"Yes, there is." Glenda placed a gentle but firm hand on Rachel's arm. "Don't hurt my son." She'd reached a level of sternness, but the crusty spirit crumbled to supplication. "Please."

The woman's churlish demeanor withered and died, the prickly remarks the words of a mother who would protect her child at any cost. Miles hadn't been a child for many years, but wouldn't she protect Bug in the same way? Do or say anything out of love for her? No matter what her age?

"I could never hurt Miles." The truth left Rachel queasy.

"Good. Now perhaps you can convince him to get a haircut. He looks...homeless...worse than one of those stray animals he's always taking in."

The sudden need to get back to what she understood straightened her stance. "I understand Randall's physical therapy is coming along nicely."

Glenda's mouth opened, the words amputated before they had a chance to spew.

"I thought I heard my name."

Rachel pivoted to find Zoe acting as chaperone, a jubilant wave from the older Malone, and a quirky smile she recognized. His mother may have given Miles his steel-blue eyes, but Randall had given him a smile that crinkled the corners of his eyes. One that gave her strength and drained the feeling from her knees.

"How's my favorite nurse?"

Randall Malone had graduated from walker to cane and the tap-tap-tap of the rubber tip squeaked against the tiles as he hobbled along the hallway. Zoe's short legs worked triple-time alongside his slow, cautious gait, and every few feet she'd glance up to assure her charge was following the rules. If he decided to veer off-track, Zoe turned into a six-pound bundle of pissed off Yorkie equal to the spite of a raging wolfhound.

Rachel snapped her fingers. Zoe sprinted beside her and sat until Randall reached them. Zoe spun in circles, all bets off, her bobbed tail working overtime in a blur of wiggles. Her job complete, she was ready to socialize.

Rachel took Randall's unoccupied arm. "You and your new hip have become good friends."

"No thanks to my physical therapist." His tone had a tinge of frost that matched an exaggerated frown. "He's a sadist."

"Patrick is the best PT on staff. He isn't that bad, is he?"

"Yes." Randall wiggled his shoulders as though shooing a pesky fly. "The man's got a psychotic appetite for inflicting pain."

"Definitely a keeper." Glenda crossed her arms, the sassy remark unhindered by the brazen gesture. "I should see about hiring him full-time."

"The man's a first-class guerilla." He waved his hand in an attempt to shoo the fabricated family of the pesky fly. "And persistent. Worse than a dog with a bone and I happen to be a juicy one he's intent on gnawing on."

"I'm certain you'll survive Patrick's demands."

Glenda's long fingers tightened on her arms, fluorescent lights highlighting the deep red manicured nails. "I need to have a chat with this Patrick about upping his game."

"You'd like him." Randall leered at her. "He's quite handsome."

Glenda raised her chin in silent question.

Rachel interrupted with a deliberate, noisy cough. "Patrick must be doing something right. He's got you motoring the hallways as adeptly as a seasoned trucker I once knew." Dottie, the Woodland Hills busybody, bounced through her mind.

Randall hooked the cane over his wrist and kissed the back of Rachel's hand. "I understand it's all due to a lovely, caring nurse." He reconnected the cane with the floor and leaned into it. "Miles told me about your all-night vigil and how you talked him out of doing away with me."

Glenda retrieved her gloves. "I would have seconded that vote had Miles asked me."

Randall smacked his cane across her bottom. "No one asked your opinion."

"No one asked for your smart remarks." Glenda swatted at the cane and then Randall. "Or your licentious actions."

"But you're such a lovely opponent, worthy of my efforts."

"Quit your self-righteous attempt to sway Mrs. Caldarone's opinion or your debauched attempt at humor, or whatever you're trying to prove and keep walking. We need to get out of here or the snow will become too deep and I'll be stuck here with you all night." Glenda wiggled her fingers into her gloves.

Randall took advantage of Glenda's preoccupation and ran the end of his cane between her legs.

Glenda gasped.

He waggled his eyebrows.

She slapped his arm.

"Spending the night with me would certainly tame the fire in that hot body of yours. And your tongue."

Glenda glared at him, an obvious comeback stuck behind a tightly pinched mouth.

Rachel clamped her lips together, afraid a laugh would betray her conclusions about the droll exchange. She'd been around the elderly a long time, and though these two might come across as opposite ends of a stick of dynamite, love seeped between the teasing banter as noticeably as smoke through a keyhole.

"It'll be dark soon and the roads will be slick." Rachel steered the conversation back toward the path of civility. "You'd better take Randall home so he doesn't fall and end up back in the hospital."

Glenda grumbled. "Better here than home."

Randall mumbled something incoherent and stooped to give Zoe a nice scratch under the chin, whispered to her and prudently straightened up. "Not bad for an old man with brand-new hardware." He clicked his tongue. "And as for you," he said, giving Rachel a prolonged hug, "take care of my son. He's mighty fond of you and that little girl of yours. Haven't seen him this happy in years."

Preoccupied with her coat buttons, Glenda paid no attention, or chose to ignore her husband.

Rachel clasped Randall's hands and squeezed. Warmth crept up the back of her neck. "I will."

"And besides…" Randall straightened and took Glenda's arm, his six-foot height reduced by the forward tilt of his hips. "I need someone around who isn't hell-bent on pulling the plug."

Glenda tugged at his reluctance of forward motion. "You're worth a hell of a lot more dead than you are alive." The look she shot him was staunch but tinged with an air of greedy mischief.

A bustle of voices from the main entrance filtered into the hallway. They all turned and Zoe took off, all four legs a blur as she sprinted down the hallway and then came to a skidding halt.

Flanked by an Estes Park police officer, a man in a red SAR jacket rounded the corner.

Chris.

"No-no-no-no-no." A brew of strangled words found voice outside her head. "This isn't happening."

She couldn't be sure she'd spoken aloud. She couldn't be sure she was still standing. She couldn't be sure of anything but the world falling out from under her feet, and she latched onto Randall to steady the room.

She waited, breathless.

The men approached, but Miles wasn't among them.

THIRTY-THREE

*P*ain stabbed his chest. His goggles had taken a direct hit and sat precariously on his face. He blinked, but he was blinded by darkness and his head throbbed, blood pounding in his ears as if lodged upside-down in a dark cave.

Think, Malone. This isn't your first rodeo.

In an effort to slow his heart, he synced shallow breaths to avoid the sharp pain in his lower rib cage. Shit. He couldn't afford broken ribs.

One. Two. Three…breathe.

He couldn't be dead, his head and ribs hurt too much. Tried to move. Couldn't. Each time he made an effort, white-hot pain pierced his chest. Shit. His helmet was wedged tight. But how? Where? Rocks? Ice? At least he could breathe. Barely. But for how long? How long had he been here? Had hypothermia set in? He blinked again, ice-cold lids folding over blind eyes.

Muffled voices. Rescuers? He tried to call back, but razor-sharp pain bit into his ribcage, and snow packed against his throat and chest strangled his voice. Stuck. Pinned in an icy prison of darkness. Pinned like a fucking pretzel.

Something tugged his foot. Laughter. He's buried alive and some asshole finds it funny? His legs moved and then something brushed his ass. More muffled laughter. He had to be delusional, hypothermia making mush of his brain, and he failed to find the humor.

"Hey, Malone! Mind if I take a selfie with your ass? Quite scenic against the backdrop of the Rockies."

Shep? Was that sonofabitch laughing?

Miles concentrated, willed his legs to bend. The fabric scraped, but didn't come free. And he still couldn't talk or move his head. Or breathe without the plunging knife doing a fair job of dissecting his lungs.

"Maybe I'll post a twenty second video on YouTube instead. This baby's gonna go viral."

Fool *was* laughing. He was buried and the bastard was in hysterics. Nice, Dawson.

The weight suffocating him began to ease. At least the asshole was digging. His torso moved and then his arms, snow and ice dribbling down his neck. The darkness gradually paled, and he was able to move his head.

"You're free, Malone. Come on up for air."

He waved his legs in search of a foothold but there was nothing solid, and Shep's accompanying laugh turned to a howl. Miles forced the helmet from its tight wedge and the weight of his body threw him backward and out of the mountain's vice-grip. The light blinded him, but the mocking echo of Shep's laugh came from his right, and he reached for his buddy's hand.

With Shep's help, Miles hoisted himself upright. Dazed, he looked around. "What the hell happened?"

"Another avalanche on the opposite side of the canyon must have triggered..." Shep doubled over, laughing so hard he couldn't catch his breath, and the urge to wipe away the shitty grin curled Miles' hands into fists. Shep hauled in a ragged breath. "...must have triggered a baby one above you. You were upside down with your butt..." Another fit of laughter erupted. "...with your butt pointed to the sky. Didn't need your beacon. You were quite visible with your yellow ass shining brighter than a fucking torchlight."

Blood trickled from Miles' lip, and he wiped it with a gloved hand. What he really wanted to do was cram the damn thing down Shep's throat. "Where the hell are my skis?" He gathered his wits and took inventory of the mishap and the rest of his body. His ribcage screamed. "Holy shit-fire."

Shep pointed to a snowbank a few feet away where Miles' skis stuck at a precarious angle. "Never taken a selfie with someone's ass before." He broke out laughing again, clutching his abdomen. "It's already trending on Twitter. Here, check it out." Shep shoved the phone at him.

"You sick bastard," Miles said with complete sincerity, but Shep's laugh was contagious, and he found himself holding his ribcage, chuckling to himself. Ignoring the pain, Miles grabbed his skis. "If you're done making fun of my ass, which happens to be green not yellow, we better get out of here before I shove yours in a rock crevice." He shielded his face from the stinging snowflakes and pointed uphill at the point they'd begun their search. "Or before the rest of this mountain decides to come down on top of us."

Miles sat near an overhang to snap his boots into the bindings and came within inches of another deep crevice iced over on both sides where the bulk of the slide came down. "Damn." He surveyed the steep mountain glacier. "Another few feet and I'd have been at the bottom. Buried. Guess I was lucky my ass got crammed between those ledges."

"You're one lucky bastard, I'll give you that. You've got more lives than a cat determined to self-destruct."

Miles took hold of an overhanging ledge opposite them and peeked over. The sarcasm he'd reserved for another comeback froze. "Jesus Christ."

"What now, big guy? You want to do another acrobatic face-plant off this cliff too?"

Miles raised a hand. "Man down, Shep."

"Fucking A—"

Miles checked his gear. "Shit. My pick's gone." He wiggled his fingers and the second Shep's pick hit his hand, he clutched his ribs with the other and leaped over the side of the cliff.

"Right behind ya." Shep jerked out of his bindings, snatched his avalanche shovel, and followed Miles over the side.

With nothing to stop him, Miles slid past an arm and gloved hand protruding from the snow. He grabbed a branch to stop his downward motion and slammed Shep's pick into the ice. He jerked to a stop, crammed his boots into the incline and placing hand over pick, clawed his way back.

With the ferocity given a father to save a buried child, he dug.

Shep knelt beside the body. "That woman wasn't crazy after all."

"Keep digging."

"This shit's bulletproof."

"Dust on the crust today, buddy." Sweat prickled his scalp. "Try it with a few broken ribs."

"Been there. No thanks."

The teammates assumed the prescribed routine and had the skier's arm uncovered in a matter of minutes.

"Pulse?"

"Fuck." Miles shook his head. "We're too late. He's gone."

"Don't think it would have made a difference. He's been here awhile." Shep pointed to the skier's hand curled around a crushed beacon.

"Guess that's why there wasn't a signal." He sat back on his boots. "Better call it in and get the rest of the team up here."

Shep made the radio call and Miles continued to chip frozen snow and ice away from the body. One arm was frozen in an upward angle atypical to the normal position of a human limb—but the sole reason Miles had seen it above the ice. If winter had continued its recent brutal pattern and spring hadn't crept in early, or if the guy's arm hadn't been broken at this ghastly angle, it may have been days or weeks before he'd been seen—if at all.

Careful not to disturb the body, Miles dug. Inch by inch he exposed the skier, lying face down, helmet skewed to one side. He brushed ice crystals from the side of the man's head and traced the indentation at the temple, grateful for the gloved barrier. He'd seen his share of unfortunate skiers, but the familiarity did nothing to lessen the loss.

"Blunt force trauma."

"Ya think? This area's expert level. Probably shouldn't have been anywhere near here."

Miles didn't move the body to investigate further. He couldn't. They hadn't freed the skier's legs. Time had passed by without notice, without change, and the body lay frozen in its precarious tomb. "Had to be booking it and crashed into this limestone wall." Miles swung around scanning the area for point of entry.

"These chutes come up fast. Not for the faint of heart to challenge them."

"Let's hope hypothermia took the poor bastard before the pain got to him."

The drone of snowmobile engines grew loud and then died, the exhaust fumes reaching him before the first of the team members. With Shep's help, the two had managed to free the body at the same time the team arrived on scene.

"Some help here, guys? Need to get this guy off the mountain and ID him. Be dark soon. Let's move!"

Completely clothed in ski attire, the body was curled in a fetal position. To stop the pain of impact? To shield himself against the elements? Whatever the reason, the mountain had claimed him and buried his body within the duplicitous arms of an icy grave, the stone pillars of the couloirs the sole marker.

Shep waved Miles away. "We'll get this, buddy." He and another rescuer kneeled on opposite sides of the body. They braced themselves and took the man's shoulders. With the help of two other team members and on the count of three, turned the man to his side.

"Stop." The command was nowhere near solid, nowhere near comprehension. Miles dropped to his knees. Froze. Nothing mattered. Not the pain in his ribs. Not the dim light. Not time. Not the unstable earth.

The incident commander squatted next to Miles and shined his flashlight at the corpse, the stark light an invasion of something private, a moment of peace captured for eternity. The victim wore the peaceful smile of the unsuspecting as the mountain stopped time and enclosed him in its frozen embrace. "Whatcha got, Malone?"

Miles stared numbly at the body and the man stared back, unbroken arm bent at the elbow, bare hand clutched at his neck, the story written in opaque, unseeing eyes.

He couldn't save them. None of them. A riptide of emotions churned as the Iraqi desert met Colorado mountain and stumbled to life in his mind.

Man down! Man down! I couldn't stop the bullets. The grenades. The sniper's rifle. Couldn't stop the bleeding, my hands soaked in warm, sticky blood. I couldn't stop the hot, angry tears as I clung to Scott until his chest stilled and the soldier breathed no more.

The soldier's heart would never beat against his wife's cheek, nor would his infant son lift his chubby hands and touch the face of his father. And when they tore him away from me, I turned and buried my face in the mutt's fur. Companion. Buddy. My tether to reality. The soldier whose sole mission was to lend comfort and a wagging tail and who faced battle without hesitation, without complaint.

He couldn't save them then, and he couldn't have stopped the mountain from claiming this victim any more than he could have stopped Brenna from killing his baby.

He couldn't fix what wasn't his to fix.

Miles grabbed the flashlight and tossed it into the snow. Unsnapped his helmet and flung it in the opposite direction, the acts ungracious and selfish and yet not sizable enough to calm the culmination of years of vacillation.

Shep grabbed his shoulder and knelt, the movement as solid as the ice beneath him, bridging the past to the present. "What's up, buddy?"

∾

T he room spun. Rachel let go of Randall, groped for the wall, and slowly backed away from Chris, the red SAR jacket, and fully uniformed policeman. She didn't know the officer. Didn't want to. Didn't want to acknowledge either of them and hear their shoddy explanations. It had been Miles in the red SAR jacket and Chris in uniform that night five years ago. They hadn't come to visit. Hadn't come to say hello. They had come uninvited, digging the crater of loss deeper in her heart.

"Rachel! Wait!" Chris broke into a jog to catch up. "I need to talk to you."

She shook her head but kept eye contact. "Go home, Chris. I don't want you here."

Chris took her arm. "I'm only here to tell you we found the missing skier."

"And Miles?"

"He was fine when I left."

Her lungs collapsed and she gulped air.

"But—"

She shook her head with considerable emphasis. "What are you not telling me?" Spit thick with bile choked the question.

Chris spread his feet wide in front of her, the detective's stance. The one that rendered him a formidable fortress. "Miles went back to the scene of the avalanche."

Something in his voice didn't ring true. Miles was safe. Or had been. Had he said that to steer her off-guard? To ease her dread only to reclaim it? "What? Why?"

"The woman we rescued said another skier went down, so he and Shep went back to check. He was fine when I left, Rachel. A hard-headed ass, but fine."

"Then why are you here?" A heavy cloud of apprehension lingered in the air. "Why'd you bring a police officer just to tell me Miles was okay? Where is he?"

"Miles asked me to bring an officer. Said he'd explain as soon as he got here."

"What the hell is going on?"

"He wanted to be the one to tell you."

The evasion rested uneasily between them and she tried to reach past it and shove it out of the way. "Tell me what?"

Chris removed his beanie and spun it in a circle in front of him.

"Rachel?"

Her name echoed from the end of the hall, the deep resonance hoarse and layered in a heaviness that matched the sodden weather. But the sight of him steadied her and tipped her off balance all at once.

Zoe's ears perked and she sped off in a tangle of legs. Miles crouched and she leapt into his arms. He spoke softly to her and then secured her in the crook of his arm, oblivious to Zoe's excited whimpers and lapping up drops of melted snow. Miles closed the distance to Rachel in a few long strides, another man in a SAR jacket at his side.

Miles handed Zoe to the other man and without a word stepped to Rachel and held her tightly against him, pulling a sudden gasp through his teeth. He was here now, with her. Safe. Dripping and soggy and solidly present, she melted into him. But the wait had been excruciating. The dread unbearable.

"Well, look what the cat dragged in." Glenda shifted her purse from one arm to the other. "And you brought reinforcements, I see. Hello, Shephard."

Shep nodded to Glenda and Randall in turn. "Nice to see you both again."

"And to what do we owe the honor—"

"Mom." The salutation was short and curt. "We've come straight from a rescue mission."

"Well, yes, I see that." She scanned them both with the discernment of a pro, a skill obviously acquired through years of experience with a son returning from a mission. "But I want to know—"

"Oh for Pete's sake, woman, leave them alone." Randall thumped his cane. "Can't you see they've missed each other?"

"He's my son. I have a right to know—"

Randall took her arm. "Let's go, *Glinda*," he said with no lack of sarcasm.

Glenda jerked away. "I'll go when I'm good and ready."

"You *are* ready."

"Says who?"

"Stop!" Miles whipped around, anger dissecting his words. "Stop this foolish bickering and go home."

"Miles!" The name froze in midair. Glenda's eyes widened.

"You heard me. Go home. This doesn't concern you and I need some time with Rachel. Alone."

"But your friends are—"

"Do what he says, Glenda, can't you see the boy's feathers are a bit ruffled?"

"You too, Dad. Or would you both care for a police escort?"

The officer spread his feet, hands clasped behind his back.

"You heard the man, Glenda." Glenda took Randall's arm. "Let's go before he has us arrested for being concerned."

Randall's cane thumped in time to a missive of grumbling. The couple turned toward the main entrance and disappeared from sight.

Miles turned back to Rachel. "Rachel, this is Shep Dawson. My SAR partner. Shep, Rachel."

Shep held Zoe with one hand under her belly and reached out his other. "Nice to finally meet you. And Zoe."

"Miles has told me a lot about you."

"That's a little scary."

"It's all good." She turned her attention back to Miles and he reaffirmed his hold, the connection instant, drawn together with the force of a magnet. He flinched at the movement.

Melted snow dripped from his hair and beanie and showered a two-day stubble. She touched the cold, broken skin, wincing at the torn flesh and bloodied lip, grateful for the line of strong bone beneath. She'd never seen him directly from a mission and her heart ached. Not for the injuries that would heal in time, but the way he looked at her—drawn and tense and completely unnerved.

"You're hurt." She reached inside his coat. He winced again. "Ribs?"

"I'm fine."

"At least let me clean these cuts. And your lip."

"It can wait, Rachel."

"What happened out there?" She wiped the droplets from his face.

He lowered her hands. "We went back after a second skier."

"Yes, I know. Chris told me."

The muscles in his face grew taut and he shut his eyes briefly as if to block out the world, block out whatever had overtaken him.

"You found the skier, right?" The words landed flat and uncaring, but the gravity of something she couldn't describe lay hidden beneath the resolute man.

He caught Shep's gaze. Shep dipped his head once and backed away to join Chris and the officer.

"We found him, Rachel." Miles paused, wiping melted snow from his face as if he could wipe away the anguish stretching from forehead to chin. "We found Nico's body."

THIRTY-FOUR

*T*he words curled around her like wisps of smoke in an airless room. She didn't want to breathe them in, to allow them to settle and become real, but she didn't possess the power to disconnect her brain, to unplug the wires connecting thought to motion. And the realness of it lay splintered in his eyes, the anguish touching her in places she'd tucked away. Memories time had dulled became sharply focused and painfully deep.

"That's not possible." The sound of her words came foreign and thin, on the edge of disappearing. She backed away, away from his words, away from the resurrection of a ghost buried long ago.

"If you want…" Hesitation deepened the lines between his brows. "…I can take you," he said, his voice ragged and coarse as if coated in rust, "to see him."

"You're…sure it's him?"

He nodded, the assurance unrelenting in the small movement. "I'm sure."

"No." The word was airy and distant, a denial of something without substance or form. "I buried him once. I can't…"

"Let me help you, Rachel." Miles took her hand. She took it back. "Together, we'll get through this."

Sometimes it's hard to cry, to let an incredulous thing take hold and squeeze the life from you until there's nothing left. Sometimes it's hard not to laugh, to keep the absurdity bottled up until the craziness festers and boils over into a nonsensical noise. And sometimes it was harder to keep them from merging, to fall into the emptiness of dried tears and laughter void of humor. She recognized the significance of both, of what had happened, but at a loss as to why.

"I don't need help." She pushed up a sleeve and checked her watch. "I need to ask Grandpa to take care of Bug."

Miles reached out his hand, gave up the offer, and let it drop. "You don't have to do this alone."

"And I'll need to call Molly. And rearrange the schedule. I'll need some time. And his family. What do I do about his family?" She grabbed her head to keep the runaway thoughts from spilling out.

"I'll have Heather reschedule my appointments—"

"No!" The command sizzled in the dead space between them. "This is something I have to do myself."

"Let me help you."

"He's my husband." The word fell loose and awkward from her lips. "I don't need your help."

His eyes darted back and forth and then broke. Fell apart. Bits of blue scattered and torn and bleeding. "I don't want to interfere, but sometimes we need someone to lean on. For support."

"Don't do this!"

"Do what? Try to help?"

"Fix this. You're always trying to fix things, to fix everything wrong with your life and mine. You can't fix this, Miles. You can't fix me." The moment the words formed, the truth of them sliced through her, the need to reach out and take them back desperate but futile.

"I can't fix it, but I can be there for you."

"You should go."

"Rachel." He took a hesitant step forward and reached out to lift her chin. "Look at me. Please."

She slapped his hand and backed away, leaving bits of her at his feet, waiting to be picked up and set right. But the floor had given way, taking her back to before. Before her husband's return and what comes after. Before Miles. Before the loss of her husband. Before Desi and Ornel and countless other patients. Before her parents' deaths.

Outside, the snow continued to fall.

"I'll go." Miles raised both hands, an offer of resignation and of compromise. "But before I do, I have something for you." He glanced at the officer who nodded in response to the implied question.

Shep set Zoe down and she sat obediently between him and the officer.

Chris took Rachel's hand, leaned in, and kissed her cheek. "If you need anything, Jenni and I are a phone call away."

It was the same, this somber gesture, the same as he'd done that night and she reached up, touching the place where he'd left his sentiments. The reminder lay cold and sober on her skin, the sudden realness penetrating the membrane of time. And then he hugged her long and tight as though the connection could bridge time and express the depth of loss between them.

She attempted a smile but nodded instead.

Chris stepped away with a clap to Miles' shoulder. The officer came up beside him with a reminder to stop by the station to give his statement and the post-incident review and then extended his hand to Rachel. "I'm sorry for your loss."

She didn't take it.

Shep was the last to approach her, offering a hug that smelled of the crisp outdoors and fresh snow and somehow, if it had an odor, of defeat. "I'm sorry, Rachel. If there's anything I can do, Miles knows where to find me." He released her, reluctantly it seemed, and then turned to Miles. Their handshake was short-lived as Shep pulled him one-handed into his shoulder. "Call me. I have a feeling I might need to buy you a drink."

"Make it a fifth and you're on."

"You got it." Shep slapped him hard on the back. "Improvise. Adapt. Overcome."

Miles nodded.

Walking shoulder to shoulder, the threesome was soon out of earshot. Shep turned and gave a quick salute.

Miles tipped his head in silent acknowledgement, turned back to Rachel, and led her inside the nearest empty room. Zoe followed at Rachel's heel.

Restlessness brewed in the taut lines of forehead and mouth as he unzipped his jacket and reached into an inside pocket. "This belongs to you."

A gold chain slipped through his fingers and hung there, stretched to full length. The room held no light save the overflow from the hall, but even in the pale light, the gold ring dangling at the end gleamed.

Recognition broke through the paralyzing stupor. "His ring."

Their rings had been a gift from a dying patient, the chains from Nico's grandfather, and they'd hung around their necks until they were married and sized to fit.

"Nico was holding it...when we found him." He lowered his head as if the weight of the small object was too much to bear, closed her hand around the ring, and then folded his around hers.

The metal still held the warmth from Miles' body, his touch a solid testament to the realness of him, a paradox to a ghost freed. A ghost whose reappearance shattered the stability of her world.

She uncurled her fingers and traced the ring's contours with a thumb, the nicks and scratches a reminder of time shared and time lost. "He wore it around his neck when he skied. Said it got too loose in the cold and he was afraid he'd lose it."

The gold band caught the light as it had that night at the waterfall, as magical now as the sprinkling of stars had been then, his words as clear as that April night.

"It's not yours to keep, but to protect while we're apart. It's my promise we'll be together soon."

He'd given her his ring—the mate to hers—to wear around her neck until they'd been reunited a few weeks later. And for the second time, he'd given it back.

'Til death us do part.

Voices, laughter, and the murmur of daily rounds borne on the air and giving life to the walls dissolved into the quiet. A quiet too profound to be real.

She draped the chain around her neck and clutched the ring, the nicks and scratches vividly etched in the metal and on her heart, but the song written there remained a shadow of a distant memory.

"Did he...did he suffer?"

A moment's hesitation softened his features. "I can't say for sure," he said, splaying his fingers. "But even if...hypothermia can set in fast. It's like going to sleep."

Her affirmation came as a subtle nod.

"He was a good skier. Had his beacon on him. He was prepared. Did everything he should have."

No tears fell. Had she hardened so much she'd become immune to his loss? A shiver pearled over her heart and she backed away, afraid of the truth. Afraid she'd forgotten and terrified she hadn't. Afraid to succumb to a future with another man whose loss would be paramount to a lifetime of grief. He'd taken hold of her hand and steadied her through a bitter ordeal, offered himself and his commitment, his word, to stand by her. And now she would give back the one thing she could. She would honor him by letting him go.

"I have to go. I...I can't do this again..."

"Don't do this. Please don't shut me out." Urgency reflected in eyes as unsettled as a restless sky reaching for a break in the storm.

"I can't...be with you."

"Jesus, Rachel." The exclamation fell heavy between them, part plea, part prayer. "Don't let this tear us apart, destroy what we have." He took a step toward her. She backed a step away. "We'll get through this. Together. Nothing is impossible if we share the burden, Rach."

She turned on him, the sharp remembrance of the name another had given her. "Don't call me that." The remark fell cold and cutting with enough force to bruise him. She gripped the ring, her nails digging crescents in her palm.

Openly disturbed by her tone, his expression crumpled, drained of everything he was and would be, and took with it a piece of her heart.

"I told you before...I told you I couldn't love you."

"You can't mean that." The question formed, parked, and answered itself in the anguish in his eyes.

"I can't love you."

Miles yanked the beanie from his head. Water sprayed from the wool, a baptism of the cold, cruel words. "You're hurt. And angry. And God knows what else is going through your head right now. I'm not a shrink, but I get it. I understand." He lowered his voice to the one reserved for soothing a wounded animal. "But I'm not leaving you, Rachel. Not now. Not ever."

The wound had been reopened, the loss an abyss too deep to ignore. To keep it from claiming her again, she could do nothing else but let him go. "Do I need to spell it out? I can't love you, Miles. I don't." The saying of it nearly brought her to her knees. "Please go." She turned away, but Miles stepped in front of her.

"I'll fight for you, for what we have. I never gave up. I never gave up the search for Nico so you'd have closure and because without hope we have nothing." The depth of his soul painted his words in painful truth.

To hell with closure. Hadn't she convinced herself she'd done that? Closed the lid on an empty casket and buried her husband? She wanted someone to tell her this was a mistake, it wasn't him but some cruel joke the mountain had chewed up and spit at her. But if it was, why did it feel like an avalanche hurling down the mountain to consume her?

The words Miles had spoken that day at his cabin came spilling back.

"The mountain doesn't fight fair. It can be cruel and unforgiving. God knows I've pulled more than my share of casualties from its bowels, but I couldn't...I can't give up. Maybe...I don't know...if I give up on him the mountain wins."

The mountain hadn't won. But neither had she. She'd buried her dreams along with an empty casket, but renewed loss weighed too heavily, a burden she hoped never to carry again—the weight too great to bear.

"Let me by." She scooted by him, but he took her arm.

"When my father was dying you told me there's always hope. I never gave up on finding Nico and I won't give up on us. I've wanted you since I held you the night he went missing, but I couldn't do anything about it then. But I can now and I'll fight for what's right. What we have. But I can't fight a ghost."

The memory of that night came again, the chill of loss a challenge to the life that grew inside her. And her hand cradled the emptiness of her womb, yet she rejoiced in the realness of her daughter. His legacy. His flesh and blood. A tether. A lifeline to the past.

Miles brought her near, the motion as magnetic as it was troubling. "I made a promise," he said and kissed her firmly, soundly, the tomorrows and yesterdays consumed in the passion of now, of one kiss, one moment forever gone and forever remembered. And then he released her, leaving no question he'd offered her the freedom to accept him or let him go. "I promised you red skies. I promised to love you always and I can't let you go, Rachel. Not like this." His voice turned thin, the fight draining with each word.

"It's not your choice to make."

Questions darkened his eyes, the loss sharp and deep, the color of the shadows littered across the snow in the forests he so loved.

"The choice is mine." Her voice softened and hardened all at once. "And I choose to let you go." The saying of it seared a scar on her heart, but the decision had been made.

Her parents had died and left her alone. So had her husband. Twice. She couldn't risk the chance of another loss. She had been forced into being alone so many times by necessity, but this time the choice was hers. One made before it tore her completely apart.

The light in his eyes flickered, taking a little of her with it as it died.

Without looking back, she left the room, left Miles, and left her heart to die at his feet. In its place she'd left the remnants of his— broken perhaps, but given time and space, would heal without her.

THIRTY-FIVE

*T*he last time he'd been here had slipped from his memory.

The late morning sun did little to warm the boulder Miles leaned against, tossing pebbles into the glassy water. Lazy ripples bled in widening circles, a parallel to expanding doubt.

The Chapel on the Rock had been his refuge when Brenna ripped his heart out and left him with a loss he didn't know how to grieve. Eventually, the ache lessened, and he'd lost track of time between heartbeats, and his visits here grew less frequent. And then not at all.

The circumstances had been different then, but the grief today was as unforgiving as the mud and slush he'd trudged through to seek solace in the mountains.

Ten days had passed.

Ten endless days of keeping his mind off Rachel and on his work: Mrs. Menske's two Corgis whose gastrointestinal problems would subside if she'd stop sneaking them table scraps; spays, neuters, and routine checkups he could perform with his eyes closed; an all-nighter with a mare whose foal decided to deliver breech—exhaustion had consumed the last of his resolve and he'd broken down at the live, healthy birth, a small token within his control; and the constant drivel from Heather urging him to get the hell off his ass, find Rachel, and win her back.

Easier said than done. Given a good round of competition, he'd be the first to sign up, but he had this thing about competing with ghosts.

With the exception of the occasional bird scavenging for nesting materials, the chapel grounds were deserted—unusual for a Saturday so close to the summer season. Snow melting from nearby Mount Meeker tumbled over rocks and trickled into the lake and the sough of the breeze through the pines whispered secrets only the forest could decipher.

"Ah, yes, the sights and sounds of the forest in spring are most delightful."

Startled, he turned toward the interruption. A frail, aged man leaned on his cane at the edge of the water not far from where Miles stood.

Miles secured his footing, made his way over the boulders, and came face to face with a tired face lined with the roadmap of many years. "Can I help you, sir?"

"It is not I for whom assistance is required."

Miles surveyed the surroundings, but the chapel grounds were as deserted as when he'd arrived.

"Does the fragrance of tomorrow not dwell among the whisper of the pines?" The old man breathed in and briefly shut his eyes, black coat parting in the breeze. "Ah, the chill of a late spring morning, no longer the bite of winter but most assuredly not quite spring," he said, gathering his coat tighter around him. "The narrowest of windows when the pregnant earth awakens and gives way to impending rebirth."

Early meadow grass poking through the muddy patches of snow swayed gently in the breeze.

"I can't argue with that. Spring is a time of renewal." The last pebble in Miles' hand broke the surface of the water with a rich plunk.

"It is most assuring, is it not?" The man swept a palm in a wide span indicating the perimeter of the open meadows.

The comment left him chewing on the bitter aftermath of its meaning. "For some."

"Ah yes, perhaps not as promising to those who carry burdens of which they do not openly speak." Wiry, old man eyebrows met in the middle of his face above weary eyes that burned through his and touched a place far removed from conscious thought. "Though you do not share your concerns, Miles Andrew Malone, the prognosis for which you ponder is not as grim as you fear."

Questions churned in the growing junk pile inside Miles' head. "Wait a sec—"

The eccentric old man raised a hand. "Allow me to introduce myself. I am Wilford Langhorne D'Ambrose, at your service." He took hold of his cane, folded an arm across his waist, and bowed deeply, black coattails nearly reaching the ground. He rose, the cane's footprint leaving a marked indentation in the muddy earth. "But for all intents and purposes I am simply Ambrose." Wisps of silver hair lifted in the morning breeze.

"Have we met?" Though the face bore a spark of recognition, there could be no way he'd have forgotten this enigmatic gentleman.

"Not in the manner of which you speak, we have not."

"How'd you know my name?"

"Ah, yes, an engaging question indeed." Ambrose waved a hand, knots of aged knuckles apparent through thin leather gloves. "The how is neither here nor there, only that it is so. Though my eyes have grown weary and my ears have strayed beyond my chin, little is known of you for which I am not privy."

Miles leaned against a boulder, eyeing him quizzically. "And it seems you know why I'm here?"

Ambrose nodded, a slow, methodical movement meant to acknowledge and dismiss, but only raised more questions. "Indeed, I do."

"This is…weird." He couldn't honestly admit it had been nice meeting him. It was as odd and far-fetched as stabbing a voodoo doll and expecting the victim to collapse. But the man wore the haggard appearance of one who'd walked a thousand miles to get here and he couldn't leave him alone. Miles slapped his thighs. "Is there something I can do for you? Escort you inside? Take you back to your vehicle?"

Ambrose looked up from under a bank of unruly eyebrows, a faint smirk curling an abundant white mustache. "There is indeed something you can do for one as old and decrepit as I."

Miles extended a hand in an offer of assistance. "You name it."

The mud gave with Ambrose's full weight, the tip sinking out of sight. "Grace me with your presence for a few moments longer," he said with a mechanical wink.

Miles raised the sleeve of his leather jacket to check the time. "I don't have much time." Aidan's pregnant mare wasn't going to foal today, so checking on her could wait. But the old man didn't know that. "I should get back to the clinic. I have a mare ready to foal."

Amusement glinted in weary blue eyes. "The clinic at which you care for our four-legged friends reserves its Saturdays for emergencies, does it not? And the foal of which you speak shall not make an appearance today."

Miles resigned himself to the odd man whose insights did little to squash an uncomfortable worm in his gut. He crossed his arms, waiting for the next absurd speculation.

"This is your place." Ambrose waved a hand in a semi-circle. "The place you come to be alone. To give your troubles to the mountains."

Miles couldn't deny it, yet his response remained silent along with an increasing pile of questions.

"You need not confirm nor deny, for the truth is in your silence." Ambrose shifted his weight. "You have come today to contemplate things for which you should not."

Miles raised a palm. "Please, sir," he said, keeping the sarcastic lilt to a minimum, "do tell."

"The situation for which you grieve will right itself. Give her time to process an overwhelming development. Do not allow this minor mishap to consume what is meant to be."

Minor? Having his heart ripped in two ranked a few notches above 'minor'. "I believe I've heard enough." Miles zipped his jacket and took two steps backward toward the chapel.

"Ah, yes." Ambrose twisted the long handles of his mustache. "It is your privilege to dismiss my intentions."

"How could you possibly know what's going on? What I'm thinking?" Miles shoved his hands in his pockets, watching him with growing interest and a deep sense of sympathy.

"I speak of Miss Rachel."

Miles glanced up at him, then dug a toe into the mushy earth. His heart thumped against his ribs with a growing urge to stop this insane attempt to dissect his thoughts and read them aloud.

"Life is a vicious circle."

The truth of this hung in the air, but he ignored the compulsion to quantify it by saying so.

"Therefore, we create imaginary circles within our circle." Ambrose sketched a wide arc in the air.

"You're talking in riddles."

"Circles are barriers created to keep what we cannot endure hidden from those around us, to keep them at a safe distance. Or perhaps from ourselves, locked away until someone or something breaks the circle and sets them free."

"What's this got to do with Rachel?" Miles blew into his hands to chase the chill.

"Miss Rachel guards her circles with utmost care. There has been but one to have ever broken through." Ambrose crossed his hands over the cane's curved handle. "That man has fulfilled his destiny."

Miles didn't need an interpreter to figure out who Ambrose was referring to, and he straightened at the presumption. "Nico?"

Ambrose narrowed his eyes, heavy eyebrows huddled together in agreement. "The one destined to break through her circle has done so. But she has chosen to close herself and her circle once again. And now I speak to the one destined to remain inside her circle for all of time."

"That's where you're wrong. She wants nothing to do with me."

Ambrose stooped, picked up a small stone and tossed it into the water. It broke the surface, raising a wide set of ripples that sparkled in the sun. "Is the stone visible?"

"No, of course not. It's under water."

"Do you see the ripples?"

"Sure."

"Do you hear them?"

The question needed no answer.

"Not unlike the stone, Nico Armani Caldarone is gone and the ripples he created are no longer seen, nor are they heard. Yet they remain." Ambrose turned a wary eye to Miles. "And you, son, have cast your own ripples and broken through where none have done so."

His skin crawled. He'd been the one to take her to the prison. He'd been the one who put her through hell. "I don't know if what I did was such a good idea."

Empathy spilled from the ancient eyes. "Some things, though difficult, are indeed necessary. As is your patience."

Miles took a deliberate step forward. "If you're somehow all-knowing, which is a crock of shit by the way, then you know I've been patient. I waited for her, given her time to grieve her husband." The term rolled bitterly off his tongue, the muscles in his jaw jumping. "Five years of not knowing if she'd ever get over him. Haven't I proven my patience?"

"Indeed, and therefore you shall have the honor of calling upon it once more. Do not let your impatience stand between the two of you."

"What the hell are you talking about?"

"I speak of an enigma from which she could not be spared. I speak of a discovery meant to be. I speak of her need to close the circle on the past and open it to the future."

Miles jerked his head toward the old man. "She was supposed to be subjected to the discovery of Nico's body? To face the bastard who raped her? To be put through the pain of burying her husband not once but twice?"

"Indeed, it is so."

"This is insane."

"Only when life's shadows fall at your feet and obstruct your path will the doors of your destiny open." Ambrose made his way to the rock and let his weight fall against it. He removed his gloves, stuffed them into his pockets, and then held out a hand palm up, tilting it back and forth. Gnarled and deeply lined, his hands wore the skin of the aged, pale and marked with dark purple veins.

Antsy to be free of the peculiar man, Miles started to walk away, but the mystery of his ways held him captive.

"Patience, son." Ambrose placed an index finger to his lips and continued the odd tilting gesture with his other hand. "They will come."

A line from *Field of Dreams* sprouted from his memory, though he was certain Ambrose hadn't meant dead baseball players. Miles shaded his eyes and glanced around with an inward chuckle at his own foolish behavior.

"Ah, yes, precious ones." One by one red spotted beetles landed on the old man's hand, as if summoned by some unheard call.

A practical scientist by nature, Miles shook his head at the unusual occurrence. "It's too early for ladybugs."

"It is never too early. Never too late. If you believe."

"Somehow I don't think I have a choice."

"You do not. There is merely what is and what is not. None of us can escape the inescapable, those things set in stone—the memories from which we hide. But we can choose what is not yet memory, that which will be."

"The future? No one can foresee what's to come."

Ambrose's wary eyes settled on him, and a boyish grin crept to the corners of his mouth, the bushy mustache rising with the effort. "Perhaps."

Miles dragged a hand over his face. "You can't seriously believe you can foresee the future."

"Perhaps one cannot choose their future, their destiny." He turned back to the ladybugs. "Perhaps it is merely the path chosen for you so you may change where it leads."

One by one the ladybugs took to flight.

Save one.

"She is special." Ambrose raised his hand to observe the tiny ladybug up close. "She who has left her imprint upon your heart."

A lightning bolt of awareness opened the parts of him closed to the teachings of an eccentric old man. He spoke in riddles, but he also spoke from his heart, a common link Miles hadn't allowed to connect. "Yes. Yes, she is."

"Ah, yes. I believe you have chosen your path."

"What do I do?"

"The way through," Ambrose said, placing a hand on Miles' forearm, "is to allow her to experience the pain. Her way. In her own time."

"But it's killing me."

"You are her strength. And she, yours."

"I can't bear to see her go through this again, to grieve all over."

"You are her future. When she has given what she must to the past, she will embrace the future."

"She made it quite clear she didn't want me. Gave me no choice."

"Life will always offer a choice. Now you must make yours. One that will alter the course upon which you shall meet your destiny." The intensity in ancient eyes matched the tone of his voice.

"No one can alter the future."

"Perhaps it is not the altering of our future, but the shaping of it. Given choices, decisions are made. Actions taken. Consequences encountered." Ambrose punctuated the reply with a pointed jut of his chin. "Each of our decisions creates one form of reality. One future. Another choice, another path."

Miles kept his gaze glued to the earth, the solidity in stark contrast to the questionable insights of the frail man.

"Consider for a moment," Ambrose said, peering anxiously over half-moon glasses, "if you choose to end the life of a loved one too soon—"

Miles squared his shoulders. "You have no right to bring that up."

"Ah, yes. I have indeed encroached upon the boundaries of moral behavior. Gone beyond, perhaps. However, would the outcome of such behavior not create another reality? One parallel yet opposite the path you have walked?"

The muscles in his jaw tensed as he digested the suggestion, the guilt a heavy burden he hadn't fully processed.

"There is but one answer."

Miles looked up, grateful the old guy had veered from something he had yet to forgive himself for. "And that is?"

"The answer lies in a force more powerful than is humanly understood. The force of which has puzzled the greatest of minds throughout the ages. It is indeed the greatest force. The greatest gift of all."

The philosophical part of Miles' brain rarely functioned on a good day, and not at all on a bad one. He'd skimped by in his college philosophy classes with the help of the woman who'd walked out on him. The bitter taste of it flooded his mouth.

"I told you, Rachel doesn't believe me when I tell her I love her." An unforgiving ache penetrated his bones.

"You must believe enough for both."

Miles massaged his temple as if willing his brain to accept the odd musings.

"Convincing you is quite a challenge, Miles Malone." An articulate laugh accompanied the statement. "A trifle hardheaded, as they say."

"I've been called worse."

Silence stretched between them, the breadth of its meaning wider than the lake, higher than the mountains surrounding them, the small sounds louder, the quiet bigger, the air heavier.

Ambrose broke the awkward span. "Memories speak in voices no one hears save the bearer. Sometimes they speak softly. Sometimes as harshly as a bitter winter wind. Memories hold us in their power and it is often the freeing of them that is the way of recourse."

"But I've—"

Impatience brewed in Ambrose's tone and held steady in his eyes. "You, my son, have led her to a freedom she has never known. Freedom to look beyond her fear. Freedom to love again, fully and completely. Allow her time to set aside one last fear."

"I've given her my word I'll do anything to keep her safe."

"Of that, there is no question, and she has laid the fear of an unthinkable demon at your feet. However, she harbors one borne of much deeper beginnings. One that is too great for her to bear. She would instead choose to set you free so she may live without the fear of losing another whom she loves deeply. The reality associated with the discovery of Nico's remains has given life to that fear."

"We don't know how many days we have left on earth." Miles slapped his thighs. "She knows that. I know that. But I swear I'd never leave her."

"It is not in the saying of the words, but the action for which they stand. It is as simple as one kiss." Ambrose placed the tip of his cane against the rock, hemming Miles between him and the lake. "Listen to what I say and it shall be so."

Miles' patience had run headlong into the stream and slipped away as easily as a leaf in the current. "You don't understand."

"Miss Rachel tells you she cannot love you, is this not correct?"

Miles studied him with reverent appreciation, but qualified the action with a skeptical eye. "How'd you know that?"

"I have had the honor to know Miss Rachel far longer than time itself. I know of her heart and of her soul."

Miles held back a laugh, not one of ridicule but of respect. "I wish I could say the same."

"Ah, but you shall." The mischief of the boy within played across his features. "It is written in the stars and recorded in the heavens. It shall be given freely with the kiss of true love and remain for all time."

"Sounds like a fairy tale."

"There is much truth in fairy tales if one chooses to see beyond the fantasy."

Miles toyed with a chuckle, this time with no restraint.

"Love is the essence from which all is bound and is the life force that shall outlast time. You cannot escape your destiny, Miles Andrew Malone, healer of wounds. You must not shy from the half that will complete your destiny."

"How am I supposed to do that when she won't have anything to do with me?"

Ambrose held out his hand, the ladybug skittering across a mound of swollen knuckles. "One kiss will not be the end, but the beginning, for love is ageless, and whoever mends her heart completes my work."

He gestured for Miles to extend his hand. The ladybug spread her wings and landed on his. "Good luck will come by way of the ladybug, so the legend says. Give your special Ladybug all that is in your heart. Love her as your own."

Bug's image came as real as if he held her in his arms. Her laughter, cheerful as the chatter of birds. Her smile, bright and warm as the morning sun. "I already do." The ache of truth threatened to burst from his heart and spill into a pile of broken words.

"If you love something Miles Andrew Malone, you must let it go. And if it returns on its own, it was meant to be yours. Always. And in all ways. And so it shall be."

The odd man's ramblings collided in waves of confusion and comfort and an odd craziness he couldn't explain. The old guy was a blend of omniscience and cryptic wordsmith and as mysterious and colorful as the northern lights.

Miles stretched his hand to the sun and the ladybug flew away. When the tiny red speck disappeared, he turned back to the old man. "Ambrose, how—?"

The question fell from his lips unfinished. How long had he been in his little trance? Long enough for the old guy to reach the chapel? He scanned the area. Squatted. Mud closed around his finger as he skimmed the shallow depression. There were no other impressions, no footprints save the ones where the old man had stood next to him.

Miles sprinted to the chapel, yanked open the door, and waited for his eyes to adjust to the light filtering through the stained glass, blinking to hurry the process.

The old man was nowhere to be found.

THIRTY-SIX

The ghost of remembrance swirled around her. The notes etched in the granite headstone played his song on her fingertips, the wind the echo of his whistle. Now and then when she least expected it, the slightest of movements would lift her hair, a momentary tickle on her cheek—the ghostly kiss of a thousand butterfly wishes.

She wasn't afraid of ghosts. How could she be? Each time she looked at her daughter, her husband peered back at her through the deep, knowing eyes he'd given her. Bug's smile held the same mischievous quirk as her father's, the one that had eventually lured Rachel to his bed and the making of their little girl.

There seemed more to it than grasping at distant memories, the way you wake from a dream and desperately try to grab the edges to hold onto the realness and will it into being. No, she wasn't afraid of ghosts, but she couldn't say the same for disturbing those she'd buried in an empty casket.

Rachel sat cross-legged at the foot of the headstone of the man who had given her his name and blessed her with their daughter. She wrapped her sweatshirt tightly around her, but it did little to comfort the chill.

Rachel clutched the ring hanging around her neck. A tear painted her smile and then darkened her jeans and she traced the outline, the circle damp and already cold. "She has your eyes, you know. Big and soft as chocolate suede...like yours, but inquisitive, and heaven help her she's got your strong will. She reminds me of it, of you, every time she doesn't get her way." She sucked in a ragged breath in place of a laugh. "And when the sunlight touches her hair, it sparkles as if it's been dusted with copper. The same way yours did. But she's been cursed with my curls. I'm sorry, I know you loved them, but she won't when she's older. And when she smiles in her sleep it takes my breath away..." Her words grew quiet. Motionless. Stuck. She swallowed past the thickness. "She takes my breath away because I see you and I know you're there, holding her while she sleeps."

Rachel plucked a sprig of an eager spring weed, tearing it into a neat green pile by her ankles. "She's got your lovely olive skin, long fingers, and she jabbers sometimes, but she's thoughtful too. She's a beauty at four and at fourteen she'll be attracting boys the way a flower attracts bees. You'd be worried." She lifted a shoulder and let it drop. "We call her Bug, Grandpa and I, because she's fascinated by anything that crawls, especially ladybugs. I named her Nicole. After you. But you know that already, don't you?"

A hand gently squeezed her shoulder. "He knows, Button." She didn't shy from his touch but at the way the disease quietly vibrated through layers of cloth, skin, and muscle and tightened the noose around her heart. "Nico is here with you and Bug and always will be."

"You were right, Grandpa."

"I surprise myself sometimes." The corner of his mouth quivered with the small upward turn. "What about?"

"You refused to let me see Mom and Dad before the funeral, and I hated you for it."

"I'm sorry, Rachel. I thought it was for the best."

"I get it now. I didn't need to see them and I don't need to see my husband. It's better to remember them as they lived."

She got to her feet and her grandfather put his arm around her, his grip solid but plagued with the tremors he tried to hide and she tried to ignore. "There's so much silence I can't hear him anymore." She leaned into the familiar nook of his shoulder. "I thought...since they found him he'd come back to me. In the silence. In my dreams."

"Sometimes we carve our dreams on our heart, to be tended with care, but we never let them go. Not completely. But we do add to them. You've never been able to Teflon-coat your heart, Rachel. You wear it like a beacon."

"I knew he was never coming back, but it haunted me for months, knowing he was out there somewhere." The truth of it found flavor in a keen bite of bitterness. "It's not fair."

"No, it's not. Many things in life are not fair, yet we deal with the inequities and move on. But picking at the scabs of an old wound aggravates the healing, brings the pain back to the surface." He punctuated the moment with a moment of hesitation. "Sometimes we feel as if we're broken and there's no way to put the pieces back together."

"I think I'll be picking up the pieces forever."

"You're a strong woman and have come so far," he said, emphasizing the last two words with a gentle squeeze on her shoulder. "It's a lifetime process, but you're healing, Button, and that's a good thing. The memories and pain will always be there, but you're no longer that broken woman."

"This is killing me, Grandpa."

"It's time to take that proverbial step forward." He took her arm and faced her. "Time to shut the door on a broken past and open yourself to a wonderful future. Open the door, Rachel. Open the door and step through it to the other side of broken."

She clung to her grandfather's hand with both of hers. "Why did they have to find his body? Why now?" The sobs came effortlessly, torn loose from the anchors time had set securely in place.

"I don't know. But there's always a reason."

"I don't know how to do this. Not again. It hurts too much."

He nodded slowly and looped his arm through hers. "Does this have anything to do with Miles?"

"He's got nothing to do with this." She spoke with an unnatural sharpness, but the mention of his name breathed life into the empty words. His ten-day absence had been like sleepwalking in a world as gray and heavy as sodden wool.

"I think it has everything to do with him. I've seen the way you look at him and he at you. Neither one of you is skilled at hiding your feelings."

Her grandfather's eyes remained guarded, truth dangling in the air between them.

"You're afraid of losing him too."

"Don't put words in my mouth."

"Then say it yourself, Button. Put the thoughts you're afraid of into words."

"I...can't." She spoke softly, the resurrection of pain and heartache echoing the betrayal attached to the words.

"You're a strong woman. Don't let the past steal your future with a good man. A man who loves you and your daughter, and will love you for the rest of your life."

"What if—?"

"That's a rhetorical question in the best of circumstances. But it's also one that doesn't deserve an answer. For in the asking, you allow the past to dictate your future."

"I couldn't bear it, Grandpa. To lose him too. I can't...I can't love him."

"Oh, my dear, sweet granddaughter. I think it's far too late for that." He hugged her, his breaths moving in and out, gathering strength and pushing back as if the force could squish the truth from her in a single gasp of air. "You already do and I'm afraid you can't turn it off like a light switch."

Sobs dampened his coat, absorbing the pain of something that hadn't come to pass. The fear of loss. The anger of losing. And the pain of those already lost. "You've lost so much." His voice had gone soft, hurt seeping into his words.

He covered her with the shelter of his love in the way only he could. She took comfort and hugged him back, wishing she could draw the poison crippling his body and expel it like a meal gone bad. It would happen again. The loss. And it would take a piece of her with him, one she didn't know how she'd live without. He'd assumed the roles of father, grandfather, protector, and counselor when she'd had none. But she couldn't bear to think of the inevitable. Not today.

"Say the words, Button." Contrary to his diminished strength of late, he held her firmly at arm's length. "For me."

The truth of his insistence was unmistakably written in his eyes. He wanted her to confess the truth, not merely to seal the future for herself, but for him. For the comfort of knowing she wasn't alone. That she was taken care of. He couldn't prepare himself without the assurance she wouldn't be alone to bear the burden. Of this she was certain.

"I love him, Grandpa." And the saying of it lifted the anguish from her heart, the admission shimmering like dew in her grandfather's eyes. "I love Miles with all my heart. With everything in me."

"And I love you, Rachel Caldarone." The words skirted the edges of reality, the voice deep and hoarse.

She turned. "Miles?"

"I believe I once said if you let me go, I promised I wouldn't be far. And I'm not one to make promises I don't intend to keep."

An extraordinary happiness encumbered Grandpa's face.

"It's good to see you, Marshall." The two men shook hands. "And thank you."

"I believe this is my cue. I've got a date with a beautiful little Ladybug, a pint of ice cream, and an unopened container of rainbow sprinkles." Grandpa kissed Rachel on the cheek and started through the line of gravestones, his gait rigid, each step taken with deliberate care. He stopped and turned slowly to Miles. "An *overnight* date."

A small smile poked through a low chuckle and Miles tucked Rachel into his side. "Your grandfather shared his thoughts with me. Told me where I could find you. I get it Rachel. And I'm willing to resign from SAR, hang up my skis, or whatever else concerns you, and

I'll be content to devote my time to you and Bug and my practice if it will ease your mind."

"I'd like nothing more. You put your life on the line every time a call goes out, every time Chris or Shep challenge you on the slopes, or when the urge strikes to tame a river in a boat not big enough for Zoe."

"Consider it done."

"I have issues, Miles. And they're selfish bitches, but those things you're willing to give up are a part of the man I love. And without them you'd be miserable."

"I'll find other ways to occupy my time."

The suggestion lingered in a small upward turn of his mouth. She allowed it to play a shivery dance over her skin and then set it aside. "I can't ask you to do that. It's too much a part of who you are."

"No matter what we do, no matter what decision we make, life has no guarantees. But I don't plan on going anywhere. Not for a very long time."

"If you love something let it go."

"If it comes back it's yours to keep."

"I pushed you away." She looked away to hide the hurtful admission.

"It hurt, Rachel. I can't deny how much. But because of it, I knew you loved me enough to let me go."

"But you came back."

"I'll always come back, be there for you, come home to you. I'll be your forever. If you want me to be."

Too many thoughts took root at once and spilled into her heart, overflowing and hard to contain. She could never forget the man whose promises had set her free in the way only he could have done, but it was time. Time to welcome those of another. "I had to come here, Miles."

"I understand. I do. I love you and want all of you, the woman complete, and Nico is a part of the package. I've no right to think otherwise."

"I had to talk to him." Unwilling to meet his eyes, she peered at the ground, her toe digging into the soft earth. "To tell him—"

"Rachel, please." He lifted her chin, his touch gentle but firm. "Don't be afraid to speak his name, to say you love him."

She held her breath.

"It's okay."

The weight of uncertainty held her motionless save for the slow side to side movement of her head.

"He deserves the respect. You can't erase him, or pretend he never existed, or deny your feelings by refusing to say his name. It didn't work with Chastain and it won't work with Nico." He took her face in his hands. "Say his name. Tell him. Tell me."

A thick sob lodged in her throat, the truth too evident to ignore. "I'll always love him." Her voice was insignificant, the reality paramount. "I'll always love Nico."

He drew her to him and she fitted herself into the hollow where shoulder met chest, taking comfort in the solid warmth. "I wasn't ready to let him go."

"And are you now?"

"There always seemed to be something missing, but I have what I need. I have closure."

"It's all I've ever wanted when it came to you and Nico."

"You're right, Miles, he's a part of me. Of who I am." The question mark no longer hung at the end of Nico's name, replaced by a simple black dot. She could let go of the man, but the remembrance would always remain. "Does it bother you?"

"Yes. And no." He reeled in a lingering pause with a pensive sigh. "I hate him, Rachel, for the grief he's caused you. When you're unhappy or in pain, I feel it in places I didn't know existed. And I hate him for leaving you, but in the same breath I love him for the same reasons."

The intensity in his words grounded her yet left her without gravity. She stared at the gravestone, solid and sure, but without the substance or power to rein in the tethers that bound her to the past. She was but a puppet, detached, invisible strings stirring her to movement.

Rachel lifted the chain from around her neck, the headstone a watery blur. "Your dreams were my dreams, my wishes yours to grant. You gave me a beautiful daughter and for that I'll always love you, Nico Armani Caldarone." Nico's ring slipped through her fingers and she draped the chain over the granite. "I couldn't say it before and mean it, but it's time. Time to say goodbye." It wasn't the first time she'd said goodbye, but this time the word grew solid, the realness more powerful yet spoken effortlessly. "Goodbye, Nico. I'll always love you, but I'm ready to let you go."

Miles took the chain from the stone and placed it back around Rachel's neck, the gold ring glinting in the afternoon sun. He closed her hand over the ring, a bold reminder of the continuous circle, the nicks and scratches of a life before, one that had been the cornerstone of the woman she'd become.

"Nico took the first step toward healing you, and for that I'm forever grateful. But I'll be the keeper of your heart, the one who will protect you from heartache and soothe the scars that will never completely heal."

She gazed up at the man with the power to unravel her, expose her, and put the pieces back together. Slowly. Neatly. And with absolution. "You want me to keep it?"

A small smile moved to his eyes, lighting them with the brightness of a summer sky and promises yet to be made. "It's a reminder. A token of the man who gave you the gift of life."

Where Nico wore a sensual half-smile or one of expressed mischief, Miles wore the one that bore the pleasures of his being. Everything he was emanated from it, marked with forty years of happiness, joy, and heartache. It was a full-on thing that spoke of adventure, spirit, and life itself, and the lines that punctuated it deep and filled with compassion. She wouldn't truly miss Nico's smile, for it graced her daughter's face—the gift of her inheritance. But the smile of the man before her, the one that spoke without words and that turned her knees liquid would be the one she stepped into the future alongside.

A gust of wind arose, riding on the chilly fringes of spring. She shivered in its wake. "I'm having his body sent to Hidden Falls. To be with his family."

Miles locked an arm around her waist in silent acknowledgment, whether from her decision, the sudden chill, or both, she wasn't sure.

She laid her hand on Nico's headstone, the offer one of all the yesterdays gone before and the tomorrows yet to be born. "I have everything I need."

And she did. The end—a crushed beacon and a gold ring clutched in death as they had been in life. The end to an era of unanswered questions. "I'll always be in love with the memory of him, but you're my life now and if I make no other promise to you, Nico will never come between us again."

"I can't ask for more than that."

She took the hand at her waist and squeezed. "Everything I need is right here." As her words drifted into the air and touched the cold granite stone, a ladybug landed on the back of her hand.

"Legend says if you hold a ladybug in your hand luck will come from the direction it flies away."

"But it's too early for ladybugs to be out, isn't it?"

"Not if you believe."

Rachel gently closed her fingers around the ladybug and out of the corner of her eye—at the edge of the wood among the shadows—a tall, lanky old man leaned into his cane and bowed deeply. She turned, but there was no one there.

Believe.

"I believe." She opened her hand and the ladybug took to flight, landing on Miles' hand. "Looks like I'm in good hands."

"Red skies at night. Always."

The memories—both good and bad—would haunt her from time to time, but Miles would be there to hold her until the nightmare faded. He would quiet the noise and fill the darkness with light. Hadn't he already? He was her knight, formed of the earth and mountains and streams, armed to catch her if she fell.

And he would love her until death took him from her. And no matter when it would be, it would never be long enough.

Rachel rose to her toes and framed his face with her hands, the evidence of his promises peering at her from within the trusses. The neatly landscaped stubble prickled her palms, the sensation both stark and fluid, a subtle reminder of the strength and compassion of the man within. Tall and graceful in stature, he was impressive from a distance, but from a few inches away the intensity was striking.

"I'm ready to go."

The depth that comes with a forest night lay upon the room, the shadows both comfort and precursor to dreams. Miles had cracked the window, selfish for the cold spring air that kept her close, kept her body feeding off his heat. The need for his touch, the need for intimacy ran deep in her bones, the hunger strong and without apology, and he'd dissolved into her in answer to her request. It had been slow and intimate, their lovemaking, the rhythm of her movements the ebb and flow of a synchronized tide.

She'd made love to him, tasting and touching and stroking, an exploration of body, mind, and spirit, composed of the tiny sounds he'd had to quiet, or accept an untimely completion. They'd become one heartbeat, one flesh, his body as much hers as hers was his. Free of barriers. Free to dream. Free to love. Two lost souls merging into one, to heal and forget and forge the future as one.

But now her fingers slowed their journey over his chest, thigh, and torso, each touch both nourishment and enticement, and an obscure sadness when they stilled. Rachel relaxed against him, her sigh rich with the pull of sleep, and her slow, even breaths a murmur on his skin. She lay curved into his side, one leg draped over his torso and an arm across his chest, her flesh the weight that bound them. He'd shared her at one time, unsure if he would ever be free of the ghosts who had come before. But he knew beyond question, beyond doubt, he'd need never share her again. He was selfish that way. And glad of it.

A finger twitched on his chest, the intimation of her dreams alive on his skin. He hoped they were kind to her, her dreams, not the nightmares that stole her sleep, but those that came with the pleasure of peaceful slumber.

He kissed her, the faint scent of hair and skin, and the heady spice of their lovemaking blended in a powerful perfume. "Sweet dreams, Sunshine." It came as thought, but spoken as a whisper of hope.

Her foot stroked his ankle timidly and she opened her eyes, the shyness blooming into dark pupils in a circle of blue.

"I didn't mean to wake you."

"I don't want to fall asleep," she whispered, her voice lulled in drowsiness. "Not yet."

"That can be arranged."

She snuggled close, nudging him in the ribs.

"Ahhh...shit-fire," he said, shying from the cheeky prod. "Ribs."

"You had that coming." She grazed a fingernail over his nipple, the instant response rising in a puddle of gooseflesh. "And that's not what I meant."

"Then please tell me before I choose to make other *arrangements*."

Abandoning the tantalizing ministrations, she tipped her head toward him. "I miss you when I close my eyes. And when I sleep."

How many times had he lain awake, the same inference dragging him into sleep? "I find it soothing to watch you fall asleep, and waking up next to you is easily the best part of my day." Miles locked an arm around her, her body warm and real against him. He drew her in and kissed the top of her head. "But it doesn't happen often enough."

They lay quietly together on the edge of sleep, the temptation pulling him under. But he fought the lure, for any time lost to sleep was time lost from her, and in the moments before he gave in, an overwhelming urge to wrap her up and protect her, to keep her safe roused him to wakefulness. He rolled to his side, sheltering her with the warm cocoon his body offered.

Soft lips kissed the birthmark near his neck, the one she'd called a teardrop, the one he'd dismissed until she'd blessed it with her touch. "I love you, Miles Malone," she whispered, her voice bathed in drowsiness.

A bounce, as familiar and unmistakable as the huge shadow shook the bed.

Rachel squeaked, more gasp than scream. "What was that?" She sat up and pulled the blankets to her chin.

"Damn dog. Where the hell did you come from?" Miles sprang from the bed and flipped on the bathroom light.

A huge tongue swiped Rachel's nose and right eye. "Gaaah!" Her surprised yelp gurgled into a breathless giggle.

"Strider, off!"

Rachel jerked her head to avoid the sloppy tongue, but it did nothing but egg the huge Newfoundland on, tail wagging fiercely at his immobile prey. She scooted back. Strider disagreed with the movement and let out a groan that matched his size, put his huge paw on her thigh, and continued his slobbery bath.

The laughter Miles tried to contain escaped in full force.

"Strider..." Breathy, unsteady giggles consumed the name and she tried to push him away, but laughter zapped her strength and it was useless to try to budge a hundred and forty pounds of Newfoundland who had no intention of leaving. "I don't need...a spit bath."

"Strider thinks you do." Miles sat on the edge of the bed with arms crossed, watching her wiggle and squirm with nowhere for her to go. "Besides, I did warn you I shared my bed."

She glared at Miles between canine kisses. Strider came up for air, licked his muzzle, and leaned his big head on Rachel's chest with a satisfied groan.

"I think he likes you."

She peeked over the dog's hairy head. "I love the big oaf too, but seriously, Miles. He's in dire need of a companion." She pointed to the dog's obvious display of affection.

"I think I'll give him another minute..." Laughter wobbled his words and they came out more a wheeze. "...to get better acquainted with our house guest."

Rachel threw a pillow at him. He caught it, but not without a grimace. "Ow! Broken ribs."

"You'll think broken ribs." She crawled from beneath the furry monster, lunged, and Miles caught her and dragged her down with him. "You are so freakin' dead meat."

The bed bounced.

Strider howled.

"Payback, Sunshine, for the Dr. Who-slash-Lecter thing."

"The way I see it," she said with a mischievous glare, " you just got deeper in debt."

THIRTY-SEVEN

*M*olly leaned against the counter, green eyes bright. "Have you seen Archie since you came back from Arizona, Rach?"

Rachel refolded the letter, stuck it in her pocket, and turned toward the effervescent nurse.

Molly wasn't your typical fiery redhead, but she was spirited and had a nose for uncovering tidbits of information—a skill she'd honed from hanging around Kitty at Woodland Hills. The two had been as close as sisters, and it had been a shock when Molly had followed her and Nico to Colorado and left Kitty behind. She'd needed a change of scenery, she'd said. But Rachel guessed a nasty divorce had been at the root of the decision.

"I have." The tension eased from her shoulders. "It's good to see him up and about again. I'm glad his little diabetes setback wasn't as severe this time."

Molly set her water bottle on the counter. "If the old coot would quit trying to kill himself with Suzie Q's—"

"I thought it was licorice jelly beans?"

Molly scrunched her nose. "He's got more junk food stashed than he does insulin. I wouldn't be surprised if his Amazon Prime account is set for auto delivery." She took hold of Rachel's sleeve, bouncing on her toes (not unlike Bug) in a whirl of excitement. "But that's not what I'm talking about." Molly's plait swung with the jerky movement, tiny misfits of hair poking out from between the heavy strands. "Have you checked out Archie's grandson? Holy crap, Rach, he's got a great backside—"

Two orderlies passed by, turned backward, and winked. Molly tucked the rest of her comment between her lips and waited for them to pass. "I mean…his jeans…he fits those Luckys nicely."

Rachel reached over and lifted her chin.

"What?"

"I think it's cute when your freckles blush."

Molly playfully smacked her hand away. "I'm not blushing."

"I take it your conclusion of said man's anatomy comes from personal inspection?"

"What?" If it was possible, Molly's freckles darkened further. "No," she said, dragging the single syllable into three, fingered the braid several times, and then whispered in Rachel's ear. "Give me time."

Rachel highlighted the observation with a judicious hum.

"Aidan's gorgeous, Rach. Straight off the Pinterest male model boards gorgeous."

Rachel tried to hide a smirk.

"What? You've got your man candy hanging on your every word, and I…"

Rachel put an arm around Molly's waist. "I'm sorry it didn't work out with Frodo."

Molly blinked once and then they both burst into unladylike snorts.

"Darrin did resemble the hobbit, didn't he? Hairy feet included."

Unable to speak, Rachel bobbed her head.

"His ego—and his list of affairs—were bigger than his balls."

"I'm sorry about Frodo."

"Don't be. It's been three years and I haven't looked back. But the buffet has limited access in Estes Park."

"It's hard in a small town."

Molly's eyes went all gooey. "*It* can get hard in any sized town, Rach, but I haven't had much luck finding one to get that way."

Rachel kneaded her temple, suppressing a laugh that desperately wanted out.

Molly took a few sips from her water bottle. "Speaking of which, are you going to give me the scoop or what? It's been a long dry spell and I'm living vicariously through you." She wiggled her fingers. "Spill."

A sudden urge to leave had Rachel's Skechers in motion, but Molly hooked a finger in her pocket. "Oh no you don't. I want details." She hauled Rachel closer by a gaping pocket. "Have you had sex with him?"

"Molly!" Younger than Rachel by a couple of years, Molly had the uncanny talent of steering the conversation back to the days of a lascivious teen when they talked about men.

"Oh, come on. Give a girl something to fantasize about. What's Miles like? Is he good?" Curiosity tinged a long exhale. "He's so big... in the shoulders, I mean. And tall. And holy crap, Rach, he's easy on the eyes. Clothed, that is. I mean...the man's a freakin' god."

She thought so too but didn't voice the thought. "Minus his super powers, he's just a vet."

"Yeah, and if my vet looked like him, my little doggie would be sick all the time."

"You don't have a dog."

Molly's shoulders met her ears. "Good thing Zoe's always around, don't you think?"

Rachel couldn't contain the spread of a smug grin. "He's an amazing man. That's all I'm going to say."

"Spoil sport."

Molly tugged on Rachel's sleeve, and the letter crinkled in her pocket. "Are you going to show that to Miles?"

An arm reached around Rachel's waist. She gasped, mentally chastising herself for the involuntary reaction she hoped would someday be a distant memory.

"Show me what?" Miles leaned in and kissed her on the cheek. "Am I allowed to do that?"

"Do what?"

"This," he said and then turned her to him and kissed her solidly on the mouth.

She breathed him in, the heady wilderness spice, clean soap, and musky redolence blending into his signature morning male scent. "I'm the supervisor. I can bend the rules if certain situations arise."

Molly made an exaggerated noise in her throat. "Breaking rules is her specialty," she said, and grabbed the nurse's tablet. "That's my cue. Later, kids. My patients call." She raised the tablet and took a few steps backward.

Rachel opened her mouth to warn her of an impending collision, but she wasn't quick enough and Molly backed into an unsuspecting visitor. The man grabbed the tablet and slipped his arms around her to keep them both from an untimely rendezvous with the floor.

The man's hair was as dark as Molly's was auburn and he towered over her by a good six inches. Molly's cheeks turned the shade of a finely blended merlot.

"Excuse me." The man gently turned her around. "I wasn't paying attention."

Molly's ears, the last piece of anatomy to do so, pinked. "Aidan!"

Though it appeared to be a conscious effort, Aidan's hand slipped from her waist. Miles approached the couple and shook Aidan's hand. "How's that brood mare holding up?"

"Keep your cell handy, Miles. She's as big as a house and restless."

"Good sign she's close or already in labor."

Aidan rubbed a knuckle under his nose. "You sure she's not carrying twins?"

"Unless the ultrasound lied, I'm sure." Miles adjusted his feet. "Twins would be a difficult birth and it's highly unusual for both foals to survive."

"She's an exquisite sorrel and a reputable producer. I'd hate to lose her or the foal." Aidan's focus shifted to Molly. "If I can't have two-for-one, I'll settle for a foal as gorgeous as its mother." Aidan followed the drape of Molly's long, thick braid. "Intelligent. Compassionate. Perfectly perfect."

Rarely, if ever, was Molly rendered speechless.

Rachel cleared her throat. "Rounds, Molly?"

Molly retrieved the tablet and turned. "Right." Aidan jogged to her side and the two headed down the hallway toward Archie's room.

"Is Molly into horses by chance?" Miles pointed his chin in the direction the couple had gone, the mystery in his question hidden in a sly smirk. "Aidan Comstock raises race horses."

"If not, it wouldn't take her long to fall in love. With horses, I mean."

"Aidan's a good guy."

"She deserves a good man." Rachel leaned against the counter. "I thought you had an appointment this morning."

"Kristina and I are meeting with the insurance adjusters on the theater damage. There's a discrepancy between what the insurance company thinks needs replacing and what actually does." Miles slipped in beside her. "Before I go, do you have something to show me?"

Rachel reached in her pocket and removed the letter. "From the Board of Executive Clemency."

Miles straightened. "Do you want me to read it or would you rather tell me yourself?"

"Everett Dumas called earlier and told me, but this is the official notification. I was afraid to read it. Afraid I'd heard him wrong." She made a conscious effort to remain resolute, but the letter trembled in her hands. "Chast..." She took in a long breath that didn't fit in her lungs. "Demetri Chastain's request for commutation of sentence was denied." The saying of it drained the heaviness from her chest. "Denied, Miles. He can't harm anyone else."

Miles embraced her, a long, breathy moan rumbling against her ear. "That's fantastic news, Sunshine."

She melted into his arms, the benefit and promise of his strength in the connection.

"The other victims have agreed to testify. Dates are set." She swallowed the memory before it had a chance to grow. "Dumas is shooting for life and he says there's no jury in the world who won't convict him."

"If anyone can put him away, it's Dumas."

"I don't know if it's okay to believe it. To hang on his word."

"It's over, Rachel. Chastain will die in prison."

"Yes, he will." She lowered her lashes. "I wondered why he looked so thin…" She fiddled with the buttons on Miles' shirt. "He applied for commutation because…he's terminal. Wants to die at home. Dumas says he probably won't make it through the trial." She looked up then, concern narrowing his eyes. "I wanted revenge. Wished him dead. Back then. But I'm a healer. I took an oath."

"You didn't cause his illness, Rachel. His psychopathic actions sent him to prison where he'll die because of them." His features softened, but his voice remained unyielding. "There's nothing more to be said."

Miles was a healer too. Had taken an oath. But the hands stroking her held no sorrow, no regret, and with a blatant disregard for the rules, he leaned in and kissed her, the claim to her future sweet on her lips.

"It's over, Sunshine. For good."

Miles' cell phone chimed. He retrieved it, the screen playing shadows on his face as he read the message. "Kristina will have to handle the insurance people alone." He brushed his knuckles along the length of her jawline. "Aidan just got word his mare is about to foal."

"Molly's shift is over in ten." She tapped a finger on her mouth. "I wonder if she's keen to watching a horse give birth?"

"Playing matchmaker, are we?"

"She has a thing for well-fitting jeans." She scanned Miles from head to toe. "She just might have a point."

Miles tossed his head back and laughed, the sensation vibrating on her cheek as he kissed her there, the humor very much alive. God she loved it when he laughed like that. The sound was bone-tingling bright, like when the sun suddenly pops out from behind a cloud after a summer rain.

He walked backward until their fingers lost connection, turned, and increased his stride.

An intense man by nature, his laugh was intoxicating and she replayed the sound in her mind and then touched her cheek, her skin still humming with the melody of his kiss.

Eight hours remained of her ten-hour shift, and his last equine delivery had taken all night. She didn't think Miles would have time to break for lunch.

Or whatever.

THIRTY-EIGHT

To separate one from the other would be as fruitful as trying to detach a dog from a particularly juicy bone. They'd made a bargain of sorts, the two of them. Bug asked and Miles said yes.

The air was ripe with the scent of pine, the sky a watercolor of brilliant blue, and insects sang in full voice. The early summer air kissed her cheeks with its warmth, and by the end of the day the sun would paint them with the first hints of summer color.

It was the same as it had always been, this place. This area of Whisper of The Pines Resort had stolen her heart as surely as the man romping in the grass with her daughter. And though she'd said she'd choose another place, Miles had come here despite the sentiment attached. He'd assured her it was big enough for new memories to squeeze in beside the old and as long as they were together, it mattered little where.

Rachel drew her knees to her chest, leaned into the old wooden bench and wondered how she got so lucky.

Perhaps it was fate. Perhaps it was the sheer tenacity of two men who'd come into her life unexpectedly and tipped her world upside down. Perhaps it was the luck of the ladybug. Or maybe it was the knowledge of what is, what was, and what was yet to come given her by a frail old man who saw more with one eye than most did with two. Never underestimate love, Ambrose had said, and the proof stood a few paces away, twirling her daughter in the air.

The jagged spires of the Rockies rose around her, enclosing the Fall River Valley in their embrace, but they no longer held her captive to their hunger. Instead, she marveled at their beauty and prayed for them to leave her man alone, to allow him the adventure and majesty woven into the fabric of his soul. He hadn't passed on any rescue missions, a testament to his compassion for others. She knew he would if she asked, but she'd promised herself she never would.

"I dreamed of Nico last night, Grandpa. It's been awhile since he's come to me in my sleep."

Rachel's grandfather patted her shoulder lightly, the tremors bleeding past the light sweatshirt, a quiet ache sinking into her heart.

"Was it the same, Button?"

"Yes. And no. He backed away this time. But I must have reached for him, because Miles took my hand and held me and made it all okay."

"Miles is a good man."

The statement held nothing but truth and she smiled, but the dream pulled it back. "Do you think Nico was trying to tell me something?"

Grandpa twirled his thumbs around each other in a steady rhythm. "Perhaps our dreams are merely the realization of our thoughts."

Bug giggled. Intermingled with Miles' deep, rumbling laugh, the melody it inspired parked a smile on her heart, scattering her thoughts. Bug plucked the giant wand from the bottle and passed it to Miles. He picked her up and together they swished the bubble wand through the air in dizzying twirls. Huge bubbles floated around them. Bug clapped wildly. Miles' laugh drenched the air. And at that moment she knew exactly which of her *kids* was having the most fun.

Strider lumbered after the bubbles with a generous woof, his body lunging in determined chase. Zoe kept stride-for-stride with the rambling Newfoundland, leaping into the air three times her height popping bubbles with her nose.

Miles set Bug and the bubble container on the grass. Bug fell to the ground and rolled on her back, hands raised to the sky. Strider initiated her with a few slobbery kisses and then stretched himself belly down on the grass, content to abandon the game. Zoe jumped on top of Strider's back, surveying the surroundings as if taking inventory of her special little world. She probably was. Strider gave a half-hearted shake, and Zoe slipped off his back and set her sights on Miles.

Noses were Zoe's thing. The hunter in her surfaced, and she crept around the two prone figures as if stalking elusive prey and proceeded to give Miles' nose a proper cleaning. He picked her up and brought her face to face, but it was Miles who covered Zoe with smooches.

Grandpa buried a wheezy chuckle in his fist. "Zoe must think Miles needs a bath."

Rachel chuckled into her jeans. "Serves him right." She tossed Grandpa a sly smile, but Strider's late-night shenanigans would remain between her and Miles.

The sun slipped in and out of the drifting clouds who'd sprinkled the highest mountains with a belated dusting of snow. Miles pointed to the sky and he and Bug were deep in conversation about a cloud that looked precariously similar to a kitten. Bug sat up, took Miles by the hand, and prodded him to do the same. The second he was upright, Bug wiggled into his lap, her small hands caressing his face.

Bug held Miles' rapt attention. He allowed her the freedom to chatter non-stop, their conversation unheard but fully understood. Miles nodded. Smiled and laughed when she did. And then she reached around and hugged his neck the way a daughter would her father. And when Miles wrapped a smile and his arms around her and stroked her wind-blown curls, Rachel's heart disintegrated, pieces of it lodged in her throat so tightly she couldn't breathe, and she pinned the moment to memory.

"I'll be okay without him, don't you think, Grandpa?" She blinked but couldn't help the gathering tears. "Without Nico, I mean?"

"I believe it with all my heart, Button. You have Miles. And Miles has both of you to care for. To protect. And to love." He looked away then, and she allowed him a moment to collect himself. "That man loves my two girls as much as I do. I can't ask for anything more than that."

"I miss Nico at times," she said, a tear slipping from her eye. "But I think you're right. We'll be okay." She'd often questioned why Nico had been taken from her, but it had become abundantly clear. Nico had been the messenger—the one who'd found her drifting through life and given her roots; Miles the deliverer—the one who'd set her free, to love completely and without fear. Ambrose had been right.

Miles took Bug's hand and the two of them trudged up the hill, one big dog reluctantly in tow, tail wagging in time to a definite swagger, the other bounding with carefree effort in front of them. Zoe reached Rachel first and leapt into her lap.

Miles bent to Rachel, the evidence of her thoughts still moist on her cheek. "You okay?"

She cupped his cheek. "Never better."

"Mommy, Grandpa, guess what?" Bug shoved her way between them and crawled into Grandpa's lap. "Dr. Miles has a s'prise for me. Can we go to his house now? Please, Mommy? It's a birthday present and I have to have it now. He said you wouldn't mind." Bug tugged Rachel's sleeve. "Can we go?"

"Your birthday isn't for another month." Rachel shot Miles a wary look, but he ignored her and dug in the ice chest and pulled out a beer. He tipped the bottle to her in a mock salute, winked, and twisted the top. "I won't mind, huh?"

Miles buried the mischief in the bottle's mouth and took a long drink, deliberately avoiding the question.

"I'm slightly concerned, *Dr.* Miles," Rachel said, pressing her thumb and forefinger together. "This sounds fishy."

"You know I wouldn't do anything Bug didn't want me to do."

"That's what has me concerned. Bug asks. You deliver."

"Actually, someone else delivered." The mischief he'd tried to conceal took up residence in his eyes.

"I didn't ask, Mommy. Promise. Can we go now?"

"Grandpa?"

"It's been a long day. I'm ready when you are, Button." Grandpa looked to Miles and attempted a deliberate cough, the conspiracy as apparent in one as the other. "And the two of you have plans later, so I'll keep an eye on our little ladybug until you get back. Or overnight, if the notion should strike you."

"I'm outnumbered three to one." She slapped her thighs. "Okay, then. Let's call it a day."

Grandpa snuggled against his great-granddaughter. "Look there, Bug." He pointed in the western sky and whispered in her ear. "A rainbow to end our day."

The rainbow stretched from peak to meadow. "It's pretty, Grandpa, but which color do you like best? I like pink and yellow but I don't see pink."

"I love them all because they remind me of you." Puzzled, Bug squirmed around to face him. "You're as lovely as all the colors put together. You're my rainbow. And if you concentrate real hard there's every color you could imagine."

Bug jumped from Grandpa's lap and twirled in a circle. "Even pink?"

"Even pink."

"I love you, Grandpa. I love you I love you I love you. Can we go now?"

"I think someone's a little impatient." Grandpa winked. "I say we hit the road."

Bug hugged Miles around the legs, nearly toppling them both with the effort. "Yippee! We're going to Dr. Miles' house for ice cream."

Strider's tongue covered Bug's face in a slobbery kiss. She squealed and burst into giggles.

Rachel tucked away a grin. "Who said anything about ice cream?"

Bug stared up at Miles. He winked and put a finger to his lips to seal their mutual agreement.

No hesitation flavored Grandpa's response. "I think that's a splendid idea."

THIRTY-NINE

They'd come from Whisper of the Pines a little earlier than Rachel had expected. Grandpa had opted to return home for a nap before his great-granddaughter arrived for the evening, and Miles had put *Frozen* on the big screen in the room he referred to as the "little theater." It would handily seat a dozen movie buffs and bore no resemblance to anything little. She'd paid little attention to the movie, preferring Miles' expressions with Bug curled in his lap describing the movie in detail.

Cold May evenings in the Fall River Valley were far from unusual, and the warm afternoon had given way to a chilly evening. They'd moved from the theater to the living room, and Miles had stoked the fire, flames quickly consuming the chill. Strider had stretched out like a big bear rug near the hearth, Zoe curled nose to tail into his furry side.

Tucked into a corner of the sofa, Rachel hugged a pillow to her chest and let the warmth and ambiance of the fire settle comfortably around her. Bug sat at the table swinging her legs, humming "Let It Go" and scraping the last dribbles of ice cream from the bowl.

Bug's tongue made one last swipe over her mouth. "May I be 'scused?"

"Yes, baby. Wash your hands."

"I'm not sticky," she said, promptly wiping them down the front of her shirt.

Miles squatted in front of the hearth and poked the pine logs, hot pitch sending up tiny embers that quickly winked out. Against the muted glow of the fire, his rugged features softened, and Rachel straightened a curl, admiring the broad shoulders and the long line of his torso beneath the sleek-fitting suit coat. *Damn.* His mere presence held the power to hypnotize.

Bug tiptoed up behind Miles. A deep-set smile punctuated his profile and he turned and caught her with a bear-like growl, tickling her sides. Bug squealed and then fell silent, giggling too hard to breathe. His face burst wide open, leaving no question to his affection.

Miles lifted the squirming form over his shoulder, brought her wiggling and squealing to the sofa, and set her next to Rachel. "Keep an eye on this little monster for a sec."

Bug flew to her feet and hung onto the back of the sofa. "Is it s'prise time, Dr. Miles?"

Miles produced a small package from atop the refrigerator and handed it to her. Bug plopped next to Rachel and tore into the package, wrapping forgotten in a shredded heap.

Bug lifted the box top. "Mommy, look! A new yellow ladybug sweatshirt." She petted the bright red ladybug on the front and then gave it a noisy kiss, and Rachel helped her pull the hoodie over her head and rolled up the sleeves. It was a little big, plenty of room for next winter's growth.

"How'd you know?"

"My mishap was responsible for ruining hers the day of the fire." He pointed to his abdomen. "Found it on the internet and Molly helped with size." He shrugged so quickly it barely registered, his cheeks flushing.

Bug leapt into Miles' arms. "Thank you, Dr. Miles. I love my new sweatshirt, and I'll wear it on every Tuesday same as before, and I promise I won't get it dirty. Know what else?"

"What, Bug?"

"I love you, Dr. Miles." She squeezed his neck, and the invisible strings attached to Rachel's heart cinched tight.

"I love you too, Ladybug," he said, his voice on the verge of cracking. He peeled Bug from him and set her back on the sofa. "I'll be right back. I have something else for you." He returned promptly and stood motionless in the doorway. "Close your eyes, Bug. You too, Rachel."

Bug plastered her hands over her eyes without a hitch, but the challenge in his voice had Rachel's radar on high alert.

"Why me? It's not my birthday."

He grimaced. "Self-defense."

"Miles?" Rachel wasn't a vet, but she recognized an animal crate, this one roughly the same size as Zoe's decorated with a huge pink ribbon. "What have you done?"

He set the crate next to Bug, and her hands dropped as if weighted with stones. Her eyes popped open, wide chocolate circles ablaze.

"Go ahead, Bug. Open it."

A small mewl came from inside. Bug opened the door and a pale gray kitten with dark gray markings tentatively made its way to her lap. In mid-gasp, Bug froze.

Rachel glared at Miles.

He set the crate aside. "She needed a home."

"She?"

"Relax. I know a good vet who will spay her and keep her healthy, and I hear he's not opposed to trading favors for cat food. Kitty litter. Whatever."

An undeniable glare twitched Rachel's eye.

"Mommy?" The surprise, question, and undeniable love spilled from her daughter in a single word. Bug had been born chattering, yet she stared at the kitten, speechless.

Miles stood with his hands in his pockets. Rachel shook her head in a slow, disbelieving back and forth movement.

"She's the runt, Bug. Smaller than the others." Bug's head bobbed, but she kept her eyes glued to the kitten who had made herself comfortable kneading her paws into Bug's legs. "You have to be gentle with her."

"Miss Heather showed me how to hold them and be nice. I'm almost five, and I know how to be gentle." Bug looked up at Miles and then to Rachel, her little cheeks rosier than the sun could color them. "Can I keep her?"

Miles screwed up his features in an unsuccessful attempt to camouflage his own excitement. Thick, tousled locks of hair separated between his fingers as he pushed a hand through it, a marked pairing of her disheveled thoughts. So much for plans. So much for standing firm. He obviously didn't share her position on restraint when it came to Bug. Her plan to instruct this man in the fine art of early childhood discipline had backfired.

The sofa cushions took the brunt of the concession as she pointedly leaned heavily into them. "Outnumbered again."

The tension visibly drained from his body. "Marshall said you'd be okay with it."

"If I recall, I said she could feed them, not keep them."

"Not all three. Just one."

Rachel planted a palm to her forehead. "Outnumbered. Outwitted. Outplayed. Do you have anything to say for yourself, Doctor?"

He shrugged. "She's a sweet kitten."

"You're a vet. Is there an animal you don't think is sweet?"

"Besides Jezebel, I've met a few that don't take kindly to my poking and prodding." He squatted beside Bug and scratched the kitten behind the ears, his big hand engulfing the silver-white ball of fur. The kitten seized his thumb, closed her eyes, and began to purr.

"Veterinary super powers at work?"

"It's been known to have its effect on humans too. One in particular gave me a nasty bite." He massaged his shoulder with the enthusiasm of a budding actor. "But while entrusted to my care, said human has a tendency to purr." Way too much campy desire gathered in his eyes.

"I do not purr." A gritty pause separated each word.

"Call it whatever you want." He stood, leaned over, and kissed the top of her head. "Definitely sounds like purring to me," he said, the words muffled in her hair.

"Mommy, please?" Bug let out a big puff of air that lifted her curls and then cupped her hand to Miles' ear. "This baby kitty will be a grown up before Mommy says yes."

Miles' strangled chuckle turned into a non-committal cough. "Well, Mom?"

Rachel coaxed Bug's unruly curls behind an ear. "It'll be your responsibility to take care of her."

"I will cuz I know how. Honest."

Zoe jumped to the sofa, her black nose wiggling as she sniffed the kitten and then licked its tiny nose. "Zoe loves her already, Mommy. So do I."

Strider wasn't about to be outdone by his appetizer-sized companion, and barged his way through the tangle of legs. The big dog laid his head on Bug's lap and nudged the kitten with a satisfied groan.

"Four to one." Rachel threw her hands up and dropped them to her thighs. "I give up."

"Happy birthday, Bug." Pleasure spilled from Miles' salutation.

Bug squished the kitten to her chest. "I can keep her?"

Rachel shot Miles a resigned look and received a smug one in return. "You can keep her. What do you tell Dr. Miles?"

"Thank you, Dr. Miles. Thank you thank you thank you." Childlike wonder shimmered not only from her daughter's big, brown eyes, but the big kid's blue ones as well. Bug snuggled the furball into her neck and rocked from side to side. "I'll take good care of her. I promise I promise I promise."

Rachel made room for Miles on the sofa and he draped an arm around her shoulder. "She'll need a name."

"My kitty is a girl. Miss Heather said so and I already named her Dory, same as the movie." Bug snuggled into her mother and handed Dory to Rachel. "The other ones are Mr. Ray cuz he teached them to eat crunchy food, and the other one is Crush cuz he's the leader and he takes them on adventures."

"They're perfect names, baby." The kitten's eyes drooped and she reinstated the noisy purr.

Miles stroked the kitten behind the shoulder. "From *Finding Dory?*"

"Uh huh. But my Dory will never have to 'member where her family is." Bug crawled over Rachel's lap and nestled between her and Miles. "Because we're her family and we're all right here." She patted their legs and tipped her head up to each one in turn. "For always."

~

Whisper of the Pines Resort took on a different atmosphere after dark. The playful flavor of the area where they'd spent the day chasing bubbles and clouds was bathed in the subtle glow from the streetlamps, and the shadows had deepened in the moon's amber wake. Rachel snuggled into him, shadows be damned.

The distant clip-clop of a horse-drawn carriage seemed the fitting mode of transportation, but she'd asked to walk instead. Huddled with her in the carriage would have been nice, but walking along the cobbled path with no one else in sight would take longer, and Miles had no problem taking his time.

He'd come here often, supporting his buddy and his crazy dream. Shep had encouraged him to stop by tonight to listen to a new song he'd written and wanted to try it out on the crowd. When Shep slipped out of park ranger mode or SAR volunteer and into that of singer/songwriter, his entire demeanor shifted. The ladies loved him. Guys loved him too—he had the uncanny ability to deliver a love song that had the women falling all over their men.

Rachel grasped his arm with both of hers. "It's lovely here at night."

In truth, he hadn't considered his surroundings; he'd favored only her. She'd worn a snug pair of dressy black jeans, calf high boots, and a sweater that fit her delightfully in all the right places, but she was covered by too much winter coat and too much scarf.

Ahead, light spilled from the windows of the spacious cabin.

"This is new."

"Logan Cavanaugh's idea. Guy's got a sixth sense when it comes to resorts." The building, modeled after the same log-siding of the lobby, sat at the end of the cobbled path near the footbridge. "Logan thought it would add to the summer visitors if they had a place reserved for dances, parties, weddings."

Rachel's sigh formed a wispy white cloud. "Perfect venue for a wedding."

"Gives Shep a place to mess around with his music. Logan didn't hesitate to hire him once he heard him sing."

The rhythm and beat of a country-rock song met them as they approached the door.

"I'm anxious to hear him."

"Just don't fall for his wiles. He's got a way with the ladies."

"How old did you say he was?"

"I didn't."

She puckered her mouth.

"He's a couple of years younger than I am, but he acts like a kid."

"And you don't?"

Miles chuckled. "Point taken."

"He's nice looking. For a *younger* man."

"Cougar tendencies, have we?" Miles made an exaggerated imitation of a purring cat.

She curled her gloved fingers into claws and growled. "I do not purr and I've got all I can handle with a certain vet who's slowly but surely spoiling my daughter."

"She deserves to be spoiled. As does her mother." He kissed her neck, the spicy scent of untamed wildflowers dissolving his words into a groan. He took her waist, opened the heavy wooden door, and led her inside, Shep's deep voice and the combined mix of guitars greeting them.

Rachel stuffed her gloves in her pockets, and Miles took her coat and scarf and hung them on the hooks adjacent to the door.

He twirled her in a slow circle. "You look lovely tonight. Your new scarf suits you."

"It was time I put the other one away. Gray's not really my color," she said, fiddling with the buttons on his jacket. "You clean up nicely yourself, Doctor."

He traced his thumb along the outline of jaw and throat and down to the low scoop of her sweater, fingers itching to explore beyond the visible. "You aren't wearing your rings."

Rachel's hand went to her neck, absent of the chain with the rings Desi had given her and Nico. "I've put Nico's scarf and the rings away for good. They're my past. You're my future." She smiled and took his hand and brought it to her cheek. "I'll keep them though. Bug may want them someday."

The reminders from the past were tucked away, the history behind them secured somewhere safe, void of the presence that kept them alive. A bubble of something, something he couldn't name spread through him like soft butter on bread. It wasn't happiness. Not really. Perhaps it was simply contentment, knowing she'd put the reminders aside for him. For them. Not forgotten, just *away*.

"One day you'll tell her the story behind them and how she came to be."

"Yes." Rachel stopped, trailing her hand along his arm. "Thank you, Miles. For understanding. You're an amazing man."

"I doubt if Jezebel agrees."

A playful nudge hit his tender ribs, but he laughed it off.

Lights hung from hand-hewn beams and a few couples graced the dance floor. Miles motioned her to an empty table with a clear view of the stage. He sat next to her, close enough to ward off any would-be pursuers.

Rachel squeezed his arm. "I think I've already proven I'm not good at anything that includes feet and requires coordination, so if you intend to ask me to dance it will have to be slow. And you have to promise you won't laugh."

"Mine aren't much more coordinated, Sunshine."

"It still surprises me, you know." She tilted her head. "That you—mister audacious—have no trouble barreling down a mountain on slivers of wood, or slithering into an ice cave with the grace of a ballet dancer, or staying upright in a tiny boat but have trouble maneuvering your feet on solid ground."

"Composite. Skis are a composite of materials."

"They're still skinny."

"And they're kayaks. Not tiny boats."

"Whatever. They're too small and they tip over."

"Would you care for something to drink?"

"Changing the subject?"

"Desperately trying to. Audacious I can handle. Dancer—of any kind," he said, wiggling a hand, "not so much. My social skills are somewhat lacking."

"Your *social* skills," Rachel whispered, "go above and beyond what you can do on the slopes."

"Your slopes are the only ones I care to prove my skills on." He brushed her soft curls aside. "Like here," he said, lightly kissing the gentle curve between shoulder and neck. And she answered with a soft sigh, her skin shivering on his lips.

"The kitten is purring again."

"I do not purr."

It wouldn't have taken much more than this subtle hint to skip the dance, strip her of those snug jeans, and have his way with her. Though having her on his arm was deeply satisfying, finding her naked in his bed eclipsed any night out. His selfishness went beyond sharing her with the past, and he'd carried it with him into the present. Wanting to be alone with her wasn't charitable. It was greedy. And when it came to her, his self-indulgence exceeded charity.

The dress jacket he'd worn with a long-sleeved shirt and black jeans suddenly seemed much too warm.

Rachel crossed her arms on top of the table. "Chardonnay sounds nice."

He touched her lightly below the ear, stood, and headed across the room. The bartender poured a glass of chardonnay, popped the top on a Corona Extra and stuffed a wedge of lime in the neck. He took a long pull, the bottle cool in his palm.

Shep ended the song with a sultry guitar run and tipped his chin at Miles.

Miles crossed the room, handed Rachel her glass of wine, and set his beer down. "Shep wants to talk to me. I'll be just a minute."

"Tell him I said he's got that sexy, gravelly voice thing going on."

"I don't know…he tends to get a big head when a beautiful woman talks to him that way."

"He's talented, Miles. And exceedingly handsome out of his SAR garb."

"And you know this how exactly?"

He must have given his reservations away, because she almost choked on her wine. "I meant he looks nice dressed up." She took his hand and gave it a gentle squeeze. "So do you. You should wear a jacket more often." She looked him up and down, and the notion to undress her as she was silently undressing him sent his blood south at record speed.

"Yeah, well, if you don't stop looking at me that way I won't be wearing a jacket." He downed another swig of beer. "I won't be wearing anything at all."

"Go." She sipped her wine and took up a wayward curl.

Shep lifted the strap from around his neck and stood his guitar in the stand. The band members followed suit, vying for first place at the bar.

Miles slapped his buddy on the shoulder. "What's up?"

"I'm glad you two could make it tonight. I've planned a special song for you and your lady and wanted to introduce it while you two were here." Shep dragged a hand across his neck and left it there. "I couldn't get the melody out of my head and I couldn't sleep one night a while back, so I spent the night writing."

"You're about half off your rocker, you crazy bastard."

"Takes one to know one." Shep's grin turned modest. "It's a song for Ladybug. For Nicole. She'll understand when she's older." Shep stuck his hands in his pockets. It's up next.

"You wrote it for Bug?"

"Yes. For both of you, too. Maybe it'll take your minds off everything that's happened recently, or put it all in perspective."

"Love song?"

"Think of it as a love story." Shep scraped a hand over his jaw. "A ballad."

"I've seen the way women react when you sing your love songs. Shit, Rachel might leave with you when she hears it."

"She might be better off with this asshole than the one standing next to me."

They exchanged a droll laugh and pulled each other into a hug and another hard slap on the shoulders.

"Rachel says you've got a good voice. Thinks you're handsome too. I think she might be nearsighted."

"Definitely needs her eyes examined looking at your scruffy ass." A sly smile that reeked of shared mischief curved Shep's neatly landscaped face, but was quickly replaced with a serious complacency. "You're one lucky bastard, Malone. She's something special."

Miles nodded, the voicing of what he already knew as warm as the alcohol swirling in his stomach.

Shep took a few steps backward and then turned and hopped on stage. In what must have been a cue for the band to return, he tapped the mic and took a stool center stage. Through the artistry of Shep's fingers, the chords came alive, the solo guitar saturating the room with seamless notes.

"Care to dance?" Miles took Rachel's hand. "I think this one has our name on it."

She hesitated, but followed him to the center of the floor. "At least it's slow."

He tucked her hand to his chest and found her waist with the other.

"Ladies and gentlemen." Shep tapped the mic and waited for the chatter to quiet. "It's an honor to have Miles Malone and his lady, Rachel Caldarone, with us tonight." Shep offered a hand in their direction and then continued to strum. Two more guitars joined, the combination of strings blending to a pleasing harmony. The drummer's swish-swish-tap rode the waves of the melody, tapping into the gentle pulse. "If not for Miles, I wouldn't have made it out of Iraq." He adjusted a boot on the footrest, the chords growing loud and then softening. He looked up, scanning the small crowd. "I owe this guy my life and it's good to see him happy. If you'll give them the floor, I'd like to dedicate this next song to them. This one's for you, buddy. Semper fi."

Miles offered a tilt of his chin and a mumbled, "Semper fi."

"For us?"

"Seems so." The melody came slow and built to a steady rhythm. Miles locked Rachel's hand in his and she nestled against him. Cradled against his chest, Rachel tipped her head up, blue eyes a kaleidoscope of brilliance above a quirky smile. "What's on your mind, Sunshine?"

She planted a kiss on his jacket. "Seems I'm not the only one here tonight who loves you."

"Shep's a crazy bastard, but he's a good guy."

"I hope he finds someone."

"He will. It's only been a couple of years since his divorce."

Rachel took his forearms, stood on her toes, and kissed him. "For healing. And because I love you, Dr. Malone."

"And I've loved you since the first time I held you, and I will love you beyond all measure of time."

Miles turned her slowly. His hands drifted to her hips and rested there, the power to hold him up residing in the feel of her surrendering to his touch. The soft strum of guitar strings and Shep's husky voice rose up around them, fusing an inward connection to the lyrics. He tucked Rachel's head under his chin and as he placed a leisurely kiss on the top of her head, movement at the exit caught his eye.

A lanky figure with disheveled silver hair tipped his head and bowed, leaning heavily on his cane. Others began to gather around them and he momentarily lost sight of the old man. When he turned Rachel back around, he scanned the room.

Ambrose was nowhere to be seen.

"Believe." The outlandish thought slipped from him, fully formed with an air of illusion yet steeped in impossible truth. Was he real? A product of his imagination? Or both? "He was right."

"Who?"

"I don't exactly know." He filled his senses with the feel of her against him, her signature fragrance, and the power of her love. "All I know is you and Bug are my life. My loves. The reason I live."

The lyrics bled from Shep's heart and soul, his voice graveled and mellow and deeply haunting.

Miles tightened his hold. The music and lyrics burrowed into his bones, haunting and real, and reflected the mood of the night and of time spent in the trenches deep in blowing sand and blood he couldn't wash away. Of incredible bonds. But mostly they spoke what he himself couldn't, of years past and the culmination of the last weeks, words Shep had plucked from his soul, written in ink, and given self-lessly back.

Miles held her close, their small movements a reflection of the crowd, a reflection of the song written for them:

I Found You
(A Song for Ladybug)

Met you on a cold, gray night
the snow a cover for your tears
hope a shelter for your fears
I was lost
lost within your heavy heart
held you tight
tight against my chest
couldn't take from you
the mountain's fierce unrest
couldn't turn the path of fate around
the night he couldn't be found

Couldn't bear the sorrow in your eyes
but no words could I say
you were his not mine to hold
I was lost
lost and couldn't walk away
couldn't save you

save you from the broken dreams
wipe away the bitter tears
that kept you from me all these years
couldn't turn the path of fate around
the night he couldn't be found

Never gave up
never gave in
never let the mountain win
never stopped searching
never stopped loving
never let the mountain win
and in searching for him
I found you

She's got his eyes, your smile, his name
and his blood runs through her veins
she belongs to him, but she's my little girl
and I'm lost
lost since my heart fell for her
and she has taken all of mine
mine 'til the end of time
you call her Ladybug, but I call her mine
couldn't turn the path of fate around
the night he couldn't be found

You've been through hell and back again
I held your hand never let you fall
she's my little girl, you're my all
and I'm lost
lost in your world
gone too far to go back when
back to when it all began—
when you turned darkness into light
when I found you on that cold gray night

the night the path of fate unwound
the night he couldn't be found

Never gave up
never gave in
never let the mountain win
never stopped searching
never stopped loving
never let the mountain win
and in searching for him
I found you

I never gave up
and you let me in
never let the mountain win
and in searching for him
I found you
I found love
love enough for two
~ shephard dawson ©2017

EPILOGUE

ONE YEAR LATER

he butterfly kite with its red, yellow, and purple wings and sweeping tails sailed across the late afternoon sky, dipping and twisting high above the sea. Its movements mimicked the queasy tidal wave in her stomach, and she looked away briefly, allowing a moment for the contents to settle. The scene on the beach below her took root, time squeezing the memory into her heart and imprinting it in her mind so she wouldn't forget a minute of their last afternoon here.

The warm breeze blowing off the Mediterranean tossed her hair, and she curled it absently behind an ear. Breathing in a lungful of the salty air, she paused, and with the exception of the tiny family on the beach, the world around her dissolved. She swam light and carefree in the momentary indulgence, as if suspended weightless beneath the turquoise sea.

Digging her toes into the warm pink sand, Rachel sat with her knees to her chest, and not for the first time in the past year wondered how she got so lucky.

Time nudged her now and then, tapping her with the icy fingers of grief. At times the nightmares caught her unaware, but their power had lessened and Miles kept her grounded, her anchor through the storm. It wasn't simply the way he looked at her or the way he held her, but the essence of power and strength his presence provided. Perhaps it was the part of him he'd absorbed from the mountains he loved. Perhaps it was the part of him left in the deserts of Iraq. Perhaps it was the sum of him—the missing piece—the piece that made her whole.

The setting sun cast its rays over the sea, spinning sparks of gold in Miles' sun-bleached hair and bathing his skin in a warm glow. He'd tanned easily, as did Bug's olive skin, darkening to a deep bronze though she'd slathered them both with sunscreen.

Miles instructed Bug how to fly the kite, and his graceful body matched the dips and turns as the kite soared above them. The kite's tails, Miles' shirt, and Bug's plaid sundress whipped in the sea breeze, silhouettes billowing against the fading day.

Marked with Bug's squeals, their laughter hung in the wind, traveled the edge of the beach, and disappeared behind the rise of staggering cliffs. She couldn't make out the words, but their actions needed no interpretation.

With Bug by his side, Miles kneeled in the sand and helped her reel in the kite, a comma pausing the end of a perfect afternoon. They set the ball of string on top to keep the kite from blowing away, and Miles took Bug's hands, engaged in a conversation of some serious nature. Bug hung on his every word. He paused, Bug's head bobbing vigorously, and she fell into his arms. He returned the enthusiastic hug, engulfing her small frame and swiping at the misbehaving curls that had come loose from her braids and danced wildly about their faces.

Miles stood then, and Bug grabbed him by the shirttail, hurrying him through the sand, her legs working overtime as they made their way up the beach.

Bug flopped herself on the beach towel next to Rachel.

"You two did great with the kite. I've never seen one sail so high."

Bug reached up to the sky. "It was sailing all the way up to heaven to find Grandpa and tell him we love him and miss him. Dr. Miles said so. Can it go that high, Mommy? Up to heaven? Do you think Grandpa saw it?"

"I'm sure he did, baby." Grief sunk its hooks into her, the ache worse for its unexpected return. "Grandpa's keeping an eye on us from heaven." The words formed hoarse and uneven but sure in spirit. And for the first time in a very long time, she embraced the idea of heaven, for it shined in her daughter's eyes.

"Grandpa said I was his rainbow and my kite has more colors than all the rainbows ever."

The words burned in the corners of her eyes, but if she cried, the colors of a perfect afternoon would surely run.

Miles brushed the sand from his shorts and bare legs and sat opposite her. "You okay?"

"Just thinking about Grandpa."

"The kite." He lowered his chin. "I'm sorry. It's only been a few months." He took her hand, the warm breeze ruffling his hair.

"It was a thoughtful gesture. Bug loved it. So did I. Grandpa would have approved."

She'd held her grandfather's hand for a long time that day, beyond the moment life passed from his body, the same way he'd held hers all those years—with the strength and courage his love provided to continue on. Miles had been there with them, his presence consuming the silence and then assuming the bond of family as her hand passed from her grandfather's into his.

Miles' expression grew quietly content. "Something else on your mind, Sunshine?"

Setting the recollection aside, she turned, tilting her head. "I'm curious." She caressed his arm, sun-kissed hair rising in the wake of her fingertip. "What has Bug so excited?"

Bug and Miles shared a mutual *I've got a secret* look. Rachel squinted at them as if she could coerce an answer by sheer force of will. Miles winked and helped her to her feet. "C'mon. I've got something to show my girls."

Rachel brushed the sand from the backside of her sundress, the breeze flowing through the gauzy material, and slipped into her sandals.

Bug's eyes widened. "Is it time, Dr. Miles?"

"A little while longer." Miles draped a cover-up over Rachel's shoulders and she slipped into it, the long sleeves a buffer to the cool sea breeze. He slipped the ladybug hoodie over Bug—the one he'd given her a year ago and she insisted on wearing though the sleeves rode too high on her wrists, the hem just above her waist. He took them by the hand and led them through a dense portion of under-brush to a small pool.

Rocky cliffs rose sharply from the Mediterranean Sea, and similar boulders surrounded the pool. The sun's dying rays sparkled on the water and fronds of an aquatic plant swayed, tickling the surface. Rachel tucked the sundress under her and sat on an overhanging ledge. Miles sat next to her.

Bug hopped from boulder to boulder exploring and humming a song Rachel recognized but couldn't place. "Hey, no fair." Bug swished a hand in the water, ripples feathering outward. "There's no starfish in here."

Rachel slipped out of her sandals and dipped a foot into the water, clear and cool on her bare feet.

"This pool is fed by a natural freshwater spring."

"It's not a tidal pool?" Rachel stretched her leg and set a foot on a mound of emerald green moss, the plant soft and spongy between her toes.

"One of the locals mentioned it and it's why I chose this beach today. I wanted it to be a surprise for Bug." He spread his palms across his knees and flexed his fingers.

"Is it time now?"

"Come sit with us for a minute first."

Arms balanced out from her sides, Bug zigzagged her way through the rocks and scooted into his lap. Miles wrapped an arm around her, the other over Rachel's shoulder.

"Do you remember when I promised to bring you a preserved scorpion?"

"You brought me one from 'Zona that time you went there with Mommy. He's triple cool!"

Rachel scrunched her nose. Though preserved in a generous amount of acrylic, it still gave her the creeps.

"And I catched a red-eyed damselfly in a jar the day before yesterday and then let her go because she might die in there." Bug pushed loose hair from her face with both hands, the skin stretching and then springing magically back.

"And I also promised to show you sparkle bugs."

Bug gasped and plastered her small, dimpled hands to her face. "Sparkle bugs live here?"

"Turn around, baby girl."

The air came alive with tiny flashes of florescent yellow-green. Bug squealed and slipped from his grasp and scampered to the far side of the pool. The tiny beetles winked off and on, and she reached for them, her mouth in a permanent gasp with no words to share.

Rachel couldn't find words. Time ceased to pass as the beetles' winking lights kept time with the melody in her heart. "They're like something from a fairy tale." She spoke, but the words came out a little wobbly. "She'll never forget this night. Neither will I."

"I wanted to make this night memorable." He kissed her temple. "But...you haven't seen a firefly either?"

"It's a standing joke at work." She paused and let loose a silly chuckle. "I'm such a world traveler. I've lived in Arizona and Colorado, traveled through New Mexico a few times and never farther east than Colorado."

"You're east of Colorado now. About halfway around the world to be exact."

"I'll have a heck of a story to tell my patients when I get back." She tossed a pebble into the pool, the ripples radiating soundlessly outward. "Seems my guy took me all the way to Italy to the island of Sardinia just to show me a sparkle bug."

"Not exactly, Sunshine." The full power of his smile never waned, but she grew conscious of her heart—a small tug, not quite an ache, that matched the shadow of doubt darkening his eyes. "I brought you here for two reasons." A strand of hair lifted in the moist air and stuck to her mouth. He wound it behind her ear, the touch delicate and laced with sincerity. "Bug needs to know her family. Where she comes from."

The hours they'd spent with Nico's family had been as anxious as it had been extraordinary. They'd welcomed them all with the exuberance of a Sicilian homecoming and had taken Bug as one of their own. How could they not? Her resemblance to Nico was striking, the Caldarone inheritance unmistakable.

But death had a way of shaping an unspoken intimacy with those it touched, burrowing in beside the joy. Tears that had threatened to make an appearance earlier made good on their promise. "I'm sorry."

"It wasn't my intention to make you cry."

She wiped the moisture from her cheeks. "Seems that's all I do these days."

"I only wanted to make sure Bug knows her family. Her heritage."

"You amaze me, you know that?"

"It's another one of my super powers."

"And cockiness."

"I try."

She shook her head, a small chuckle fading with it. "She'll know her roots, and I thank you for that. But you're her family now." The courage to say the next words had left her more than once, but it swelled inside her, painfully aware of the need to be said. "She loves you, Miles, as she would the father she's never had."

His wistful smile blossomed into a face-splitting grin. "I could never love a child more than I love that little girl. Not even my own."

The admission grabbed her heart, Grandpa's words rushing back, filling whatever lapse in faith she'd had. Maybe everything would be okay. "You can't possibly know how much I love you right now."

"You can show me." He brushed his thumb along her chin and to the base of her ear, and the playful glint in his eyes went straight to her core, an ember fanned to full flame. "Later."

Her hand crept to the inside of his thigh and squeezed. "I think you'd better focus on something else."

"I think you're right." Miles kissed her lightly and helped her to her feet. "I think it's time, Bug."

Bug threw a spree of rapid-fire kisses to the fireflies and quickly abandoned her post. "C'mon, Mommy. We need to go back to the beach."

"Finished with the sparkle bugs so soon?"

"This is more 'portant than sparkle bugs. More 'portant than anything in the whole wide world." She spread her arms wide enough to capture the entire planet in a big Bug hug.

Nothing had ever been more important than insects, but Rachel didn't argue. The sand was warm, the night was young, and she held the two most important people in her life by the hand and by the invisible strings of her heart.

Miles led them to the edge of the water, a wave striving inland trickling between her toes. The last wake of sunlight shimmered on the water, the soft ebb and flow a soothing hush as the waves kissed the sand. Sunset glowed across Miles' skin, gilding him with a warmth that softened the chiseled line of chin and jaw. His hair, the kind the sea breeze enjoyed whipping about, spilled over his forehead in golden streaks. Just the way she liked him. Messy. Wild. Completely undone and entirely put together.

But the playfulness he'd displayed a moment ago had dimmed.

He lifted her chin with the gentleness she'd come to know, but a flicker of hesitancy resided in the movement. "I thought this would be easy."

Bug yanked on his shirttail. "Now, Dr. Miles?"

He patted Bug's head and hugged Rachel to his side. "In a minute, Ladybug. I'll give you the signal."

"Miles, what's—"

He put a finger to her lips. "Men are fickle sometimes and they get this big idea in their head about what love is and they find out that the idea of being in love is somewhat different than actually being in love and then they do things—"

Rachel covered her mouth, but failed to stop an unladylike snort.

"What's so funny?"

Bug toggled between the two.

"You sound like my daughter. You're rambling, Doctor. If you've something to say, why not spit it out?"

"What I'm trying to say…" He paused and shuffled his feet, muscles tensing with the movement. "Not only do I love you, Rachel, but I'm *in* love with you." He swallowed, the motion as evident as the quaver in his voice. "I love every inch of you, every facet of who you are, and every space between. I love your daughter and I swear it will be your name I speak when I take my last breath."

He caught Bug's eye and winked. Hopping into action, she cupped her hands around her mouth in a makeshift megaphone and hauled in a lungful of air. "Ziggy, COME!"

Bug tugged on Rachel's sleeve, bouncing on her toes. "Look down there on the beach, Mommy. Quick! Look!"

A black silhouette lumbered along the edge of the waves, a small one racing beside it. "This can't be, can it?" She took a step toward them, but Bug latched onto her skirt.

"Wait, Mommy. They'll come to us."

Rachel whipped around, gaping at Miles. "Is that Strider and Zoe?"

"Closest I could come, but no, not exactly."

The big chocolate Newfoundland bounded toward them and then sat obediently at Rachel's feet, the tiny Yorkie pulling in the reins beside the big dog.

"Meet Ziggy." Miles scratched the big dog behind the ears. Ziggy groaned, eyes growing drowsy. "And the little guy is Wade. I sorta borrowed them."

Rachel kneeled, took Ziggy's head in her hands, and planted a noisy kiss between his ears. "Aren't you the spitting image of Strider. And you, little man, could be Zoe's twin brother." Wade danced on his hind legs, turning a complete circle. He sat, dipped his nose under her wrist and when she didn't respond, he nudged her again, a small box dangling from his collar.

"I think Wade's trying to tell you something." Miles raked a hand halfway through his hair and parked it there. "Maybe you should take the box?"

"Hurry up, Mommy." Bug danced on her toes, braids bouncing erratically. "Hurry up and open it!"

Rachel untied the ribbon. Miles dropped to one knee and took her elbow. Bug scooted between them and placed her hand on Miles' shoulder as if the purpose of their mission lay in the simple connection.

Rachel's hands trembled, not sure if the movement was her, the man who knelt beside her, or Bug's excited bouncing.

"Please open it, Rachel."

She did.

Fireworks of color reflected off a marquise diamond. The gold of a rising sun. The pink of the Sardinia sand. The blue of solemn eyes. And the red of a fiery sunset. Smaller diamonds set deep in the platinum band winked like a flurry of tiny fireflies. Rachel covered her mouth to contain an undignified sob but found she couldn't breathe.

"I've waited my entire life for something as real as what we have, Rachel. Are you ready to make it official? To become a family? Will you do me the honor of becoming my wife?"

"Mommy, Mommy, please say yes. I told Dr. Miles you would. He asked me first and I said yes! It was easy. I said it right out loud."

Words jumbled together in a mishmash of incoherency. Thoughts of marriage had skirted her mind, but she hadn't focused on them—until recently and only then for purely selfish reasons. She'd considered how it would affect her daughter. How it would affect her. And Miles. The connection Bug and Miles shared was special, but it was evident she'd missed the mark completely. "I—"

Miles took her hand and they rose to their feet. He waved and a shrill, distant whistle rang out and the two dogs bounded up the beach in the direction they'd come. Ziggy's ears flopped and Wade's legs blurred, running full out to keep up with his mentor.

Bug bounced on her toes, waving. "Bye, Ziggy. Bye, Wade." A muffled woof and a sharp yip answered her.

Miles removed the ring from its velvet nest. "It belonged to my maternal grandmother."

A noisy gasp escaped through her fingers. "It's breathtaking. But your mother...Glenda is okay with this?"

"The ring was her idea." He tilted the diamond to catch the fading light. "Her bark is worse than her bite. Just ask my father. This is her gift to you, her way of welcoming you to the family. They adore Bug, and I think they want both of you to be a part of our family as much as I do. So...will you? Will you honor me this day and every day from now on? Will you marry me, Rachel?"

The answer stalled on her tongue, stuck somewhere between surprise and disbelief. Her eyes settled on his, the anticipation and apprehension in them turning liquid.

"If I have to, I'll beg."

Bug balanced her weight on one leg. "Mom." The designation wasn't a question but an accusation of extreme impatience. "What exactly is the problem?" She deposited her hands on her hips and tapped her bare toes, the emphasis unapparent in the sand. "C'mon, Dr. Miles, kiss her already and make her say yes!"

Both their heads dropped, staring at the almost six-year-old as if she'd uttered a profanity. Miles palmed her head and turned it upward. "Where did you hear that, young lady?"

"Dusty. At school." Bug fiddled with the drawstrings on her hoodie. "He said his mommy and daddy kiss all the time."

Mommy and Daddy.

The significance of the words coiled around Rachel's middle. Bug had a father. In the literal sense. The man whose life had been taken before he could hold his daughter's hand; who never smelled the sweetness of her skin, kissed her button nose, or tucked her in at night; the man who had worshiped her, sang to her, and loved her from outside the womb.

Nico would never hold her hand and dance at her first father/daughter dance. Share career day at school. Dry her tears. Laugh with her. Blow bubbles in the spring air, fly kites, and pace the night away every time she went on a date. Her father would never have the chance to do those things. But the man beside her would. Because he loved her little girl. Because they had a history now.

Yes, she had a father, but she didn't have a daddy.

"I think the two kindergartners may have a point," Miles said and kissed her, the sensation an immediate balm to panic's probing fingers.

"It's about time." Bug plastered both hands over her eyes. "Sheesh, I thought I had issues."

The hunger in his kiss left her void of gravity, the tide sweeping the sand from beneath her feet. And she took his kiss and gave it back, and to hell with keeping it from her daughter. She loved this man. Loved the doctor, the rescuer, the adventurer, and the intimacy of the sensual lover. He was the keeper of her daughter's heart. Owner of hers.

A slow-motion smile matured on her lips.

"Is that a yes?"

Time moved at a crawl. Words formed and then vanished in the swirling breeze, but her thoughts matched a vigorous nod.

He slipped the ring on her finger, the diamonds no contest to the brilliance in his eyes.

Rachel twirled the platinum band, the facets cut in the diamonds catching the sparks of the dwindling daylight.

For better or worse.

She'd been blessed with the love of two men. Two men who had picked up the pieces and healed her splintered past. She loved them both in equal measure, wholly and completely, and though Nico was gone, a part of him would be with her always. But Miles would be the one to keep her warm at night. Keep her safe from the nightmares.

She smiled up at him, his face a watery portrait. "Definitely a yes."

"Yippee! Yippee!" Bug's arms and legs went all whichaway and she twirled until she landed in the sand with a plop. Rachel lifted her to her feet and held her, her little body unsteady. "I don't feel so good, Mommy."

Miles picked her up and carried her to their towels.

Rachel squatted next to her and kissed her forehead. "Can you sit here for a few minutes while your tummy settles? I need to talk to Dr. Miles."

"No fair backing out." Bug's mouth puckered. "You can't because I really want to meet my Aunt Madison. She's pretty and Dr. Miles said she'd come see us if you got married."

"Don't worry, baby. I just need to talk to him for a minute." Bug curled in a ball, humming quietly to herself. "We'll be right by the water. Your tablet is in the beach bag if you feel better."

Bug continued her self-consoling, twining and untwining the drawstrings through her fingers. Rachel kicked off her sandals and she and Miles made their way through the sand to the water's edge.

"Is she okay?"

"Just dizzy. She got a little too excited."

"Her enthusiasm is contagious."

The rhythm of the waves lapping against the shore brought both comfort and unrest—the assurance of the known and ebb and flow of change. That crazy flutter of uneasiness that came with the shift in transition.

"You seem a little distracted."

"Miles, I—" She took a step up the beach, but he took her hand.

"Is something bothering you, Sunshine? Are you not sure about this?"

The first pinpoints of stars popped into the twilight sky. The breeze off the Mediterranean blew softly against her cheek and fanned the tails of her cover-up. She looped her arm through Miles' elbow, steeling herself to the reservations she'd carried inside for weeks.

"Did you mean it when you said you love Bug...as if she were your own child?" When the words had been but thought, they hadn't sounded so harsh. Gooseflesh made a slow crawl down her arms.

Miles turned and met her eyes. "Is that what's bothering you?" His rugged features shone soft against a pale, rising moon. It wasn't the question, but the way in which he said it that lessened her doubt.

His thumbs tracked the imperceptible scar past ear and under eye and settled on her cheek. "I love you and Bug with everything in me, and I'd give my life for either of you. Nothing could change my feelings, only deepen them, and I can't imagine my life without either of you." The brief lapse stretched into his next words. "I don't know how to explain it, except by proving it every day for the rest of my life."

"Nothing will change how you feel?"

"'You call her Ladybug, but I call her mine.'" A faint smile turned inward. "My blood may not flow through her veins, but she owns my heart. Nothing will ever change that, Rachel. Shep took what I feel, what I couldn't express, and put it into notes and words in a way I never could."

Tears threatened, but she blinked them back and retrieved a photograph from her pocket. It trembled in her hand. "This may change your mind."

Moonlight caught the images. His body went rigid and by the look on his face whatever possibilities he'd imagined this wasn't one of them.

The tears she'd forced back made a grand entrance. "It was taken a few days before we left." Disgusted with her lack of resolve, she wiped the tears, but new ones fell in their place.

"When did this happen?"

A noise not quite a sob and not quite a laugh escaped with an uncertain shrug. "I'm not exactly sure."

Waves splashed over her feet, the cool water a relief to the unsettled heat of an awkward exchange—one she never envisioned having. Shadows formed in the folds of his opened shirt, the assurance of him a solid silhouette masking an opaque expression.

The scent of tropical flowers soured her stomach, and she took in a long breath through her mouth to quiet the churn. Gulls called in the distance and the tide rushed past, time as still as the hush of death, and as alive as the life inside her.

He blinked, the only movement save his trembling hands. "Why, Rachel?"

The question lay between them, a dozen answers as heavy as the mist weeping off the ocean. Doubt balled up inside her like crumpled sheets of unwanted paper. "I'm sorry, Miles." She'd been careful. Had taken extra precautions after they'd passed testing and she'd started taking birth control pills. "I was scared something might go wrong

and there's Bug. This wasn't supposed to happen, and then there's…"
Rachel bit down on her lip to keep what little courage she held onto
from crumbling into the sand.

"It did happen and you know what I've been through," he said in a
halted, gritty voice as if rusted by salty sea water.

"I do know, but this wasn't part of my plan."

"*Your* plan?" The air was charged with static, humming just beyond
the edge of perception. "It takes two to make a baby." He held up the
photograph. "When did you decide to exclude me, the other half of
this equation?"

"I never meant to exclude you. I should have told you sooner."

"Can you explain why you didn't?"

"I tried. Many times, but I was afraid and I thought tonight…but
then you asked me to marry you, and I had to know if—" She inhaled
the urge to remind him of his words, but let it out despite what he
might say. She had to know. "You said you didn't want a baby with
someone else."

"Jesus, Rachel, that's not…" The breeze whipped his hair and the
evening shadows softened the tension brewing in his eyes. "I said I
couldn't bear the thought. But a child growing inside you is more than
a thought. It's real. We made this baby together. It's flesh and blood.
Our flesh and blood."

From a distance he was remarkable, a beautifully made man. But at
mere inches from her he was stunning, despite the intensity that was
—albeit slowly—slipping away.

"How…" His throat rippled as if trying to swallow something he
hadn't had time to properly chew. "How…far along?"

Did it matter? Did it matter whether she was one month or three?
She looked away, unwilling to guess the reason for the question. "Dr.
Lecter estimates I'm twelve weeks."

She looked up then, but the photograph had captivated his attention and his expression blended into that contemplative thing she
hoped he'd pass to his child.

His fingers slid over the grainy image, tracing the lines and
shadows of skull and spine, bent knees and nub of a tiny nose. A

mental caress. A father's first kiss. And all at once a peace came over him, a look so fragile if she reached out to touch him, he would surely shatter.

He counted fingers and toes not yet defined. She counted heartbeats she'd already heard. Miles collected the first images of his child and she collected the pieces of her heart.

"From the tests and what she can tell, he's perfect."

"I'm sorry you felt you needed to keep this from me." A brief moment of hesitation stilled him, and then he tilted her chin. "He?" The word emerged, hoarse and quiet and rich in expectation, and his eyes—she'd seen them temper like this before, the steely blue going soft and tender. "Rachel?"

"A son."

An unspoken response parted his lips and then he flavored her answer in a flurry of broken conjectures. "Is there any chance...he's okay...you won't do anything..."

"He's healthy. And safe." She took his arm then, the air lifting his shirttails and exposing a finely tanned torso and the scar he'd earned rescuing Bug—one of many he'd collected fighting battles alongside her. "I could never do anything to harm him."

"And you?"

"Sick. Weepy. Starving all the time. But okay. I'm so sorry. We discussed this and we were careful. I don't know how it happened."

"I know exactly how it happened." Miles took her in his arms, the vibrations of his deep laugh and the crash of waves to shore breaking the tension and then washing it out to sea.

"Well, I do too, but—"

"It's a super power thing."

"What?"

"Super-powered sperm."

She smacked his arm.

"I guess it slipped my mind to warn you."

"What, that I'd need Kryptonite in my pills?"

"And keep it caped."

"Stop it."

"Practice makes perfect, Sunshine." Amusement that hinged on tenderness spilled into his expression. "Guess we finally got it right."

"This isn't a joke." She pulled away. "And that's not the point."

"Then what is?"

"Gray hair."

"I happen to like every one of your three gray hairs."

"That's because you don't have any."

"I do. Many." He scrubbed a hand across his chin. "And that's not the reason I find joy in the silver."

"Hmph."

He reached over, trailing a finger along her hairline. "To have you alongside me, to see the years touch you in the way only age can, means we've lived and loved and we've found the pot of gold at the end of the rainbow. Together. Nothing else matters."

"I'm too old!" She kicked at an incoming wave, the gratification instant and all at once a letdown as her foot sailed through nothing but foamy water. "I'll be forty when this baby is born."

"So?"

She wheeled around, the sand parting in her wake. "Why do you think Dr. Lecter advised the Harmony test? Sure, it told us the baby's gender, but its main purpose is screening for genetic issues for those of us a few years beyond normal child-bearing years."

He clasped both her hands and brought them to his chest, the certainty in the pledge held against his heart. "Do you love me, Rachel?"

"Of course I do, but—"

"Do you love our baby?"

She dropped her hands and splayed her fingers over her belly, cradling their baby with the love of heart and soul, surrounded by the protection of her body. "More than life."

"Then nothing else matters."

Every qualm that threatened her sleep struggled to break free, to gather and spill across the sand. A roller coaster of emotions that had at once set her afire with excitement, had at the next moment buried her under a cloud of concern.

She dipped her chin, taking refuge in the sweep of sea and sand.

"Look at me, Rachel." He lifted her chin, the movement a stilted gesture of one unsure of what she'd find. "I assumed it was the warmth of coming summer on our mountain, or this tropical paradise that had brightened your skin and warmed your smile and taken the curl from your hair, the extra fullness in your breasts from ice cream and Italian food, and Jesus, Rachel...your wanting of me." He kissed her forehead, his touch an intimate link between souls. "I've always thought you were the most beautiful woman I've ever seen, but lately you've given new meaning to the word."

"Wait 'til I'm a fat, waddling toad and can't stand to look at you let alone allow you to touch me."

"If you're uncomfortable, I'll find some way to touch you that you find tolerable. Or simply hold you. Making love isn't always about sex. Not in my book. It's about love. Tenderness and understanding. Touch." He lifted one shoulder, one side of his mouth taking up the action. "There's more than one way to make love to the woman I adore."

The moon reflected in his eyes the same way it sparkled over the rolling sea, and they bore deeply into hers with his sultry expression, and the world around her disappeared.

"This may not have been planned, but our son was conceived in love. That's what matters."

"Miles—"

"Our son," he said, the words smothered in optimism and expectation. "Yours and mine. Because we once loved and because we always will. Someone once told me love is ageless, and I didn't realize what he meant. Until now. There's a deepness to us I've never known before."

Ambrose.

Surely...

A wave lapped over her ankles, the sudden chill shattering the shield she'd placed around her heart. She'd been afraid to love him. Afraid to love their baby. Afraid to tell him. He'd given her his promise—not out of obligation, but out of love for her, for Bug, and for their son. The warmth that was the life inside her took root, the sensation fully awake, and without thought, her hand went again to their unborn child. The union of love. The gift of life. Their baby was safe, their son loved.

Our son.

As they often did in times of reflection, the early days with Bug came whirling back: the gleam in Grandpa's eyes the first time he held his great-granddaughter; her breathless giggles when Zoe kissed her nose; the intense bond when the tiny baby girl nursed at her breast, a connection that often brought her to tears; the soft depth in her inquisitive brown eyes.

But mostly she'd been scared. Alone and terrified, she'd tucked this tiny link to the past in her bed and curled around her when Nico's absence became too much.

The moon, balanced on the edge of the horizon, stretched its orange and copper reflection across the sea, and a gull's cry splintered the hush that had settled between them. "You're okay then...with this?"

"More than okay. You've given me something I've only dreamed of, and I'm a profoundly happy man." The hint of a frown touched his brow. "And I understand why you didn't want to tell me and I'm sorry I overreacted."

And then he kissed her with a full-on, piercing grin that left nothing to her imagination, crumbling her insides and leaving bits of her scattered across the sea like pieces of glittering glass. Miles slipped his arm around her waist and stepped behind her, his hands seeking, protecting what she'd been too afraid to share. She was alone no longer, and she was lost in his arms around her, his touch as natural as the swell of sea to shore.

"I didn't think this last year, this week, this day could get any more perfect. But it has, in ways I never imagined. We've found the pot of gold at the end of the rainbow, Sunshine."

He turned her around and kissed her soundly, caressing her with a passion and hunger that conveyed answers to questions unasked, dreams fulfilled and those yet to come. His entire being entered into the act, and it radiated from his body and bled into hers and brought with it something new. Something unnamed. She could stay locked like this forever and it would never be long enough.

And then he softened the connection with a flurry of murmurs not quite laugh, not quite groan, but exquisitely male. "How many men can say they've had the pleasure and honor of becoming a father—twice in the same day?"

How many nights had she lain awake imagining their son? As handsome as his father with his dusty blond hair and lively blue eyes, but maybe only a subtle version of her curls. And Bug, the over-protective big sister until the little boy grew into the height Miles would give him and then heaven forbid anyone look crosswise at his sister. And in her dreams Miles held their tiny newborn, lost in the safety of his father's big, strong hands and sanctity of his being. But their son would miss Grandpa's giant Santa smile, his patience and insight, the things he'd selflessly bestowed on Bug.

Miles had been right—she shouldn't have kept this from him. He'd been put through hell with Brenna, and she'd kept these first months selfishly to herself.

"What about Bug? What do I tell her?"

"The truth."

"I...uh...don't think that's appropriate. At least not for a few years."

"Hmm...you're right. That particular subject will never be appropriate for my little girl, but that's not quite what I meant."

My little girl.

They stood facing each other and she held his eyes as he did her hands, a moment that stretched and fell away with the ebbing of the sea. Together. Heart to heart. Hand in hand. A bridge linking past to present, the first steps into the future. As long as they shared as two halves of a whole, their world—their family—would be one.

Miles touched the intimation of his son in the photograph once more. "He's so tiny. And is that—"

"No." Rachel smiled and leaned into his side. "His boy parts are there, but they're not developed." She pointed a shaky finger. "You'll see them next time. If you want to go with me."

Joy bloomed in his eyes, but it was no match for the warmth in his smile as he handed the photo back to her. An unabbreviated grin. A daddy grin. The one that sprang from the little boy grown with a son of his own and would remain, the unseen ripples in the circle of their life.

"C'mon, Mama. Let's tell Bug she's not only going to be a flower girl but a big sister."

The other world she'd learned to live in seemed far away, a ghost-like dream that had lost its clarity as wakefulness overshadows sleep, the feel of it fading the way the sun's last glimpse had given way to the rising moon. Her life had become an artist's palette—globs of paint on an empty canvas that with time and patience and carefully placed brushstrokes becomes a vividly colored landscape filled with perspective and the minute details that render it three-dimensional.

He'd be an incredible dad.

He already was.

Miles took her hand and started up the beach, but she didn't follow. He turned to her, and the sand stirred, the earth shifting beneath her feet.

"Everything's about to change, isn't it?"

His eyes drifted over her with an extraordinary appreciation, one she hadn't seen before.

"Becoming a family will be a big change. One I welcome with open arms and full heart." Miles tucked her hand into the crook of his elbow and they strolled up the pink sand beach. "You're not alone, Rachel. There's the four of us now."

The memories he'd created for a child that had never been born would never be truly forgotten, but he'd soon hold his son and count each tiny finger as they curled around his, a bond he'd only dreamed of coming full circle, the lines and shapes of the missing pieces a vague memory. A quiet shiver tightened around her heart, and she squeezed Miles' arm in response, the idea as weightless yet as solid as the cliffs around them.

Rachel sat next to her daughter and put the back of her hand to

THE OTHER SIDE OF BROKEN

her forehead and then her cheek and pushed a stray curl behind her ear. "Do you feel better, baby?"

Bug set the tablet aside. "Yes, but you guys take forever to talk." Miles and Rachel both chuckled at the innocent comment. "But I had lots of time to think about stuff," she said, dark eyes set in serious thought.

Miles took a seat in the sand beside them. "Want to tell us about it?"

"My forever daddy gave me his eyes cuz mine are brown, not blue like Mommy's and I love my daddy and I will love him forever and ever, but I wish he could give me hugs and kisses like Amber's daddy when he picks her up from school." Bug got to her knees, twisted around, and cupped her hands to her mother's ear. "So can Dr. Miles be my other daddy? I can love him forever and ever too, can't I?" She'd meant to whisper, but the challenging smile and upraised eyebrows emphasized an obvious lack of secrecy. She turned to Miles and then back to Rachel. "Please?"

Miles glanced at Rachel and blinked. His clueless expression spelled *first time dad* across his face in a shaky, nonplussed font. Her nod back carried the pleasure of her daughter's wishes. And hers.

He lifted Bug into his lap. "Makes me very happy and I'm honored," he began, the words a little unstable, "that you want me to be your daddy." The last word was more than shaky. More than steeped in pride. More than Rachel could ask for, and she blinked back joyful tears. "Because you're my little girl and always will be. And I'll help you remember your forever daddy who gave you your beautiful brown eyes, so he's never far from your heart."

Bug raised her hands in the air and then squeezed Miles' neck. "I love you, Daddy."

"I love you too, Ladybug." Miles cleared his throat. Twice. "Is my little girl hungry?"

"Duh. How come it takes forever for grownups to talk?" Bug brushed the sand from her hands and into Miles' lap.

"But first, your mommy and I have an important question for you."

Bug squirmed. "All right," she said, exasperation filling an animated sigh. "But I might die right here in your lap because I'm starving and my mommy and daddy take a long time kissing and talking and stuff." She wrinkled her nose, toggling between the two adults.

Rachel tugged the drawstrings on Bug's hoodie a little tighter. "It'll only take a minute."

"You always say that and it still takes a million years."

Rachel withheld a chuckle and nodded for Miles to continue.

With the implication of a special kiss, he brushed Bug's nose—the same button nose Rachel wore when she was little and the reason for the nickname her grandfather had given her. "How do you feel about becoming a big sister?"

The question squashed Bug's tendency to squirm and a decisive frown wrinkled her forehead. "Do I get to make her mind me like Zoe and Strider? Not Dory, though." She shook her head, curls at the end of her braids whipping across her shoulders. "Dory doesn't mind anybody and brings me dead beetles and stuff." Her words skidded together, sparking lively twinkles in her eyes. "One time she brought us a mouse and let it go under my bed and it wasn't even dead. Mommy screamed and was really mad at Dory and I got to sleep in her bed because we didn't catch her 'til the next day. The mouse was really hungry because he ate all the peanut butter in the trap right before dinnertime and then Mommy let her go in the woods."

His mouth parted, but nothing came close to a spoken word, his apparent attempt to raise his grade another notch in Parenting 101 quickly deflating. Rachel waited, raising an eyebrow as slowly as he calculated a response.

"I s'pose you can bring me a little sister. Do I have to share my room?" Bug's bottom lip puckered into a serious pout.

Miles shot Rachel a questioning look as if willing a smidge of parental advice from her, but she politely ignored the request. "We have lots of rooms. You don't have to share, but what would you say to a baby brother instead of a sister?"

"Yuk. No. Boys are gross. We can we trade, right?"

"That's not exactly the way babies work, Bug." He kneaded his temple with an index finger, the question obviously more complicated than he'd imagined. "I think you're stuck with a brother."

"Dogs and cats have lots of babies." She tried to scowl, but it was more excitement pinched into a question. "Why can't we pick a sister instead? Zoe is a girl and so is Dory. Mommy said girls are okay cuz we can have them spaded."

Rachel tucked a laugh behind tight lips.

If it was possible, even the stubble on Miles' face turned a lush shade of pink. "It uh, doesn't work quite the same way as a litter of pups or kittens."

The answer churned in the little quirks of her face and eyes, and then she took Miles' face in her hands, securing his attention with a thoughtful squint and deadpan pout. "If I say okay to a yucky brother," she said with weighted hesitation, and then let go of his face, "can I have a pony for Christmas?"

Miles ruffled her hair with a laugh to match and kissed his little girl's nose. "We'll see what Santa has to say about that."

Bug nodded once, a dramatic bob of the head, and her shoulders rolled into a punctuated shrug. Miles winked and gave Rachel a look steeped in candid affirmation.

And then he stretched a hand over Rachel's belly. "May I kiss my future wife and mother of my children?"

"I think I'd like that very much."

"Yuk, yuk, yuk." Bug covered her eyes with both hands.

"Hello, Sunshine," he said and kissed her again, Bug's giggles the background music.

"If the first one was hello, what was the second one for?"

"Healing. For family. For red skies at night. And for always."

THE END

Did you enjoy Miles' & Rachel's story?

The biggest compliment you can give an author is to share the title on

social media and leave a review on Amazon, BookBub, and
Goodreads. Nothing fancy, a sentence or two why you enjoyed the
book. It only takes a minute and is priceless to the author.

Happy Reading!

AUTHOR'S NOTE

Sexual assault (in any form) is a serious crime that is devastating physically and emotionally. If you, a family member, or someone you know is or has been a victim, please do not hesitate to contact the **National Sexual Assault Hotline: 1-800-656-HOPE (4673)** or **RAINN** (Rape, Abuse and Incest National Network www.rainn.org) to seek help in your area. Whether you're looking for support, information, advice, or a referral, trained specialists are ready to help 24/7. It's confidential and free.

You're not alone.

Help is out there.

ALSO BY SUSAN HAUGHT

A Promise of Fireflies

Whisper of the Pines, Book 1

(*Ryleigh & Logan's story continues in*

Christmas Under the Tuscan Stars)

In the Shadow of Fate

A Promise of Fireflies companion~always FREE

A Thousand Butterfly Wishes

Whisper of the Pines, Book 2

Outside the Lines

Whisper of the Pines, Book 4

Christmas Under the Tuscan Stars

Whisper of the Pines, Book 5

Dream Believe Write

Writing Prompts for Fiction Writers

Sign up for Susan's **Love is Ageless** newsletter to stay updated on all sales, giveaways, new releases, and inside peeks at scenes that ended up in the slush pile.

www.susanhaught.com

susanhaughtbooks@gmail.com

The Story Behind the Story

I DIDN'T WANT to write this story—but my readers wrote to me, asking me not to abandon Rachel, to please give her her "happily ever after."

I DIDN'T WANT to write this story—the subject matter is a difficult one and I did everything in my power to forget about it, to put it out of my mind. But it haunted me. Haunted my dreams. Haunted my writing.

I DIDN'T WANT to write this story—because I've been there and I knew it would dredge up memories I've tried to forget for forty-seven years. Though I bear no physical scars, the scars live within, their damage at times far worse than the physicality of that night. I've forgiven the man who raped me, but the memories of that night will always be a festering wound, one capable of healing completely only when my lungs cease to draw breath.

LIKE RACHEL, I thought it was my fault. To this day, I still feel that way at times even though I know it's not true. But when you're sixteen, your world view isn't the same as when you're older, and in all fairness, I was still a child. I told no one. I lived with it alone until one night shortly before I was to be married, I broke down and told my future husband. He had a right to know. I won't go into details, but he was my savior, my Miles, and looked beyond the victim and saw the woman who'd had something terrible happen to her and loved her anyway.

BUT THIS NOVEL isn't my story. It's Rachel's...and she's a hell of a lot stronger than I could ever be. My circumstances were far different than hers, but many times during the writing of her story, I found myself back to that night, writing through a waterfall of tears. The loneliness. The guilt. The embarrassment. The idea that if I scrubbed hard enough, all traces of that night, of *him*, would swirl down the drain into the dregs of the sewer. It didn't work that night, and I know it never will. It's just a little easier to live with after all these years. And with Miles by her side, Rachel will find it a little easier too.

I DIDN'T WANT to write this story—but now that I have, I think it was my way of letting go. I'm finally able to talk about it without the ugly feelings resurfacing to the point I can't breathe. Though Rachel and I are nothing alike, we share something very special...when the time was right, we told our stories, and though the memories will never be too far from conscious thought, we both have our "happily ever after".

I DIDN'T WANT to write this story—but I did, and it's for all the victims out there, for those who live with and love the victims of any kind of sexual assault, for those who've come forward and those who suffer in silence. It's for victims past, present, and future. We share a bond—one I don't wish on anyone—but a bond nevertheless. You're not that tiny grain of sand out there, alone. We're in this together, one of thousands in a great big sandbox.

I DIDN'T WANT to write this story—but I did. For you—because it's not your fault.

From my heart to yours,
Susan
#MeToo

ABOUT THE AUTHOR

Susan Haught writes deeply emotional stories of family, friendship, and the healing power of love. A multi award-winning novelist and Australian black liquorice connoisseur, Susan believes Love is Ageless and has the power to change lives--one step, one touch, one kiss at a time.

Susan has been chosen three times as the recipient of the New Apple Award for Excellence in Independent Publishing for *A Promise of Fireflies*, *A Thousand Butterfly Wishes*, and this book—*The Other Side of Broken*. *Vicious Circles*, a fictional story about the deceptions faced in the midst of spousal abuse, was a finalist in the Writer's Village International Short Story Contest, and Susan's writing earned her the title Best Writer in the Best of Rim Country Reader's Choice Awards. Her website was named as one of The Writer Awards Top Author Websites.

When Susan isn't writing, you'll find her tending her garden with a notorious brown thumb or escaping into someone else's words. She enjoys mentoring new writers, and she's always on the lookout for the best in Australian black liquorice and ways to spoil her grandpuppy, a feisty Yorkie named Ryleigh. Yes, her son named his gorgeous Yorkshire Terrier after the main character in *A Promise of Fireflies.*

Susan and her husband call the mountains of Arizona home where they raised one son. They spend their spare time catering to a high-maintenance princess, their Shih Tzu, Mercedes, and on FaceTime with Ryleigh...and their son!

Learn more about Susan's award-winning *Whisper of the Pines* series, sign up for her *Love is Ageless newsletter*, or download her *FREE* companion book by visiting

www.susanhaught.com
susanhaughtbooks@gmail.com

Happy Reading!

facebook.com/SusanHaughtBooks

twitter.com/SusanHaughtBKS

instagram.com/susanhaughtbooks

ACKNOWLEDGMENTS

To my readers—without you, none of this is possible. A writer spins a tale with his heart and soul, and without someone to read the words it's nothing but pages and ink. Readers like you give it life. CHEERS! to each and every one of you. You guys rock!

No book is born without a support system. From the first cells of an idea to the long labor of birth, these people have stood beside me and held my hand through the process. And at times, it's not easy being around me.

I raise my glass (with a nice chardonnay) to my two men first and foremost—Bruce, my DH of forty-four years who's everything to me and when I'm hunkered down to write, has become a trusted grocery shopper who finally knows the difference between red romaine and red leaf lettuce. The produce guy can't fool you any longer! You're my dust-bunny buster, dragon-slayer, my biggest cheerleader, and carry the weight I sometimes find too heavy to bear. Most of all, you keep me grounded. I love you—yesterday, today, and tomorrow.

And to my son, Adam, my loudest cheerleader—I'm so proud of the man you've become. You face life head-on with a smile, and with more ambition and courage than I could ever dream possible. You're an amazing daddy to a sweet, snugly, half-crazy Yorkie for whom Zoe is modeled. Zoe popped up in A Thousand Butterfly Wishes with so much potential as a lead character, I had to keep her story alive. It was a blast bringing her to the page once again, and I thank you for not rolling your eyes at my requests for photographs of my precious grandpuppy. I love you and Ryleigh (aka Zoe) with everything in me.

To John Lee and David Francis of the Larimer County Search & Rescue (Estes Park, Colorado) who answered all my crazy questions about rescue missions and dangerous ski areas. You both were instrumental in helping me give wings to this portion of the story. I applaud the LCSAR for their courage and compassion every time they answer the call and put their lives on the line "so others may live". Stay safe out there.

Many thanks to Matt Bielke, who took the time to review the rescue/ski scenes with a keen eye, and set me straight on terms and situations so my words would ring true.

To the legal expert (who wished to remain anonymous) of the WFWA (Women's Fiction Writers Association) who helped me discover I knew nothing about the legal system. Thank you for your patience with my ignorance, answering all my questions, and steering me in the right direction.

To the Gila County (Arizona) District Attorney's office, whose team helped me tie up the loose ends of the legal aspects of this story and bring them to full light. I commend you both for all you do to bring justice to the victims. Thank you, and God bless.

To Hannah Milnes at the Arizona Board of Executive Clemency for information concerning parole hearings (or lack of) in the state of Arizona. Your help was instrumental in bringing life to this portion of the story.

To Dawnie Steadman at the Forensic Anthropology Center of the University of Tennessee. Frozen dead bodies aren't a usual topic of conversation, and you helped bring authenticity to a crucial part of the story. I also owe a debt of gratitude to Kara Braden, fellow author and good friend, for asking her experts in this area as well. The information both ladies provided added a touch a realism that I couldn't have done without them.

I could not have seen Zoe through her medical issues without the help of a special DVM. He wished to remain anonymous, but I hope he knows how much I appreciate him taking my limited knowledge of canine brain trauma and giving it an authenticity I never could have on my own. My deepest thanks for taking the time from your busy schedule to offer assistance.

It's been twenty-four years since my son was an almost five-year-old, and I owe Pamela Donovan, Kate Murph, Elizabeth Mackey, Laurie Sneezy, and Karen Frewin a big HIGH FIVE for filling me in on the things little people say these days. Bug's character adopted bits of dialogue from the many suggestions you gave me, and did so without a hiccup! Like they say…kids say the darndest things!

To my fantastically insightful beta readers Anne Pisacano, Brandy Bell, and Arlene Hittle whose feedback had me freaking out, but when I buckled down and put their thoughts into action, the characters and story came full-circle. I couldn't ask for anything more. You guys are priceless to my stories, and I love you for it.

To Elizabeth Mackey—you have a knack for taking my ideas and turning them into stunning book covers. I can't wait to see what you come up with next!

To Michelle Kowalski—again my deepest thanks for taking my love affair with the comma and giving it a dose of Xanax. I hate to think how many times you rolled your eyes. And for taking the rough edges of this manuscript and hemming the loose seams with your expertise and love for the written word. The manuscript would be a train wreck without you.

To Karen Phylow—my go-to proofreader who finds the smallest details that slip through the cracks.

My fondest wishes go out to each and every one of you. Like they say, it takes a tribe to write a book. It certainly does in my case. Take care all, and God bless.

Susan

A SIDE NOTE

I had a lot of help with this story—from the legal aspects, reading and listening to victims' stories, learning how a frozen body would look if discovered years later, to the dangers search & rescue volunteers face. It was a heart-wrenching, yet amazing journey.

Though I received accurate information from the people who offered assistance, I've taken liberties as most authors do to enhance the story. I thank these people for their expertise, and any and all discrepancies are mine alone. Please thank them, and slap my hands if something doesn't ring true.

Flattop mountain and The Drift in the Rocky Mountain National Park are very real, but I don't know if there's a Devil's Horn, nor do I know if a glacier exists in that particular area. Miles' and Shep's downhill excursion was the product of my imagination, as was the name of the cliff they recklessly skied off of. I needed to introduce Shep (who will grace the pages of On Wings of Dragonflies) who's penchant for adventure (aka danger) outshines Miles' by a long shot. I think you're going to like him.

I've never had to spend time in a prison (EEP!) and I admit I got a little sick to my stomach at the thought of visiting. I've driven by the Arizona State Prison in Florence, and that was as close as I ever want to get. It truly did elicit a sense of foreboding I've never felt anywhere else. That being said, I'd like to thank Troy Hayden of FOX News for taking us inside the prison via YouTube (watch it here). Again, I've taken liberties for the sake of the story—I believe there are classrooms, but the one-way mirror came solely from my imagination. All other inequities are mine alone.

The same goes for the hearing scenes. Hearings are heard by the Board of Executive Clemency, and are conducted via videoconferencing. Rarely, if ever, do victims attend a hearing with the prisoner in attendance. Rachel needed to face Chastain, so Miles brought Logan (A Promise of Fireflies) into the story to pull a few strings. Logan can be quite persuasive, and when Miles sets his mind on something, he gets it done. I also took the liberty to have the attorney (now DA) who prosecuted the original case attend for Rachel's sake, and to inform her of the new developments. Attorneys are allowed to be present at hearings, but rarely do they attend. Besides, I love Everett Dumas. He's a pretty cool guy with a giant heart, and my heart goes out to him.

I couldn't have brought the story to life without an amazing amount of help. But please remember, this is a work of fiction, and the liberties I've taken helped to bring the story alive.

Any factual or creative embellishments are mine alone.

DID YOU KNOW...?

The very first therapy dog was a World War II Yorkie. His name was Smoky and you can read his story in its entirety. I adore the photo of him curled up in a military helmet. It is also reported Sigmund Freud kept a chow named Jofi in his office during psychotherapy sessions. He believed the dog calmed his patients, and his diary notes form the basis of modern-day pet-assisted therapy.

Therapy dogs are often used in hospitals, care facilities, nursing homes, etc., to cheer up patients, but are not considered by law to have the same status as a service dog. However, their presence is widely known to help in the healing process.

Whiskey lollipops are a thing. Really. I pinned the recipe on my Pinterest board NomNomNom because, you know, whiskey.

A group of ladybugs is called a "loveliness". And some ladybugs are pink. I pinned some interesting things on *The Other Side of Broken*, a board I have on Pinterest for all things that inspired me while writing this novel.

Some beaches along the coast of Sardinia (Italy) are pink. It's true! They get their hue from broken coral pieces, shells, and calcium carbonate materials. See for yourself on my Pinterest board Bucket List

Damselflies are similar to dragonflies, but are smaller, have slimmer bodies, and most species fold their wings along the body when at rest. Heck, I thought they were female dragonflies!

Fireflies can be seen in Italy, and in my research of Sardinia, I found a travel blog whose author said they saw fireflies while visiting. They discovered a freshwater pool near the Mediterranean and as the sun went down, the fireflies emerged.

If a ladybug lands on you, it is said your wish will come true. If caught and then released, the ladybug will fly to your true love and whisper your name in his/her ear. It is also believed the direction a ladybug flies is the direction from which your luck will come (old ladybug legends).

Ladybugs aren't really bugs. They're beetles, and are sometimes called ladybirds.

Avalanches are caused not by noise as is commonly assumed, but by four factors: a steep slope, snow cover, a weak layer in the snow cover, and a trigger, and on average kill 150 people a year worldwide.

Ladybugs "bleed" from their knees when threatened. A foul-smelling hemolymph will seep from its leg joints, leaving yellow stains on the surface below. It is said to deter predators.

Butterfly Wonderland (where Rachel & Miles visit) is located in Scottsdale, Arizona, and is the largest butterfly conservatory in America. The Native American butterfly legend I found there was the spark that ignited the story behind *A Thousand Butterfly Wishes*. Visit Butterfly Wonderland on the internet sometime if you can't get there in person.

The MegaDog (heaped with mac n' cheese) is an actual item on the Diamondbacks menu, but it's only available at Salt River Fields during spring training, not the regular season at Chase Field as I portrayed in this novel.

The Arizona Diamondbacks debuted as a team against the Colorado Rockies on March 31, 1998 to a sold-out crowd. Arizona lost the home opener 2-9. The Rockies and Diamondbacks are both in the NL West Division, and have met nineteen times every year since 1998.

The Arizona Diamondbacks and Colorado Rockies share the spring training facilities at Salt River Fields at Talking Stick in Scottsdale, Arizona. The Salt-River Pima-Maricopa Indian Community partnered with the DBacks and Rockies, and built the first MLB spring training facility on Indian land in the nation.

Improvise, Adapt, Overcome ~ the unofficial motto of the United States Marine Corp was made popular by the Clint Eastwood movie, *Heartbreak Ridge,* in 1986.

A medical corpsman in the U.S. Marines is extremely rare. The Marines rely on the U.S. Navy for their field medical officers, called hospital corpsmen. Navy corpsmen are assigned a Marine field unit and offer medical support during operations and battle.

Now you know..........Research can be such a blast!

PLAYLIST

THE OTHER SIDE OF BROKEN

Songwriters are modern day poets, their words straight from their
soul. With each note, they give them wings to touch our hearts.
When I hear these songs, Rachel & Miles
are right here, beside me.

- Say You'll Never Let Me Go ~ James Arthur
- One More Light ~ Linkin Park
- Inner Demons ~ Julia Brennan
- The Fighter ~ Keith Urban/Carrie Underwood
- Stuck on You ~ Lionel Richie
- Broken ~ Lifehouse
- Demons ~ Imagine Dragons
- Fight Song ~Rachel Platten
- Pieces ~ Rob Thomas
- Fix You ~ Coldplay
- Heavy ~ Linkin Park
- Let's Hurt Tonight ~ One Republic
- Bleeding Love ~ Leona Lewis
- Fells Like Tonight ~ Daughtry
- The Sound of Silence ~ Disturbed

- Superman Tonight ~ Bon Jovi
- Try ~ Pink
- One Call Away ~ Charlie Puth
- Never Let You Go ~ Alex Band
- Between the Raindrops ~ Lifehouse
- New Divide ~ Linkin Park
- Maps ~ Maroon 5
- Savin' Me ~ Nickelback
- Set Fire to the Rain ~ Adele
- Forever Yours ~ Alex Band
- I Can Take it From Here ~ Chris Young
- Never Gonna Leave This Bed ~ Maroon 5
- You Run Away ~ Barenaked Ladies
- Unsteady ~ X Ambassadors
- Can't Fight This Feeling ~ REO Speedwagon

Made in the USA
Monee, IL
28 March 2021